NICE
GUYS
FINISH
DEAD

NICE GUYS FINISH DEAD

AN ALBIE MARX MYSTERY

DAVID DEBIN

Turtle Bay Books
A DIVISION OF RANDOM HOUSE
NEW YORK
1992

Grateful acknowledgment is made to the following for permission to reprint previously published material:
LEONARD COHEN MUSIC: Excerpts from "Bird on a Wire" by Leonard Cohen. Copyright © 1968 by Leonard Cohen/Stranger Music, Inc. Reprinted by permission.
JON LANDAU MANAGEMENT: Excerpts from "No Retreat, No Surrender" by Bruce Springsteen. ASCAP. Reprinted by permission.
MCA MUSIC PUBLISHING: Excerpts from "Hello, Goodbye" words and music by John Lennon and Paul McCartney. Copyright © 1967 by Northern Songs. All rights controlled and administered by MCA Music Publishing, a division of MCA, Inc., under license from Northern Songs. Excerpts from "Born to Be Wild" words and music by Mars Bonfire. Copyright © 1968 by Duchess Music Corporation. Rights administered by MCA Music Publishing, a division of MCA, Inc., New York, NY 11019. Excerpts from "Within You, Without You" words and music by George Harrison. Copyright © 1967 by Northern Songs Limited. All rights controlled and administered by MCA Music Publishing, a division of MCA, Inc., under license from ATV. All rights reserved. Reprinted by permission.
PEER MUSIC: Excerpts from "You Are My Flower" by A. P. Carter. Copyright 1939 by Peer International Corporation. Copyright renewed. International copyright secured. All rights reserved. Reprinted by permission.
SPECIAL RIDER MUSIC AND BIG SKY MUSIC: Excerpts from "Percy's Song" by Bob Dylan. Copyright © 1964, 1966 by Warner Brothers Inc. Copyright renewed by Special Rider Music. Excerpts from "The Man in Me" by Bob Dylan. Copyright © 1970 by Big Sky Music. Excerpts from "Sweetheart Like You" by Bob Dylan. Copyright © 1983 by Special Rider Music. All rights reserved. International copyright secured. Reprinted by permission.
WARNER/CHAPPELL MUSIC, INC.: Excerpts from "In the Midnight Hour" by Wilson Pickett and Steve Cropper. Copyright © 1966 by Cotillion Music, Inc., and Irving Music, Inc. All rights administered by Warner-Tamerlane Publishing Corp. All rights reserved. Reprinted by permission.
WARNER/CHAPPELL MUSIC, INC. AND JONI MITCHELL: Excerpts from "Woodstock" by Joni Mitchell. Copyright © 1969, 1974 by Siquomb Publishing Corp. All rights reserved. Reprinted by permission of Warner/Chappell Music, Inc., and Joni Mitchell.

Library of Congress Cataloging-in-Publication Data
Debin, David.
Nice guys finish dead: an Albie Marx mystery / David Debin.—
1st ed.
p.   cm.
ISBN 0-679-40141-5
I. Title.
PS3554.E1762N53   1992   813'.54—dc20   91-51048

The text of this book is set in Garamond Stemple.

For Gary G. and Gary D.,
Julia P. and Julie G.

They say that Patriotism is the last refuge to which a
      scoundrel clings,
Steal a little and they throw you in jail, steal a lot and
      they make you a king.
There's only one step down from here, baby, it's called
      the land of Permanent Bliss,
What's a sweetheart like you doin' in a dump like this?

Bob Dylan, "Sweetheart Like You"

The winds of Belief are blocked by the mountain. High in
the Windshadow lives the Divine Salvia.

Ahmet Ludi, *A Heretic's Handbook*

NICE
GUYS
FINISH
DEAD

CHAPTER 1

I arrived at Linda Selby's house about eight and found her hanging in the living room. She was a short girl and always hated having to look up at everyone, but that night she had one hell of a height advantage, dangling a couple of feet off the floor like that. I don't mean to be glib about death, particularly someone else's, but it's a defense mechanism for me, this glibness, and I need all the reinforcement I can get at this point. Things haven't exactly been going my way lately and this thing with Linda Selby was one more setback.

I only knew Linda a year or so and our relationship was more hers than mine, but she was a damn fine woman, dedicated to making this planet habitable again. Chief Seattle said, "We don't inherit this land from our parents, we borrow it from our children," and though she had none of her own, Linda believed the children deserved better than this garbage dump we were giving back to them. The problem was, she took it so much to heart that she must have finally decided that nothing she could do would turn the tide.

So when I walked into her house and those glassy, dead

eyes bored into my heart, it was all I could do to leave her hanging up there, humiliated, while I waited for the police.

Now they're here and they're not making my day either. This billiard-topped bully, Lieutenant Danno, reeks of arrogance and stale English Leather.

"Albie Marx. You're the guy who wrote that book, what was it, something about a mouse . . . ?"

"Roger Wellington Rat."

He scratches his bald head. Or is he polishing it? "That's it, Roger Rat. I remember you from the sixties. You were that fuckin' hippie rabblerouser, right?"

"Good memory, Lieutenant. I see they haven't raised your elocution requirements since then."

Danno does not like a smartass. I do not like cops. Advantage—Danno. "I haven't seen your ugly face in a long time, Albie. What have you been up to?"

"A little of this and a little of that." Why can't I give this creep a straight answer?

"You making some money? You think you could spring for some new clothes?"

He must be referring to my old jeans and jean jacket and my worn Tony Lama boots. "Old is *in*, Lieutenant. Why encourage more new production when the world is crammed with perfectly good things already?"

I'm watching the cops behind him work around Linda's still dangling body. A photographer's flash bounces off Danno's gleaming pate and into my eyes. "How did you know the victim, Albie?"

"We were friends." What business is it of his what our relationship was?

"Good friends?"

I don't like the way he says *good*, with those skimpy eyebrows leering away at me. "Friends," I say.

"Were you fuckin' her?"

How do I respond to that? "It's getting late, Lieutenant. I just lost a friend and I need a drink so if I seem a bit grumpy it's just that I get negative when I have to waste time with a cretin like you. May I be excused now?"

"Look, you phony intellectual Marxist prick, right now you're up to your eyes in shit."

"At least you're not a racist."

He looks me up and down and then smiles, wide, appreciative, showing big, horse-sized choppers. I feel like offering him an apple. "You're a character, Albie. You used to be one smart fuckin' media clown. We'll see how the old dance works if the new tune happens to be homocide."

"Are you implying Linda didn't kill herself?"

"I'm implying that you better answer my fuckin' questions."

"Her brother was killed in a car crash last week. She was depressed. She wanted company. She called me and I came over and found her like this. I called you people. That's the story, beginning, middle and end."

"What time did you get here?"

"I already told your guys, around eight-thirty."

"Where were you before you came here?"

"Home."

"Was anybody there with you?"

"My cat." Already he's checking for an alibi. What is he not telling me?

He inspects something harvested from his ear. "You said the front door here was unlocked?"

"How else would I get in? I don't have a key."

"That's what I wanted to know. That's all for now, Albie. We'll be in touch." He turns and starts toward the small knot of men working around the spot where Linda's body is being freed from the pink terrycloth noose. Suddenly he turns back to me. "What was it they used to tell Roger all the time? 'A rat by any other name . . .'?"

" 'Is still a rat.' I thought you people only read *The Enquirer* and *Penthouse.*"

"That was a pretty good book, Albie. You should have quit while you were ahead."

But you can't quit while you're ahead, can you? Unless you really quit, like Linda did. Or Janis. God, I haven't thought about Janis in a while. But she's never too far away, as near as an oldies radio station or a sixties album collection. One week, seven days out of sixteen thousand, less than five hundredths of a percent of my life was the time I spent with her. Yet how many hours have I remembered her, dreamt of her, used her to summon those lost feelings of youthful righteous invincibility? She was the white queen of soul and she took a little piece of my heart but she gave me a lifetime of courage in return.

Shit, the old sixties miasma again. The thing with Janis, the trips with Leary and the bunch, hippies and yippies and acid-rock groupies. And *Roger Wellington Rat.* My biggest hit. My only hit. Hey, they say all you need is one.

I really hate this, my sick fascination with the sixties. Who I was, who I thought I was. I guess we all thought we were more than we turned out to be. I guess that's the big letdown, the one that won't quit. We thought we were so great then. We could touch the stars. We were Love, we were God, we were Music. Everything was of the same fabric, we were only one thread each, but oh, what a miraculous tapestry we all made together. Then Reality set in. While we were making love, Someone Else was making money. While we were making music, Someone Else was puncturing the ozone. While we were being God, Someone Else was killing the dolphins. Sure, we stopped the war. And we helped our black brothers and sisters into colleges and voting booths. But we exhausted ourselves. We made the big push and it didn't go far enough. And there, at the end of our line, was Someone Else, ready to take over again.

Did I know Abbie Hoffman? Yes, and loved him. Abbie and Albie. Jerry Rubin used to say we ran the gamut, from A to A. If official history ever reflected the truth, Abbie would have been acknowledged as one of the great freedom fighters of the twentieth century. But, poor Abbie, for all his flag-shirted, pig-nominating clowning, he took it too seriously. He finally killed himself because he found out that higher consciousness in this new age is mostly a vanity label, like Polo or Guess? We used to say, you are what you eat. Today, you are what you wear.

Twenty-five years ago, I wrote a book about a rat with an inferiority complex who learned that the world will perceive you the way you perceive yourself. It was a pretty good concept, particularly in those days when blacks and women and alienated youth were openly dreaming of freedom and equality. It hit just right in the public's third eye and I became an instant celebrity, along with the likes of Peter Max, Rod McKuen and Tiny Tim.

The initial thrust of the book's impact carried Roger and me through most of the seventies but by the end of the decade we were beginning to experience the intellectual backlash that identified people of the sixties as a bunch of cultural fossils with tie-dyed brains. Naiveté, which had its own charm and cache in our decade, became laughable in the seventies and a crippling disability in the eighties. The author of *Roger Wellington Rat* was typecast into a time and a way of thinking that made him unpardonably obsolete.

Fuck it. Have a drink. Do what you can. So what if we didn't take this world into Nirvana. Maybe if we save a kid from starving or save an elephant from being butchered or stop a bomb from being tested we're doing all we have to. That's what I've got to tell myself, being in the Protest business or, as Shrike, my editor, calls it, the Great Consciousness Movement. He rescued me from my comfortable obscurity, living on the paltry royalties from *Roger,* to write a column for his underground glossy, *Up Yours,* an exercise in alternative journalism that is read by several hundred thousand people a month.

Mother Jones, High Times and *Spy* all owe a debt to *Up Yours,* in continuous print since 1964 on the heels of the Kennedy assassination. Shrike hired me to write a monthly column, the old yippie soldier spewing a tell-it-like-it-is-before-it's-too-late harangue.

Yeah, I made my debut in the sixties and slept through the seventies in a fog of indifference. It wasn't until the mid-eighties that I decided to make my comeback.

I met Linda Selby at a Christmas party last year, given by a local chapter of Greenpeace, donations accepted. I get invited to every new-wave fundraiser. Since I've had my column, I've become one of the high-profile bigmouths for the new Protest Movements.

Though she was smaller than petite, Linda was a very attractive girl, with long black hair and dark, almost black really, impassioned eyes. But very serious, very somber. She was almost forty and from what she told me, had managed to pretty much totally avoid men up to that point. She'd had only one lasting relationship, a disastrous affair with a well-known city official who promised her everything and delivered what politicians usually deliver.

After him, she retreated to a stance of sexual indifference, but she wasn't without a strong current of passion, which she channeled directly into the issues and causes in which she believed.

"It's so horrible what we're doing to this planet," she would say, and it came straight from the heart. "The way we treat animals is just a symptom in our society, like child abuse and rape. We kill the trees, cut down the rain forest, destroy the ozone, poison the water, all in some crazy obsession to dominate nature. Why can't man stop wounding the earth? Why can't he let her heal?" She'd look so sad then, as if all this were being done to her personally.

"That's just what man does," I answered. "Man wounds, woman heals."

"But that's changing, I can feel it. People are becoming more aware."

"What they're doing is saving their own asses. Suddenly they're afraid they won't be able to breathe the air outside their own window so they're thinking of doing something about it."

"But that's the point, isn't it?"

"The point is to realize that nature is always sacred and not just when you're being threatened. Can I get you another drink?"

"No, thank you. My name is Linda Selby, by the way."

"Albie Marx."

"You're Albie Marx? God. I'm sorry, I didn't know. I read your column in *Up Yours* all the time. I've been a fan of yours for years." She looked at me with eyes that were as close as they could bring themselves to seduction. I get a lot of seduction from forty-year-old ladies of the movement.

"Let's not date ourselves," I said lightly, preferring not to think of my glorious past.

"I still have my first copy of *Roger Wellington Rat*," she

persisted. "That book meant so much to me. Being short. You know."

"Do you live around here?" I asked, as I finished my Corona. I felt like getting drunk, so drunk, and making love to this wide-eyed woman-child.

"West Hollywood," she answered. "And you?"

"Los Feliz. Excuse me, my glass just became empty." We went to the bar. A shot of Cuervo Gold, with a Corona chaser. My fourth? Fifth? Doesn't matter. I'll run an extra couple of miles tomorrow.

"Albie . . . " The dark eyes were pulling me in.

"Yes, you can come home with me tonight," I answered.

She laughed, a little too self-consciously. "Was all that true, about you and Janis Joplin?"

"My claim to fame."

"I just always wondered. She was so incredible. And you were my favorite author. I wondered about the two of you together."

"Whatever feels good, believe."

"You don't have to talk about it."

"But you'd love to hear the dirt."

She looked at me as if I'd farted, then she turned to go.

"How would you like to go somewhere where we can do some serious drinking?"

She stopped and turned back. "I don't really drink."

"I'll drink your share. What do you say?"

"I have friends here I haven't said hello to."

"We'll meet out in front in ten minutes. That enough time?"

She was trying to figure out what I meant to her. How she could fit me into her life. Whether she had enough room, could take the pain, wanted to make the effort. I could sense her whole being involved in the calculation. She kept her eyes tilted up at me, and they were fascinated, afraid and warm.

"How old are you now?" she asked. Not an aging hippie's favorite question.

"According to the stars, my mother, my boss, my last lover or the little boy who's trapped inside this decaying body?"

"According to your heart."

The thought passed through my head, *I like this girl.* "You know, you're playing with fire. Well, more like hot coals. Smouldering coals."

She smiled, a real smile, without the fear and self-consciousness, and reached out her hand. I took it.

"If I give you my number, will you call me?" she asked.

When I was younger I wouldn't have let the night get away without taking her to bed. Now . . . Now, it doesn't seem to matter as much.

I'm driving down Sunset and I'm thinking about Linda and I'm looking at Spago and a billboard for Madonna and a silent couple in an Acura and I'm wondering where all the Meaning went. It's early, I'm dangerously sober, I know a million things I shouldn't and someone's trying to hang a murder on me.

Wait a second, what am I talking about, "murder"? I don't care what Danno thinks, he didn't know Linda. I could tell him about her lifelong depression and the battle she constantly waged to keep from going under. I could testify to the many tearful times she had threatened to give up and turned the conversation from planet annihilation to self-annihilation. I could point out to him that statistically, according to the *American Journal of Psychology,* after guns and drugs the noose is a woman's favorite way out of this madness.

But somehow I don't think it would do any good. He has it in for me and he knows something he's not saying. Maybe it has to do with Newt.

Linda's brother, Newton, or Newt as he hated to be

called, was shorter even than his sister. Not quite a midget
was Newt but, in Napoleonic tradition, possessed of a con-
suming need to compensate for altitude with attitude. Linda
called me at the office last week. Newt was in town and he
wanted to meet me.

"You never told me you had a brother."

"He works for the government," she said, as if that explained it.

"What branch?"

I heard her cover the mouthpiece, then answer, "I don't
know. I can't say. Would you be willing to meet him?"

"I've never been big on government types."

"He has information that will interest you."

I looked at my watch. I'd been sitting around nursing some
coffee and stale donuts all morning. My column was due for
print and I had nothing to rant about, nothing I believed
would make one bit of difference in this Joyless New World.
Maybe Linda's brother would say something to spark an idea.
He had to be an improvement on the blank sheet of paper
leering at me from the platen on my typewriter. I agreed to
meet him.

I was to drive to the Pacific Coast Highway, park in the lot
next to the Sand and Sea Club and wait in my car. What is
it with these government boys? They always have to create a
drama. Why couldn't we just meet at a bar somewhere? Fortunately I had a pint of Cuervo Gold in the glove compartment
of my faithful old '66 Jag 3.4, and the wait was no less
unpleasant than sitting in my office, acting like I was thinking.

It was December and the beach was stark, even though the
sun was out. The sun was always out. They say it never rains
but it pours in Southern California. I actually couldn't remember the last time it rained, it must have been six or eight
months ago. The water problem was so deep and depressing
that nobody wanted to be associated with it. It never appeared

in the papers, politicians didn't talk about it, not one environmental group demonstrated about it. Everyone knew we desperately needed water and everyone figured it would come from somewhere. After all, didn't we appropriate the Colorado River and use it to turn a dull, brown desert into the glamour capital of the world?

I watched the gulls messing around with the garbage cans on the bare beach and today the sun looked cold. There was a deep brown cloud out to sea, a grimy film that people insisted on calling "haze," and it sapped the sun's heat and stole its glory. People jogged back and forth in their new nineties bodies, intense fitness freaks and voluptuous girls who went to bed with men other than me and forced me to wonder what went wrong with myself as I took another warm pull on my trusty Cuervo.

There were several other vehicles in the lot with me, one faded red pickup that looked like it was there since *Beach Blanket Bingo.* Pretty soon a boat of a car, a Lincoln, pulled up beside me, driving itself, with no one at the wheel. For a second I imagined I was on *Candid Camera,* then the driver's door swung open and a five-foot pip-squeak popped out and headed for the beach without so much as a glance in my direction. He was wondrously small but stocky as a baby bull. It was impossible to tell his age and I got the stone feeling that this was no one to fuck with. His walk was confident, strong and purposeful. He wore a gray suit and dark tie and black wing-tips that dug deep into the sand as he made his way toward the water's edge. Somehow I knew it was him, the brother who worked for the government.

As I took a last slug and shut the bottle away, I had a premonition. Having anything at all to do with this banty rooster would most certainly lead to confronting things in my life I had been putting off for years. I could be safe, I thought, could leave my demons unmolested, could start up the car and drive back to my office and write my column. I could fire away at the "well-informed" couch potatoes who knew nothing about the thousand-year drought they were about to reckon with. I could berate the indolent bastards with a torrent of guilt-seeking prose, a fire and brimstone harangue to take action before it's too late, to take to the streets and fight to the death for an end to golf courses, lawns and swimming pools.

But I didn't really give a damn. Not really. I wanted to think it was because it wouldn't make one bit of difference what I wrote. I had to think that. Because if that wasn't it, then it meant that I just didn't care. And that would most certainly be the end of the line. Come on, let's face it, they don't know, they don't want to know. If Lincoln were giving the Gettysburg fucking address on TV, the poor, happy idiots would be grabbing their remotes, scanning for a wrestling match or maybe a rerun of *Wheel of Fortune.*

I got out of the car and headed for the water. My life was a mess and you don't clean up a mess by avoiding it. Up close, the sand was sootier than it looked from afar. There were little ice cream sticks and asphalt coals and food wrappers and beer bottles and all kinds of things an alien from another planet would try to explain after the human race was extinct.

As I walked I started to clean up the beach. I grabbed one of the heavy trash cans that sat strangely empty and dragged it behind me, loading in all the refuse I could reach. Occasionally I glanced toward the ocean at the little man who stood, his back to me, looking out on the roiling brown water.

Maybe it wasn't him, I thought, and all of a sudden felt stupid. What kind of asshole was I, cleaning up after a herd of pigs and watching a strange midget stare at a filthy ocean? I got mad at myself, called myself a bunch of dirty names and started to overturn the barrel of garbage.

Then I felt eyes on my back, felt them as surely as I felt the cold sun on my face. I released the can, straightened up and nonchalantly dusted myself off. I pulled my last stick of sugarless Care Free bubble gum out of my pocket, dropped the wrapper in the can and chomped down. Casually glancing back toward the parking lot, I spotted a new arrival, a plain blue Ford with two men in front, wearing ties and jackets and shades. They were staring straight at me and it didn't take a genius to figure they weren't a couple of fags out for a matinee. These were the real McCoy, the bloodless ones who come for you when you've outlived their tolerance.

Now I felt challenged and it pumped me up. I hated all those fuckers in blue Fords and passionless faces and even though I'd become a disgraceful parody of what I once was, there was still one little living piece of me that would go through the fires of hell if it meant sticking it to those swine and everything they stood for. I picked up a driftwood stick and strode to the sea, bursting to tell the little rooster what I thought of him and his associates.

When I reached within a few feet of him he spoke, projecting his words out where they would be absorbed by the pounding surf.

"Understand, I'm first and foremost an American."

I looked at him for the first time and, behold, there were sad, salty pools in his big little eyes.

"I'm proud of my team and I'm proud to play for the biggest and the best on the planet," he continued, as if I weren't there. "Make no mistake, God is still on our side."

"Your friends in the Ford don't look very saintly."

"Sometimes the beacon of democracy shines on things better left in the dark. Sometimes even I have my doubts."

"Don't make me laugh," I said, using my driftwood stick to scoop up a discarded prophylactic that was lolling on the hard, gleaming sand at our feet.

"Word has it you can't be trusted. Is that true?"

"Absolutely."

"Good. It takes a weasel to deal with weasels."

"Flattery scores no points with me," I replied, flipping the distended condom around on my stick. "Just say what you have to and be done with it."

His voice tightened. "I'm dealing with maximum flap potential here. Compromising my people."

"What people are those, Newt?"

"Newton."

"Whatever."

"Big people. Bigger than me."

I didn't have the heart to tell him that included most everybody.

"Look to the NSB for an Executive Action under NSC 10/2."

"What is this, a civil service exam?"

"Marx, if this operation wasn't sicker than you and your anarchist friends, I wouldn't even spit on you. As it is, I find you revolting and stupid. But you might just clog up the works. I have to take that chance."

"Your courage overwhelms me."

"You know, my sister said underneath all the bullshit, you're really a nice guy."

"Is that supposed to be a compliment?"

He gave me a look of remote contempt and shook his head. Then, turning to head back to his car, he added, "There's a key in that scumbag you're playing with. Use it."

Sure enough, sequestered in the tip of the rubber was a small, locker-sized key. That little pervert. I had made it a rule not to do business with the government for this very reason—they always leave you holding the bag. I secured the key and chucked the condom into the water.

When I turned back toward the parking lot, the driverless

Lincoln was pulling out onto the Pacific Coast Highway and the blue Ford was following indiscreetly behind.

Maximum flap potential, NSB, Executive Action, NSC 10/2, a key in a scumbag and a couple of geeks. Maybe it all made sense, but not to me. I stopped at a liquor store for some C & C—a new pint of Cuervo and a pack of Care Free bubble gum.

Okay. NSB equals National Security Board. Established in 1988 by a secret presidential directive after the Iran-Contra mess to provide an additional layer of executive deniability in classified covert intervention, particularly in the area of foreign military operations. The NSB is the most covert of all intelligence units, its operation so classified that even the CIA is denied access.

"Look to the NSB," Newt had said, "for an Executive Action under NSC 10/2." An Executive Action could be anything from an assassination to an invasion. NSC 10/2, as I vaguely remembered it, was a secret National Security Council directive which authorized the DDO, the Deputy Directorate of Operations division of the CIA, to engage in a wide range of covert activities, including propaganda, sabotage, demolition, economic warfare and other forms of subversion against hostile states. The CIA had been created by act of Congress in 1947, which specifically defined its activities as limited to intelligence collection and analysis. NSC 10/2, part of the CIA's "secret charter," was thus never authorized by Congress or the American people. Surprised?

So what was the big deal? The NSB was running or planning to run an unauthorized subversive action against some "hostile state." What else is new? What aspect of this by now commonplace scenario had pushed little Newt over his moral threshold? And where in the haystack was the mysterious lock

that awaited the slimy little key that rested in the pocket of
my jeans?

But all that was last week and right now I'm headed for a place
called The Rock on Santa Monica Boulevard, a bar and eatery
where, if you're lucky, you can pick up a girl with tatoos and
if you're not, you can get knifed in somebody else's bad movie.
They have the world's greatest jukebox with a playlist that's
remained unchanged since "In A Gadda-Da-Vida" got installed in 1968. That's how long I've been going there and, like
a bed you still sleep in that's played host to a multitude of
lovers, every stool, every song, every drink holds the ghost of
a sexual encounter.

My editor, Shrike, likes to ride his Harley through the
streets like the man he wishes he was and stop at the The Rock
for some tough talk and Jack Daniel's. He's there at the bar
when I walk in, black hair pulled back in a ponytail, black
leather jacket, black pants, boots, shirt, cigarette lighter—the
Dauphin of Darkness.

"Marx, you scumdog. Get over here and give me a kiss."

I laugh and shake my head, which is the only way to react
to Shrike. Leon the bartender sets out my usual, Cuervo Gold
and Corona.

Shrike is unwinding from the rigors of overseeing *Up Yours.*

"Did you know that sixty percent of the Amazon land is
owned by one percent of the population, mostly foreigners,
predominantly Japs? Japs, Marx! The Japs have their hands on
forty percent of the world's oxygen supply! They've got us by
the lungs! Let them have Columbia Pictures and Rockefeller
Center, they can ice-skate and colorize movies forever for all
I care. But *air,* Marx, they're destroying our AIR!"

Shrike is now off his seat, leaning over me and blowing hot
sour-mash bourbon and cigarettes in my face. I try not to

recoil too visibly—a man should be able to take it and, after all, Shrike is my boss.

"Marx, I'm doing an entire issue on the Japs, I'm going to dig up every fact and figure I can get my hands on, I'm putting the entire research department on it. I'm going to bury the bastards. And you're my emotion man, Marx, your column sets the stage. I want you to whip them up for me, make them feel threatened, victimized, condescended to. Get them angry and paranoid of anything that's yellow and smiles a lot."

I down my first shot of tequila and acknowledge Shrike in all his slathering hyperkineticness. "We'll get 'em, boss. We'll roast 'em good."

"You don't understand, Marx, you don't comprehend. Satan, thy name is Sony. The devil's forces capture our souls with Nikons and crush the American dream with Hondas. These are the Armies of Darkness. Marx, you don't look too good. Is something worse than usual happening?"

"Not really. I found a friend of mine hanging from the end of a rope a few hours ago."

He cocks his head and looks at me, wondering if I'm jiving or telling the truth. "That's rough," he says, testing.

"Rough," I repeat, and I'm thinking about Linda and me having breakfast in bed and watching *The Newlywed Game.* Shrike's fading fast as Linda turns to me with a mouthful of croissant and slips her hand between my legs and the host is asking one of the girls, where's the strangest place your husband ever made love to you? And I get this searing deep painful feeling of loss as the girl answers, "I'd have to say in the butt, Bob," and Linda's sweet, childish laugh starts to dissolve in my mind and Shrike belches smoke in my face and asks if I'm all right. I gulp down the rest of the Corona and Leon sets me up again.

"Shrike," I whisper, and he leans his head close. "I think they're out to get me."

"They've always been out to get you, Marx. That's why your readers love you."

Pursuing the most horrifying scenario, I ask, "What if they say Linda was murdered and try to prove I did it?"

"Did you?"

"Go to hell." I empty the second shot glass of Cuervo.

"Did your friend kill herself or not?" Shrike wants to know. He's becoming intrigued.

"Another tequila, Leon. Make it a glass of tequila. No, make it a pail. A pail of tequila and a brace of hookers."

"Okay. Let's assume for a moment that she did not kill herself and that someone other than you killed her. Here." He shoves a napkin in front of me and hands me a ballpoint. "We'll do a right-brain exercise." Good old Shrike, new wave to the bitter end. "Without thinking, write down real fast four names of people who by the wildest stretch of the imagination, could have wanted her dead. No thinking, just writing."

"Nobody wanted Linda dead—" I try to say.

"Write," he orders.

Without thinking I write four names on the napkin.

"Good," he says. "Let's see what you have." He picks up the napkin and reads. "Nat Bostwick."

I shake my head no. "Her boss. Not a chance."

"Harry Ballister. Is that the city councilman, Harry Ballister?"

"He jilted her. If anything, she'd want to kill him."

"Maybe she had something on him."

"Maybe."

"Sarah Myerson."

"Her best friend. A pea for a brain but a stand-up lady."

"Sally Keester. *Keester?*"

"Aptly named. Her next-door neighbor. They hung out a lot. Sally needed her company, she wouldn't do it."

He looks at the napkin, disappointed. "Maybe we should try a left-brain technique—"

"Nobody killed her. She was depressed about the world. She was depressed about her brother."

"Why her brother?"

"He was killed in a car accident last week. Little Newt. Little Newt, the CIA man."

"A brother in the CIA. This gets more interesting."

"I'm glad you're having fun, Shrike."

"What kind of car accident?"

"He turned on the ignition and the car exploded."

He digests this news, then drinks down his Jack Daniel's and mourns, "Why is it always the little guy who gets buried?"

"You knew Newt?"

"You, Marx, you!"

In the pregnancy of the pause the Beatles drift by from the jukebox . . . *"You say yes, I say no, You say why, I say I don't know . . ."*

Shrike looks like he's about to recite Dylan Thomas, "Do not go gently into that good night," but instead just averts his gaze and silently dabs at his eyes with a napkin. The man has soul, whether he knows it or not. And I'm thinking to myself, *I* should be the one crying, it's my friend who is dead. But I don't.

I'm not as drunk as I have to be to go home so I get into my car and head back down Sunset. I turn on the radio and the talk show guy is hammering, "Come on now, admit it, doesn't sex with the same person get really boring? Were human beings really meant to be monogamous? Do you really want to spend the rest of your life having sex with the same person?

I say no. What do you say? In L.A. the number is 280-TALK, in the Valley, 985-TALK, in the desert . . ."

He takes some calls and I drive along and pretty soon I'm in Linda's neighborhood and some self-righteous insomniac from West Covina is saying that the thousandth time he makes love to his wife is better than the second time he makes love to anyone else.

Linda's street is quiet as I drift by and turn down the radio. Her little Spanish cottage is sadly still and dark, and I'm just starting to feel the horrible ache in my stomach, the sheer physical pain of loss, that up until now I have tried to deny.

Then comes a déjà vu, that feeling that this has all happened before, and I play this game where I tell myself if it's happened before I must be able to guess what will happen next, if I could only concentrate. In this car, on this street, feeling this pain, what's next, I know what it is, it's happened before and I have the feeling it isn't good. But I can't remember it or think of it or whatever you do in a déjà vu. So I pull over down the block and wait for it to pass and wonder if that's what I did before that I'm having so much trouble remembering now, pull over and wait for it to pass.

Cleaner than cyanide in Kool-Aid, the déjà vu dissolves, but it leads my mind to another time, another death. I knock off the lights and the engine and, sitting there in the throbbing blue-blackness, watch myself opening the door to Janis's hotel room and seeing her sprawled on the carpet like a broken puppet. My heart starts pounding like it did then, like it did when I saw Linda dangling from the living room fixture with eyes like golf balls, her lovely smooth legs hanging still and lifeless.

Fuck you, I think to God. Fuck you, fuck you, fuck you, fuck you! And you suffer swine to live. Don't ask me for anything, don't ever ask me for anything because you take and you take and what do you give? Calvin Klein, car phones and crooked Christian theme parks? You're wrong, you stink, you're no good, you're no good, you're no good, baby, you're no good. I have no problems talking to God like this, we have an open relationship and we're both free to express our feelings.

Having righteously dispensed with the Almighty, I look across at Linda's house. I'm here because I figure that if she really did herself in, she would have left me a note or a letter, some message of explanation or farewell. Lieutenant Danno and his hounds wouldn't have found it, there's a secret opening behind a framed Nirvana Rock Festival poster in the bathroom, where Linda and I always left messages for each other. If she had anything to tell me, that's where it would be.

I get out of the car and slip through the shadows to Linda's back door. I have to walk down the driveway and under a gallery of elm trees and I try not to breathe heavily or make my bootheels click on the asphalt. I realize I should have taken another hit on the Cuervo but a mind that feels like the inside of a torn pocket can't think of everything, can it?

I look over at the house next door and see Sally Keester sitting at her kitchen table, crying. Sally looks and dresses like a forties B-movie femme fatale and, watching her through the window, crying alone in the brightly lit kitchen, I feel like I'm in a museum after hours, spying on one of those heartbreaking Hopper paintings coming to life in the night.

Negotiating the area between the two houses, I find the key Linda kept under the rock by the back fence and let myself in. I locate the flashlight on the shelf by the door and make my way into the kitchen, careful to point the beam low.

There in the kitchen, leaning against a wall, is the sign Linda carried at a demonstration the other day, against a well-known research facility where they experiment on dogs.

"What kind of experiments?" I had asked.

"Head transplants."

"Head transplants?" I repeated dumbly.

"They put a German shepherd's head on a beagle. And a doberman's head on a collie."

"No sense of aesthetics."

"All in the name of medical science. In the name of humanity. It's so sick. These people are Nazis. They've got to be stopped." And it was always Linda out there on the protest line, trying to stop them.

She came home from the demonstration more deeply depressed than I'd ever seen her. The police had treated them like criminals, arrested a few and broken it up.

I tried to pick up her spirits but just made things worse. She wanted to know why I didn't come to the demonstration, why I was all talk and no action. She wanted to know why I couldn't commit to anything, why I never once said "I love you," even out of simple consideration. She wished I would just finally let go, "come out of denial" and open my heart to my feelings. I told her that survivors in the nineties don't walk around with open hearts and I wasn't quite ready to become a whipping boy for the types of assholes who exploited humaneness. She said I was confusing "surviving with living," that I was watching life instead of experiencing it, and wondered how she could have become involved with someone so hopelessly closed off. I was starting to feel really bad, like everything she said was true and everything I answered was just petty defense.

I tried to take her in my arms but she asked me to leave. She wanted to be by herself.

"Great solution," I said, stung by the rejection. "Be alone with the person who makes you most miserable." And I left.

Remembering that conversation and my overwhelming need to defend myself in the face of her honesty, I get a guilty chill and think that she'd still be alive if it weren't for me. My temples pounding, I head for the bathroom, filled with the hope that I won't find a suicide note, that, ugly and foul as it sounds, somebody else took Linda's life.

Following the beam of the flashlight, I move through the living room, carefully skirting the area where I found Linda's body, so many eons ago this very evening. In the dim aura of light I can make out the markings left by the police. What could Danno possibly have on me I wonder, as I enter the bathroom.

Hoping against hope to find the cupboard bare, I reach behind the Nirvana Rock Festival poster, into the little niche in the wall, and come out with a small slip of paper. It's too small, I'm thinking fervently, to be an explanation of life and death. I straighten the poster back up and shine the light on the little white paper, a "While You Were Out" message detached from a telephone message book.

"Hollywood Post Office, 343 N. Gower Avenue, Box #2323." In Linda's handwriting. That's it. No "My darling," no "Your little girl," no poetry, no profound saying for the day—just that.

I'm wondering what the hell it all means when I suddenly hear a sound, a kind of thud, like a cat jumping down from a sink, but I know it isn't a cat because Linda didn't have a cat and because I hear a man's voice grunt, then curse in a bare whisper. I panic. Quickly I look at the message and memorize the box number. 2323. Two three or not two three, that is the number. Got it. I stick it in my mouth and I'm swallowing it just as the lights go on.

"Having fun, Albie?" Lieutenant Danno asks, his deep, unreadable eyes raking me over pretty good.

"Albie! I didn't know it was you," exclaims Sally Keester, her face still puffy from sobbing. "I saw a light in the window and called the Lieutenant."

The yellow slip of paper is halfway down my throat and refusing to go the rest of the way. I want to give some slick excuse for being there but all I can do is choke and cough.

"Are you all right, Albie?" she asks, concerned. The paper is wedged in my throat I can only shake my head no. "I'll get you some water," and she hurries off to the kitchen, leaving me alone with Yul Brenner's twin brother, whose sympathy for my imminent suffocation is obviously at low ebb.

"Did you find what you're looking for?" Danno inquires, as I gasp for air. "Is it something you'd care to share?"

I want to tell him that I wouldn't share a shit sandwich with him but what I actually try to say is that I came to get some notes I need for my column, some facts and figures that I'd left with Linda. My voice sounds like a kazoo as the air whistles past the paper stuck in my throat. I start to cough again and I'm probably turning blue but Danno just stands there eyeing me coldly. Sally comes back with the glass of water and I try to get it down without spraying them both. She looks so concerned that I feel obligated to indicate that I'll be all right.

Danno remains unmoved. "Maybe you'd like to level with me about your relationship with the deceased."

By the way Sally blushes I can tell that she's told him everything she knows and more.

"We were friends," I manage to say, finally getting some unobstructed air to my lungs. "We liked each other. Surely you've had that experience with *someone*, Lieutenant."

"You were the one who found Janis Joplin's body, weren't you?" he asks, and now I know what's bothering him. It never was proved if Janis shot up alone or with someone—or if someone else shot her up.

"Now we have Linda Selby," he continues. "That makes two for you, Albie. Most people never get one."

"I don't see the correlation, Lieutenant."

"I think you will, Albie. Just be patient."

An hour later, I'm sunk into Sally's couch, finishing the last of her tequila. It's not Cuervo Gold but at this point what does it matter? Sally is sitting across from me in an armchair, dozed off. I invited myself over when Danno showed us out of Linda's place. I was too revved up and lonely to go home. Great company Sally turned out to be. I'd get the hell out of here if I had the energy to get up off the couch.

Sally looks a lot like Lana Turner, that kind of down-and-dirty untouchable blonde that you know is a maniac in bed but would be afraid to ask for a date. She's big enough to break a small man in half and I've fantasized making love to her, pictured us in a secret tryst, meeting secretly in a motel room to spare Linda's feelings. Now that Linda's gone, the idea of meeting Sally in a motel room doesn't have the verve it used to.

The booze has me bleary but the events of the day are starting to sink in and I'm wondering, what the fuck have I gotten myself into? The last things I need are trouble with the law and political intrigue. Haven't I had enough of all that? I'm just starting to get back on my feet and get some momentum, after my hiatus of the eighties. I found a voice again, even if I don't believe in it. I don't have to believe in the dignity of man anymore. Why should I be different from everybody else? It's time for me to be happy too, let the needs of the planet be serviced by others. Look at Linda. She cared, she cared completely, and what did it get her? A man who can't say "I love you" and a death without honor.

But I can't convince myself of any of this. The real me isn't the drunk who can't face himself but the man who won't stop.

The real me has to keep fighting, has to stand guard. This thing we call freedom is too easily pulled over our eyes. As long as we're reasonably happy we think we're free. Only we've accepted Someone Else's definition of Happiness—a job, a vacation, a six-pack of beer and cable TV—while Someone Else goes about scooping up money and grabbing more power and running this world any way they see fit. It may not be the end of freedom and it's a lot better than a pickaxe in Siberia, but can it possibly be what humanity has arrived at after four million years of evolution? A world full of obedient, TV-glazed consumers? Isn't there something a little bit . . . higher? I may not be happy but I'm free. Isn't that better than the other way around? Besides, what is "happy?" Cows are happy.

CHAPTER 2

Nowadays Walter Bates practically lived in the White House basement. Of his own choice and design, his office was small and functional, exemplifying the Spartan approach he took to his work. From 0600 hours to 2400 hours (he put himself on military time when he came to work at the White House), Walter was at his post, designing the machinery that facilitated the plans of the captains of state, the architects of civilization, and when sleep became a necessity, the Snooze Room was right down the hall.

Walter was known to be brilliant and highly disciplined, and though he'd never been to war, or even in the military, he liked to think of himself as brave and warlike too. But he gave himself credit for knowing that whatever anybody is, they can never be perfect, so he always ended his memos with CYA. Cover Your Ass.

You hear that one all your life. Until you learn it. Then you know. Keep your nose clean and don't fuck up, his dad used to say. But we all fuck up once in a while, so CYA.

Things were coming down to the wire and he felt strong. Now he needed to hear from that little twit he placed on the senator's staff. Rosenbaum only had Ivy League pretty boys working for him so this Greenfeder was a perfect plant. Maybe Rosenbaum will fall in love with the kid. Then they'd really have that phony New York Jew by the balls.

So many strings leading out from his fingers. So many possible endings. But the one he loved most was the image of himself in the office next to the chief of staff, J.T., his teacher and mentor—two walls away from the President himself. The advertising business had had its moments, he and J.T. had played with some major accounts, but never anything like this. Here on the Staff, we play with *armies.* Here in the White House basement, we *make the rules.*

He smiled deep inside. This will be some campaign. Bigger and better than all the rest. With ample rewards. Ample. And this committee vote is the crucial first step. SCOLD, the Senate Committee on Legalization of Drugs, is making its recommendation today. They could be voting right now. As soon as they do, Greenfeder will be on the horn. The kid's on top of it.

He went down the list of committee members. Seven Democrats, six Republicans, with Rosenbaum chairman. J.T. and his hounds have been squeezing these bastards from morning till night. If they recommend, both Houses will follow and the stage will be set. Yes, they'll recommend. When J.T. wants something, J.T. gets it.

He remembered the days at the agency, when J.T. knew every rep, creative director, writer, director, producer, editor, all the way down the line, on every account. He read every memo, played every jingle, screened every daily and when he wanted something added or changed—he called personally and told them what to do. It was a style that kept him on top on Madison Avenue and it was clicking on Pennsylvania Avenue as well. J.T.'s been on the phone day and night with one bag of wind after another, telling them exactly why they should vote to recommend Legalization.

The whole plan is beautiful, the way it's playing itself out. Take St. John for instance, the mad chemist—one day he's on his high horse about ethics and mind control and the next his lawyer is cutting a deal for stock options into the year 2020. J.T. just scares the shit out of people.

His intercom buzzes. "Greenfeder on three."

He picks up the phone. "Yes?"

"*Yes.*"

"Perfect."

He hangs up. It's getting closer, he thinks gleefully, exerting steel will to keep from rubbing his hands together. The first major piece is in place. He'll get the particulars momentarily. It will be hell for anyone who voted No. J.T. never forgets and J.T. never forgives. Senators, governors—even the President— have all been on their oratorical knees to J.T.

And why not the President? J.T. created him, didn't he? "You sell a president like you sell a deodorant," J.T. once said. "Nobody cares what a deodorant is made from, they don't want to know the names of the chemicals and the reactions they cause. People want *hope.* They want to be just like the darling, happy, actors they see in TV commercials.

" 'If Right Guard makes me sexy and popular, I'll go out and buy it. If Donald Cale makes me proud and secure, I'll go out and vote for him.' "

And vote for him they did. In record numbers. If a presidential campaign is the Heavyweight Title Match of advertising, then J.T. is the undisputed Champ. What is his secret? To J.T., the commercial is a "magic bridge," where you take your target market from fact to dream to illusion—the illusion that your product will make the dream come true. They don't buy apples, they buy vitality. They don't buy a Cadillac, they buy superiority. They don't buy Donald Cale, they buy a kinder, gentler prosperity. A galaxy of ideas. A hundred bulbs of light.

And now, Walter rhapsodizes, another great victory for J.T.'s incomparable team—Legalization. But careful—don't get carried away by today's vote. It's a long way from committee to congressional approval, a mother of a course with traps and obstacles of every kind. Yes, it's exhilarating to birdie Hole 1, but that guarantees nothing. On this course, each hole is tougher than the last. You've got to keep your head down and follow through. And remember to CYA.

Which reminds him of Newt. Why had he trusted the little traitor in the first place? Lucky thing Newt wasn't *his* man. J.T. himself picked Newt from the jingle pool and assigned him to the National Security Board. But the operation is mine, Walter firmly reminds himself, ergo, so is Newt.

He doesn't know what paperwork, if any, Newt had managed to smuggle out of the office. Walter tried never to spell anything out too clearly, in writing or otherwise, so that only the person for whom it was meant would get the full meaning. But sometimes . . . you just can't be sure.

He knows of Newt's meeting with Albie Marx. But what information did Newt divulge? No documents were passed. No physical contact was made. Besides, Newt hated Marx's type and all that it stood for. From sixties drugged-out radical to shrill nineties voice of doom, Marx was the self-appointed raving alcoholic conscience of the middle and underclass, of environmentalists, Naderites, commies, faggots, Jews and the rest of the filth. Newt had to be in some state of mind to allow Marx within ten miles of him.

Well, Walter wouldn't worry too much about Albie Marx. He's a harmless bigmouth. A drunk with delusions of grandeur. And now, with the icing of Newt's sister, he'll have his hands full with the L.A.P.D.

His private phone, the direct line to J.T., beeps.

"It's *yes,* J.T."

"Good. We're in gear. Did you get the count?"

"On your desk in ten minutes."

"What about St. John?"

"Set."

"We'll need push money for the media heavies when we sell the Crisis."

"Give me a number."

"Three mil."

"No problem, J.T."

"You're showing me something, Walter. I like what I see." The line goes blank.

Walter's chest swells. That rare compliment came from the most powerful man on the planet.

CHAPTER 3

"Air Quality—Unhealthful," according to the Los Angeles weather service, and I'm into mile four of my eight-mile run. Deep into my lungs and into my bloodstream I draw the excretions of millions of fuel burning engines, uncounted toxin spewing factories, and every slimy operation that makes provision in its budget for "EPA relations."

I'm high in the hills over Hollywood, in Los Feliz. Once upon a time, in its golden years, Los Feliz was so desirable that the great Frank Lloyd Wright erected two of his masterpieces here. Will and Ariel Durant spent thirty-seven years in these hills, living into their nineties, falling deeper and deeper in love and turning out volume upon volume of the history of civilization. W. C. Fields and Douglas Fairbanks Jr. drove their Deusenbergs here, through massive, iron-gated entries, to estates rivalling any in the movie star pantheon.

Not that it's exactly a war zone now, but the prosperity that created these lovely, winding roads and gracious, hillside homes long ago fled west, to the insular safety of Beverly Hills and the once purifying breezes of the ocean. Now, most every house has a security system with armed response and decorator window bars.

My morning runs vary according to how much I drink the day before. Some of the steeper grades are truly punishing, which I love, because only a thorough and complete exorcism of the spirits of Cuervo, in liquid form through the pores, will allow me to indulge them again. This is the secret of being a fit, healthy drunk.

Running is also a time for meditation, reflection, examination. A time for being alone and chewing on your options. Along about mile five, I realize that the post office box number in Linda's last message is the answer to the mystery of little Newt's key.

I'm chugging up the hill toward my house when I spot my cat Tank on the front step, squinting reprovingly at me through his one good eye. A grizzled old hunter is Tank, a big, kick-ass tom, with chunks of his ears lost in battle and a tail with more kinks than a car phone antenna.

My little house is actually the caretaker's quarters of a great old estate, built in the twenties by a newly landed oil baron and long since abandoned to a succession of owners who went broke trying to maintain it. Through it all I've hung on to my domain, this large one-room cottage with a kitchenette, bathroom, floor-to-ceiling stone fireplace and spectacular views of Los Angeles, or whatever you can see through the blanket of grime.

I haven't seen Tank in a couple of days and he's laying this guilt trip on me with that look, but I'm not buying into it. He has his life and I have mine. Hey, there are plenty of times when I can use someone around and where is he? Out getting laid, picking on birds, duking it out with the neighborhood ringtail—like the Beatles say, the love you take is equal to the love you make. I don't see him going out of his way to make life less empty for me.

"What is it with you? You want food, right?" I tried to encourage him to be vegetarian but it's not in his makeup. He wouldn't touch the stuff I put out and only ate mice and birds. Now that I've gone back to liver and fish platters, I see him more often.

Sopping with sweat, I find the last can of catfood and dump it onto a plate for him. He never so much as says thank you. The red light is blinking on my message machine and I don't really want to hear anyone's voice but since my life is such a muddle of shit right now I throw peace of mind to the wind and hit the playback button.

"Something to think about, Marx," comes Shrike's sickening peppy voice, "for your lead-in to the Jap issue. Hypothetical question: What if the Good Lord, being preoccupied with some other cosmos or galaxy for a minute, had given the world the Tokyo Project instead of the Manhattan Project? Gave the Nips the atom bomb first. What kind of restraint would *they* have used? They'd have nuked us off the fucking planet! We're so goddamn complacent, we take it for granted that we got the bomb first. But what if we didn't? Might be interesting to draw some conclusions. Check you out later. Oh, by the way—how's the murder case coming?"

Thoughtful of him to ask.

"Hi, Dad, it's me." My son, Freedom Marx, now known as Jonathan Grant. I can see why he'd change his first name, but the Grant part, that's pure rebellion. What's wrong with Jonathan Marx?

"This treatment you sent me. I can't recommend this." The kid's twenty-three years old, a minor executive at Disney, and I gave him a treatment of an idea I had for a film called *Dodgers,* an adventure about an underground network of draft dodgers in the future, when the United States is militarily annexing all of Central America. Not so farfetched, right?

"This isn't a Disney picture. Why don't you write something nice? We're looking for a romantic dra-medy caper. Something for Goldie Hawn. I can't recommend this, Dad. It's so . . . depressing. Give me a call. I'm open for lunch on the fifth."

That's three weeks from now. But what can I expect? I haven't been the world's greatest father. He may be a mindless slimeball, but he's my son. My only child. A product of the Chicago Democratic Convention of 1968, where I avoided being beaten to a pulp by the police in the park by screwing his mother, a yippie freak, in a clump of bushes at the edge of the lake. Defying convention to the bitter end, we finally got married—after five years of peaceful cohabitation, bringing up the child we named, in honor of our passion, Freedom. The marriage lasted six weeks.

I'm heading up the steps of the Hollywood post office, just a couple of minutes after opening time, and wondering who belongs to the limousine with the city official plates parked in front. My question is answered as I step through the front doors. Passing me on his way out, his wimpy puss all wrapped up in some self-important psychodrama, is Harry Ballister, city councilman, bulwark of conscience in government. He was also Linda Selby's lying, cheating ex-lover. We've met but he doesn't notice me. With what's probably going on in that conniving cerebrum of his, he wouldn't notice his own mother. Funny coincidence, both of us being here this particular morning.

"Good morning, Councilman," I say, ripping him out of his dyspeptic self-absorption.

"Good morning," he replies brightly, with the automatic cheerfulness of the inveterate politician.

Before he can hurry on, I nail him with, "I guess you heard about Linda Selby."

He stops and looks at me, scanning his mental Rolodex for my name and face. In a matter of seconds his expression speeds through preoccupied, cheerful, surprised, and calculating and finally settles on noncommittal.

"How do I know you?" he asks.

"Albie Marx. I took your place in Linda's bed."

"Good to see you Albie," he says and reaches out to shake my hand. No way you putz, I think, as I let him dangle his pink manicured paw in the air. You have to hand it to these bastards. I hit him with one of my best shots and the fucker didn't blink.

"I heard about Linda this morning. I was devastated. What made her do such a thing?"

"She got tired of the bullshit, Harry. She was too sensitive for this world. You remember, don't you, how vulnerable she was?"

"She was a heck of a girl, a real jewel. The Lord works in strange ways, I see that every day. All we can do is keep fighting the good fight. I know you believe in that, Albie, I've read some of your work."

"Do you *feel* anything, Harry? Does it hurt that we've lost someone who really cared about this world? Or are you really as phony and scummy as Linda said you are?"

He can't duck that one. But he does.

"Nice seeing you, Albie. If there's anything I can do, give me a call."

I watch him hurry down the steps and slide into the waiting limousine, another perk paid for with my fucking taxes. You can't rattle these guys, they have you by the balls and they know it. What was he doing here? Buddha said, "There are no coincidences."

Though it's early in the morning, the building is beginning to bustle. I reach into my pocket and bring out Newt's key. Two three or not two three, that is the number. As I head for the boxes I'm starting to feel watched. It's all in my head I tell myself, I'm getting paranoid. Not that I ever stopped being paranoid. To this day I can't see a police car in my rearview mirror without feeling a cold bolt of fear in my stomach.

Searching for 2323, I keep looking around, hoping to catch someone in the act of spying. I realize I'm making quick, furtive motions with my head, like a barnyard chicken, so I stop. Nobody pays any attention to my chicken routine anyway, this is, after all, Hollyweird, where behavior isn't considered abnormal unless it involves an AK-47.

I locate number 2323 and slide the key into the lock. It fits and it works and the little door opens. I look inside and—it's Mother Hubbard time. Just some dust and that's it. This is a bitch. What do I do now?

I think of Harry Ballister. Did he get here before me? Was there anything here to begin with? Is Linda's final epistle a code I misread, meaning something entirely different?

I'm standing and staring into the box, like if I look at it long enough something will appear. There's a young girl standing nearby, in her early twenties I'd say, and she's apparently wondering what's with me, staring forlornly into an empty post office box.

I sneak a good look at her and realize that this is no ordinary girl. This is a major piece of work. She's got a real pretty face, kind of open and round, with perfect olive skin and big, really sensitive brown eyes on the order of Linda's. In contrast to the softness of her face, her brown hair is cut short and hard, and it's flecked with just about every color of the rainbow. She's wearing the shortest acceptable skin-tight miniskirt and a purple leather motorcycle jacket. Her ass and her legs are worth doing time for.

She catches me looking and walks away. I get that horrible feeling of being a dirty old man. I want to tell her I'm not what I look like, I'm still young, I'm still crazy, I can still fuck all night.

Nothing hurts more than getting older, and to my lasting regret it was my generation that made it a crime. "Never trust anyone over thirty," we declared with the incurable optimism of youth, never stopping to think, in our rush back to Eden, that time catches up with us all.

Goddamn, I miss Linda. She understood all these feelings. She was soothing. She understood the process somehow, the stages and phases and metabolic transformations. I could be old or young with her, each had its charm. Now, what?

"Mr. Marx?" she asks, as I step out into the Hollywood haze. It's her. The colors in her hair are more electric in the daylight, like they're vibrating. Or maybe it's me that's vibrating.

"Who may I say is calling?" I ask, trying to appear indifferent while my heart is about to explode out of my chest.

"We have to talk." And she starts off down the steps. Like I'm supposed to blindly follow her. She gets to the sidewalk and looks back at me. "Are you coming?"

"Who are you?" This kid is a little too confident.

"Don't be a jerk, okay? This isn't a game."

I think to myself that of all the insane situations I could have fallen into, this at least has some heat. I join her on the sidewalk. "Do I get to know your name, or do I address you as Ma'am?"

"My name is Mariah. Where's your car?" I hear the words in my head, "the rain is Tess, the fire's Joe and they call the wind Mariah."

I decide to play this one out and I lead her to the Jag. She opens the door and gets in without a word. I get behind the wheel and start up the engine.

"Where are you going?" she asks, as I pull out into traffic.

"Wherever's right," I reply, figuring it's eight o'clock in the morning, I'll stop at the first open bar that isn't crawling with degenerates.

"Let's go to your place," she says, without even looking at me.

"What is this? I don't even know you. We're not going to my place. We're not going anywhere. You have something on your mind? You want to talk? Talk."

I glance at her and I see that she's struggling with some giant emotion that's getting the best of her. But she squashes it down, without knowing I've seen the struggle.

"You made my mother very unhappy," she says harshly.

Her mother? What now? A paternity suit at my age?

"But for some stupid reason she loved you."

"Who is your mother?" I hear myself ask wearily. Why do women have to be so fucking complicated?

"Linda was my mother. Linda Selby."

For a second I'm blown away.

"Don't tell me you forgot her already, you son-of-a-bitch. She's only been dead for twelve hours."

This is all I can take. I jerk the car over and pull on the handbrake. "Who are you?" I demand. "Just who the hell are you?"

"Linda's daughter," she repeats, and suddenly her cool facade crumbles and she starts pounding the dashboard. "And now she's fucking gone! She's gone! She's gone!"

I grab onto her wrists but I have no leverage and she's stronger than she looks and I'm weaker than I look. She clips me in the nose and I see stars and now I'm warding off blows that hurt, really hurt.

"Hold it!" I shout, trying to defend myself without punching her. "Come on, stop it!"

It takes me a minute but I finally subdue her, all the while checking my windows to see that this scene in my car isn't attracting attention. Her fury spent, she pulls away and huddles over on her side of the car, marshalling her feelings for battles to come.

"Linda never told me she had a daughter," I say softly. "Or a son, or any kid. Forgive me if I'm having a hard time digesting this."

"I don't give a fuck what you digest. I just want to find out what really happened to my mother."

"Not any more than I do!" I'm suddenly shouting. "And I've had it with this bullshit game!" I grab her wrist tightly, painfully. "Now who the hell are you?"

That does it. She comes totally apart. If she's ever going to tell the truth, it's now. I know a little about people and this kid's defenses are down.

Through the profound relief of her sobs she's blurting, "I just got to know her . . . They never told me . . . She gave me up for adoption . . . I found out last year . . ."

All I can say is, "But she never said anything. Why didn't she say anything to me . . . ?"

The car is vibrating with a thousand raw nerve endings. I keep seeing Linda, motionless, pitiful, her neck at an impossible angle, eyes bulging and glassy. Nothing makes sense, nothing computes. And this magnificent creature across from me. All youth and pain and beautiful skin. I'm anguished and frightened and indescribably horny. How can I think of sex at a time like this? Because this girl is *hot*.

We end up in a booth in a Hollyweird Boulevard coffee shop. There's a mental escapee in the next booth playing with his hair, which completely covers his face. He winds it around his fingers, draws it away from his eyes like draperies, then lets it flop back again. The waitress, who's probably served every pathetic creature out free on the street, is treating this guy like Mr. Joe Average and taking his order.

I'm watching all this because he's sitting right behind Mariah and I'm doing everything I can not to fall into her eyes. I can't stop all the buzzing that's going on in my loins but I can at least keep it confined to that area. First of all, to her I'm an old man. Second, she's Linda's kid. Third, she's the age of my son. Bottom line, I don't have the time or the energy to fall in love. Which is what a night with this person would lead to. Guaranteed. So I'm holding back, I'm putting a governor on the old flirty looks, I'm facing the situation that *does* exist, the continuing mystery of Linda Selby.

"What were you doing at the post office?" she has the nerve to ask. Those big, brown eyes of hers aren't so sensitive right now, they're hard as brass. She's leaning toward me, her hands with the dadaist fingernails clasped tightly on the table in front of her.

"Let's just cut the shit," I say. "What did you take out of the post office box?"

"My mother said you're a cold customer."

"*Cool* customer."

"She said cold."

"She may not have gotten everything she wanted from me, but she never called me cold."

"Defensive," she taunts.

"I'll take the rap for a lot of things, but I'm not cold."

"You can't fuckin' take it, can you? You hold onto that sixties flowerchild shit like it's really still you. Why don't you admit you're as mean as the rest of us?"

It's almost heartbreaking, hearing the kid describe herself like that. "How old are you?" I ask. "Twenty-two? Twenty-three? What do you know about anything?"

"What are you? Fifty?"

"Do I look fifty to you?"

"You look like a hundred and fifty to me."

At this moment an angel of mercy appears in a waitress uniform. "What's it gonna be for you's?"

"Espresso," says Mariah and the waitress gives her a don't-bust-my-balls look. "Coffee."

I order coffee and I'd love to have a donut but I'm thinking that donuts go straight to the love handles and a man who looks a hundred and fifty better use some restraint. Although I can probably run farther than her twenty-year-old boyfriends. And last longer in bed.

"Look," I begin in a peacemaking tone, "I feel as rotten about this as you do, whether you believe it or not. You came looking for me, I didn't come after you. You must have known about the P.O. box or you wouldn't have been in the post office. If you have something to tell me, tell me. If you have something to ask, ask."

Now those eyes are really taking the measure of me. "She didn't kill herself."

"How do you know?"

"She wouldn't. She just wouldn't."

"How can you be so sure?"

"She was excited. She said she was going to blow the lid off something. She was excited, she was *not* suicidal."

She pulls a folded-up manila envelope out of her purse and drops it on the table. "Uncle Newt gave me a post office key and told me if anything happened to him, to make sure you got this." And she bites her lip to keep away the sadness.

I want to take her hand to comfort her but I'm afraid I'll never give it back, so I busy myself with opening the heavily sealed envelope.

"I'll find out who did it," she vows to herself, staring intently at her iridescent fingernails.

Making my way through the heavy tape I get the envelope

open and slide out a thin sheath of papers with a topsheet that reads, "TOP SECRET CLASSIFIED INFORMATION— U.S. GOVERNMENT PROPERTY."

"What is it?" she asks, clearly counting herself a part of the intrigue.

"Heartburn," I answer. Now aware of an even bigger mess than I thought I was in, I quickly scan the coffee shop and the street for any government geeks who might be in attendance. The maniac in the booth behind us is trying to eat a soft-boiled egg through a curtain of greasy hair.

"Aren't you going to read it?" she demands. This kid has no idea of the problems you get when you fuck with the government. "You want *me* to read it?" she asks impatiently, reaching for the documents.

I hold them away from her, under the table, then lift up the top page. It's an offical memo on plain stationery, which has been shredded then painstakingly pieced together with scotch tape. Without my reading glasses the print all runs together and dances around. I curse my eyes and dig into my jean jacket for the ten-dollar specials I get at Thrifty. I put them on and glance involuntarily at the girl.

"They say the eyes are the first to go," she says without humor.

Go to hell, I think, and peer back at the memo.

TO: J.T.
FROM: W.B.
RE: *NICE* CAMPAIGN

J.T.:
STORYBOARD FINAL. SCOLD TO ROLL OUT PRELIM O.K. HOUSE LEAK PLUGGED. ST. JOHN PLAYS FOR OPTIONS. TASK FORCE LONG-BOMB READY ALERT. PHOTO OPS NEGATIVE. CHEM-TECH PSYCHOGRAPHICS AVAIL FOR YOUR

EYES ONLY. LUDI TO BE SANCTIONED. CYA.
W.B.

Stapled to the memo is a separate FBI document entitled:
LUDI, AHMET. CLASSIFIED.

Ahmet Ludi? There's a name I haven't heard in years.
Why would he be involved with the government? He left
the country twenty years ago, didn't he? And never came
back. I'd do the same thing if I had the balls. Then again,
where would I go?

"Well?" she says. "What does it say?"

I signal for the waitress to bring the check. "I'll take you
home."

We're out on the street and I'm opening the door of the car
for her and she says to me, "When I want to go home, I'll let
you know." And she gets into the car and closes the door by
herself.

We're driving through Hollywood again and even though
it's still morning I want my Cuervo and Corona cocktail. The
Up Yours offices are nested in the top floor of an old three-
story brick building on the corner of Van Ness and Santa
Monica, just a couple of blocks from the recording studio
where Janis recorded her last track back in October of 1970.
The good old days. When a "cocktail" was heroin in one arm
and LSD in the other.

Not one to exchange pleasantries, Mariah nods curtly when
I introduce her to Shrike.

"Mariah's mother was my friend who—" I look at Mariah.
I am about to say, "killed herself," maybe because I still can't
imagine someone deliberately stringing Linda up, but the grief
in Mariah's eyes takes my voice away, like a TV actor when
the sound suddenly goes out.

Shrike guesses my meaning and assumes the pontifical
expression he believes her tender age warrants. "Death is the

stage direction of Life," he coos sepulchrally. "One body exits, another enters. The show goes on." He imagines this brilliant epiphany will clear everything up for her.

"I don't believe in reincarnation," she answers, her voice flatly unimpressed.

He flashes me a glance of assumed collusion, which I do not endorse, then asks, "Do you believe in God?"

"I believe in Darwin," she replies, "survival of the fittest."

"But you don't rule out God?"

"I rule out *your* God."

"You don't believe in anything higher than yourself?"

"What are you, a missionary?"

"When I deal with a savage, yes."

"Why are you so interested in what *I* believe? You know all the answers."

Shrike objects. "I'm always willing to hear another side."

"You're full of shit. Nothing I say is going to change the way you think."

This hits him where he lives. He's built his whole persona on having an open mind. "Albie, would you say I'm a reasonable man? Do I hold onto ideas out of ego?"

"Don't drag me into it," I declare. "You can take care of yourself."

"I believe in a Force that sustains the Universe," she volunteers, "but it makes no judgments about right and wrong or good and evil—you don't come back as a guru if you're 'good' or a rattlesnake if you're 'bad.' "

"There's no 'good' and 'evil'?"

"Those are words—they mean different things to different people. There's just a Force. Or a Consciousness. Anyone can tap into it and become more powerful. What they do with that power is never judged."

"So you can be Ghandi or Hitler, it makes no difference?" I ask, intrigued.

"Not in the long run," she answers.

For a twenty-two-year-old, she's pretty opinionated.

"Then why are we here?" Shrike asks, rising to his most poetic stature. "On a small ball of rock, circling an inconsequential star, in a medium-sized galaxy, in a universe vast beyond anyone's imagination?"

"To keep each other busy," she answers, "Until the sun burns out."

That's about as bleak as it gets, I think. I wonder if all the kids nowadays feel like that.

"I'll make you a proposition. If you'd be willing to put that on paper, I'd be willing to publish it," Shrike offers magnanimously, to prove his open-mindedness.

"For what reason?" she responds. "To use up more paper?"

He finally gives up and focuses on me. "I want you to see something," he says, and takes us to a small room where Myoshi, the art director, is finishing a rough of next month's cover. It's a drawing of an Americanized Japanese family, mom, pop and a couple of kids, watching TV in their American living room, with needlepoint pillows, bowling trophies, and plates with the handpainted portraits of American presidents. The one off-key note is in front of the fireplace where a bearskin rug has been replaced—with the hide and head of an American human.

"What do you think?" asks Shrike.

"You did this?" I say to Myoshi. "These are your people."

"This *art*," he objects. "This my job."

"You're one to talk," Shrike butts in. "I suppose you've never put down a Jew."

He has me there. I can do, as they say in show biz, twenty tight minutes on Jews. When does a Jewish man stop masturbating? When his wife dies. But seriously folks, I mean no harm.

"Great work," I say to Myoshi. "Try making the tongue

hang out." I pat him on the shoulder and I'm surprised at the steel cable tension of the muscles under his floppy Missoni shirt. I've got to get to a gym, fast.

When Mariah heads off to the ladies room Shrike looks at me with one big, black eyebrow arched to his hairline. "A little jaded for you, wouldn't you say?"

"It's nothing like that," I retort, surprised by my anger at the innuendo. "The kid needs help. Her mother and uncle just died violent deaths. That doesn't exactly promote an exalted view of the world."

"I think she had those opinions already."

"Leave it alone, all right? I'm here for your political expertise." In his twenty-five-year career in underground journalism, Shrike's written political articles for every dissident rag from *The Nation* to *Mother Jones*. I give him the Top Secret memo. "What do you make of this?"

He takes the page to his desk where he studies it intently.

Mariah comes back from the john and sees him reading the memo. "What the fuck are you doing?" she hisses in my ear while she digs her nails into my arm.

"He's a political analyst," I grunt and wrench my arm free. I can allow leeway for grief but this girl's going over the limit. If I didn't feel so much like spanking her I'd kiss her so hard she'd think I'm Muhammad Ali.

"This is a classic," Shrike chuckles, shaking his head as he reads the document. "campaign . . . storyboard . . . photo ops . . . psychographics . . . it's pure agency lingo. Madison Avenue shop talk."

"What does it mean?"

"It looks like a practical joke to me."

"And if it isn't?"

He shrugs. "Who knows? J.T. could be John Thomas."

"The White House John Thomas?"

"President Cale's chief of staff."

"What makes you think it's John Thomas?"

"It's the right frame of reference. He comes out of advertising."

"That's right," I recall. "The whole White House staff comes from advertising."

"He ran BBD&O for years. He's the genius who created the Isuzu commercials. A major slimebucket. He ran Cale's campaign. He's running the country."

"It makes sense. A ravenous consumer society controlled by a ravenous marketing mind."

"Which came first, the buyer or the seller?" Shrike quips rhetorically. He looks again at the memo. "I wonder if 'Ludi' means Ahmet Ludi . . . Where did you get this?"

"It's a put-on," says Mariah, snatching the paper from his hands.

Shrike reaches for the memo but she steps back with it. He looks at me with giant question marks.

"Come on, Albie," she says to me, like I'm her little French poodle, then turns and splits.

Shrike is confused but impressed. Watching her depart, that incredible body swaggering off down the hall, all he can say is, "Unbelievable ass."

"You think it's the real thing?" I ask, preoccupied with the secret memo.

Eyes glued to her fabulous behind, he replies, "You can't fake *that*," with the solemn reverence of a Sistine Chapel tourist.

We're walking back to the car and she's bringing up all sorts of memories and vague stirrings of feelings in me. For instance, right now I'm thinking of my girlfriend Barbara Goldstein's apartment on Avenue H in Brooklyn, where I grew up. It's exactly January, 1958, and we're watching saucer-sized snowflakes glide by the window, piling up in great drifts on the street four stories below. We're completely alone, her father's at work and her mother's gone shopping. The Shirelles are asking, "Will You Still Love Me Tomorrow?" on the phonograph. The radiators are turned all the way up, the windows are getting steamy and pretty soon we're touching and rubbing and humping and grinding and I'm coming in my pants and I'm *still staying hard.*

I have never gotten laid by anyone but a hooker and I tell myself this is it, I am finally going to put my dick in a white girl, a virgin no less, I am finally going to come with my eyes open.

I've got my finger in her sweet, moistening pussy and delighting in the pungent smell that embraces us, and I finally manage to get my pants open and free my raging tool from its Fruit of the Loom straightjacket.

Suddenly and without warning, she removes my hand from between her legs, smooths down her skirt, sits up straight and says, without looking at my poor, double-crossed dong, "You won't respect me."

Standing there with my mouth open and my balls turning blue, I knew at that moment I would never give my respect to any woman who had to ask for it.

Mariah doesn't ask for respect. She could give a rat's ass what I think of her.

I ask her how it is that, in the year I knew Linda, Mariah and I never ran into each other, why Linda never mentioned her name. She tells me that twenty-two years ago she was delivered of Linda, who was just seventeen, in a Los Angeles hospital, then whisked off by a couple named Annie and Paul to a place in New York called Merrick, Long Island, where she was brought up and cared for but never informed that she was adopted.

It was only when she herself got pregnant at the age of

eighteen that Annie, in her distress, lamented to Paul, "like mother, like daughter."

Unlike Linda, Mariah didn't have the baby, but that experience led her to the Pandora's box of her past, which took another four years to pry open. Finally, last year, it revealed the identity of her real, blood mother. She secretely contacted Linda by phone and told her she was coming to meet her.

When the two finally met it was an emotional bloodbath. Linda had been twenty-one years in denial about giving her child away and Mariah had been building a rage about being abandoned.

"She was too guilty to deal with me," Mariah states flatly. "She totally gave herself to her causes because she had nothing in her personal life. When I showed up she was forced to question everything she was doing. It was almost too painful. The only real thing in her life was you—and you never gave back what she gave to you."

My first impulse is to deny that smug summation, but maybe she's right. God knows I've never been able to maintain an honest, open, loving relationship beyond the time it didn't suit my needs. Yes, I *thought* I was giving, I acted like I was giving, I could have explained in detail each action and reaction proving my position. But you can't give unless you can feel. And as I get older, I'm growing horribly certain that my feelings—the basic, raw produce of my soul—joy, happiness, love, pain, anger, fear—are locked up, tighter than the proverbial drum, in the knotted form of some soul-searing scream or yell, somewhere between my groin and my chest. And that if I don't find a way to break these feelings out and live them, or scream them, in their purest state, I will never know what it is to truly love or be loved.

"We decided to keep our relationship private," Mariah is saying, "until we felt secure enough to come out with it. I never even told Paul and Annie."

"So you were out here to visit?" I ask.

"I decided to move out for good at the end of the year, and I came to see her, to tell her I was coming."

It was during this stay that she met "Uncle" Newt. She was with Linda when news came of his death. And now she, Mariah, is the only surviving member of the Selby family.

"Where are you staying?" I ask.

"I'm not staying anywhere. My bag's at her house but I won't stay there."

"We'll get you a hotel room."

"You must have room for me," she says. "I'll stay with you."

Why are you doing this, God? What do you want from me?

CHAPTER 4

Councilman Harry Ballister went over that phone call to Linda for the fiftieth time. He had called her because he was horny, but also because the Waste Disposal thing was getting so scary, he needed to go lay his head on an understanding breast. And who better than Linda, the Earth Mother, who had loved and comforted him so many times before?

Yes, he had dumped her, but not maliciously. Their affair had simply grown stagnant. Not from her end, perhaps, but certainly from his. So what was he to do? Continue to act like everything was hunky-dory, effect some phony charade of sex and manners? Would that have been fair to her? He had always played square with her, his conscience assured him. When he said, "I love you," he meant it. When he kept on saying it after he meant it, he did it to keep her happy. What more could she ask?

Then he began seeing Lesley. Lesley was English and smelled like musk and she used wonderful words. She went to the gym every day, and had a sleek, strong, athletic body. Lesley made him feel like that student he was long ago, burning with curiosity and always aroused. He didn't tell

Linda about Lesley, what good would that have done? It would only have hurt her.

But it would have hurt her more if he simply said good-bye. So he continued to see her, blaming official demands for the reduced regularity, and gave equal time to Lesley. Was it his fault that Linda was too insecure to demand more attention? She was getting quality time, wasn't that enough? His sex with Lesley made him hotter for Linda and vice versa. They were equal beneficiaries of each other's desire.

Then Lesley found out about Linda and threatened to break up with him. What could he do? He didn't want to lose either one, he'd become so dependent on both of their love. But if he had to give up one of them, he knew it would be Linda. But then what if he and Lesley went along for a while, and it didn't work out? He couldn't go back to Linda. Unless.

Unless Linda was so hopelessly in love with him that she'd take him back no matter what. He had to protect himself, didn't he? Why should he be left all alone if choosing Lesley was a mistake?

Appealing to Lesley's compassion, he told her he couldn't just tell Linda good-bye and walk out, it would destroy her. He had to have a weekend to gently break it to her. Lesley understood, even praised him for his unusual sensitivity.

He took Linda to the most romantic place he could think of, an intimate resort called Two Bunch Palms out near Palm Springs. He got a room with a fireplace and treated her to massages and facials and then he made love to her like he'd never made love to her before. By Sunday evening she was glowing like a cheerleader at the Rose Bowl. Finally, it was time to go home.

In the car back to L.A., an ocean of tears suddenly welled up in his eyes. "Overwhelmed" with respect for her, he confessed to having an affair with another woman and told her of his painful decision to see that relationship through.

Linda was shocked. She had no idea. How long had this been going on? Was it someone she knew? What had she done wrong? Yes, she could see how upset he was, how difficult this was for him, but couldn't he give her another chance?

A man has to do what a man has to do, he told her resolutely. But the thought of losing you is too much to bear. If this other relationship doesn't work out, he asked, would you be still there for me?

That may have been taking it one step too far, he reflected later, after he'd dropped her off. She suddenly clammed up and stared stoically out the window the rest of the way home. When he pulled up to her house he tried to take her hand, to share in her misery, but she left without a word.

Sex with Lesley (as with every other woman in his life) eventually began to lose the sharp edge of passion, so he secretly started up with Dawn, a new, young secretary he had recently hired. But younger girls were not really for him, they were too moody and he always found himself trying to guess what they really wanted, instead of what they said they wanted. It was exhausting.

Then Lesley found out about Dawn and it all got ugly. Lesley refused to acknowledge the realities of life and turned violent and vindictive. She wrecked his house, threatened Dawn with a can of Mace, then ransacked his office.

He had to fire Dawn, who appeared to be having a nervous breakdown, and when he was putting his office back together, discovered some very sensitive information was missing.

Waste Disposal, Inc., a giant sanitation concern, was vying for the right to operate a new toxic landfill to be located in the hills dividing L.A. from the San Fernando Valley. He had promised them his support and in response they contributed some cash to his campaign chest. It wasn't as if they had bribed him. He was supporting them anyway, nobody made them return the favor. The whole city council did business that way. After all, it was impossible to live on what the city paid. Public opinion had forced them to cap salaries and ban honorariums. How did people expect their public servants to make a living?

What Lesley took from his office were some very incriminating ledger sheets giving a one-sided picture of his relationship with Waste Disposal. She was well aware of what they were and, knowing her frame of mind, Harry had to get them back right away. Used in the wrong way, they could literally destroy him.

He tried to find her but she'd disappeared. Not home, not at work, not anywhere. He was frantic. He couldn't sleep. Every horrible scenario did a loop through his mind, playing over and over. Which is when he called Linda. For comfort. For a moment's safe haven. She couldn't turn him down after all they'd had together, could she?

"Hello?"

"Linda, it's Harry."

Silence. Then she started to laugh. It was a good laugh, a rich laugh and he felt his stomach do flip-flops.

"What's so funny?" he asked, not really wanting to know.

"You are, Harry," and she laughed again. "Lesley told me you'd call."

He was stunned. Lesley and Linda? But they didn't know each other.

"We've been friends since you and I broke up," she informed him.

"She never said anything to me," he offered lamely.

"Men like you never see beyond your own little world," she chided. "You have no idea what a woman thinks."

He was beginning to get angry. He had called to offer his company and she was saying things that hurt his ears.

"As a matter of fact, she stopped by a few days ago. She dropped off some fascinating reading material."

Harry's heart froze. Oh, God, don't let it be. Don't let it be. "What kind of material?" he asked casually.

"Mostly numbers," was the answer, the answer he dreaded. "I really must go, Harry. Thanks for calling." And she hung up.

No matter how many times he went over it, it still came out the same. She had it. He needed it. He had to make her understand.

Then he was standing in her kitchen, shaking like a leaf. Linda was hanging in the living room, in no shape to do any more talking. Rustling through her papers, wearing Linda's rubber dish gloves so as not to leave fingerprints, he noticed the yellow carbon copy of the message in her telephone ledger: "Hollywood Post Office, 343 N. Gower Avenue, Box #2323."

He was there the next morning, using all the persuasion of his official persona to talk the corpulent post office clerk into opening the box for him. But, like all minor civil service bureaucrats, post office workers are made of stone. The fat lazy cow was immovable.

All wrapped up in figuring out a way to force the issue, he ran into Albie Marx on his way out. Marx was one of those people, a carping fingerpointer of the antiestablishment establishment, who always made his skin crawl. These whining faultfinders never *did* anything, just screamed themselves hoarse criticizing others. Unfortunately for dedicated public servants like himself, their hue and cry was not always ignored, resulting in catastrophes like salary caps and banned honorariums.

He would have given anything to know if Marx had the key to box 2323, but the man was so foul and insulting, there was nothing to do but smile and get out of there. A cold sweat swept his forehead when he imagined his ledgers in the possession of Albie Marx.

CHAPTER 5

Mariah wants to stop at the death house to pick up her suitcase. I try to talk her into checking into a motel, tell her I'll pay for it, but she says she'd rather sleep on my floor than "some fucking cold room." Sure. It'll wind up being me on the couch and her in my bed. And I'll be up half the night, trying not to think about her in my bed.

As I'm driving I'm sneaking glimpses of her out of the corner of my eye. She seems to have pulled into herself, found some transcendental spot where she can be summoned at a moment's notice, while everything sorts itself out. Even in repose, her defiance defies small talk. Her toughness, her existential inflexibility, her determined rejection of our phony value system, all haunt me like memories of who and what I used to be.

There's a Springsteen song, "No Retreat, No Surrender," that speaks of positions taken in the crystal clear crucible of youth, ideals that define the forces of good against the forces of evil, that should always be fought for, never abandoned. But is it a fair and reasonable directive? Hasn't Eldridge Cleaver retreated? Hasn't Jerry Rubin surrendered? Haven't fifty million bucks made "The Boss" slightly more willing to do what it takes to make the next fifty million? Can anybody blame them?

Something happens as the decades of one's life peel away, leaving a smaller and smaller center of concern. For nearly everyone, the primary concern of that primeval center narrows down to pure physical comfort.

In my twenties I slept on communal floors and trembled with fear and elation following Martin Luther King into Selma. I took psychedelics and wandered sleepless and unwashed through the high California desert, ruthlessly pursuing Divine Revelation and Universal Love. In my thirties I envied the Punks and poked a hole in my ear. I got dragged off to jail chanting "Death to Reagan," and I fasted and spent a month in the streets with the homeless.

Now that I'm forty-seven, the only discomfort I let myself endure is the effort of writing my column, my meager attempt to inspire awareness that has all the effect of pissing in the ocean. I don't care as much as I used to, but why should I?

And why should the presence of this girl, with her fuck-you attitude toward the world, provoke in me such remorse for having retreated and surrendered? If I can forgive Cleaver, Rubin and Springsteen, certainly I should be able to forgive Albie Marx.

I pull up at Linda's house and let Mariah out. She goes to the front door and as I watch, pulls a key out of her purse, unlocks the door and vanishes inside.

I'm tuning in to 97.1, the "classic rock" station, when I spot Sally Keester, her magnificent fanny cavorting within the confines of a silk Chinese kimono straight out of a Rita Hayworth flick, sneak out her house and scuttle across the driveway, disappearing into what I assume, from my position, is Linda's back door. I wonder if she knows Mariah is in there and, if she does, if they know each other. Is there something going on between them? Is there something I'm not being told? Is the sky brown?

Crosby, Stills and Nash are asking Judy Blue Eyes, "*Where are you going now my love? Where will you be tomorrow? Will you bring me happiness? Will you bring me sorrow?*" as Mariah trundles back out of the house hauling a well-worn suitcase. I get out of the car to open the trunk and notice a quick movement of the drapes in Linda's front window. Good old Sally—the blunderbuss of discretion.

Well, they don't know I know they were in there together, and I'm not about to let Mariah know I know it. If she wants to say something, fine—if not, it's another hole in her story, which is starting to look more like John Lennon's Albert Hall every minute.

I take the bag from her, toss it into the trunk and, though I hate to waste rubber, take off with a perversely deliberate squeal of the tires. Mariah gives me a puzzled look but I say nothing and drive straight to the Landmark Motel on Sunset and pull up in front.

"Do you need any money?" I ask.

She's not thrilled about this but it's clear that I'll breach no more discussion about sleeping arrangements. She seems to soften a little.

"What are you going to do?" she asks.

"Find out where I stand with the police."

"When will you call me?"

"I don't know."

"You better not disappear on me," she warns.

"Who said we were a team?"

"Whoever knows that we have those files," she answers, and gives me what I assume is her trump card look.

Dragging her bag out of the trunk I'm already asking myself

why I'm not taking her home with me. Because, I inform myself, as if myself didn't know it already, I want her too much.

Tough as she is, she's had a hard time and I'm starting to feel bad about leaving her alone. "I've got to see some people and make a few calls," I explain, in a voice full of compromise. "Get yourself settled and I'll check with you later."

"When is later?" The kid never relents.

"Do I have to give you a time?"

"No, I'll give you one. Six o'clock."

Why argue? I'll say six and call when I call. "Fine. Six o'clock. What name will you be under?"

"The name I was born with. Selby."

For the first time it occurs to me to ask, "Did you ever find out who your father is?"

"I'm working on it," she replies, lifting her bag. And she heads into the lobby, to the admiring stares of a couple of drooling jamooks at the front desk.

After a minute I realize I'm standing there like a protective father, watching through the front window as she asks for a room and waiting to see that she gets one. I wonder, is this concern strictly paternal, or am I actually growing attached to her?

I want to get home and go through my phone book for the number of a certain lady, whose name I can't recall, with whom I spent one outrageous night in drunken debauchery, only to find the next morning, when she strapped on her .38, that I'd gone down on an officer of the L.A.P.D.

Though it was just a one-nighter, and I felt used when she didn't call again, I hope she'll remember the ecstacy of that evening, and make up for her thoughtlessness by getting me info on Linda's case.

From Los Feliz Boulevard the Jag chugs up onto Valley Oak Drive and I'm three or four twists of the road from my house. It's hard to believe that mere hours have passed since this morning's run, and in this short duration I've obtained Newt's secret documents and become infatuated with Mariah. Did I say that?

My foot reaches for the brake to stop, turn around and go back for her, but my mind regains the upper hand and asserts the more pressing need to deal with the Danno situation before it gets out of control.

I deposit the Jag under the carport and check the mailbox in front. The usual junk flyers, coupons, donation requests, a big, screaming envelope announcing that, "Albert Marx of Los Angeles California May Have Already Won the Publishers Clearing House Twenty Million Dollar Sweepstakes!"—God, I could use that twenty million, it would give me just the cushion I need to stop everything and write the book that will make me a household name again. Yes, I wrote *Roger Wellington Rat* in a week, but that was before I found out how hard writing is.

The last piece of mailbox flotsam is a *Soldier of Fortune* magazine addressed to "Tank Marx." Shrike promoted a free subscription for me when I was researching mercenaries in Zimbabwe and I gave them the name of my cat. I can imagine who they picture they're dealing with when they send out the issues. He's even received "Dear Tank" letters from the editor, providing special information on who's fighting who and who needs replacements.

The other reason for the subscription is that I figured if someone is casing my place for a heist, a *Soldier of Fortune* magazine addressed to someone named Tank might be enough to make them think twice.

I'm flipping through the pages of heroism and devastation as I open the front door and it's a good ten seconds before I look up and see the disaster. The place has been ransacked. Nothing's been spared. Every drawer has been violated. Closets, cupboards, cabinets, wastebaskets—the cushions have been pulled off the sofa, jars and vases smashed—even the wall-to-wall carpet's been pulled back at the corners.

Involuntarily my hand tightens on Newt's envelope with its secret documents, in the stack with the mail. I think of Shrike and his theory that it could be some kind of practical joke. But this wreckage wasn't wrought by jokers. These fuckers are serious.

Then I hear a sound at the back door, like a board creaking, and I'm moving in that direction, picking up speed and licking my lips, like a hungry grizzly after a deer. Somebody's going to pay for this.

I fly through the door and see a flash of his back as he runs alongside the house and turns onto the street. I want him so bad I don't think of the danger, I just take off at full speed.

He's jumped into a car, some Japanese make, and as I reach the street, I have the horror of watching the son-of-a-bitch, wearing a rubber Freddy Krueger mask, bearing down on me before I lurch out of the way at the last possible instant. He roars by me, clipping my hand, and flies away down the hill. I run to my car, start it up and pull out of the carport.

I'm still moving backward when I throw it in first and leave what little rubber I have left plastered to the street. The Jag is in shock as I trounce the accelerator and take off after the masked man and the thought passes through my mind, "Do I really want to catch this maniac?" but the answer must be yes because I'm driving like it's the fuckin' Grand Prix and I'm madder than hell and I'm screaming my lungs out and it fuckin' feels great!

We fly through Los Feliz, tearing around hairpin curves like *Bullitt,* gears whining, tires squealing, the whole nine yards and I'm thinking Mariah should see me now, she should be hanging on for dear life and realizing how crazy I am. It won't be as exciting in the retelling—a dog is lazily shuffling across the street right in front of me—I jerk the wheel and start spinning—the front tires catch the curb and bounce up and over, pointing straight down the steep hillside—miraculously the car's hurtling downhill without overturning and I'm frantically grabbing to fasten my seat belt and there's a house right in front of me, a backyard fence with a pool and a couple of guys kissing on a rubber raft and I don't even try the brake it's so hopeless and the two guys hear the car and look up with saucer eyes and they dive underwater as the Jag hits the fence and slows down but keeps coming and I can't believe this is happening to me cause it's just like a movie and everyone knows movies aren't real and the car actually bounces along the brick decking and past the pool and smashes through double sliding glass doors into a kitchen where I see a naked guy lighting candles on a birthday cake just before the Jag plows into the stove and I knock myself out on my custom wood steering wheel.

CHAPTER 6

I'm lying on a gurney in a busy corridor in St. Vincent's Hospital, kind of hazily enjoying an assortment of white-clad fannies sashaying this way and that, when it occurs to me that I'm feeling a deep throbbing that's anything but sexual, starting in my left hand and pulsating all the way up to the top of my head.

"And you may ask yourself, Well, how did I get here?"

I attempt to sift through my memory and I get sucked into a giant black hole that has pulled in and pulverized the last few hours of my life and when I come out on the other side I'm looking at some guy with a giant erection throwing a birthday cake up in the air.

"And you may say to yourself MY GOD!, What have I done?"

Jesus Christ . . . my house, the chase, the dog, the hill, the pool . . .

"Mr. Marx? How are we feeling?" I fight my way back to the moment and discover the lovely pink face of a Nurse of the Cross. The face next to hers belongs to Mariah.

"Who got me out of the car?" I croak, as if that were the

most critical question of all. Birthday cakes, erections, those guys with my unconscious body . . .

"I understand that it took the fire department a good twenty minutes to cut your door open," the nurse informs me, and I experience a deep sense of relief.

"How long have I been unconscious?"

"About three and a half hours. Are you in a lot of pain?"

I look at Mariah and imagine I see actual concern on her beautiful face. "My hand and my head," I answer, checking back in with the painful throbbing.

"I'm afraid you've broken two fingers—your ring finger and pinky—and we had to put a few stitches in your forehead. Other than that, you're good as gold."

I look at my left hand and indeed, the last two fingers are enclosed in a splint.

"Your daughter's been worried to death," she says, glancing sweetly at Mariah. "She rode in the ambulance with you."

My "daughter" smiles at me and I wonder what in the world I am doing, being involved with this person.

"Can I take him home now?" the person asks in a convincingly worried voice.

"Anytime he feels strong enough. I'll be at the central nursing station, just call if you need me." To me she says, "Try to act like an adult next time you get behind the wheel of a car. Will you do that for me, Mr. Marx?"

"I'll make sure he does, Sister," Mariah promises.

When the good nurse is gone, I fire away. "You're pushing the envelope, my friend, you're raising more questions than you can answer. You're in too many places at once."

"I tried to catch you when you drove off from the motel," she explains. "They had no vacancy."

I remember watching her through the window. There didn't seem to be any problem.

"I grabbed a cab to your house but you were tearing out of

the driveway like a madman. By the time we caught up, you were parked in some guy's kitchen and he was calling the police." She concludes, in what I detect is a possibly semiauthentic tone of concern, with, "You were totally unconscious. You could have died."

"So naturally you had to tell them you were my daughter," I challenge.

"I told them that so they'd let me stay with you. It was the easist thing to say."

"Do you always say the easiest thing? Doesn't the truth have *some* trivial value?"

"Are you angry because I was worried about you?"

"I'm angry because I'm in a hospital with broken fingers and a megaheadache talking to somebody whose identity is a total mystery to me."

"You know who I am. You just can't handle me caring about you. It's too much responsibility. You'd rather be drunk and alone."

"Don't play Psych 101 with me," I retort through the pounding in my head. "I've been analyzed by masters, I don't need your Cliffs Notes on Freud. What else did you tell the police?"

She just looks at me. "Do you want me to take you home or not?"

"Do I want you to take me home or not?" I repeat, as if she has asked the stupidest question in the history of stupidity. "Yes. I want you to take me home."

She checks me out and has someone call for a cab. The parts of my body that haven't been bruised, lacerated or broken are all agonizingly stiff and I feel like the Tin Man in *The Wizard of Oz* as my little Dorothy helps me out of the building and into the taxi.

"They gave you some painkillers," she tells me, "in case it gets bad."

"We'll get some tequila and have a party," I groan, sinking into the corner of the seat. "I hope you didn't say anything to the police."

She gives me a dirty look. "I told them you were visiting friends."

"I don't find that funny."

"Can I at least ask what that car chase was all about?"

"You have no idea? It couldn't have something to do with a friend of your uncle's, could it?" I answer, with all the irony I can pile into my voice.

"You think they were after the documents?"

"The documents!" I remember suddenly and sit up painfully. "They're in my car!"

She just smiles smugly, then extracts from her purse the by now well-worn manila envelope and wags it in front of me. "Nobody questioned giving your mail to your daughter."

I've got to hand it to her. She's so smooth she makes it look easy. She's got more levels than Sybil. I'd like to get to know a few of her.

We get to my house and put the couch together so I can rest my bones while she does what she can to straighten up the wreckage. Tank wanders in, cocks his one eye at Mariah and wanders back out again. He doesn't understand women, first they're nice then they're mad then they're affectionate then they're distant . . . so he keeps his distance. Just like his dad.

"Was that your cat?" she asks.

"He's a Virgo. Can't deal with untidyness."

She seems to accept that and I drag myself off the couch to turn on the TV and pick up a black telephone book lying where it was thrown on the floor. Luckily, whoever hit the place, if they did any pillaging at all, left my book behind.

The *Evening News* is on and, as I leaf through my book, the entertainment they serve up as fact forms a familiar backdrop of sound.

Now what was the name of that cop I gave head to all night? Over the years you meet all kinds of women in all kinds of situations and I try to file their numbers in some kind of workable order. If I can't remember the last name, I look for the first name; if I can't remember either, I look under the place where we met; if I was drunk as usual, and remember none of the above, I look under distinctive characteristics like "Screamers" or "Amazons."

There's only one name under "Cops," Stevie O'Donnel, and there's two numbers, work and home. I dial the work number, Precinct 4 of the Hollywood Police. I give her name and someone puts me on hold. Then she comes on, still with that sexy voice.

"This is Stevie. Can I help you?"

"Hi, Stevie. This is Albie Marx. Do you remember me?"

"Who?"

"Albie Marx. We met at a bar one night. About six months ago. The crazy writer with the Cuervo shooters?"

"What did you say your name is?"

"Albie. You remember?"

"Alvy?"

"*Albie,*" I repeat, mortified. "I ate your pussy for six hours straight."

"Oh! *That* Albie! I remember you. It's been a long time. How have you been?"

"I had a sprained lip for a while, but other than that, terrible."

"I'm sorry to hear that."

"You could have sent flowers."

"After one date? What can I do for you, Albie?"

"There's a Lieutenant Danno, with Homocide, who's trying to convince me I murdered my friend. I wouldn't kill a Republican, much less a friend. This guy has it in for me."

"I know Danno," she says. "A hard man."

"You know me pretty well, right Stevie? You know the intimate Albie Marx. Do I seem like a murderer to you?"

"Not really."

"Well, I'm not. I lost a good friend and I'd like to know what happened. Is there any way you could find anything out for me? Anything at all?"

"Like what?"

"Like anything."

"I don't know. What's the victim's name?"

"Linda Selby."

"What's your number?"

I give her the number and thank her profusely in advance. She tells me she promises nothing but will check into it.

"Another one of your conquests?" Mariah asks when I hang up.

"Yeah," I grumble. "She barely remembered my name."

"This is interesting," she says, picking up a framed snapshot of Janis and me taken in front of Janis's psychedelic Porsche. "Janis Joplin. And some hippie."

"That was twenty years ago. In my drug phase."

"You both look wasted."

"But we're having fun."

"You just look wasted."

"We were moody. Would you get me that bottle over there?" She hands over the Cuervo Gold and I enjoy a deep, burning slug. "She used to say, 'Why not sit back and enjoy it, as long as you know you're gonna crap out in the end anyway?' And she'd hit the Southern Comfort."

"She died of a heroin overdose, didn't she?"

"She died of self-loathing and fear. She was all raw emotion.

A child who couldn't control her feelings. Felt all the time like she couldn't live up to being 'Janis Joplin.' " I take another swig and it doesn't burn like the first one. "But she had her moments. You'd look at her singing and you couldn't believe the sound that came out of that little body. It drove people wild. She was hot. Too hot. She burned herself out. Like that sun of yours."

"Where were you when she OD'd?"

"That's between me and God." I work on the bottle again.

"Are you going to drink that whole bottle?"

"Don't worry. There's more in the pantry."

"That's not what I had in mind."

"Well I don't need a mother, I've already got one." The words are out of my mouth before I realize I'm saying them. She can't hide the hurt when she hears the word *mother*. Or am I just imagining that? Anyway, I can't let it stay that way. "I'm sorry," I say softly. "I'm a real asshole."

"So am I," she responds flatly. "That's why we get along."

"We do?" I'm surprised that she thinks so.

She snags a copy of *Up Yours* from the floor and thumbs through the pages till she gets to my column. "Welcome to The Holy War," she reads.

"That's an old issue," I inform her. "It was provocative when I wrote it."

She goes on reading. "This country is in the throes of suffering a tragic loss. The Russians and their corrupt brand of communism have sunk into a quagmire of economic disintegration. Our arch enemy has fallen without a shot being fired.

"With this loss of the always imminent Threat of War, posed by the once-powerful Evil Empire, our own Military-Industrial Complex, which in the past five years has spent over two *trillion* dollars, needs major new justifications for its gluttonous appetite.

"In an era when social programs are slashed, when there is no money for drug *rehabilitation,* when there are more homeless, schoolless, hopeless people than ever before, when the planet itself is crying out for Mercy, for its forests, its rivers, its farmland—this Military-Industrial *conspiracy,* this privately run, members-only, racketeering, profiteering, self-aggrandizing, 'protector' of freedom and liberty, finds itself foraging desperately for an enemy.

"But it can't be just any enemy. It needs an enemy that will inspire Americans, tired of phony wars on behalf of Big Business, to a higher call, a call to protect the very fiber of our society.

"The President and the Businessmen who advise/control him and the Generals who get rich off the Businessmen realize that America, which for so long has defined its morality, economics and national image as Freedom's Bulwark against Communism, must now create a new enemy, equal in immorality to the old.

"Enter our modern Holy War. We have been told that crack and cocaine, which flow into America from various Central and South American countries, are destroying America's youth and therefore its future. (*We have not been told of the CIA's collusion with and profit participation in these drug rings.*) Tomorrow or next week or next month or next year we will be told that unless we send in our troops and install 'freely elected leaders' (American puppets whose radio, TV and violently coercive political campaigns are financed by the CIA), the very Soul of America will be threatened.

"Yes, the story goes, once we eliminate the (wrong) drug cartels and restore these countries to their 'rightful rulers' (along with making them safe for American Business/Plunder), we will in the end be able to pull back our armies and give them the opportunity to 'determine their own destiny.'

"And so Communism-as-Enemy is replaced by Drugs-as-

Enemy without dropping a stitch. And, as usual, the true culprits, the Greed, Racism and Arrogance of our Elected Officials/Rulers, *those vices that engender the demand for the drugs in the first place,* will be the true beneficiaries of this new Holy War.

"So that's the report from this mountaintop. The question I leave you with is this: What will *you* do when your child is sent to Peru to give up his or her life for democracy? Think about it."

She looks up from the magazine. "What a bunch of horse-shit."

"You disagree?"

"People want to get high, they don't care if it comes from Thailand or Colombia. They're fucked up behind *life,* not politics." She throws the magazine on the coffee table. "You people blame everything on the government. It's all mental masturbation."

As she says this, the Network News Washington correspondent is reporting that SCOLD, the Senate Committee on Legalization of Drugs, has recommended unanimously for Legalization.

Then there's a wild news conference with a haggard Senator Rosenbaum explaining that there are certain specific guidelines issued by his committee, based on extensive information and research, which remove from consideration dangerous substances like cocaine and heroin, barbiturates and amphetamines.

The Network correspondent comes back and predicts that the recommendation will precipitate violent debates in Congress and lead to a multibillion-dollar research free-for-all in the race to discover the perfect legal drug.

"Guess I'm not the only one jerking off," I say. "Let me see that memo."

She frowns and digs the documents out of the envelope. I'm

squinting down at the dancing letters and I realize I don't have my glasses. I look up and she's holding them out to me.

"Don't anticipate me like that," I complain. "I don't know you that well." I put on the glasses and read: SCOLD TO ROLL OUT PRELIM O.K. "That's the Senate Committee on Legalization of Drugs. This memo is dated three weeks ago. Which means today's vote is just part of somebody's overall plan—what this memo refers to as the *NICE* CAMPAIGN, whatever that is."

I scan the rest of the short message. HOUSE LEAK PLUGGED must mean somebody in Congress with a big mouth has been shut up. CHEMTECH PSYCHOGRAPH-ICS . . . Psychographics, if I remember correctly, are psychological demographics worked up by ad agencies to sell different product lines. What could they be selling? Would the government sell drugs? Does the Pope wear a funny hat? LUDI TO BE SANCTIONED. *Sanctioned* is an agency word for eliminated.

"They're going to kill Ahmet Ludi," I tell Mariah.

"Who is Ahmet Ludi?"

It occurs to me that she's too young to remember. "He was the greatest record producer in the history of rock 'n' roll. Nobody's heard from him in years."

"What made him so great?" she wants to know.

I look at the file attached to the memo. It's got an official FBI stamp. LUDI, AHMET. CLASSIFIED.

"Ludi, Ahmet; born, December 25, 1932, Chicago, Illinois.

Father: Esai Ludi; born, Izmir, Turkey, March 15, 1900; died, Chicago, Illinois, March 13, 1955.

Mother: Avria Hemjani Ludi; born, Izmir, Turkey, July 24, 1907; died, Palm Beach, Florida, March 13, 1960."

It appears to be an informal biography.

"Father, E. Ludi, born Sunni Muslim in Turkey, raised in high mountains between Aegean and Anatolian regions.

Thinly populated area specializes in grain and livestock, produces much of Western world supply of opium. Married A. Hemjani (15), immigrated to U.S. in 1922. Settled in Chicago, 1923, worked various jobs as laborer, craftsman, etc. 1930–33 suspected of illegal transportation of liquor in violation of Volstead Act. No arrests, no convictions. Opened legal liquor supply business 1933 at time of Repeal.

"First child, Tara Ludi, female, born 1930. Ahmet Ludi (Muslims name first male child Ahmet) born 1932. Attended Chicago public schools.

"Father opened 'Southside' nightclub, 1946, catered to blacks. Club became well known for rhythm and blues music, featured leading performers of the time. Ex-precinct police officer states nightclub also known for prostitutes and drug dealers although Ludi did not encourage such activity. Ludi believed to be promiscuous with many black females.

"Ahmet Ludi attended Franklin High School, 1946–50. High school records give no indication of intellectual precociousness. Maintained average grades. Classmates interviewed remember 'fast cars, fancy clothes,' masculine attractiveness.

"1950 E. Ludi started 'Ludi Records,' to record performers who worked in his nightclub. Ludi worked for his father, learned all aspects of record business. Company moderately successful. E. Ludi died 1952, leaving company to family. Control assumed by only son, Ahmet.

"Ludi Records' first release under Ahmet, 'Rock All Night,' 1952, acknowledged to be first rock and roll record (preceeding Bill Haley and the Comets' 'Crazy Man, Crazy,' 1953).

"1953–1958 Ludi wrote, produced and released twelve #1 records, more than any other contemporary. Ludi also produced first rock and roll show (1955), with Chuck Berry, Bill Haley and other leading artists.

"Ludi continued to release records and produce rock and roll shows. Mother died, cancer, 1960. Sister died, auto accident, 1961. 1962, Ludi sold Ludi Records, claimed it had become too big and commercial.

"1962–1964—unable to certify his whereabouts. Best information leads to pilgrimage to parents' birthplace in mountains of Turkey. Assume he acquired extensive knowledge of opium at this time.

"1964 Ludi appeared in London, often in company of Beatles and Rolling Stones. Considered a legend by then, was sought out as producer by groups, managers, record labels. Worked only as creative advisor.

"1967, arranged for Beatles to go to India. Came back to London for recording of *Sgt. Pepper,* then returned to India. Remained until 1969. Scattered information leads to belief that he lived alone, emulating Indian holy men and experimented freely with various indigenous psychedelics and hallucinogens.

"1969 Ludi (age 37) returned to U.S. Promoted Big Sur 'Nirvana Music Festival,' three-day outdoor rock concert. (FBI informers at festival reported highly suspicious nonviolence by concert-goers, even among hard-core activist groups.)

"1970 arrested in Los Angeles for possession of heroin. Charges dropped due to Illegal Search and Seizure violation by Los Angeles police. This is last time seen in U.S.

"1970, passport accepted by Libertad (small, undeveloped island in Caribbean northeast of Honduras, Latitude 16 degrees North, Longitude 82 degrees West). Passport never renewed.

"1986 (in absentia) first person inducted into newly formed 'Rock and Roll Hall of Fame.'

"CONCLUSIONS/SPECULATIONS: By virtue of his history and mystique, Ludi has become a cultural icon for many individuals of his generation. One of the older secretaries in this office recalls meeting Ludi at the Nirvana Festival in '69 and attests to his personal charisma and 'animal magnetism.' (This secretary's clearances have since been reviewed and revalidated.) His personal fortune has been completely depleted by gifts and donations to various ecological and esoteric organizations. The IRS has no outstanding claims.

"Ludi is a very private individual, requiring great isolation from society in general. It is assumed that he is still on the island of Libertad.

"ADDENDUM: Ludi's presence on Libertad has been confirmed by one Irmgard Menglemann, traveling with Felix St. John, NSB scientist on official field trip. Menglemann was able to obtain several excerpts of Ludi's writing, from a text titled *A Heretic's Handbook*. Excerpts are here included."

I hand Mariah the biography and flip through the excerpts from Ludi's book. By this time it's seven-thirty and I'm rapidly fading. It's been twelve hours since I arrived at the post office early this morning. Not exactly a typical day in the life of Albie Marx, I say to myself as I take yet another sweet pull on my friend José. I'm getting too old for the fast lane. I belong in the lane reserved for slower vehicles and trucks.

My eyes settle on a verse in the Ludi excerpts, preceded by the brief instruction: "CHANT UNTIL MESMERIZED."

> You are my flower,
> That's bloomin' in the mountains so high
> You are my flower,
> That's bloomin' there for me.
> So wear a happy smile and life will be worthwhile
> Forget the tears but don't forget to smile.

With a start, I recognize the words. It's an old Blue Ridge Mountain folk tune by A. P. Carter. I should play the record.

My brain tells me to get up and go to the stereo but my body is saying it's had enough for one day. I let the pages slip

through my fingers and don't even bother to take off my
reading glasses as I close my eyes and . . .

I'm running for my life through the streets of Manhattan.
David Duke and his neo-Nazis are after me, they know I'm
a Jew. I jump on the ferry to Liberty Island. I'm panicked and
feverish as I run to the Statue of Liberty, pursued by the
shouting racists. Climbing, climbing, to the top of the statue,
their voices and shouts closing in. Now panting, sweating,
lurching outside, onto the deck of the crown, three hundred
feet high, I look down at the concrete below. Duke bursts
through the door and sees me. I pull myself onto a point of
the crown as his Nazis come for me. I have only one choice
to avoid being taken. I can't let them get me. I jump. I'm
floating then tumbling then plummeting down, down, then
SMASHING into the hard ground, the life flowing out of my
body, I'm dying, I'm dying, I'm dead.

I'm alive. My soul is alive. In another body. I am another
person. I am not Jewish. I am a blue-eyed, blond Protestant.
I work in an office. I work for some average American Protestant Jew-hating businessmen. I'm starting to worry. What if
they see through me? What if they suspect? What if they find
out I was a Jew in another life? The paranoia is unbearable.
I can't look them in the eye. My fear and guilt are overwhelming. I've got to escape. I've got to get away.

I'm running through the streets of Manhattan—
ENOUGH! I can get out, I can escape, I just have to make
the effort . . .

I claw my way back to consciousness. What was that all
about? The ultimate paranoia—fear of being persecuted for

what you were in a previous life. Could you be any more paranoid than that? Sick.

I'm on the couch where I passed out. From here I can see Mariah, asleep in my bed, her close-cropped, rainbow-topped head resting lightly on my pillow. She's even more beautiful in repose, relieved of the ruthless burden of consciousness.

Though she's just a kid, the age of my son, when she's awake and energized and in my face, her strong presence demanding, challenging, confronting, she can be surprisingly intimidating, the type who wears you down till she gets what she wants, like her mother might have been if she hadn't given up on herself early in life.

But what does this girl want? Why glue herself to *me?* Does she expect me to solve the mystery of Linda? Or does she suspect me of being her killer? Can I trust her? Is she out to get me?

Or is she, under all that self-assurance and bluster, reaching out in her way for friendship? Or validation? Or *love?* Forget it, Albie. This girl has too much going to fall in love with *you.*

But maybe, if I had a better image of myself, if I felt really *capable* of solving the mystery, if I felt *worthy* of being her friend, I would feel less threatened and more encouraged by her power. If I felt strong within myself, her strength would amplify, not diminish, mine.

She does look delectable in that bed. There's nothing I would like more than to crawl in there with her. What time is it? My watch says 12:35. And I'm wide awake. This has been happening a lot as I get older, whenever I have too much to drink, when I go to sleep drunk, I wake up in the middle of the night, my mind going a million miles an hour, and can't fall asleep till five or six in the morning, which renders me dopey and groggy when I get out of bed at seven for my morning run.

Well, I'm not going to lay on the couch all night, staring

up at the ceiling and fantasizing making love to Mariah. I force myself to sit upright and everything hurts, each bump and bruise roaring its protest in my brain. My two broken fingers are throbbing like five times their size and each throb reverberates with a needlelike stab in the stitched-up gash on my forehead.

I force my way through the pain to get to the phone and quietly call for a cab. I don't want to wake Sleeping Beauty because it will mean dealing with everything that's going on and that's the last thing I want to do right now. I need some distraction.

The cab drops me off at The Rock, where I note Shrike's big black Harley parked in front. I hope he doesn't start the Jap Rap again.

"What the fuck happened to you?" he asks when I get inside and I realize I must look like I smashed into someone's fist. "Has Iron Mariah been venting her existential rage on our poor little writer?" I choose not to respond. "Put that on my bill," he tells Leon, who is already setting my Cuervo and Corona on the bar. A redhead several seats down smiles at me.

"I got an interesting call today," Shrike is saying, as if all I want to do is hear about his life. "From a big downtown lawyer."

I smile back at the redhead and hold up my glass in a mimed toast to friendship. She reciprocates.

"He wanted to know if I would be interested in selling the magazine." This he says with the assurance that it will get my ear. Just to disappoint him, I gesture to the redhead to come and sit next to me. "This was definitely not a crank call," he adds, hoping at least to arouse some job insecurity in his bid for attention.

"Sell," I tell him, "and get a condo in St. Tropez." He sees this is going nowhere and returns to his discussion with the biker next to him.

The redhead, who's running a little long in the tooth but might by some stretch of a sexually deprived imagination be described as voluptuous, slinks over and smothers the barstool beside me.

"Where do I know you from?" she asks in a badly disguised New York accent. "You're familiar t'me."

"Not as familiar as I'd like to be," I reply in my Groucho voice, and waggle an imaginary cigar.

"What's that—Groucho?" she asks, and I know there will be no subtlety tonight.

"Can I buy you a drink?"

"Wouldn't you care t'know my name first?"

No, I would never care to know your name. "Let me guess," I say. "Could it be . . . Elsie?" She shakes her head no. "Adolph?"

She laughs a kind of sharp hocking sound. "Adolph?" She slaps my arm playfully, her long crimson nails lingering a meaningful fraction of a second too long. "Do I look like an Adolph?"

Don't make me answer that. "Leon, a drink for *Mein Kampf* over here."

She hocks another laugh. "A comedian. What's your name?"

"Albie."

"Come on."

"Really. Albie."

"Albie. I like that. Mine is Tina. Pleased t'meetcha, Albie."

"Pleased t'meetcha, Tina."

By the time we get to her place we're so blasted I'm doing material like "Pleased to *eatcha*, Tina," and the two of us are cracking up like school kids. As if that isn't hysterical enough, when I'm trying to get my hand with the two splinted fingers down the back of her pants, she screams that I'm tickling her pubic hair and starts hocking that laugh and I'm hocking like her and we just can't stop laughing and fall on the bed clutching our sides and gasping for air.

And somewhere the Observer in me is watching this joke and shaking his head and thinking this is Nowhere, this is Empty, this has No Soul.

Tina drops me off at Rent-A-Wreck on her way to work and I thank her and I crack her a joke and she hocks me a laugh and we both know we'll never see each other again. We took refuge in the feel and the touch of each other, in our tastes and our smells and our mutual sounds of pleasure, but we were about as intimate as strangers on a subway. But we had fun, didn't we? Do we have to have everything? Does every liaison have to be a love affair? What's it all about, Albie?

The Rent-A-Wreck guy is showing me several reasonably clean cars when I suddenly remember I didn't use a rubber with Tina. Even though I tested HIV negative four months ago, who knows where she's been? What a wonderful new world. We've come all the way from Hippies to Yippies to Yuppies to Baggies. God, I hate those things, it feels like you're fucking with someone else's dick. But I'd better wise up. This is the nineties, not the sixties. Free Love isn't free anymore, one mistake and you pay with your life.

I consider renting a Honda or Toyota, just to get a rise out of Shrike, but decide on a quick little white Mustang, five or six years old but hot to trot.

I get home to find Mariah on the couch with Tank. The tube's tuned to CNN and she's reading *Roger Wellington Rat.* The scrubby old tom is passed out on his back, feet sticking up in the air, his one good eye rolling back in his head, purring like a Peterbilt. Fuckin' cat, he never did that for me.

The place has been nicely tidied up and I'm all set for a hassle about where did I go and what did I do, but all she says is, "I hope you used a condom."

"I went through a six-pack," I answer, ready to do battle for no good reason. Why am I so hostile?

"You look terrible. Did you get any sleep?"

"As needed. I see you wormed your way into his heart," I comment, indicating my blissed-out tomcat.

"He just wanted his tummy rubbed," she says in neo-babytalk, plunging her hand into his mangy undercoat. "Doesn't he?" Tank cranks up the purring decibel.

"Thanks for straightening up the place."

"I can't stand clutter," she shrugs.

Our attention is attracted by CNN, where the effects of SCOLD's recommendation are being discussed and dissected. The morning anchorman is quoting a recent piece in *The Christian Science Monitor,* "American voters now believe that drug abuse and trafficking are the most important international challenge their nation faces, more serious even than nuclear war and environmental destruction."

"They did it!" I shout. "Those fuckers did it! *'More serious than nuclear war and environmental destruction!'* Their fucking P.R. never fails them! We're a nation of sheep! Fat, dumb, obedient *sheep!*"

"In response to this challenge," the newsman is saying, "the Senate Committee on Legalization of Drugs yesterday recommended *for* Legalization, the most radical stand yet taken in this nation's war against drugs."

"If they only knew what we know," I lament to Mariah.

"What do we know?"

"It's a plot! It's always a plot with them! A conspiracy. They've probably got some fucking drug, who knows what it is? They'll make robots out of everybody."

"As if they needed a drug to do that," she muses.

"If I could figure out what their game is, I'd write a story that would blow their cover sky high, a fucking tornado of truth."

"That might be dangerous," she says, in a voice much older and harder than her years. "You'd be putting your life on the line."

Now Senator Rosenbaum is on, not haggard like he looked last night outside the committee room, but fresh, coiffed and in command, wearing an understated silk tie and an eighteen-hundred-dollar suit.

"In the likely event that our recommendation is passed by the House and the Senate, President Cale will impanel a blue ribbon committee, chaired jointly by the heads of the Food and Drug Administration and the National Institute of Health, along with the surgeon general, to determine what drugs will be made available on a nationwide basis.

"My colleagues and I have been assured by John Thomas, the President's chief of staff, that President Cale will fully support any decision made by this distinguished committee."

"I can't take this," I say, snapping off the TV. Why do events I have no control over bother me so much? I look at my phone machine where the blinking red light tells me people have called. "You didn't answer the phone?"

"Was I supposed to?" she asks.

Actually, I'm glad she didn't. Who knows what she would say to people? I hit the playback button. The digital readout says I have four messages.

"Hi, Albie . . ." A sexy, sleepy female voice which I don't recognize. "Albie . . . Are you there? . . . Shit." Click. I have no idea who it is.

"Hi, Dad, it's me. Listen, I can't make that lunch on the fifth, Eisner wants me at Goofy's birthday party. How about next month? The eighth? I'll get back with you to firm it up. Ciao."

"My son," I explain to Mariah. "We're very close."

"Mr. Marx, this is L.A. Vehicle Impound, we have your automobile here, a black Jaguar. Ask for George. The number is 452-2608. You'll need to bring two hundred dollars in cash." I scribble a note to call my insurance guy.

"Albie, this is Stevie O'Donnel. The news is not good. Call me." Fuck. Back to Linda. Well, what did you think, asshole? That it would all go away?

I dial Stevie's number. After a minute I get her on the phone.

"Stevie, it's Albie."

"I don't want to talk on the phone. Do you want to meet me somewhere?"

"Anywhere you say."

"My shift is up. How about my place?"

I scratch down the address and arrange to meet in an hour.

"I'm going with you," Mariah says.

"She won't talk with you there," I argue.

"It's about my mother, damnit! Not about you getting laid!"

"I'll ignore that statement. She's doing this as a favor to me."

"Really? What does she get in return? Half a six-pack?"

Wow. She's actually jealous. I know jealous when I see it. It makes me feel kind of good, even with all this horrible stuff going on, like maybe she could even go for me.

"You better shower," she says, like it's all decided. "You stink from last night's perfume."

Maybe I'm barking up the wrong fantasy.

We pull up to Stevie O'Donnel's apartment building in Venice. These little one bedroom cubicles used to be dirt cheap, now you wait on line for them at twelve hundred a month. The good news is, for those who crave the calming effect of the pounding surf, they overlook the ocean. Working in Hollywood, living in Venice—its a long commute for Stevie, not to mention a change of cultures. A cop with a beach girl mentality. That's probably why we hit it off.

"I want you to wait here," I tell Mariah.

"You're not my boss or my father," she retorts and opens her door.

"Let me point something out to you," I say, holding her arm. "I have the utmost respect for your grief, but grief doesn't give you the license to act like you do with me. Respect is a two-way street. I'm not some twenty-year-old punk whose testosterone's running away with him. I'm not falling all over you. You don't have me by the balls. If you want something from me you ask for it civilly, okay? You act like a human being when you want something from me? Do I make myself clear?"

"What are you, Albie? What is this image you have of yourself? You're talking to me like some kind of fucking *adult.*"

"We all have to grow up sometime, kid."

"You're spouting the rules and regulations you used to despise. I read your book, I know who you *were.* What do you think, I won't respect you if you're not some kind of super-macho-Romeo? If you're just Albie? Albie who hates bullshit and rules and believes what he says has meaning?"

"When I was your age I believed everything I said. I thought I was so fucking right and look where it got me," I answer, hearing twenty years of disappointment and cynicism in my voice.

"And when did you decide you were wrong? When everyone told you you were full of shit? Who said you had to believe *them?* There must have been someone in that drug-ridden body who believed in himself. Don't fuckin' order me around, Albie. You don't have the weight."

I have never been talked to like this. I'm not sure how to react. I want to punch her in the face. I want to scream at the top of my lungs for her to get the hell out of this car and my life. Who the fuck is she to say these things?

But I do want to grow. Everyone deserves a chance at *real* love, not just puppy love or worship love or lust love or any of the other tip-of-the-iceberg loves. I do want it all, once in my life. And maybe, with this girl's help, if I face myself and let go the defenses, I will see who it is that deserves this love.

All right, so I won't punch her in the mouth.

Stevie answers the door barefoot, wearing tight jeans that round out her ass and firm it up just right and a T-shirt that screams big, luscious nipples. Her eyes go from anticipation to annoyance when she sees Mariah.

"This is Linda Selby's daughter," I explain. "She'd like to know what happened to her mother."

She looks from me to Mariah then back. "Were you in an accident?" she asks, eyes on my forehead.

"I hit a stove doing forty."

She gives us a cop's shakedown look, then says in a confidential tone, "I can't say anything in front of her."

"She's okay, you can trust her," I assure her.

"My name is Mariah," Mariah offers. "Anything you say will be between us. I need to know what happened to my mother."

I reinforce this with a look of solemn confirmation. Stevie, who was in the mood for more than just talking, is hesitant.

"She's had a hard time," I tell Stevie. "It's a long story but she just got to know her mother when this terrible thing happened. It's really important to her. She'll keep her mouth shut."

Stevie takes a breath and considers the situation, then decides to go with the flow. She bites the bullet and lets us in.

The fire in the gas fireplace is dancing and licking the firelog and the ocean is pounding away in the big picture window. The only thing missing is Stevie naked on the couch, her fingers locked in my hair as I bury my tongue in her. Mariah is looking at me and I know she knows what I'm thinking. I hope she also knows that I'm happy to do without it.

We sit down on the couch and Stevie sits opposite in a white wicker chair. "I don't know that much," she begins, "but it wasn't a suicide."

Though this doesn't surprise me, it's like she tripped an adrenaline valve. My heart takes off like a rocket car and the blood goes careening through my body like the Indy 500. Somebody actually murdered Linda.

"She was dead before she was hung up. That was confirmed by the coroner. They're getting court approval for a complete autopsy."

I look at Mariah. Her expression doesn't change. She's all business.

"Do they know how she died?" she asks Stevie.

"They think they do."

"What do they think?" I urge.

She searches my eyes and answers, "Heroin."

"Heroin? Are they sure?" She's checking me out hard. I didn't do it, Stevie, I swear I didn't do it. "Linda never took drugs. She wouldn't even smoke a joint."

"Maybe she had no choice."

Idiotically I ask again, "She OD'd on smack?"

She nods. Mariah gets up from the couch and walks over to the window. She's looking out at the ocean with her back to us and I'd bet my last royalty check she's losing the battle of the tears.

"Danno's got a hair up his ass about you. I don't know his case but I hope you have a lot of right answers."

My mind goes to a documentary I just saw, *The Thin Blue Line,* where a poor son-of-a-bitch was convicted of a murder he didn't do because some cop wanted his ass. A cold sweat breaks out along my hairline.

"Why the fuck is he after me?" I ask, masking my fear with belligerence.

"Nobody knows Danno, nobody gets close to him. But they respect him. He's tough."

I'm looking at Stevie and all I can focus on is that somebody shot Linda up and tried to make it look like suicide. But who?

I think of the list I made with Shrike. Sally Keester, no. Sarah Meyerson, no. Nat Bostwick, owner of the popular health food restaurant where Linda was hostess—he had a crush on her but would he shoot her up with heroin and hang her from a fixture? Not likely.

Then there's Harry Ballister. Hard to picture Ballister with the stomach to do someone in. But who knows? And what was he doing at the post office yesterday? Does he know about Newt's files? And if he does, why would he want them? Is Ballister somehow involved in this government plot? Did he kill Linda because she knew about the plot and his involvement in it? And if he killed Linda, did he kill Newt too? My head is spinning.

"You want a glass of water, Albie?" Stevie asks.

No, I want my mommy.

We walk out of Stevie's and the sun is shining but there's a cloud over my heart. If I weren't so fucking mad I'd be overwhelmed. All the nightmare memories of Janis's death are coming back on me, of her body on the hotel room floor, her face bloody from busting her nose when she fell—of that bare, bright room, where the cops tried to scare me into saying I gave her the heroin, I shot her up, I killed her—all that shit I thought I'd finally put down is swirling around in my head again, but this time I'm not scared, I'm fucking furious. Whoever killed Linda will pay—I make this promise to you Linda, and to myself and to Mariah.

Why does this Danno have it in for me? He brought up the Janis thing the other night, but I don't remember him from back then. Of course, I was so spaced out in those days I hardly remember anyone. But the police always make an impression on me and Danno is one cop I wouldn't forget.

It all comes down to Authority Figures. Like all good rebels, I have a profound loathing for authority, probably mixed with a deep-seated fear as well. There was never an ass I could kiss. Maybe if I'd been a little less arrogant and a little more realistic, I might have had an easier time of it. Might have avoided the hard times and the drugs. But I was never a "Yes, Mister—No, Mister" man. My father tried to beat it into me but my mother told me I had to answer to no one. He was an alley cat and she solved her loneliness by playing the two of us against each other like some bizarre love triangle. It made him jealous enough to take her to bed and show her who was more of a man. But it also made him real mad at me. I learned to hate authority. These days I tell myself, what the hell, he wasn't so bad. Lots of other guys would have taken a powder. He stuck around and took it like a man. Brought up a family the best he could. Now they're a little old couple who live in San Diego. Obla-dee-obla-da.

We're getting into the car and Mariah spots a pay phone down the street. "Albie, I'll be right back, I have to make a call."

"Right now?"

"I just remembered, I have a friend back East who I promised I'd call and if I don't do it now while I see a phone I know I'll forget again. Can you wait two minutes?"

"Sure. Go on."

A *friend.* Probably her boyfriend. Good. Maybe she'll decide to go back to him and let me sort out my life on my own. All this spiritual growth is wearing me out.

Look at her, leaning against that phone booth with the phone in her hand. She looks like one of those ads for jeans or fast red cars. The type of babe everyone dreams of having. Gorgeous, young, independent, with a tight pussy and a fuck-you attitude toward everyone but her man.

That hair. She's got more colors than a Seurat. How did she find all those colors? I couldn't even name them all. And those eyes. What am I going to do about those eyes? I can't look in them anymore, it's like staring into the sun, you go blind and look away. Just once I'd like those eyes to look at me like they would die if I told her we'd never see each other again.

Fuck it, I'm not going to do this. This girl and I have crossed paths accidentally and we'll work out our business and be done with it. As Dylan said, "Heart of mine, if you can't do the time, don't do the crime." Besides, you dolt, she's calling her boyfriend, remember?

She hangs up, looks around warily, like she ripped off the phone company or something, then walks back my way. The way she walks. She's so fucking strong, you gotta love it. What the hell, we're in it for the ride, let's go for it.

"Did you get your friend?" I pout, as she gets into the car.

"Yes. Thanks."

"He must have been thrilled to hear from you."

"Who said it was a 'he'?"

"It *was* a he, wasn't it?"

"Yes. And he *was* thrilled to hear from me. He'd been waiting for my call."

"Well, I'm glad you made someone happy." And I throw the Mustang into gear and screech off in the direction of Hollywood.

CHAPTER 7

Lieutenant Joseph Danno sat at his desk and focused. When Joe Danno focused, no amount of extraneous activity could distract him. Ringing phones, cursing hookers, screaming crack addicts, crying mothers, all faded into the river of nothingness that existed outside his body. Within, all was reason, all was fact.

Fact: According to the coroner (soon to be conclusively verified by autopsy), the victim was deceased before the noose was placed around her neck. Fact: The victim's blood analysis revealed a fatally toxic level of heroin (which converted to morphine after entering the body). Fact: The brachial cephalic vein in the victim's right arm showed a fresh puncture mark. Conclusion: Death by heroin overdose.

Fact: Cloth fibers found in the victim's bedroom were verified to contain crystallized particles of chloroform. Fact: Similar fibers of the same chloroformed cloth were found on the nose and mouth area of the victim's face. Fact: Fibers of the bedroom carpet were found on the victim's bare feet. Conclusions: The victim was chloroformed, probably in her bedroom. Awaiting autopsy to confirm.

Fact: No signs of struggle were discovered in the victim's bedroom or elsewhere. Conclusion: The victim allowed the killer in, probably willingly.

Fact: The victim's body was reported at eight-thirty P.M. by Albie Marx. Fact: Coroner fixed approximate time of death at seven P.M. Fact: The victim's neighbor, Sally Keester, reported being in victim's house and talking with victim at approximately six P.M. Keester entered through back door and left through front door and verified that both doors were usually kept locked and were locked at the time of her entrance and exit. Lock is push-button type which remains locked if not changed manually. Fact: Albie Marx stated he had no key to victim's house and entered through unlocked front door. Conclusion: If the killer did not deliberately unlock the front door before leaving, Albie Marx is lying.

Danno put his open hand on the back of his clean-shaven skull and rubbed up and over the crown of his head, all the way down to his forehead and then back again. Then he opened the process to a circular motion, including the sides all the way down to his ears and the back of his neck. He loved the feel of the smooth skin stretched tight over the heavy bone of his skull. He had been blessed with a large, dome-shaped cranium, a powerful and intimidating force, and when he ran his razor blade over the areas where hair would still grow if allowed, he was reminded of the warhead of a torpedo or, when he narrowed his eyes and added an inscrutable look, an Oriental assassin.

If the pre-autopsy report was wrong and Linda Selby wasn't dead prior to hanging, it would be possible that she committed suicide by shooting up with a big dose of smack and then hanging herself. It's even possible that she poured some chloroform onto a rag in her bedroom, walked downstairs, shot up with heroin, stood on a chair with a noose around her neck, then chloroformed herself, knocked over the chair and hung.

That's what you'd call a suicide and a half. But she'd have dropped the chloroformed rag when she hung and no rag was found at Linda Selby's feet. Nor was a hypodermic turned up in the search of the house and its environs.

He could see why someone might need chloroform to get a needle into Selby's arm, but why go the hanging step? To make it look like suicide? People don't chloroform *and* hang themselves. Well, killers aren't all that smart, are they, or there'd be more killers than cops. Danno really liked this case, it appealed to his sense of high drama. And the presence of Albie Marx made it just like a Greek fucking tragedy.

Albie Marx. The weasel had changed a lot in twenty years, but Danno could still picture him down to the smallest detail, down to the "Hoffa For President" button he wore on the lapel of that pretentious black frock-coat he used to go around in. Albie was a mass of hair then, all wild and unruly, with a red bandana and a cock-sureness to his eyes that was mostly a memory when they met up again, a couple of nights ago.

Marx had failed to remember him though, and that was good. Of course, he hardly resembled the Danno of 1970. He too had hair in those days, bushy brown hair that grew in profusion around his great balding crown, and his uniform was standard flowerchild issue, bell-bottoms and tie-dyes. He was with Hollywood Undercover, a "narc," and he wasn't above planting a lid or a gram on someone who deserved to be busted. Joe Danno had a personal vendetta against all who used or dealt drugs—his seventeen-year-old sister, who had run off with a musician who once played for Janis Joplin, had been killed trying to fly off an overpass on the Pomona Freeway, out of her head on LSD.

On the night of October 3, 1970, Danno was in the hotel apartment of an alleged drug dealer named Howard, an old Beatnik-turned-Hippie, a remnant of the Lenny Bruce crowd who was said to supply smack and cocaine to L.A.-based rock stars and their friends passing through. Just before midnight, Howard received a phone call, informing him that Janis Joplin had OD'd on heroin. At twelve-thirty A.M., a full half-hour later, her body was first reported. By Albie Marx.

It was never shown that Howard provided the fatal dose that killed Joplin, although Danno eventually got him sent up on another deal. And Howard claimed not to know, and finally died without revealing, the identity of the mysterious caller.

But everyone knew Joplin and Marx were having this wild affair, and Marx's discovery of the body was enough to warrant trying to scare something out of him. It wasn't Danno's case but he felt the connection between his sister and drugs and Janis Joplin, so he was in the interrogation room when Albie was brought in, all puffed up with phony defiance. He never interrogated Albie himself, so Marx didn't recognize him the other night. But Danno never let go of the feeling that it was Marx who made the call to Howard. And if it *was* Marx, Danno guessed, then he'd either supplied or administered the fatal dose. Like the acid-head boyfriend who killed Danno's sister.

Marx, of course, denied everything, denied making the call, denied using heroin, and there was never any evidence to prove otherwise. It was the final ruling of the chief medical examiner that Janis Joplin died of an accidental overdose of heroin. The Los Angeles coroner also made the point that alcohol was present in her blood and her liver showed the effects of long-term, heavy drinking. She was twenty-seven years old.

So it was settled, and Marx went on his way, but Danno wasn't satisfied. He kept an eye on Marx on and off for a while, through his contacts, but could never get anything on him. Marx stayed clean and was seen around less and less. Danno assumed he'd been so spooked by the Joplin thing that he gave up drugs and dropped out entirely.

He hadn't heard a peep out of the dirtbag until only a year ago, when one of his buddies pointed out Marx's column in *Up Yours* magazine. Danno had always had an open file in his mind when it came to Marx, a particularly painful file because it reminded him of his dead little sister, so he noted the loudmouth's return to the world with great interest. And now it turns out, Linda Selby died of a heroin overdose. Sounds familiar, doesn't it? So Albie Marx was back in his sights, and he was lining up directly in the cross hairs.

CHAPTER 8

Harry Ballister could give a perfect description of quicksand now. Every time you fight to extricate yourself you sink in deeper. And it all started with Lesley, it's all her fault. If she hadn't freaked out over his affair with Dawn, everything would be sunshine and flowers.

Now he's sitting behind his desk looking into two faces of stone. Expensively dressed, they sport gold Rolexes and diamond rings, and one of them is graying at the temples like an elder statesman. If he didn't know who they are, he'd think they're highly paid corporate executives. But these fellows aren't talking profit margins and deal points. Their conversation is angled more toward the visceral side. As one of them is describing his personal technique for pulverizing an elbow, Harry's mind is clawing in panic for a way out of this chaos.

Waste Disposal sent these two over when Harry placed a call to their West Coast V.P. and told him he had to vote *against* granting Waste Disposal the new toxic landfill contract. He explained that he had a problem with missing files and had to vote "No" in order to protect himself—for the record. If the accusation was made that he'd accepted money from Waste Disposal, he could deny it and point to his vote as proof of noninvolvement. He would pay back the money they gave him immediately.

Unfortunately, as he was informed by the two men in his office, Mr. Conroy and Mr. Barnes, Waste Disposal has a policy of no refunds, no returns. They even offered him *more* to keep his vote. When he balked at their generosity, the talk turned to bodily parts.

Barnes, the more distinguished of the two, is saying to Conroy, "Do you remember the mayor of Tuscaloosa, James? The gentleman was made of pig iron. Took me four hefty whacks to put a dent in his collarbone."

"You threw your back out on that, didn't you?" Conroy responds sympathetically. "Swinging that heavy lead pipe."

Harry shudders so hard he can feel his teeth rattle.

"Occupational hazard," philosophizes Barnes. He turns back to Harry. "So, Councilman Ballister, we don't want to take up your time with old war stories, we know you're a busy man. We just came to pay our respects and hope you will think about us when you cast your vote Friday. We'll be thinking about you and wishing you the best."

"Is that your wife?" Conroy asks, pointing to the framed photograph of Lesley, flexing her muscles on Malibu Beach.

"I'm not married," Harry answers, thinking he will destroy the picture the minute they leave.

"Well, give our regards to your parents then," says Conroy, rising. "Waste Disposal believes in the strength of the family."

He doesn't have to show them the door. He's surprised how gracefully they move for cavemen.

The quicksand is sucking him deeper. One thing leads to another and thwop! You're under. Now he has Conroy and Barnes in his life. If only he hadn't called Waste Disposal. But he had to cover himself. Especially after that call yesterday from Lesley.

"Hello, Harry," she had intoned, in that superior British accent.

"Lesley! I've been searching all over for you! I miss you," he cried. She had called him out of the blue.

"It seems I underestimated your ambition. I never thought you would . . . go that far . . ." She was choked with emotion.

Harry was surprised she'd be so upset over his taking money from Waste Disposal. "I'm giving the money back, Lesley," he promised. "They're not getting my vote."

"Screw the money, Harry! You think I care about your petty bribes? How could you do what you did to Linda?" She tried but failed to stifle a sob. "That poor, darling girl who cared only for healing this planet. Was your miserable little career worth a life like that?"

He finally caught her drift, understood what was making her so melodramatic. "You think I had something to do with *that*? You think I would kill Linda for some stinking ledgers?"

"You *killed* her?" she gasped. "I assumed you drove her to suicide."

Uh, oh, Harry thought. Better tell her about his talk with the chief of police. "It looked like suicide. But I was talking to Herman Baddely, the chief of police, about some totally different matter and somehow her name came up, I don't remember how, I think he'd met her with me a long time ago and anyway, he told me she was deliberately, you know, murdered . . ."

"Harry, you bastard!"

"It wasn't me! Why would I kill Linda? Are you crazy?"

"Crazy enough to keep the originals of your precious ledgers!"

"Lesley," he began, in his most endearing, seductive, confidential voice, "You're the only one. I left Linda for you. I left Dawn for you—"

"You expect me to fall for that tommyrot?"

"Come on, you know you're still nuts about me. Wouldn't it be better to just give up this act and come back . . . ?"

"Oh! Go to hell, Harry!" And she slammed down the phone.

He cursed himself up and down. He'd mishandled her again, been too forceful. She was still out there, a loose cannon.

That's what made him call Waste Disposal, he was frantic to cover himself in case Lesley or anyone else released the file publicly. How could he know the damn call would backfire, that the gangsters would hold him to his word.

But it was true what he told Lesley about Herman Baddely. The Los Angeles chief of police had volunteered the information about Linda. Harry, of course, told Baddely he hadn't seen or spoken to Linda in ages and was shocked to hear of her death. But now the chief of police was in the mix with the rest of them.

And then he had to sit at his desk like a good little boy while Conroy and Barnes had their good-humored chat about elbows and collarbones. The thing is getting totally out of hand. He has to do something. But what?

There's nothing he can do about Waste Disposal.

If he can get Lesley on the phone again, he can reason with her, maybe even talk her in, so to speak. If he can get her to meet him, he's sure he can put it all right with her. They were crazy about each other, weren't they? The thing with Dawn was a mistake, a freak. He'll show Lesley what the real Harry is like, the Harry who knows how to love a woman. And then, when he gets Lesley under control, who else could possibly hurt him?

Albie Marx.

Does Marx have his ledger? Did he get it from Linda? Their meeting in the post office, the morning after Linda's ugly demise, could not have been mere coincidence. Marx was there for a reason, he didn't just stop by at seven A.M. that very morning for stamps.

If Linda had stashed Harry's file in the post office box— and if Marx had the original of the yellow carbon copy Harry tore out of Linda's phone book—then Marx now had the file. Two *ifs* don't always make a *then* but in this case Harry had to assume the worst. And the worst was that Marx would come out with a full-scale exposé in that cheap crusading rag he worked for.

Could he make some kind of deal with Marx? If he went to him, man to man, and promised him anything to lay off, would Mr. Morality lower himself to preserve a good man's reputation? Or would the bastard just turn up the heat and gloat that much more? Of course he would.

No, there was no deal to be made, no middle ground. It was total deliverance or total disaster. But it was a crazy chance he took, searching Marx's house. And he almost got caught. If only Marx had been crushed or decapitated in the crash, things would be back to normal. But no. Right now, at this very moment, Albie Marx is putting together the story that will destroy his career and ruin his life.

I have to take care of Albie Marx, Harry thinks feverishly, *I have to stop him.*

CHAPTER 9

"Air Quality—Unhealthful to Critical," according to the Los Angeles Weather Service and I'm into mile four and wondering why I'm preserving my liver by sweating out last night's alcohol at the cost of killing my lungs by sucking in this greasy inversion sludge. I guess it's because lungs, you can picture what they do, you can figure lungs out, they can be fixed, worst comes to worst, you have one to lose. But you only get one liver and once it starts slipping, you're a long shot.

Way down below I hear the beeping siren of an emergency vehicle and I figure it's the paramedics again, riding to the rescue of some poor golden-ager whose lungs have refused to accommodate any more filth. It's becoming commonplace in L.A. to see paramedics rushing all over with respirators. If I were cynical enough, or had some spare cash, I'd invest in oxygen tanks. Pretty soon everyone will have one.

I'm running in the middle of the afternoon to be by myself and meditate on my circumstances. In the summer I hung out in Woodstock, I came to know a Tibetan monk, Rinpoche, who lived in a monastery in nearby Mt. Tremper. Rinpoche meditated six full hours each day, day in and day out, and was the most well-adjusted human I've ever known. Those were my psychedelic years and the instant Perfection of Peyote was a lot more exciting to me than Rinpoche's Work-a-day Bliss, so I insisted on hacking out my own inner pathway instead of following his. But some of his pronouncements I do still remember, the most profound of which will always be, "You are not who you think you are."

That much I thought I knew from my tripping, but Rinpoche's words sunk much deeper than I was capable of diving at the time. A couple of trips on mescaline can reveal many things under the layer of our concensus reality, but it can't replace twenty-five years of six-hour-a-day meditation, and Rinpoche pointed out that meditation is the *only* way to discover who you truly are.

Accepting his premise for the sake of philosophical discussion, I asked him a question which made him smile in a way I will always carry with me. I asked, "Even if I meditate six hours a day, how will I *know* when I know who I am?" And he answered, with that amused, sweet knowing smile, "You'll know."

So, even though I like to say that running is the secret to being a fit, healthy drunk, I also think of it as my time to meditate toward an understanding of who I really am. Unfortunately, my mind is always so occupied with this constant sea of troubles, upon which I always seem to be floundering, that today I have as little idea of who I really am as I did when I thought I knew who I thought I was. You get the picture.

After we left Stevie's, Mariah and I went to the Lazy Leek. That's the upscale vegetarian health food restaurant in the designer area of West Hollywood, where Linda worked as a hostess. I had to get a reading on Nat Bostwick, her boss, to gauge his potential as a suspect or put him out of my mind altogether. Bostwick is a fifty-five-year-old muscle builder, one of those Jack LaLanne types who can't stop impressing you with his strength and conditioning. He once towed a rowboat full of concrete from Alcatraz to San Francisco, all by himself, with his hands tied together. A determined, powerful man, full of phony, I'm-better-than-you smiles.

Nat was in love with Linda from the moment he hired her. She never encouraged him, but she kind of liked him, with all his foibles, because she was a compassionate, loving person. She made it plain that their relationship was strictly platonic. Nat isn't the sexual harassment type so he left her alone, but never gave up his romantic ideas and, even when he did nothing but look at her in that way, it made Linda uneasy.

When Linda and I got together, Nat got nuts. First he took the fatherly approach, counseling that I was wrong for her, bad for her, poisonous, destructive, a liability and a fraud. When that didn't work he decided to lay back and wait, but his preening peacock mentality made it impossible for him to be in the same room with me without glaring and strutting in his unintentionally comic way, trying to make me feel threatened. I always think of Nat as the classic Paranoid-Narcissist, so in love with his own reflection that anyone who doesn't feel the same way is either stupid, misguided or a mortal enemy.

When Mariah and I arrived at the restaurant, the staff was still buzzing about a shooting which took place there the night before. Can you imagine the level of stress in this world? Designer vegetarians shooting designer vegetarians. Over what? Too much kelp in the quiche?

Nat wasn't there, he was giving a statement on the shooting to the police. We ordered the "power brunch" of tofu eggs and soy sausages with twelve-grain toast, sesame butter and a bottle of nonalcoholic wine. I was working on this fashionable feast when Nat Bostwick struck.

I remember seeing, out of the corner of my eye, a body hurtling through the air, then feeling the impact as it landed on my shoulders, crunching me down into my chair, which

shattered and sent me to the floor with the murderous mus-
clebound maniac on top of me. I remember the excruciating
pain when his knee slammed down on my two broken fingers,
mashing them into the floor. I remember thinking, what will
Mariah think of me if this idiot beats me senseless in front of
everybody?

That question was answered immediately. Before Nat could
land one crazy blow, he was suddenly bellowing like a bull
and clutching his nose, which was magically spouting blood
like an overturned fire hydrant. So quickly that almost nobody
saw it, Mariah had delivered a perfect karate kick with the heel
of her boot, square in Nat's schnozzola. As I watched in
wonder, cradling my two wretched fingers in my good hand,
she knocked him flat on his back with another powerful kick,
right to the sternum, and jammed her knee in his neck to keep
him pinned.

Then one of Nat's muscled-up busboys charged her head-
on but Mariah, who, it turns out, is a third-degree black belt,
leveled him with an upward karate punch to the area which
causes the most pain. At this point a third vegetarian bully, the
biggest so far, came at her from the blind side, but before he
could get there I slammed the bottle of wine upside his head
and he dropped like a duck shot out of the sky. The collision
of bottle and skull ended the brief battle with a profound and
final *thud.*

At that point no one knew quite what to do. The designer
vegetarians in the restaurant were horrified. Nat was trying to
get up but Mariah had her boot planted on his neck and he
was making no progress. He was making a lot of noise,
though, through the fountain of blood.

I looked at our waitress who was standing there gaping and
said, very calmly, "Check please." Then I heard people running around in back and phones being dialed.

With a shaking hand, the waitress passed me the check

which she'd scrawled in a writing I couldn't possibly read. I thought of putting on my reading glasses but it occured to me that would do irreparable harm to my new tough-guy image, so I dug out a couple of twenties and threw them on the table.

"We'll be back," I said to Nat, who was glaring at me with hatred from beneath Mariah's boot. "Better get that nose under control." And we walked out. Like they do in the Westerns. The guys in the white hats.

Out on the street I was sky-high. My adrenaline was threatening to lift me right off the ground. "Where did you learn to fight like that?" I asked my new tag-team partner, who was remarkably relaxed.

"New York City subways," she answered with a curt little smile. It wasn't good enough.

"Who are you?" I asked. "Girls from Long Island don't fight like that."

"You know who I am. You're just confused by seeing a woman fight like a man. You'll get over it."

"I'd like to know *why* you can fight like a man. I mean, you're fucking combat ready."

"Albie, that was basic karate. A side kick, a front kick, an upward block and a punch. I've taken karate for years. It's a sport, like fencing. I enjoy it. You could have done what I did with enough training. Why do you have to make such a mystery out of my ability to defend myself?"

Sure, Mariah, anything you say. But she was good. She was very good. A twenty-three-year-old girl, she couldn't weigh more than 120, had easily disposed of two well-conditioned muscle men. Her streetfighting instinct was too well developed to attribute to some karate class on Long Island, even if she'd taken it for years. This girl had practiced for real somewhere.

We pulled away from the restaurant as a police car pulled up and I knew that I'd eventually have to pay the bill for our donnybrook. So many things were happening so fast that I suddenly felt the pressing need to be alone and think, so I headed back to my place where I could go for a long meditative run. On the way home we swung by the Vehicle Impound Lot, where I gave the guy fifty bucks extra to see that the Jag got to the body shop.

Now I'm into mile five and reliving the brawl in the restaurant and I swear to God I feel like Clint Eastwood. I still believe in nonviolence, but that fight could be a high point of the decade for me. Not that I'd want to make a habit of it. Once is enough. If I leave the fight game a winner, my heroic image of myself will be set for life. But wouldn't Rinpoche say, "You are not your image?" And wouldn't he be right?

The question right now is, does Nat's attack on me enhance his potential as a suspect in Linda's murder? And if not, where do I go from here? I sure as hell can't sit around and wait for Danno to put all his pieces together and present me with an airtight case.

I'll bet that Nat Bostwick attacked because he blamed me for Linda's death. My verdict on Nat is, with all his muscles and temper tantrums, he's still a pussy. It takes a more desperate, pitiless type to commit murder, and Nat Bostwick is too much in love with himself to be that desperate. Which leaves me where? With Harry Ballister?

Was Harry after Newt's file at the post office yesterday morning? It's for sure he wasn't there by coincidence. Could he be mixed up in the National Security Board operation? Why else would he want the file?

Let's say he's involved. Newt knew it and told Linda. She confronted Harry and he panicked and killed her, then tried to make it look like a suicide. Unlike Nat, Harry *is* that scared, desperate type who would stop at nothing to protect himself from a threat, be it real or imagined.

But if Harry killed Linda, did he kill Newt too? According

to Linda, Newt was car-bombed last week, after he and I met at the beach. I can't see Harry changing a tire, much less wiring up a car bomb. That had to be the work of those two in the Ford, the geeks who followed Newt out of the parking lot. So, maybe it was them and not Harry who killed Linda.

But Danno's got it in for *me,* and my pointing a finger at somebody else, with nothing to back it up but Newt's memo, will only make Danno more determined to hang me. And if I give the memo to him, that will be the last anyone will see of it. God knows that's happened before. The term *Classified* has protected the guilty, from presidents to assassins, more times than any of us will ever know. That's exactly the reason Newt got that file to me.

Let's face it, the memo is the only thing I have to work with. As far as I can see, I have only one course of action—to get out there and pry the lid off "Campaign NICE," then see what crawls out. If I'm lucky, the worms will reveal themselves. What other choice do I have? It's a tall order, tilting at government windmills, but this is my life and it may be the last shot I get.

I hear a car screeching up the hill behind me and I turn to look. The driver is wearing a rubber Donald Duck mask. Just before the panic kicks in I think of my son working the room at Goofy's birthday party. Then I realize that the guy in the Duck mask is pointing his car directly at me and coming fast. What am I, Target of the Month? What is going on here? Is Mercury in retrograde, or what?

I turn on the jets and sprint onto the sidewalk but the Duck will not be denied. He takes a driveway ramp full speed and veers onto the sidewalk behind me. He's bearing down, bumping and swerving crazily along the pavement. I can't make a dash for a house because they're all fenced off for security. The steel monster is snapping at my heels and the hungry roar of its engine is filling my brain. If you think you know terror, try being chased down a sidewalk by a speeding car.

I head back into the street but there's nowhere to go. The opposite side of the road is faced with the sheer wall of the hillside, no sidewalk, no driveways, no houses, just steep stone and shrubbery. The car jumps the curb and screeches back into the road after me.

I'm running in the middle of the street with the Duck right behind me and my only chance is to get back to the sidewalk but it's not really a chance because he's too close on my ass and it's just a matter of seconds before he gets to me and then—from the opposite direction—a huge boat of a car suddenly rounds the curve up ahead and looms giant in front of me—there's no one at the wheel, no one that I can see, but the car is coming right at me and I'm caught between Ghost Car and the Duck and I ready myself to be pulverized between the two behemoths . . .

In that eternal moment allotted to dead men, between their final two heartbeats, I confront all the "searing regret" (Richard Ford's term, not mine) that a man must face down in order to survive. And I think of my son, and how I would have rescued our relationship if only I'd been given the chance.

The Ghost Car reaches me first and I press myself against the hillside wall hoping he'll miss but he doesn't even try for me, just keeps going straight at the Duck who is coming at me from the other direction and suddenly they're heading dead on at each other, the Ghost Car challenging the Duck to a deadly game of Hollyweird Chicken.

Ducks aren't known for their balls and this one turns out to be no exception. He swerves to the right to avoid the collision, causing two wheels to jump up on the curb, then flies along on a tilt, taking a row of mailboxes and garbage cans with him. The Ghost Car keeps going and disappears around the downhill turn while the Duck Car rights itself and takes flight, vanishing around the uphill turn. I'm standing there in my jogging sweats, my knees quivering like they're doing the Charleston, thinking that maybe if I'd become a doctor like my mother wanted, I wouldn't be living a life designed by Franz Kafka.

Suddenly I recall Newt's caustic comment to me on the beach that day—"My sister said underneath all the bullshit you're really a nice guy"—and in one terrifying flash I see clearly exactly what that meant to him: Nice guys finish dead.

"Somebody tried to kill me," I announce to Mariah when I fall back into my house.

She doesn't hear me. She's eating popcorn and going through my record collection. Half of them were made before she was born, including the one she's listening to now. Dylan is twanging, "*. . . One of my friends is in trouble deep. Turn, turn, to the rain and the wind . . . ,*" from way back in '63, the year of King's March on Washington, my first time in that awesome, corrupt city. Will I have to go back there to sort out this government intrigue?

"What did you say?" she asks, chomping on one of Orville Redenbacher's crunchy morsels.

"*. . . Tell me the trouble, tell me once to my ear . . .*"

"Somebody tried to kill me."

"*. . . Turn, turn, turn again . . .*"

"Somebody what?"

"*. . . Joliet Prison and ninety-nine years . . .*"

"Kill me! Will you turn that fucking thing off!" She hits the eject button and shuts Dylan's big yap. Joliet Prison and ninety-nine years. Danno's Valentine wish for me.

"Some psychotic in a Donald Duck mask tried to run me

over! Actually drove up on the sidewalk after me! Look at me! I'm shaking!"

"You're all right. Calm down."

"Calm down? Some fuck tried to run me over! You want me to calm down? I was a cunt-hair from death!"

"Did you get the license number?"

"Are you kidding? All I could 'get' was out of the way. If it weren't for Newt, I wouldn't have gotten that. Jesus Christ—Newt!"

"What do you mean, 'Newt'?"

"It must have been Newt in that car. It had to be Newt."

"Newt's dead."

"How do you know? Did you see the body?"

"He was blown to smithereens."

"Then someone put him the fuck back together again. He cut off the guy in the Duck mask and saved my life."

She looks incredulous. "You saw Newt?"

"Did I say I saw him?"

"Did you?"

"No."

"Then why are you so sure it was him?"

"Because I know a midget driving a car when I don't see one."

"But they told me he's dead," she insists.

"Dead midgets don't drive like that. It was Newt all right, I'd bet my cat on it. They must have fucked up. They must have blown up some other poor schmuck. You think car bombers are infallible? If they were such geniuses would they be car-bombers? Poor Linda believed it. She got all depressed for nothing."

"Is it possible you're right?"

"Oh, I'm right. He's alive and he's out there. A little Lone Ranger on wheels."

"I have to know."

"Well, if you see him first, thank him for me. I was so scared I just about shit my shorts. And I thought I was a hero in that restaurant today, I really thought I was tough. Forty-seven years old and I'm still trying to bullshit myself. *Hero?* Come on, I'm a middle-aged writer! Middle-aged writers don't beat up bodybuilders! Middle-aged writers don't get chased by cars! Did you ever see a middle-aged writer being chased by a car? How did I get into this? Who asked for this *mishegaas?*"

"Albie, relax, you're giving yourself a heart attack."

"Action-adventure is not my strong suit, okay? You like streetfighting, fine. You go solve Linda's murder on your own."

"It's my fault someone tried to run you over?"

"It's your fault I was starting to think like a tough guy. I am not a tough guy."

"What are you, a coward? A weakling? A victim?"

"Yes! What of it?"

"Then how do you explain *this?*"

She shoves a book in front of me, a coffee table edition of great '60s photographs. It's open to a black and white picture of a long line of southern blacks, accompanied by a handful of whites, facing down a phalanx of tight-lipped Alabama cops in full riot gear. The photograph is remarkable in that it totally captures the palpable violence in the air. Two of the black people in the foreground are carrying an American flag, but the most prominent face in the photograph is covered in bright, clown-white makeup and has "VOTE" written in big black letters across the forehead. The unmistakeable owner of this crazy, brave face is me, Albie Marx.

"Is that a coward?" she demands to know, her finger jabbing at the ancient image.

"I don't know," I answer dumbly, suddenly exhausted by life.

"Don't quit on yourself, Albie. It's a long track."

"*Too* fucking long."

"Who *is* this guy?" she still wants to know, not giving up on the photograph.

"A clown," I answer, failure and regret dripping off every letter of the word. "He was not who he thought he was."

"Fuck that. Fuck who you thought you were. Did you do what this picture says you did?"

I look at the image on the page and try to see through to the reality. How do I know when I know who I am?

"Is this you in the picture, Albie?"

"Yes."

"Are you standing up to those fucking pigs?"

"Yes."

"Are you risking getting beaten with clubs? Getting kicked? Shot? Where is that courage coming from?"

She's driving hard. My heart is pounding and the sweat is pouring off me in rivers. How many roads must a man walk down before he calls himself a man? How many dues must this Jew pay before he can sleep on the sand?

"You never gave up, Albie. You just took a break. You needed it. You deserved it. Now it's time to go back into battle."

Back into battle. I think of Newt and the two geeks wearing shades in the Ford, and John Thomas, of Watergate and Contragate, of Keating and BCCI and the S&L scandals, of the obscene financial gap between the rich and everybody else, of blacks killing each other over drugs, of political manipulation and Madison Avenue politics, of the insidious new high-tech tyranny over the mind of man. I hear Eldridge Cleaver's words ringing in my ears: "We must take a revolutionary position against everything that exists on the planet earth today!"

Where do we draw the line, God, when do we stand up

and say, "No, you can't fuck up our world anymore! You can't sell us drugs and you can't hoard the profits and you can't start wars and you can't put our freedom to sleep!" And why, God, does it have to be *this* run-down antique, this once braveangrydedicatedfoolishproudarrogant relic, who gets the nod, in the last of the ninth, with bases loaded and nobody out? Where are the kids who should be fighting for the planet they're inheriting? Is anyone out there? Is it all up to the old guys? I did this already, why do I have to do it again? Don't they have eyes? Ears? Mouths? Are they all watching *The Simpsons?* Playing Nintendo? Cruising the mall? Wanting to be Madonna? Do they think their supply of air, water and uncontaminated food will last forever? There are dues to pay, my children, and nobody's paying them! *That's* what the National Debt really is—who's going to pay when Mother Nature presents the bill?

Mariah is watching me as all this zooms through my head. She's a good little motivator. Streetfighter, existentialist, motivator. I wonder what else she is. What difference does it make? She's here, she's beautiful and she cares. If I were to live my life, as Don Juan suggests, as if each moment is my last, does it matter if Mariah isn't who she says she is? As long as she supports and encourages me, why should I care who she is?

"You're wondering about me, aren't you?" she asks, with those X-ray eyes. "You're asking yourself, 'Who is she? What does she want from me? What am I getting myself into?' The call is yours, Albie. If you want me to leave, I'm gone. I won't guarantee how long you live after I go, but you're a big boy, you've played for big stakes before. Say the word. It's up to you."

God, how I love this girl. I'll probably never come out and say it, but I refuse to deny the feeling.

"Albie, you look like my dog. What are you so sad about?"

"I'm not sad. I'm happy."

"You don't look happy. Do you want me to leave?"

"No."

"You want me to stay?"

"Yes."

"Then why are you looking at me like you're off to the guillotine?"

Because—I'm losing my head over you?

Mariah has a way of relating to Tank that reveals her soft side, the little girl in her. Here's this salty old cat, this refugee from the garbage dump, who never trusted a woman in his life. And here's this hard-core girl, a third-degree black belt existentialist, who probably never gave half as much to a man as she knew she would get. Neither has any reason to like, much less trust, the other, but something in their chemistry attracts them. She rubs him and he rubs against her, she strokes him and he takes loving swipes at her and she talks baby talk and he makes sounds out of Catnip Nirvana. Why do they feel so safe with each other? What instant recognition tells them they belong together? I wonder if he'll go off with her when this is all over.

When this is all over. If it's ever over.

I get out of the shower and Mariah casually asks me more questions about Newt while she scratches Tank's ears. Was anybody with him? Was anybody following him?

"Like who?" I ask.

"I don't know. Anybody."

"Like two assholes in a blue Ford?"

"Did you see them?"

"Do you know who they are?"

"How would I know who they are?"

She's impossible to corner. She's going for something and I wish I knew what it is. I don't know what she knows. I wonder who she really thinks bumped off her mother. She's not the type you can ask direct questions to, she gets her hackles up too easily. Maybe if I lead her around through the back . . .

"I have a plan," I tell her. "The only thing we have to go on is the fact that Linda left me a note with the location of Newt's file. I can only assume that the file has something to do with her murder.

"Okay, so what's in the file? A memo referring to a secret operation and an FBI profile of Ahmet Ludi. And what is the only name that links the two documents? Felix St. John. The memo says, 'St. John plays for options,' and the profile says that a companion of Felix St. John, an *NSB scientist on an official field trip,*' confirmed Ludi's presence on the island of Libertad.

"That makes St. John a prominent player, someone who's probably got a whole lot of answers. If I can locate him to ask the questions."

She looks at me long and hard. "That's your *plan?* To locate Felix St. John?"

"Yes," I answer defensively. "To find out what the NICE operation is about. And hopefully, who killed your mother."

Her lips form an infuriating little smile. She's not over-whelmed with my strategy.

"And if you found him," she asks in the tone one takes with a child, "what makes you think he would tell you anything?"

"That's a positive line of thought," I reply angrily.

"Do you have a positive answer?"

"I'll jump off that bridge when I come to it."

"Brilliant."

"I haven't heard any ideas out of you," I retort.

"Okay, let's say you found him and he *did* tell you what he knows. You think Danno cares about government conspiracies?"

Why is she asking so many questions? I'm Albie Marx, not Sherlock Holmes. "I can't go to Danno and tell him I know who murdered Linda. He'll laugh in my face and slap on the cuffs. I have to lay it all out for him. When he sees the players he'll realize I don't fit in." That sounds pretty feeble, even to me, but what are my alternatives?

"Do you know who the killer is?" she asks bluntly.

"I have my suspicions."

"Harry Ballister?"

There she goes again. She's a fucking mind reader too. "What do you know about Harry Ballister?"

"I heard him trying to talk the clerk in the post office into opening Newt's P.O. box. He announced his name like he was King of Los Angeles."

The bitch. "I don't believe you! That's critical information! Why didn't you tell me?"

"I was getting around to it."

"When? When I'm in the gas chamber? You know something? We're not on the same team. You don't give a flying fuck about me."

"Because I don't shoot off my mouth with every thought that goes through my head? Besides, I don't believe Harry killed my mother."

She's driving me crazy. "What is this, a game to you? Why bother asking questions when you know everything? Why not shoot off your mouth just enough to tell Danno who did it and go back to New York? What are you hanging around wasting your time for?"

"Because I don't know who did it!"

"Well, what are the possibilities? Harry Ballister, the guys following Newt, Nat Bostwick . . ." She's looking at me with a fixed stare. "Or *me*," I say. "Maybe you think I did it."

"I never said that," she responds levelly. "But I'm not stupid enough to think I can solve a murder and overthrow the government too. Why don't you bite off something you at least stand a chance of chewing?"

"You know what's wrong with you? You don't have any confidence in me."

"*I* don't have any confidence? Didn't you just tell me you're a coward, a weakling and a victim?"

"That's what I mean! You keep bringing up the negatives!"

"You're impossible."

"And what are you? Sally Field?"

"I don't care what people think. I don't need to be liked. And at least I'm straight with *you.*"

"Are you really?"

"Are you straight with me?"

"What's the difference? You can read my mind."

"Give me a break, Albie."

"We're fighting again. Do you notice we always end up like this? Why? Why is it always a fight?"

"Because you're so insecure."

"Oh, it's all me, right?"

"No, it's not all you—"

"Well, it *feels* like it's me. If it *isn't* me you should tell me, cause you're getting all the goddamn negative benefits of it being me, so it might as well be me. And I'll tell you something else, pal—if you keep this crap up, it goddamn well *will* be me!"

And with that I slam the fucking door behind me. Why are women so infuriating?

I call Shrike from a pay phone and tell him to meet me at The Rock. I want someone to drink with and he's always good for that.

The place is quiet when I walk in out of the daylight, and squint down the bar at Leon. "Leave the bottle," is all I say as he's setting me up and I head for the men's room. Why does she get me so out of control? One minute I'm a marshmallow and the next I'm a kamikaze. She always says the thing that sets me off. Does she do it on purpose? I know, it's a woman's idea of control. If she can get you leaning in eight different directions, you're always off balance. That's what their famous "moods" are all about, keeping you guessing. Because without the whole dog and pony show, they're afraid they won't last. You'll figure them out. They'll become predictable. You'll get the upper hand.

Fuck it, have a drink.

When I come back out Shrike is there in his usual seat at the bar and I'm actually glad to see him. A vision in black and he's all mine.

"Hope you're not waiting for me to get started," I say as I sit on my chair and swoop up my Cuervo in one fluid motion.

He looks me over, kind of shaking his head and going tsk, tsk. I down the Cuervo and take a great long slug from the bottle of Corona. Then I fill up the shot glass again.

"To John Shrike, the man who brought me back from the dead. May he never have to do it again."

Shrike lifts his glass of Jack Daniel's. "To Albie Marx, the most persecuted human being in the history of his own imagination."

And we down our drinks. Shrike goes to the juke box and the cheap bastard actually throws in a quarter. What does he play? Cheerful old Leonard Cohen.

"Like a bird on the wire, Like a drunk in a midnight choir, I have tried in my way to be free . . ."

And cheerful old Albie Marx and cheerful old John Shrike start to hum along with that old funster, Leonard.

"Like a baby stillborn, Like a beast with his horn, I have torn everyone who reached out for me . . ."

This music is not an *upper*, you know? Did we actually *listen* to this back in '69?

"Did you do the Jap column yet?" Shrike asks.

"I've been slightly distracted lately, boss. Nothing important, just trying to stay off death row. I'll have it in time."

"That won't be necessary. The issue's in limbo. I've been meditating on it. There's a possibility I may be wrong about the Japanese. Did you know they gave fifteen million dollars to the United Way last year?"

"Toyota spends more on Super Bowl spots."

"Over three hundred million in corporate philanthropy."

"Cheap P.R."

"I'm just trying to be fair. We can't go off half-cocked. We have a responsibility to our readers."

Leon refills Shrike's glass and offers one of his rare observations. "The public opinion polls list Japan as our least trusted ally. One poll said they're a greater threat to the United States than the whole Middle East."

"Thank you, Leon," Shrike says happily, "you just made my point. If the public thinks something is true, count me out. I'm a shepherd, not a sheep."

"Little Bo Shrike," I say, but he doesn't hear. He's onto the next thing, and he's workng himself up.

"But I've come up with a great new hook for the issue, and you're going to love it, Marx—'The Killing of an Activist.' We do your friend Linda's story! Great, right? We immortalize her. Her work, her beliefs, her desires . . ."

"You're not a shepherd, you're a fucking vulture."

"It's a great story! Starring our own Albie Marx. Mystery, drama, passion, it has it all! And it's unsolved. If it sells big, we can do follow-ups. Take it through the arrest, the trial, the conviction—then, if the killer gets the death penalty, we can do a whole protest issue on that! The potential is limitless!"

He's looking at me expectantly, like I should be jumping up and down with excitement. Doesn't he realize this is my *life?*

There's something very fishy about this, even fishier than usual. Shrike's *always* had a thing about the Japanese. All of a sudden he's talking about their charitable contributions? Two days ago he'd have jumped on those figures to prove that they're not only buying our land and our businesses, but our minds as well.

But what's wrong with them buying everything? Everything in America is for sale, isn't it? That's free enterprise. That's the system. If Joe Blow, whose family has lived in this country for four generations, four generations of assembly-line workers for General Motors, is out of work because GM can make more money copartnering with the Japanese in Mexico, that's free enterprise. GM doesn't owe Joe Blow dogshit. If Joe Blow can't pay his mortgage, sell the house to someone who can. Or give it back to the bank—the bank Mitsubishi just bought. If Joe Blow's family fought in World War I, II, Korea and Vietnam, so what? Money talks, memories walk. Beautiful, isn't it? Joe's father loses his legs defeating the Japanese in the South Pacific, then they come over here and take his son's home without bloodying a bayonet. Joe's a lucky guy, he and his family are homeless, but he still has his limbs. Go get a job, Joe. What? You've never done anything but assembly-line work? Well, get your ass to Mexico boy, there's plenty of factories there. Twelve bucks a week's better than nothing at all.

Shrike doesn't know it, but I just wrote his column for him. Too bad he doesn't want it anymore. Why is he changing horses in midstream? I recall a conversation he began with me last night.

"You mentioned something about selling the magazine," I venture.

A twinge of discomfort flickers in his eyes. "That may not be serious," he answers. "My lawyer is handling it."

"Who's the buyer?"

"I don't even know yet. But the fact is, we have to put out an issue next month and your friend Linda will make a great cover story. I love that, 'The Killing of an Activist,' don't you?"

"You're a piece of shit."

"If you really cared about her you'd know what this would have meant to her. She'll become an inspiration to people all over the country. Her courage and dedication, her desire to heal—why should she die for nothing? Why not make her death mean something? Can you argue with that?"

If I really cared about her . . .

"You did care for her, didn't you?" he asks, his eyes glued to mine and his Jack Daniel's breath boring into my nostrils.

If I really cared . . .

She was ready for a relationship. I should have been. She was willing to take the risk. I wasn't.

"But I swear by this song, And by all that I have done wrong, I will make it all up to thee . . ."

Maybe Shrike's right. She wouldn't have wanted to be a martyr, but if her death can make people think about what they're doing to themselves and their planet . . .

"If I have been unkind, I hope that you can just let it go by . . ."

Was I unkind? Or was I protecting myself? Why did she stick with me? Because she knew what I didn't—that I was finally ready for love.

"If I have been untrue, I hope you know it was never to you . . ."

What does that mean, untrue? Other women? Or secret

thoughts? Did I look into her eyes and listen to her hopes for our future together and promise that everything would be all right—while I was plying myself with excuses for not falling in love? Is it possible that I loved her and never even knew it?

Shrike is filling my shot glass as Leon plunks down another Corona. Linda hated my drinking. I was never a mean drunk, I was always relaxed and amusing, but the alcohol was a buffer between me and my feelings, an emotional painkiller. Like drugs, but legal. Maybe, if I had been on the wagon, Linda and I would have had a real love affair. That would have been nice.

It's deepening L.A. night, I'm at the reins of the Mustang and Shrike's riding shotgun. We're on an amusement park ride called the Hollywood Freeway, ripped out of our gourds, flying through the turns with the rest of the traffic to the rollicking beat of k. d. lang's band on the country-western station, "... *the big-boned gal, no doubt she's a natural, shakin' and fakin' and swingin' on a broken heart* ..."

Shrike's playing a harmonica he grabbed from the Harley's saddlebag and stomping his foot and we're off to do some breaking and entering at the office of Councilman Harry Ballister. It's incriminating evidence we're after and we fear nothing and no one.

The music propels us along in the dazzling thrall of a necklace of diamond headlights and glittering, swaying clusters of ruby-red taillights, stretching forever before us. The rumbling trailer trucks are giant prehistoric ants that we speed by in the darkness, and the bright roadside signs call out, proclaiming their readiness to fill your needs ... Best Western ... Chevron ... McDonald's ... California Federal ... Familiar symbols that tell you you're safe, they're out there, you're not lost, you're not alone ... We're doing 75, synchronized to the dance of traffic, rolling in, rolling out, fast and sleek in the

sable night . . . The Broadway . . . May Company . . . Denny's
. . . Taco Bell . . . They're always with us, always there for us.

A bouffant blonde with the dim, good-natured face of a
New Jersey receptionist turns to look as we come up alongside her white convertible, and Shrike gives her a big, lewd
smile. She smiles back, showing small, needy teeth, then flips
on her signal and moves across lanes toward the oncoming
exit and Shrike's gaze follows longingly but he doesn't say
anything, just goes back to playing his mouth organ. And I
think of her apartment and her smell and her lips and her
tongue and her clothes and her underwear and her skin and
her breasts and her nipples and her stomach and her pubic
hair and her clit and her vagina and her ass and her asshole
and it's done and I'm back in the car with the music and
Shrike and the glittering strands of red and white lights.

The address from the phone book leads us to Ballister's office
building. When I see it's a new high-rise security complex I'm
discouraged, but Shrike, ace investigative reporter, won't be
denied. He directs me around to the subterranean parking
entrance. The heavy iron gate is shut tight and forbidding. We
pull up to the automated box where you slide in your parking
pass, and Shrike hands me a blank plastic card to insert.

"Open Sesame," he says confidently, and the gate groans,
then slides open obediently, innocently admitting the two
desperadoes in the Mustang into the bowels of the building.

The parking garage is fluorescently bright and empty, except for a few scattered vehicles belonging to late-working
type A's. We park and take the elevator up three levels to the
elegant lobby, where a security guard requests our signatures
for his ledger. I scrawl "Butch Cassidy" and Shrike signs "The
Sundance Kid" under me. The guy doesn't bother to look.

The office directory lists "Ballister, Harold, Los Angeles

City Council," in room 6334. We get into the elevator and I push the button but nothing happens. Shrike inserts his skeleton card into the automated after-hours slot. He does it so naturally that I'm thinking he's almost *too* good at it. The elevator cranks up and delivers us to the sixth floor.

"Let's find a janitor's cart," Shrike says as we step out onto the lushly carpeted landing.

I had sobered a little in the act of signing in back down in the lobby, but I have the bottle with me and Shrike and I pass it back and forth as we walk down the empty corridor.

"I hate fucking politicians," he says, making a face at the taste of the tequila. "They're more dangerous than priests."

"What priests do *you* know?"

I hear loud music, somewhere up ahead. As we come around a corner we spot what we're looking for. Three quarters of the way down the hall is a large janitor's cart, towels, rags and cleaning utensils piled high, parked beside an open office door. A ring of keys dangles from a hook on the cart's side and a Mexican polka plays from a portable radio sitting on top of a stack of paper towel refill packages.

It turns out the cart is just three offices away from 6334, which is Ballister's office, so we have some waiting to do. Shrike locates a stairwell and we sit on the landing and share the Cuervo.

"Fucking Ballister's a piece of shit," Shrike says, and lights up a Camel.

"I didn't know you knew him."

"I don't know him. I don't have to know someone to know he's a piece of shit."

Interesting philosophy. "Is that the 'Objective Journalist' speaking?"

"That's my Shit Detector speaking." He sticks his head out the door and peeks down the hallway. "Few minutes more."

We sit in silence for a while. Shrike goes into his thoughts and I go into mine. Danno won't wait much longer to make a move. I have to be ready, because when he comes he'll be charging hard. When he accuses me, you can bet he'll have the evidence to back him up. I'll need something solid on Ballister to fight back with.

"Let's go," Shrike says, grinding his cigarette underfoot.

The cleaning cart's gone and rounded the next corner. I wait at Ballister's door as Shrike stalks the cart then returns with the ring of keys. He unlocks the door, tells me to get started, then goes back to replace the keys.

Inside the office I switch on the light. It's a luxurious suite, too good for a pig like Ballister. There's a roomy reception area with a couple of desks, a kitchen, a private bathroom and a large, open office with a panoramic view of the city. The carpet is rich and the furniture first rate.

I go into Harry's office which is impeccably neat and orderly. The walls are laden with degrees from colleges and law schools, plaques and awards from civic and charitable organizations, photos of a well-dressed and affable Harry at benefits and affairs with various show business personalities— Larry Hagman, Angela Lansbury, Bob Eubanks, Neil Diamond, Jerry Lewis—and, in the most prominent position of all, an autographed picture of Harry shaking the hand of President Donald Cale, with none other than Chief of Staff John Thomas standing beside them.

Could they be talking about NICE, I wonder? A bumbling, mid-level bureaucrat recruited by the most powerful men in the nation to play some critical role in the mysterious drama of NICE? Is it too far-fetched? Did Nixon employ bumbling mid-level Cubans to burgle the Democrats? Did Reagan hire bumbling mid-level arms dealers to bargain with the Iranians? In these times the far-fetched is tame and the bumblers still bumbling.

Harry's desk is compulsively tidy, with not so much as a

scrap on top, so I methodically go to work on the drawers in search of something I can use. As I'm pawing my way through Harry's stuff, I catch a glimpse of Shrike in the outer office, coming out of the bathroom with paper towels bunched in his hand and passing by Harry's door.

Harry's desk drawers yield nothing more than office supplies, general personal effects and a copy of *The Price of His Toys,* a glossy catalog of overpriced novelties for the obscenely rich, tucked under a stack of personalized stationery. I move to his mahogany file bureau and thumb through the folders, reading through anything that looks halfway promising. Outside I hear Shrike pecking away on the secretary's typewriter.

I'm engrossed in what appears to be an incredible proposal for a new, believe it or not, "toxic landfill," to be located atop the hills between L.A. and the Valley, when Shrike comes in and tells me to hurry it up, the security people will be making their rounds soon.

I speed through the rest of the files, finding nothing relating to Campaign NICE, John Thomas, Ahmet Ludi, Felix St. John or anything that can link Ballister to the secret operation. I tell myself, he's got to have *something* in writing, but I can't find it. Meanwhile, Shrike is busily rummaging through the cabinets and closets.

I'm just about finished in Harry's office, having turned up nothing even remotely useful, when Shrike calls to me from the kitchen.

"Look at this," he says as I get to the door, "I found them behind the refrigerator." How did he know to look behind the refrigerator? He's holding up two rubber masks—Freddy Krueger and Donald Duck.

So the masked man is Harry Ballister. It was Harry who ransacked my house in search of Newt's memo. And it was Harry who tried to run me over this afternoon. The son-of-a-bitch must be in way over his head to be this desperate. And if he's desperate enough to kill me because he figures I have Newt's file, wouldn't he be desperate enough to kill Linda if he thought she knew something too? I guess when you're dealing with the President of the United States the thought of fucking up can be pretty unnerving.

But if Harry did kill Linda, how would I prove it? How would I prove he tried to kill me? The masks won't do me any good, it's my word against his. Somehow I think Danno would side with the councilman.

"Put them back," I tell Shrike, "just like you found them."

"Do they mean anything?" he asks.

"Yeah—he's getting a head start on Halloween." I don't want Shrike knowing too much, he's the type to go off half-cocked and send up a warning flare to everyone involved in the NICE conspiracy. I'm not quite ready for that yet.

Shrike looks at the masks again, then reaches to put them back where he found them. Suddenly he freezes at the sound of Mexican music right outside Ballister's office door. "Quick, the lights!" he whispers and we lunge for the switches. We get everything except Harry's inner office before a key is inserted in the lock. We dive for cover, Shrike into the bathtub and me under the secretary's desk as the door opens and the security guard and janitor stick their heads in.

"You left a light on in here, Geronomo," the guard says to the janitor, and walks into Harry's office. I'm under the desk and something stinks to high heaven but I don't know what it is. Maybe the guard farted.

"Come on man, I got three more floors to do," the janitor complains in a heavy Spanish accent. The guard turns off Harry's lights and I'm sweating like a donkey under the desk and starting to feel nauseous from the strange odor.

By the light of the outside hallway spilling into the office,

I can see the guard's feet stop for a moment in front of the desk. Oh, God, what if he finds me?

"Something stinks in here man," the guard complains to the janitor. "Did you clean this office?"

"Yeah, man, I cleaned it. Come on, I gotta finish."

"You know whose office this is, Geronomo?"

I'm starting to gag from whatever it is that smells. I wish this fucker would go already.

"This is Councilman Ballister's office. He's your elected representative, Geronomo."

"Yeah, well no wonder it smells in there, man. Let's go."

I'm literally holding my mouth closed with my hand to keep from gagging out loud. And keeping my eyes on the guard's polished black shoes. I assume he's taking a last look around, then he proceeds to the door. When he finally closes it behind him, we're thrust into total darkness.

I hear Shrike come out of the bathroom. "Don't turn on a light," he says. "We'll split in a minute."

"Do you smell that?" I ask, feeling my way to the door to join him.

"What?"

"Smells like shit," I say.

"Shhhh!" He waits a moment, then opens the door and peers out. "Let's go," he says, and we move out into the hallway and run to the stairwell. Even with all my jogging, the excitement has me palpitating all over, and we fly down the six flights of stairs like schoolkids pursued by a teacher.

We hit the lobby and slow it way down, walking normally past the guard with the sign-in sheet, nodding goodnight, then taking the elevator down to the lot and the Mustang. A minute later we're out on the road, headed for the freeway and back to The Rock.

"I love close calls," Shrike says, and punches up the radio. "Too bad you didn't find what you were looking for."

"Yeah," I repeat, "too fucking bad."

But all I can think of are the two rubber masks and the sheer desperation Ballister must be feeling to have tried the things he's tried. And what he'll try next.

I leave Shrike at The Rock around midnight. He's hitting on some black biker chick, I think she said she was in a rock and roll band or something.

I'm headed for home. The exquisite edge of the tequila has worn off and now I'm just dull with the alcohol. I turn on an all-night talk show and people are calling in to find out what to do about the spraying. The Mediterranean Medfly, recently discovered again in L.A., is threatening to multiply and cross over into the San Joaquin Valley, home of California's multibillion dollar fruit farms. In order to fend off this costly invasion, large sections of Los Angeles and the San Fernando Valley are being sprayed daily with malathion. People are warned to cover their cars and stay indoors during spraying times.

The authorities have assured everyone that malathion is harmless to humans. Most of the sheep have accepted this explanation, but to the great irritation of the authorities, a few problem people keep asking how it can be that a substance which peels the paint off your car and gives your dog emphysema has no effect whatsoever on the human body.

The government "authority" on the radio is explaining that, given the minuscule doses of spray each person is exposed to, there's no chance of damage to human health.

Someone calls in and asks if malathion isn't the same compound used in World War II nerve gasses developed by the Germans. The government guy says they'll have to ask a chemist about that.

As I'm heading into Los Feliz, a chemist calls and verifies the last caller's point about the nerve gas. The government guy says that it may be so, but the doses are so small as to render the nerve gas harmless to humans. The spraying will continue.

I'm chugging up the hill toward my street when a cab passes me on its way down. You rarely see cabs in these hills, much less after midnight, and I glance back through my rearview mirror but it's gone around a turn.

On an instinct I decide to follow and see where it goes. Maybe it has something to do with me and maybe it doesn't, but I have nothing to lose and Mariah's probably sleeping in my bed so I'd just have to flop down on the couch anyway. I wheel the Mustang around at the first available driveway and follow the cab at a respectful distance.

The cab makes its way along Franklin, then down to Hollywood Boulevard, then down again to Sunset. The talk-show host is having a screaming match with a guy who calls him a piece of "anti-God-Liberal-slime" for complaining about the Crystal Cathedral. The Crystal Cathedral is an all-glass church, run by the honkiest white-bread preacher for rich, white Republicans, and yesterday it received the only dispensation against malathion spraying granted anywhere in Los Angeles. Can you imagine cleaning thousands of gallons of goopy insecticide off a glass building the size of St. Patrick's? That's a lot of squeegees.

The cab pulls up in front of LeDome, a high-priced Hollywood restaurant, fronted by soaring marble columns and frequented by high-level show business swells. Nobody's spraying malathion on this place either.

As I watch from my vantage point down the block, who do I see jump out of the cab, take a quick look around and hurry into the restaurant? Take a wild guess. Talk about hidden agendas, this girl Mariah's a regular Mata Hari. What is she up to now? I'm dying to know who's she's meeting, but I don't want her to see me.

LeDome is a large, opulent place, luxuriously appointed and composed of a number of faintly lit rooms, the respect of privacy being one of its primary appeals. You enter into an open reception area, then have three choices—to the left and right are various well-padded rooms of the restaurant, or straight ahead is the massive, round, leather-wrapped bar, where self-annointed "producers" and sugar-daddy-seeking "starlets" are forever doing the Hollyweird Waltz.

Round walls shield the bar from the other rooms, so that once I'm assured that she's not in the bar, I plant myself on the most secluded stool and order my usual. From this spot I can peer around the walls and see without being seen. And when I get around to doing just that, what I see is Mariah, easy to spot with her rainbow hair, at a table, her back toward me, deep in conversation—with a midget named Newt. Uncle Newt. The dead secret agent. The half-pint responsible for getting me into this mess. I *knew* he was driving that car today. If these two are deliberately gaslighting me they're fucking with the wrong guy.

"Aren't you Albie Marx?" a voice suddenly inquires.

Startled, I whirl around to discover a good-looking redhead, around thirty-five, scrutinizing me over her martini.

"Yes, you are Albie Marx, aren't you," she declares in a sexy British accent.

Where do I know her from? She's got a body I wouldn't forget—not if we spent a night together.

"I don't expect you remember me," she says modestly. "We only met once. At the home of a mutual friend." And suddenly, for no reason, her eyes get all teary. She chokes out the words, "Excuse me," and digs for a hankie.

"Are you all right?" But the tears don't stop. Wait, I know, I remember. "We met at Linda's," I recall.

"Yes," she manages to sob from behind the hankie. "Poor Linda."

Poor Linda. Yes, poor beautiful Linda. In the swirl of my problems have I forgotten to grieve? This woman cries for you and I have yet to. I will though. I will cry for you, Linda.

"I'm Lesley Wentworth," she says, blowing her nose.

"Yes, I remember—Lesley. It's good to see you. I wish it were under different circumstances." She nods in agreement. That's right, she's a friend of Linda's. I vaguely remember meeting her one night when I'd had a few. Of course, that could have been any night.

She's still mopping her face when I suddenly remember Mariah and Newt. I turn away from Lesley to peer around the wall again. The table is empty. They're gone. Fuck! I jump off the stool and survey the restaurant. Nowhere. Gone. Maybe I can catch them. I dig in my pocket and throw a ten-spot on the bar.

"For hers, too," I tell the bartender, indicating the bleary-eyed redhead. To Lesley I say, "I have to be going. It was really good seeing you."

She's trying to ask me something but it's too late, I'm gone, out the door, into the street, eyes peeled for Newt and Mariah. They're nowhere in sight. They must have spotted me. Damn-it! How could I let myself get distracted?

Depressed, I start back to my car, kicking myself all the way. If I hadn't squandered my attention on Lesley, who's a nice enough person but means nothing to me, I'd know what Mariah and Newt were up to, and maybe even how it involves Harry Ballister.

Reaching my car it suddenly dawns on me that, seeing me at the bar, Mariah must have headed straight home. She couldn't have much of a head start. I'll beat her to the house and confront her when she comes in. Then it will all come out, all of it.

I jump into the Mustang and rip out of my parking spot, flying like a Santa Ana toward Los Feliz. Mariah and Newt. What could that mean? He's her uncle, she says. But why would she meet him secretly? After all, he saved my life. Why wouldn't they include me? We all want to catch Linda's killer, don't we?

The cops are out in force tonight, so I have to slow down on the main streets. I'd never pass the Breathalyzer test in the shape I'm in. I'm driving with one foot on the gas and one on the brake, straining to get above Franklin and give the Mustang her head. This confrontation can't come fast enough for me.

When I get up into Los Feliz, I let her out all the way, leaving rubber on all the turns. Normally I'm a careful driver, squealing tires have never been one of my favorite things, but since this crazy thing started I'm becoming Mario Andretti.

The house is dark as I turn onto my street. Not a light, not a sound. I think I've beat her home. I turn off the headlights and the engine and let the Mustang glide into her stall under the carport. Noiselessly, I get out, close the door and make my way to the front door. It's locked, a good sign. I let myself in and my eyes adjust to the inner darkness.

Then I hear a sound. Breathing. Someone's here with me. My body tenses. I move warily toward the far wall where the bedroom light panel is mounted. Reaching the switch, I steel myself, take a breath, then—throw on the light.

There she is. In my bed, under the covers, pretending she's fast asleep. It's an old kid's ploy, I remember my brother and I used to do it when we heard my father come stomping down the hall with a belt in his hand. Most of the time it worked. But it's not going to work for her. Not tonight.

I go to the bed and take a good hold of the covers. I don't

see her clothes by the bed and I doubt very much if she had time to take them off. Faking sleep, fully clothed, praying I'll let it slide. But I won't. I rear back and rip off the covers.

She's buck naked. And acting like I dropped a bomb on the bed.

"What the hell are you doing?" she sputters, blinking against the light. "What's the matter with you?" She grabs hold of the sheet and wrenches it back to cover herself. She's looking at me like I'm a flaming maniac. "Are you drunk again?"

I shout in frustrated anger, "I know where you were! I fucking followed you!"

"You're out of your mind," she says quietly. "What are you on? You're taking more than tequila."

I'm enraged. "Don't give me that! Don't change the subject! You took a goddamn cab to Hollywood and back! I saw you! I followed you into LeDome! I saw you with Newt!"

She closes her mouth and looks at me like she's watching some kind of incomprehensible machine have a mechanical breakdown. It's breaking down right in front of her and she hasn't a clue how to fix it.

"Don't look at me like that, goddamn it! You beat me back here and pretended to be asleep! What do you take me for, a fucking idiot?"

"I don't take you for 'fucking' anything." She swings her legs over the side of the bed and, wrapped in the sheet, stomps to the closet.

"What are you doing?" I demand.

"Getting the hell away from you," she answers, and grabs a bunch of her clothes. The sheet is restricting her movement and she becomes angry and flings it away. Her nakedness is mesmerizing.

Before she gets into her panties, I see that whatever I've imagined about her body is insufficient. She's all rounded and curvy, round and curvy and young and tight. Her skin is olive perfection and her pubic hair is spectacular, thick and black, curling into wonderful mysterious crevices. Her breasts are beyond air-brushing, full and firm with strong, uplifted nipples. She is the most beautiful woman I have ever laid eyes on. She is getting dressed and leaving me. I do not want her to leave me. I can put up with her secrets but not her absence.

I try to reason with her. "Forget it. Forget I yelled. Let me try this—I'm in a fix. I might have to go to jail for the rest of my life. Or get the death penalty. For sure it's going to be something that won't be laughs. All I'm asking of you is, if you know something, tell me. If you can help me, help me. I have nothing but respect and admiration and good feelings for you. Will you do that? Will you help me?"

"I've been helping you, Albie. You've been sucking my tit since I met you. I don't know what else I'm supposed to do. I give you the file. I save it from being confiscated. I save you from getting the shit kicked out of you. If that's not helping, tell me what is." She stands there defiantly, clad only in panties, her young breasts thrust challengingly out at me. I can't seem to get my mouth to work. She senses victory.

"Don't leave," I manage to say. "I don't want you to leave."

She regards me thoughtfully for a few interminable moments. "Then can I go back to sleep now? Is it asking too much to be spared a drunken rage in the middle of the night?"

What am I supposed to answer to this? Maybe she's got a twin sister. Who the hell knows? Who the hell knows anything anymore?

The light is streaming in the window and the ringing telephone is rattling my synapses like a radio sound-effect man's tin thunder-sheet. My two broken fingers command me to lie still or face the consequences. I remember attempting to masturbate with my good hand, being all out of rhythm and trying to force it, then passing out with the image of Mariah in her silk panties draped over my tequila soaked brain.

What time is it?

It's too bright.

Why doesn't she answer the fucking phone?

I hear her pick it up. "Hello? Who wants him? Hold on." She brings the phone to the couch where I'm planted in the sweat and rubble of last night's nightmares. She's wrapped in my white terrycloth robe, and with her rainbow hair, I think of an ice cream cone with sprinkles.

"It's Danno," she says sotto voce, covering the mouthpiece.

My heart sinks. I knew this was coming but I hoped for more time. I take the phone. "Yes?" I say, trying to excise the hostility from my voice.

"Good morning, Albie. Detective Danno here. I was wondering if you wouldn't mind doing us a little favor."

What does he take me for? "Anything I can do to help, Lieutenant."

"It's for the boys in the lab. They're working real hard on the Selby case and I'd like to give them a hand putting some pieces together."

Forcing some pieces together would be more like it. But I have to play this game. "What do you need?" I ask amiably.

"Not much. A few hairs."

Uh-oh. I suddenly feel the crushing weight of circumstantial evidence coming at me like a boulder rushing downhill. "Hairs? What kind of hairs?"

"The kind I wish I had, Albie. Head hairs."

"Head hairs?" I sound like an idiot, repeating everything he says, but he's got me off balance.

"And a few pubic hairs too, if you don't mind. For my scrapbook."

This guy is a motherfucker.

"Do I have any choice in this?" I ask.

"I can get a subpoena."

Get a lawyer, you idiot, an inner voice shouts. "I'll get back to you this afternoon. How's that?"

"Call me by three and I won't feel ignored."

"I'll call you by five."

"You're tough, Albie. Five it is. Talk to you then."

Conversation over. I feel like vomiting.

"He wants hairs?" Mariah asks, looking concerned.

"He wants my head. I need a lawyer. What time is it?"

"Nine-fifteen."

I dial the magazine office. "Shrike, it's me. I need a lawyer."

"Great!" he enthuses. I recall last night's conversation about "The Killing of an Activist." No wonder he's so happy. "I have a guy for you. The best. Wait a second, I have his name right here . . . Arthur Gruntman. Great criminal lawyer. He's in the Movement."

"Really? Maybe he'll donate his services." But I wouldn't bet on it.

"His number is 464-1515. Arthur Gruntman. Give him a call."

"Arthur Gruntman—464-1515," I repeat for Mariah, who writes it down on a piece of paper. "Thanks."

"When you come in today, we'll lay out the new issue. It's gonna be a blast."

"Thanks for the number, Shrike," I repeat, and hang up. Does the man have *no* sensitivity?

"I have to get untracked," I say to myself as much as to Mariah. "This thing's coming down and I have nothing to defend myself with." Then I add, "You do what you need to do, but I have to get to St. John. He's the only lead I have."

"I agree."

"You *agree?* Suddenly you agree? Why? What did Newt tell you?"

"Don't start, Albie," she warns.

"All right, forget it. You never saw Newt. You want to be a mystery woman, that's your business. Mine is to find Linda's killer."

"Whatever you think, our goal is the same."

She hands me the slip of paper. Arthur Gruntman. 464-1515. I dial the number.

"Gruntman and Sachs, please hold."

I haven't uttered a word and already I'm on hold. I have to hand it to lawyers, they treat everyone the same—like dog-doo. To add insult to injury, they play Muzak in your ear. Thirty seconds go by while I listen to 1,001 strings mangle my youth with a limp-dick rendition of "I Want to Hold Your Hand." But then, I tell myself, John Lennon liked Muzak.

"Gruntman and Sachs, sorry to keep you waiting, may I help you?"

"Arthur Gruntman please."

I'm switched to another secretary. "Arthur Gruntman's office."

"Arthur Gruntman please."

"Who may I say is calling?"

"Albie Marx. John Shrike, from *Up Yours* magazine, gave me Mr. Gruntman's name. I have an urgent situation."

"One moment please, Mr. Marx." Her tone doesn't reflect my urgency.

"Albie." His voice is deep and immediate.

"Arthur?"

"I'm a great admirer of yours. *Roger Wellington Rat.* A classic."

"Thank you."

"And John Shrike. What can I say about John Shrike?"

"The less said, the better," I joke, and he laughs knowingly. "I'm in big trouble, Arthur, and I need to talk to you about it."

"When can you get to my office?"

That's all there is to it. We agree to meet in an hour. I feel slightly relieved even though I know, in the long run, the only one who can help me is me.

CHAPTER 10

Mariah and I are sitting at Gate 23 in the American Airlines terminal, waiting to board Flight 2242. A passenger waiting nearby is watching one of those coin-operated TV's and my attention is caught by a report on the news, quoting Undersecretary of State Elliot Charmburg as saying, "We are keeping a close eye on recent developments in Libertad."

"Did you hear that?" I ask Mariah.

"What?"

"That news report. They mentioned Libertad. That's the island where Ahmet Ludi lives, where St. John saw him. Some kind of 'developments' there."

"It's starting," she says. I glimpse an imperceptible shadow flicker across her eyes.

"What's starting?"

"Operation NICE. It's out of the gate. We're running out of time."

"I told you that two days ago," I moan.

"You were right," she says, as if she knew it all along, then turns her attention back to the Ahmet Ludi file.

I can't win with this chick. Fuck her. My mind goes back to our meeting with the lawyer. Gruntman.

Gruntman was smart and fat. Very fat and, I suspect, just as smart. He weighed about 350 and had a giant head that must have held at least twenty pounds of brains.

He told me that Danno couldn't just come out and subpoena my hair. That would be a violation of the fourth amendment. But he could get a search warrant and collect hair from my house. I'd love to see Danno on his hands and knees, picking up pubic hairs in my shower stall. Fat chance. He'll make somebody else do it.

And, Gruntman added, there was an outside chance, depending on the judge and the persuasiveness of Danno's argument, that the warrant might give him permission to take hair directly. What's he going to do? Come in with a barber? Call Jon Peters, we need some of Albie's hairs. It's not funny but you gotta laugh.

Other than that, the only way Danno could get my hair would be to formally charge me with the crime. Which would really be horrible. What would it take, I asked Gruntman, who compulsively ate diet candy all through the meeting, for Danno to charge me with murder?

"Probable Cause," he answered. "And if he's collecting hairs, he's building up to Probable Cause."

"What if he doesn't charge me, but tells me to stay available?"

"You're free to come and go as you please. But if they *do* charge you, they can say that flight after being told to stay constitutes an awareness of guilt. They can make that argument. Are you planning a trip?"

With Mariah's help, I told him about John Thomas and Newt's files, Harry Ballister and Felix St. John, Freddy Krueger and Donald Duck. He listened deeply, never pausing in his constant demolition of diet candy.

He was intrigued by the Ballister element. He knew Ballister by reputation, had met him once at a fund-raiser, and agreed that he was the desperate type, the type to do anything when threatened. He also knew Harry was tight with Herman Baddely, the chief of police and, unless we could back up whatever suspicions we had, we might do ourselves more harm than good by accusing Harry this early in the game. We agreed to hold back on that front and also that Gruntman would deal with Danno from now on, that I wasn't to say a word unless Gruntman was present.

By the time we left his office, he had managed to fill an entire wastebasket with diet candy wrappers. As a friend of Shrike's, an admirer of my work, and a member of the Movement, Gruntman agreed to take my case at the cut-rate price of $400 an hour. My mother was wrong about being a doctor—I should have gone to law school.

Having Gruntman on my side made me feel a lot better. He was going to dig and find out what they're planning for me. In the meantime, after hearing the story from beginning to end, he didn't dissuade us from going after St. John.

That left us with the question of how to go about it. Surely the National Security Board would know where to reach him. But how could we get it out of them? They don't just give out information to anyone who asks for it. They have to know you, you need *clearance.*

I thought of suggesting that Mariah ask Newt, but that would only have started a fight. Best leave the Newt thing alone, until she decides to come clean on her own. Besides, it's kind of exciting to know I have a guardian angel floating around out there, a cavalry of one to come to my rescue when the savages attack.

Back at my place, the answering machine had been using a lot of tape.

"Hello, Albie, this is Lesley Wentworth, we had a drink in LeDome last night . . ."

Mariah looked at me with disgust. Another piece of ass, I could see her thinking.

". . . I was wondering if you might like to stop by my flat for a drink. Or I could come to you—" I hit the fast forward and cut her off. Why inflame things between Mariah and me by making her listen to some woman's proposition?

"Mr. Marx, this is Jonathan Grant's assistant, Marcy Kennerly." Marcy Kennerly? The little pisher has an assistant? "Jonathan wanted to know if he could move your lunch date to the nineteenth. When he made the appointment for the ninth he forgot that Mr. Katzenberg's spiritual teacher is giving a three-day executive seminar at La Costa. If the nineteenth works for you could you give me a call to confirm? Thank you."

The nineteenth? Maybe he can come to my arraignment. If he isn't diddling Minnie Mouse on Eisner's couch. We've got to get this relationship together.

"Mr. Marx? Are you there? This is Ralph Pierson at Jaguar Body Works. Your insurance company wants to total your 3.4. It's gonna cost eighteen thousand to put it right. They'll give you fifteen-five. I can cherry it out but it's gonna cost you around three grand out of pocket, with your deductible and all. What do you want to do? Call me. 464-8969."

I'll spend the dough, that's what I'll do. The car means more than dollars and cents to me. Fucking insurance companies. Do they ever lose?

"Hello, Albie. Joe Danno here. One thing I forgot to mention when we spoke this morning—don't leave town. Talk to you at three."

At *five*, Joe, we said *five*. Asshole. I could just about feel his hot, skinhead breath on my neck.

"Albie? This is Sally Keester. I have to see you. It's important. It's around eleven now, I have to go out for something but I'll be home by noon. I really need to see you."

Mariah was giving me that look of disgust again, and I let her do her act. I didn't mention the other morning, when I saw Sally sneak into Linda's house while Mariah was there. Instead, I played as dumb as she probably thinks I am and explained that Sally was Linda's next-door neighbor and probably had something relevant to get off her chest. Mariah acted like she didn't appreciate the idiom, but at least the explanation diffused her phony dudgeon.

Then I got on the phone and called a list of scientific and government agencies, The National Institute of Health, the U.S. Department of Scientific Research, the National Alliance of Scientists, the Foundation for Science In Industry and a dozen or so others—none had Felix St. John on their rolls. None had ever heard of Felix St. John. How could a man so important be so unknown?

By the time twelve o'clock rolled around, we had gotten nowhere and I was so frustrated that I was openly hostile with anyone who denied knowing Felix St. John. Mariah finally suggested that I go to Sally's while she took over the phone work. That sounded fine to me. Finally, we were functioning like a team.

Sally Keester was wearing a classic forties pink sweater that she must have bought at one of those Beverly Hills collector's shops, the kind Lana Turner wore when they dubbed her "America's Sweater Girl." A tight skirt from the same period rounded out what was already rounded out to begin with. You could find a lot of things wrong with Sally but her keester sure wasn't one of them.

I figured it was a healthy sign that I could still get turned on in spite of my problems, so I let myself go with the flow and didn't try to turn myself off by thinking of fat girls or Willie Mays. Whatever happens happens, I reckoned.

"I hope you don't think I'm . . . crazy for wanting to see you," she breathed, and the tone of her voice gave the word *crazy* a dimension I hadn't noticed before.

"I'm learning that nothing is 'crazy' anymore," I assured her. "You're looking quite well."

"Thanks," she said modestly. "Can I get you something?"

How about two Quaaludes and you sit on my face, the old Albie answered from a decade ago. "Sure," the new Albie said, pleased with his spiritual progress. "But I polished off your Cuervo the other night."

"I bought a new bottle."

"Not just for me, I hope."

"Would that bother you?"

"Not enough to keep me from drinking it."

I followed her into the living room, wondering when the game playing would stop and she'd get to what was on her mind. As I watched her pour my drink, it occurred to me that the word *voluptuous* should really have an 'm' in it—she was truly *volumptuous*.

She set the shot glass and the bottle down on the coffee table and sat next to me on the couch. She always smelled so good. What was that perfume she used? And what did she want from me?

"Detective Danno was here yesterday, Albie," she began, looking me straight in the eye. "He told me that Linda didn't kill herself. Were you aware of that?"

"Not at first," I answered, downing my drink and pouring another. "What else did the son-of-a-bitch have to say?"

"He told me how she died. What kind of low-life would do something like that?"

"What did he tell you?"

"That someone killed her with heroin. I'm sick thinking

about it. They knocked her out with chloroform and stuck a needle in her arm. It's so wrong. So unfair. I'm very angry."

Chloroform? I hadn't heard that before. Made perfect sense, though. Neither Ballister nor anyone else could have gotten that needle into Linda's vein if she were awake. How did Danno interpret the chloroform in terms of me? If I needed the chloroform, at least he can't think we were shooting up together. But how did it relate to him wanting my hair? I was getting exhausted just thinking about it.

"I knew about the heroin," I yawned.

"Albie—he also told me that it was you. That you killed her." This was said in a nonjudgmental tone, but something far back in her voice gave off a faint whiff of accusation.

"Is that why you had to see me?" I asked, sinking back into the sofa's soft pillows and peering at her from under knit brows. "You want me to tell you it wasn't me?"

She searched my eyes so ruthlessly I felt like asking her for a warrant. "Yes," she finally said. "Tell me it wasn't you."

I closed my eyes against the weariness. "It wasn't me." The nights of tossing and turning were catching up with me. I wanted to plunk my head down in her breasts and sleep for a month. "I didn't kill her . . . I loved her . . ."

Next thing I remember, Sally was shaking me, calling my name, shaking me, shaking me . . . "Albie, wake up! Wake up! Albie!"

"What . . . ?" I must have blacked out. Too much pressure. Too little sleep. Too much booze. "What did I . . . black out?"

"Black out? You've been dead to the world for three hours. You scared the hell out of me."

"Three hours . . . ?" I felt like a thick misty fog had invaded my brain.

"You looked exhausted so I figured I'd let you sleep for a while. Then I couldn't wake you up. I was about to call an ambulance."

"No. No ambulance. What time is it?"

"Ten to four. Are you all right?"

"I'm stacked up over Kennedy. What happened? Did I just fall asleep?"

"We were talking, you closed your eyes and you were gone. Just like that."

"It's four o'clock? I have to get home."

"Do you think you should drive?"

"I'll find out, won't I?" I answered, struggling to my feet. Maybe I'm getting a brain tumor. Maybe I should see a doctor.

"Let me help you," she offered, taking my arm.

"No, I'm fine. I can make it." I shook the cobwebs from my head. "Can I have some water?"

She ran into the kitchen to get me a glass of water. What's happening to me? Should I be worried?

"Here," she said, handing me a glass of what passes in Los Angeles for water. Polluted as it was, it felt good going down.

"Thanks. I'm sorry I fell asleep on you."

"That's okay. I got what I needed. Thank you."

I guess what she needed was to hear me say that I didn't kill Linda. I'd say it all day if I had the time, but the clock was moving inexorably toward five, the time I told Danno I'd call, and I'd made no progress. I said good-bye to Sally and carefully guided the Mustang back home.

When I got back, Mariah had a big shit-eating grin on her face. She had finally found an organization who knew Felix St. John and had willingly given his address and phone number.

"Who?" I asked. "Who gives out numbers like that?" If the information was indeed correct, I was willing to bet that she got it from Newt.

"The National Society of Inventors," she answered smugly, as if she had really done some detective work. She handed me a paper—Felix St. John, 757 Maple Street, Philadelphia, Pennsylvania. 215-694-3948.

"I don't buy it," I said.

"What do you mean, you don't buy it?"

"You know what I mean. You didn't get this from any 'National Society of Inventors.' "

"No? Where did I get it?"

Why did she insist on playing this game? All right, I figured, I'll call the number. I dialed. The phone rang. A woman answered, a fierce fräulein with a proud German accent.

"Hello?"

"Is this the St. John residence?"

"Yes."

"Felix St. John?"

"Yes. Who is calling?"

I looked at Mariah. Her eyes said, "See?" I returned to the German.

"My name is Albie Marx. I'm a reporter with *Up Yours* magazine—" The line clicked and went dead.

I realized I was staring at the phone like it had turned to shit in my hand. "She hung up," I said. But it was Felix St. John's number, no doubt about that.

I should have been thrilled that she'd located him, but my own frustration had mounted to the point where I had to get some satisfaction. I wondered if I should bring up the Newt thing all over again or just let it slide. She'd never admit to getting St. John's number from Newt, so what could I do? I asked for the number of her "National Society of Inventors."

"You still don't believe me?" She was beginning to lose her temper.

"Would you believe you if you were me?"

"Here. Call them." And she threw the pad at me.

"Good bluff. But I call." Which I did. And was embarrassed to find she was telling the truth. It *was* the National Society of Inventors and, though they had no other information about him, they did give me what they had as St. John's current address and phone number.

"I suppose you want to apologize now," she said, as if she would never accept it, even if I did.

"Not right now. But I'll take a rain check."

"Asshole," she said.

I looked at the clock on the kitchen wall. "It's four-thirty. Danno will be calling in half an hour."

"What are you going to do about it?" she challenged. "Tell him to screw off?"

"Nah, that's too easy. That's *your* style. I'm going to do something that will really fry him."

"What's that?"

"Get the fuck out of town."

Albie Marx, tough guy.

So here we are at the airport, waiting to board our flight to Philadelphia. Mariah's reading the excerpts from Ahmet Ludi's *A Heretic's Handbook* and I'm agonizing over the fact that we're running out of time.

Without any warning, an overwhelming sense of sadness abruptly sweeps over me. I can't say that any one thing is the trigger for it, but I'm suddenly covered in this shroud of despair. Everything going on in front of me is flooded with the stark spotlight of insignificance. The airport terminal becomes an anthill, crawling with two-legged creatures scurrying this way and that, doing their business, nibbling away at the seconds and minutes and hours of their lives.

The sad feeling invades my throat, my chest and my stomach and I feel the need to let go, to let it all go. I mutter to Mariah that I'll be right back and go into the men's room, into a stall and shut the door.

I'm just in time. The tears explode out of me, pulverizing the dam of denial, drowning all resistance. I put my elbows on my knees and hold my head in my hands and let it come, deep and wrenching, an avalanche of helplessness burying my phony bravado in quake after quake of heaving sobs.

CHAPTER 11

Lieutenant Joseph Danno enjoyed playing the part of the mystery man. No one he'd ever worked with knew any more about him at the end of a case than they did at the beginning. Since he had started out as an undercover narc, a cop on the streets alone, he'd never had to put up with a full-time partner and that suited him just fine. Danno wasn't a lover of humanity, and most cops were no better than criminals, except that they happened to work for a company whose business it was "to protect and serve."

He got a good laugh out of those Hollywood cop movies where they threw two completely unsuited people together who pissed and moaned about each other for an hour and a half before saving each other's lives. Every year they came out with a crop of those pictures and they were always the same. Did people really buy that? What bullshit. He wouldn't trust anyone he *knew* with his life, much less some trigger-happy glory hound. The difference between a real cop and a movie cop.

There was one person, though, who thought she had his number, and for the sake of serenity during the few hours he wasn't at work, he let her believe it. That was Patsy, his wife, an opinionated bigmouth and mother of his two teenage sons.

Eighteen years ago Danno had an experience with Patsy that he mistook for love. She was much younger, slimmer and quieter then. He was thirty years old, a loner, and his hair was falling out in great, horrifying clumps. He had never felt a great craving for female company, and the few sexual adventures he did have fell far short of what they were cracked up to be. So, the experience of not wanting to get rid of Patsy as soon as he got to know her made Danno think that he'd finally found love.

What he did find was someone to take care of his personal needs while he spent sixteen hours a day chasing criminals. And, as a byproduct of sharing the same bed, they produced a couple of boys, Sonny and Bruno, neither of whom he ever got to know or understand. One had a haircut where the sides of his head were as bald as his father's but the top stood as high as a birthday cake. The other wore an earring with a cross so heavy and large that a full-grown parrot could perch on it. Like 90 percent of their schoolmates, Bruno and Sonny couldn't tell you what continent they were on, the names of the last three presidents or add up the price of three ice cream cones without a calculator. They were beyond his comprehension and, more and more when he was home, he retreated into the comfortable sphere of his thoughts.

And his thoughts these days revolved around Albie Marx. Patsy called it "obsessing," and maybe he was, but Marx was worth it. In Danno's mind, it was Marx and his ilk who were responsible for Sonny's and Bruno's boldfaced rebelliousness. The hippies and yippies of Marx's glory years made rebellion and distortion so attractive and commonplace to the kids that it got to the point where parents nowadays thought it natural for their kids to go around with birthday cakes on their heads. We're not only talking hard-core inner city kids here—we're talking white kids, with their parents, at shopping malls, going around with birthday cakes on their heads. Society was totally out of hand and Danno had a responsibility to see that the perpetrators did not go unpunished. So when Patsy accused him of "obsessing" over Albie Marx, he took it as validation that he was doing his job.

Now he was sitting in his backyard, which his dog and the gophers had long ago destroyed, on a rusted metal chair, sipping a Bud and going over the case against Marx for the hundredth time.

(1) He has no alibi: Selby died at seven P.M. Marx reported the body at eight-thirty P.M. He claimed to be working at home from six P.M. until the time he left for Selby's but has no witness to corroborate.

(2) He has a motive: A lover's quarrel. Sally Keester will testify that Selby told her she and Marx had quarrelled and that Marx had attempted to smooth it over with physical affection but Selby had asked him to leave.

(3) He lied to the police: Marx claimed that Selby's front door was unlocked. Sally Keester will also testify that it was locked when she left at six P.M. This means that Marx concealed that he had access to the victim's home, which translates in court to a conscious awareness of guilt.

(4) Fingerprints: Marx's fingerprints were found all over Selby's house, even on her vibrator. (God knows what the two of them did with that piece of equipment.)

Everything was falling into place. Even though they still hadn't come up with the chloroform container or the fatal hypodermic syringe, Danno felt he was almost ready to take his case to the city attorney and ask for a charge of first degree murder.

The L.A. city attorney, Ira Franklin, was an ex–federal prosecutor who wouldn't bring charges unless he was convinced he could win. Not that he always won, but he insisted on going into each trial loving his chances. That made life miserable for seasoned cops like Joe Danno, who didn't need trials to know who was and who wasn't guilty.

The hair samples from Albie were to be his clincher. Upon examination, foreign hairs had been found on Linda Selby's clothing. Then, the coroner reported finding some small, partial stalks under her fingernails. The roots were distinct, round and fresh, indicating they had been pulled from the follicle, a probable sign of struggle.

Danno was wild with excitement. If he could match the hairs under her nails and those on her clothing to Albie Marx, his case would be tight enough to march into Franklin's office and demand an indictment. There were also some pubic hairs found in Selby's bed and, to further bolster his case, Danno wanted to match those up to Marx as well.

Then he made a bonehead play. He called Albie on the phone, gambling that the fool's self-destructive arrogance would lead him to volunteer his hair, in defiance of being the prime suspect in the case. The call was supposed to make Albie think that a refusal to cooperate would look like the act of a guilty man.

But the move backfired. Next thing he knew, he was fielding a call from Arthur Gruntman. Gruntman was a fat piece of shit but one of the most successful criminal lawyers in the business. He'd been getting people off on this or that technicality since Danno was out on the streets. And he always made it look easy, even in cases where the evidence was legitimate and clear as rainwater. Gruntman told Danno if he wanted Albie's hair, he'd have to charge him with murder.

Danno was suddenly stuck between a rock and a hard place. City attorney Franklin would put him through hell handing down a murder charge without the overwhelming weight of evidence on his side. The last thing Franklin wanted to do was tackle Gruntman and lose, particularly in a high profile case,

which Albie Marx's presence determined this to be. The press
would be all over this one, digging up the past, digging up
Janis Joplin, digging up Danno himself, and Franklin
wouldn't go out on a limb with a limp case. There was only
one thing to do and Danno did it as soon as he got off the
phone with Gruntman.

He called his strongest ally, the one person who wanted to
see Albie nailed as much as he did. From their talks and the
information he had given her, Danno knew she was convinced
of Albie's guilt, and she'd offered to do anything she could to
help. Danno didn't know and didn't want to know what in the
past had turned her so sharply against Albie. Maybe it was a
case of a woman scorned. Whatever the reason, Sally Keester
listened intently as Danno laid out the situation and told him
she'd call him back. A few hours later she did just that.

"Hi, it's Sally."

"Hello, Sally."

"Can you come by right away? I have what you need."

"What is that?"

"His hair."

She had gotten a fast-acting sedative from her brother, a
pharmacist, which, when mixed with alcohol, worked instantaneously. Albie took a nap and Sally took a snip. She let him
sleep off the mickey and then sent him packing.

Danno was no fool, he knew the Doctrine of the Fruit of the
Poisonous Tree—illegally seized evidence cannot be used in
court. But Sally would keep her mouth shut and the lab would
do him a favor and compare the hairs. If the comparison came
up positive, he'd have the confidence to demand that Franklin
get him an unrestricted search warrant. Then he'd have Albie by
the long hairs, the short hairs and every other kind of hair.

Poor Albie. A descendant of Samson should have had the
presence of mind to recognize a Delilah when he saw one. But
that's the way it goes. Some Jews never learn.

CHAPTER 12

Sally Keester sunk deeper into the steamy tub brimming with fragrant bath oils and luxuriated in the silky texture of the delicious warm water. She ran the tips of her fingers along the smooth, firm skin of her calves and thighs and renewed her promise to her body that she would never let it get old. As long as she could remember, she'd nutured and pampered this body, to the exclusion of things some people felt more important.

It was on the farm in Twin Falls, Idaho, that she first learned the awesome power of such an instrument. Anything on two legs and male would turn into a moose on the first day of fall from so much as a whiff of her sweet pubescence.

One football player drove his father's tractor into Snake River just because she asked him to. Another fool carved her name on his chest—she laughed when it came out backwards—he did it in a mirror. A forty-year-old farmer offered her father fifty-two heifers and a liter of prize-winning bull sperm for her hand in marriage. In Twin Falls, Idaho, no price was too steep for the privilege of popping the cherry of the fabulous Sally Keester.

But men and their antics held no interest for Sally. All she cared about was movies. Movies on the little black and white TV her mother smuggled into her room, movies at the Snake River Cinema every Friday evening at seven—before she could even read, she was collecting vintage fan magazines from the forties and fifties and, by the time she was seventeen, had so totally identified with another Idaho farm girl, Julia Jean Turner, that she left home and headed for Schwaab's in Hollywood, hoping to be discovered at the soda fountain, just like the famous director Mervyn LeRoy discovered Julia Jean. Then, she imagined, her Hollywood mogul would make her a star and change her name from plain old Sally to something more exotic, more romantic, like they changed Julia Jean Turner's to Lana.

Well, she made it to Hollywood. And *discovered* she was. At Schwaab's. At casting calls. At parties. At orgies. The sex didn't move her but it seemed like the only thing everyone who was anyone wanted to do. And they all wanted to do it with her.

Once, when she confided her dream to a well-known agent who had just devoured her ample behind like a bum at a banquet, he suggested changing her name from Sally to Lotta—then laughed himself into an emphysema attack while she laid there, mortified.

Men in the right positions had responded to her like the boys in Twin Falls, but as soon as the Hollywood boys got what they wanted they were suddenly so busy with their next film project, they couldn't find two minutes to return the calls of the fabulous Sally Keester.

Eventually she managed to meet one producer who, in exchange for her willingness to participate in some very bizarre sexual behavior, pulled a few strings and got her into the Extra's Union. From then on, she worked often enough as an extra to earn a decent living and still tell the people back home she was in the movies.

What hurt was the heartbreak of giving up her dreams. And who was to blame? The men who used women, abused them, made all those promises and never called back. And precisely because she hated them so, she devoted herself as never before to the attainment of physical perfection.

Freed from the panic of depending on their whims and largess for her next meal, she encouraged their attention and inwardly smirked at the lengths to which they would go for a touch, a caress or a peek at what lay under her titillating Lana Turner skirts and sweaters. She never gave in, she just watched them squirm. It was as easy and diverting as pulling the wings off flies.

Then she bought this house and met her new next-door neighbor, Linda Selby. Linda was into causes, like animal rights and the environment, which didn't really interest Sally. But, like Sally, she was a woman on her own, strong in her resolve and distrustful of the intentions of men. In that first year they got to know each other and became best of friends.

They were such opposite types, a big curvy blonde who loved soap operas and a dark, intense brunette who marched in protest rallies. As time wore on, and Sally became more enmeshed in Linda's life, she began to worry about Linda's safety at these protests and rallies, where the police were always angry and rougher with the demonstrators than they needed to be.

For her part, Linda loved Sally's concern, you might even say needed it. She even convinced Sally to march with her outside the UCLA animal experimentation labs. Sally went along to make Linda happy, but really to be her protector. None of the men who had ever been in Linda's love life had marched side by side with her in protest, and she was deeply moved by Sally's dedication. Their relationship grew and flourished and blossomed—they were beautiful twin petals in a perfect red rose.

Then tragedy struck. Linda met Harry Ballister at a political fund-raiser. He wasn't the handsomest or the sexiest man around but he had the gift of gab and his political status admittedly gave him a certain charisma. Linda was charmed by the snake. She bit into the apple and got hooked on the councilman. He slithered into her life and, just like that, Sally was history, her relationship with Linda wilted on the vine, leaving behind only thorns in Sally's heart.

Sally saw in Harry what Linda myopically missed. He was one of the pigs, the type of man Sally had learned to despise and distrust. She knew in her heart that he would inevitably hurt her dear friend but there wasn't a thing she could do about it, except wait with excruciating patience for the end to come. Finally, as she knew he would, Harry dumped Linda.

Sally was reborn. First she instilled in Linda a powerful guilt, built on the pain she had made Sally suffer and Sally's unheeded I-told-you-so's about Harry. Then, when she was sure Linda was good and hooked, she began reeling her in with her special brand of love and attention. Just when it seemed Linda was all hers once more . . .

The man syndrome struck again. Linda fell again, this time for Albie Marx, a drunk and a drug addict, an over-the-hill hippie who screwed anything that wasn't nailed down. It was a slap in the face to Sally that Linda would choose a gross womanizer over the selfless, revitalizing love that Sally so openly offered her.

Sally pressed Linda at every opportunity, every time Marx's Jaguar wasn't sitting there, leaking oil in Linda's driveway. They argued and fought and Sally recited chapter and verse of Marx's sordid past, the women, the drugs, the deadly affair with Janis Joplin. Finally, it all got too much and Linda blew up. She ordered Sally out of her house and told her she never wanted to speak to her again. Sally was humiliated. And incensed.

All that was academic now. Linda was dead. But that wasn't enough. Sally wanted more. Albie Marx wasn't a murderer but he still had to pay for his sins against women.

After he staggered out of her house, stoned out of his mind on her brother's sedative—she had a hard time trying not to laugh out loud—she made the call to Lieutenant Danno.

Now it was merely a matter of time before the chapter was closed on this painful but liberating phase of her life.

CHAPTER 13

Harry Ballister sat in his shrink's waiting room, absently thumbing through a copy of *People* magazine and wondering how much he could tell Dr. Patchman without feeling overexposed. He'd already filled the psychiatrist in on selected details of his Waste Disposal crisis, but should he go so far as to tell him the really intimate things, like yesterday's attempt to murder Albie Marx?

It wasn't the threat of legal prosecution that made Harry hesitate to divulge his heinous act. The confidentiality of the doctor-patient relationship was legally protected, like that of a lawyer-client or priest-parishioner. What it really boiled down to was, what would Dr. Patchman think of him if he knew he was a murderer? Would he be angry? Repulsed? Derisive? Unimpressed? Would he drop Harry as a client?

He needed Dr. Patchman more than ever now, more than he'd ever needed him before. The constant threat of being exposed as a crook, scorned by his peers, publicly censured—the fearful Sword of Damocles which hung mercilessly over his head had brought him to the brink of nervous collapse. His once superior mental faculties were in such a state of imminent breakdown, that the only person who could possibly keep the complex machinery running was Dr. Steven Patchman.

Harry had been depressed for nearly a week, but he knew he was starting to crack when he arrived at his office this morning and found Phyllis, his new secretary, ashen and sick to her stomach. Someone had broken into his office during the night and left a foul-smelling large manila envelope, which Phyllis had found sitting on her desk when she came in, addressed thusly: "To Councilman Harold Ballister. Important Overnight Delivery. Contents Fragile, Do Not Bend or Squeeze."

What she found in the envelope was an unbelieveably large, truly massive human turd, still soft and pliable though not, thank God, warm. By what hand this awesome specimen was delivered to Phyllis's desk was a mystery defying solution. The only clue was the enclosed note, which was typewritten and unsigned. It read:

"Dearest Harry, I have been an ardent admirer of yours for many years. I am a white male sculptor, very good looking, and in honor of your recent victory at the polls I have made this sculpture for you.

"I feel it's my best work as it came straight from the gut. It embodies your wonderful earthiness, your willingness and desire to push through from the dark into the light, your no-nonsense approach to life, your dignity, your principles, and your courage to be what you are. I just wanted to share it with you because you inspired me to make it. If we could have lunch sometime I would promise to work up another one, even bigger and better than this, depending on what we eat. Your Secret Admirer."

It was too sick for words.

Over the years, Harry had become such a prominent figure in Los Angeles, that his first reaction was the anonymous prankster could have been almost anybody. In politics you learn that people are scum and will do practically anything to air their opinions. Maybe it was just some disgruntled citizen expressing himself the only way he knew how. Or maybe it really was a sculptor with a misguided sense of aesthetics. He'd seen stranger things in his time. Didn't some artist shake Congress all up with a National Endowment for the Arts financed "sculpture" of Christ drowning in the artist's own piss in a mason jar? He wouldn't put anything past an artist.

Then it occurred to him. What if Albie Marx was behind it? What if Marx was trying to soften him up for the upcoming Waste Disposal scandal? Get him off balance, a few jabs, a few body blows, some shit in the mail, then—POW!—the knock-out punch. It could have been Marx. Maybe Marx figured out who it was in the Donald Duck mask, trying to crush him beneath a speeding automobile.

The Donald Duck mask! Oh, no! He ran to the kitchen and looked behind the refrigerator. Both masks were there where he hid them, undisturbed. He was safe. It wasn't Marx. Marx would have found the masks. Harry was relieved. For a moment. Then all of a sudden he was shaking with anxiety.

That was when he called Dr. Patchman for an emergency appointment. The doctor charged time and a half for unscheduled meetings but at this point, money was no object. Harry was fighting for his sanity.

Dr. Patchman opened the door to his office and a patient stepped out, dressed in a suit and tie and carrying a briefcase. A typical-looking businessman, you'd never have guessed he was in psychoanalysis. He shook Dr. Patchman's hand.

"Thank you, Steve, I'll see you on Tuesday."

"Yes, Tuesday," Dr. Patchman said, and the man walked through the waiting room and out the door.

Steve? That guy called Dr. Patchman "Steve," Harry thought feverishly. I've been a patient for five years and I still call him Dr. Patchman. How do I get a self-image like that?

"Come on in, Harry," Dr. Patchman said, standing at his door.

Harry got to his feet and self-consciously strode past the doctor into his office. Would he have the guts to call him Steve?

"So?" Dr. Patchman said, settling into his armchair. "It's been a rough day?"

"And it's only two o'clock," Harry said. "I can't take any more. I'm coming apart. I'm losing control."

"Perhaps you'd like to talk about it."

"I told you on the phone what happened this morning. What was left in my office last night." Patchman nodded.

"Well, right after I spoke to you I got a call from a friend of mine, well, an acquaintance. He's a TV producer, he has a weekly sit-com. We go out for dinner together every once in a while, we talk some business, exchange some phone numbers of ladies we know. He asked if I broke up with Lesley. I told him yes, a while ago, but I was thinking of getting back together with her. I asked him why he wanted to know. He tells me he saw her the other night at LeDome. She was sitting at the bar having a cozy drink with Albie Marx. Can you believe that? Lesley and *Albie Marx!* Together! They had to be planning something. I'm telling you, they're out to get me. They'll ruin me with those Waste Disposal papers. They'll bury me. For what? I got a stinking twenty grand. Twenty grand is nothing! I know council members who wouldn't take a call from Waste Disposal for less than thirty. So what did I do that was so wrong? But that's not the way Marx will make it look. No. He'll make this into the scandal of the century. Crooked councilman. Mafia connections. Toxic landfills. He'll make it sound horrifying. I'll get crucified. I'll have to resign from the City Council. Get lawyers. I'll be convicted in the press before the trial even happens. It will cost me a fortune in legal fees and the best I can hope for is probation. My career will be ruined. I'll probably be disbarred. What will I do? What am I suited for? I'm not going to be a bartender, I'll tell you that. Why is this Marx trying to ruin me anyway? What did I ever do to him? I didn't take Linda away from him, I fucked her long before she met him. Maybe I ruined her for him. We had pretty hot sex, you know. Maybe compared to me he was nothing in bed. Maybe he couldn't satisfy her. Is that my fault? Why take that out on me? Linda and I had chemistry. It's a fact of life. Don't go destroying someone's career because they're a better lover than you are. I don't know. I'm really depressed. I miss Lesley but she hates me. Dawn's so mad she'll probably file sexual harassment charges. And Albie Marx has information that could put me behind bars. What would you do? If your career was threatened? By someone who hated you? Someone who's known for going after public servants, politicians, whatever. And now I find out this man is secretly seeing the one woman I could ever love. What am I supposed to do? What would you do? If he was walking across the street in front of you, and you were in your car, half out of your mind with fear of losing your lover, your career, your identity—wouldn't you consider running him over? Don't tell me it wouldn't enter your mind. You wouldn't be normal if it didn't. I'm not saying you would do it but if you didn't think about it, there would be something wrong with you. Am I right? From a psychological viewpoint? You'd have anger, right? You'd want to express it. You'd jam your foot down on either the accelerator or the brake, depending on how repressed you are. I'm right, aren't I? After five years of treatment I know a little about psychology. So I tried to run him over. You can't say it wasn't rational. I did what a man has to do. Protect my territory. It's man's oldest instinct. Self-preservation. And wouldn't you know it? I missed. I was so blind with rage that I totally missed. So here I am.

I couldn't even run over the man who's trying to destroy me. And now this Lesley thing. I can't take it, Steve—"

"Excuse me?"

"I said, I can't take it, Steve."

"You've never called me Steve before. Why did you call me Steve?"

"The guy before me called you Steve. Is it okay?"

"Well, what does 'okay' really mean? I just find it interesting that you called me Steve."

"Can I tell you the rest of this?"

"I want to talk about this Steve thing. You must have changed the way you feel about me. I sense you feel closer to me. More at ease."

Harry tried to explain it was simply a matter of doing what the last guy did but Patchman insisted on spending the rest of the hour discussing their relationship, himself, and his feelings about being named Steve.

By the time Harry got back to his own office, he was soaked through and through with nervous flopsweat. Nothing had been accomplished except Patchman now insisted on being called Steve.

Phyllis the secretary had recovered enough from this morning's shit delivery to give Harry his only message. Chief of Police Herman Baddely had called. He thought Harry might be interested to know that the police were talking to Albie Marx about the Linda Selby case.

My God, Harry thought, will it ever stop? The cancer is growing. Marx might even tie him into Linda's murder. And he had been worried about graft and corruption. How about *murder?* How scary was being disbarred compared to a one-way ticket to death row? That settled it. Marx had to go and he had to go *now.*

CHAPTER 14

Walter Bates had the TV in his office tuned to C-Span, the live feed of the opening of the House and Senate debates over the Legalization of Drugs.

Congressman Tad Seriovitus, an intolerable bore from Rhode Island, was making his opening remarks.

"The Senate committee tells us the time is at hand to legalize drugs in this country. But do they tell us what drugs they would legalize? Prescription drugs? Recreational drugs? And if they're talking about *recreational* drugs, do they include those drugs which are known to cause brain damage, disability and violence?"

No you fool, Bates thought, why would we want to cause brain damage and violence? We want to make people happy. We want to insure a peaceful society, not encourage a more violent one. We want all Americans and, ultimately, the world, to experience a lasting euphoria, to eschew violence and rebellion and to march side by side in a worldwide society of consumers, dedicated to goodwill, free enterprise, and product identification for all.

Seriovitus pushed on. "And which companies will get the

contracts to make these drugs? The ones who spend the most money right here in this building! And that will buy profits that will forever define the term *obscene!*"

You moron! Profit is what the world is all about! Didn't the Communists learn that lesson, after it was too late? If they'd concentrated more on profit and less on ideology, they wouldn't have lost their half of the world. Don't people care about profits in Rhode Island? How did this fatuous Liberal ever get himself elected?

"I tell you, these new legal drug cartels, *legally* buying senators and congressmen with their new mega-profits, will be a greater threat to this country than the Colombian drug barons ever were!"

Incensed at the analogy of politicians to drug barons, Seriovitus was hooted and shouted down by Democrats and Republicans alike.

The hearings were turning into a circus, but that was to be expected. The bottom line was that J.T. had enough votes in his pocket to push the bill through. Bates therefore turned his attention to matters that needed it.

J.T. had given the green light and the Libertad "crisis" was off and running. The first report of hemispheric differences was manufactured out of an innocent reply by the government of Libertad to a State Department request demanding more land for the new American naval base planned for the island.

The Libertad government replied that no additional land would be ceded over without intensive internal debate. This was reported on American television, after a State Department briefing, to be a move by Japanese-led elements on the island to establish their own military base in the Caribbean.

Miffed and confused by the American tradition of disinformation, the Libertad government naively issued an official statement that they would stand up for their right to do whatever they wished with their own land.

That's when the American media's insatiable appetite for crisis, any crisis, paid off. The declaration by Libertad of its sovereign rights was played out on TV and in the press as a thinly disguised attempt by the "natives" to sell America's prospective naval base to the Japanese, who were currently in the midst of rebuilding their awesome military machine. That was a serious matter. Things would start popping now.

And Bates had his fingers on all the buttons. The U.S. 82nd Airborne was standing at ready-alert in Grenada, some three hundred miles from Libertad. He awaited only a call from J.T. to send them into action. A designated CIA assassin on special assignment with the 82nd was prepared to carry out the sanction of Ahmet Ludi.

And the reclusive Felix St. John was on twenty-four-hour call, ready to be shipped out to Libertad to begin setting up the Chemtech lab and refinery, the facility at which the strange scientist's personal creation, the soon-to-be-legal new wonderdrug called NICE, would be synthesized and processed.

That's when the real fun will start, Bates thought, when he and J.T. get to do the thing they do better than anyone else—create the Grand Illusion, the packaging and selling of NICE.

People won't buy NICE, they'll buy Happiness. Peace of mind. Idyllic images. Escape through refreshing sleep. And the Happiness they'll buy will in no way diminish their health and efficiency. All it will diminish is maladjustment and unruly ideas. Everyone will feel good. No one will complain. The blacks will love it—they'll take it like candy, leaving crack and heroin behind, wallowing contentedly in their filthy ghettos, never knowing or caring that nothing has changed.

And the homeless, that whining army of drunken bums—with NICE they'll think a cardboard box is as wonderful as

a six-bedroom home in Grosse Point. Everyone will feel good.
No one will complain.

And, as if the cake needed icing, those properties of NICE
which amplify bright, sparkling cheerfulness to the eye of the
beholder, which transform a simple Doublemint smile into a
blazing effulgence of pristine beauty, will make everyone, rich
and poor alike, ever more receptive to the onslaught of TV
commercials showing the people as they aspire to be, beautiful, happy and fragrant, with all of the comforts and luxuries
Americans rightly deserve, a triumph for Free Enterprise and
a billion more products for the Eternal Suckling. Overnight
Chemtech will become one of the world's giant companies.
And Walter Bates is in on the ground floor. He's got a piece
of the action, a sliver of unimaginable profits. This time he's
working for Number One.

Stop, Walter! No daydreaming!

Resolutely summoning back his composure from such in-
fantile flights of fancy, Walter looked again at the TV. Congressman Seriovitus was droning on.

"Since 'recreational' drugs are not used medicinally but to
help people escape from themselves, then how can we build
a better reality here on earth? By using drugs to soothe
people's conscience so that they do not have to face the
consequences of their greed, exploitation, ruthlessness and
indifference? I tell you, by legalizing drugs we will be legalizing indifference. Legalizing corruption. Legalizing and supporting a decadent and destructive life-style for all
Americans!"

A decadent and destructive life-style, Bates echoed silently.
The phrase made him think of Albie Marx. Bates had been so
busy with the hard details of the campaign that he'd let the
whole Marx thing slide. That's all he'd need, at this stage, to

have an Albie Marx come up from behind and bite him on the ass.

He decided to assign a tail to Marx and the girl. At this point he couldn't leave anything to chance. In the brief time he'd been in the covert business he'd learned one thing for absolute certain—you can never be *too* covert. He placed a call to his Los Angeles bureau and arranged for someone to be assigned the detail. J.T. would have called it a redundant use of man power. Bates still called it Covering Your Ass.

CHAPTER 15

I don't know how long I stayed in the airport men's room after having my big cry. I know that I felt a lot lighter. I had released a lot more than tears. It was like there had been some kind of knot in my chest, an actual physical knot, caused by the constant constriction of muscles around my heart.

I remember all the times as a child, when my father humiliated me by shouting at me or spanking me in front of my mother, when I screamed voicelessly, in my heart, "I hate you, I hate you, I hope you die!"

And the times when my mother chose him and his bewildering masculinity over me and my constant neediness, and I pleaded silently in my very core, "Don't leave me, please, don't leave me!" All that expression, all that emotion—it never got past my chest.

Can you imagine the effort it took to hold all that in? And the physical damage that was wreaked on the parts of my body that shouldered the heaviest portion of the load? Years and years of shutting down, constricting, tying the feelings up in a knot so they couldn't run wild.

Growing older didn't change things. By adulthood constricting was second nature, it took less effort but caused the same damage. On those rare wonderful occasions when I cried in a movie I thought I was having a major emotional experience. But it was a speck, a tiny crystal on the tip of the psychic iceberg which was growing larger and colder and more impenetrable under the surface.

When Janis died I plummeted into a sea of anguish. Yes, I *cried*, but we all cried, we cried together because it was more than the death of one special person, it was the beginning of the end of a brief period of spiritual freedom and conscious awareness the intensity of which mankind had never known.

"And I dreamed I saw the bombers riding shotgun in the sky, Turning into butterflies above our nation."

I cried for Janis and I cried for Albie and I cried for the creeping despair that heralded the utter rejection of Aquarian ideals in the seventies and the total moral, ethical and scientific corruption of the eighties.

"We are stardust, We are golden, And we've got to get ourselves back to the garden."

Joni Mitchell wrote it and we all sang it. But what happened? Twenty-plus years later we stand amidst the debris of thoughtless, irreversible damage to our planet, rampant greed, inflation and depression, consumerism at any cost and horrifying, insidious new forms of mind control.

My heart has cried over these horrors, but crying for the losses of humanity doesn't have the charge of crying over the loss of deep, personal love. The love of a mother. Of a father. Or a lover.

We're sitting in row 34 of the American Airlines 747 jumbo jet winging us to Philadelphia International Airport. The plane was two hours late taking off. We were told by one of the flight attendants that with the exponentially burgeoning

air traffic, a mere two-hour delay is as close to schedule as
flights leaving Los Angeles have a right to expect. She also lets
on that most of today's air traffic controllers have no more
than a high school education and are not required or able to
read anything more complex than a sixth grade reader for
their exam. Makes you feel comfortable circling Kennedy,
right?

I don't like flying. The thought of entrusting my life to
some martini-drinking pilot, some Corvette-cowboy NASA
reject from Newport Beach, does not fill me with unbounded
confidence. My defense is to get sloshed the minute I step on
the plane and stay that way the whole trip. That's why I fly
American. They carry those magical little bottles of Cuervo
Gold. And I've had about three of those babies by the time we
reach cruising altitude. I'm in the window seat, Mariah's in the
middle and next to her, on the aisle, is an athletic-looking guy,
about thirty-five, in a well-tailored suit. His name is Tom Rush
and he's a salesman for a high-priced line of women's sports-
wear. I know that because he gave me his card and invited
Mariah to his showroom in downtown Manhattan. He tried
to chat her up but when she ignored him he went back to his
Sports Illustrated. I'm sitting quietly and staring out the window when she turns to me and asks, "What happened to you
in the terminal? You came out of the men's room looking like
you swallowed a ghost."

"More like I threw one up."

"Were you sick?"

"The truth? I've been holding a lot in. A lot of feelings.
About myself. About Linda. About you. I took an emotional
dump."

"It must have felt good." I shrug. "You never talk about my
mother, Albie. Did she mean anything to you? Ever?"

I peer out the window again at the breathtaking clarity of
the sky and the thick, heavy cloud cover that stretches forever

below us. The dark world under those clouds has only the memory of these beautiful, clear skies. But that memory gives them the knowledge that sooner or later it will be sunny again. A kind of scientific description of hope.

"There's always sunshine up here," I remark. "There's always perspective. I didn't have much perspective when I was with your mother."

"What didn't you see?"

"I didn't have the balance she did. I didn't see both sides of the clouds. I saw the gloom of living on earth at a time like this. The gloom of being Albie Marx, Herald of the New Apocalypse. Linda saw the darkness like I did, but she knew the sunlight was there too. A woman needs sunlight."

"And a man doesn't?"

"A man's raised to think all he needs is strength, ambition and ruthlessness. A man who doesn't have the so-called 'killer instinct' may as well not get out of bed in the morning. The 'good' parents, the ones who want their sons to survive and prosper, teach them the killer instinct—win at all costs. Only problem is, when you know what the killer instinct is, and the damage it can do, you're always afraid someone will use it on you."

"Even a woman?"

I look at her with an ironic smile. "No. A woman would never use, manipulate or deceive a man. I know *you* wouldn't, right?"

She ignores the thrust. "So you were afraid my mother would hurt you if you were sunny and open with her?"

"It wasn't a *conscious* fear," I answer.

"Oh, I see. If it's not *conscious* you can blame it on society and your parents."

Good point. "I never thought of it that way."

"Well, think of it this way—if you don't take responsibility for the way you feel and the way you act, whether it's conscious, subconscious or unconscious, you're never going to think enough of yourself to get out from under those clouds."

"You're a regular fountain of wisdom."

"I'm young but I'm learning," she says without sounding defensive. "Here. Read this." She hands me a page from *A Heretic's Handbook.* Ahmet Ludi invites us to sing along to a Reggae beat:

> Don't believe in ma-ma
> Don't believe in pa-pa
> Don't believe in po-lice
> Don't believe in coun-tries
> Don't believe in Je-sus
> Don't believe in El-vis
> Don't believe in T-Vs
> Don't believe in theo-ries
> My Heart
> I'm believin' in *my* Heart
> Only my Heart
> Tells me who I should be.

"He sees very clearly," she says. "Right to the heart of things."

"Not exactly the sentiments by which an orderly society is run."

"But hardly enough reason to kill him," she says, betraying surprising anger.

"I agree. I mean, I can see where he'd be persona non grata with the establishment heavies, but is this little book really dangerous enough to warrant assassination?"

"That's what we have to find out," she answers, with fierce determination.

"You're starting to sound like a journalist."

"Why not? We're onto a major story, aren't we?"

You know what? She's right. And so was Shrike, I now realize, when he delivered his "Killing of an Activist" spiel at The Rock the other night. Some very powerful people are invested in this scheme. If it all came out and could be proved, it could irreparably damage Cale's administration. Yes, this could easily be the story of the year. Year? Fuck—the decade. Hey—maybe I'm sitting on a Pulitzer Prize.

"What are you thinking?" she asks.

"I'm trying to make four ones equal four. What do Harry Ballister, Ahmet Ludi, Felix St. John and John Thomas have in common?"

"NICE," she answers. "And Albie Marx."

"Albie Marx . . ." I repeat, deflatedly remembering my pathetic reality and feeling like a fool for fantasizing about a Pulitzer Prize. "I remember him. Wasn't he the guy who cried all the way to the gas chamber?"

"That was another Albie Marx. The one *I* know saved millions of people from mind control drugs and rode off into the sunset with his adoring princess."

"That's the story I'd like to hear," I say gratefully, leaning my seat back and fluffing my pillow for a much-needed nap. "Tell me that story."

It's snowing in Philadelphia and we circle the airport until the plane is nearly out of fuel and the galley is totally out of tequila. You're going to have to pour me off this flight, I tell the stewardess, who comes from South Carolina and lives in Brooklyn. I give her my number in case her next L.A. over-night gets too tame for her fiery Southern spirit. She thinks I'm cute. I think I'm a corny old drunk. She promises to call. I hope she doesn't.

I wedge myself into the head to unleash my swollen blad-der. As I'm watching the alcohol flow out of me I suddenly ask myself, *why* am I doing this? Why do I continue to anesthetize my feelings with tequila when what I really want is to feel them? Why, when I have been given an incredible opportunity to fall in love and write the most important story of my life, am I acting like the same old self-destructive Albie Marx? Isn't it time to grow up?

It's not only snowing in Philly, it's four A.M. and a bitter 13 degrees. I've lived in California so long I almost forgot why I moved there. Now I remember. Good thing Mariah checked the weather and we stopped at an Army surplus store on the way to the airport. We'd be dealing with frostbite without our heavy green air force parkas, thermal long underwear and snow boots.

We head straight from the terminal to Budget Rent A Car where my last valid credit card gets us a filthy new Ford. It also comes back to me that there's no such thing as a clean car in this part of the country.

Luckily, Gruntman has given me his home number, so before we take off I put in a call. It must be one in the morning in L.A. but you couldn't tell by the way he sounds.

"Albie." The voice again, deep, immediate and reassuring.

"I'm freezing my balls off in Philadelphia, Arthur. Any developments?"

"I talked with my friend in the D.A.'s office. Danno's going to court for a warrant to search your property."

"I hope he cleans up afterwards."

"He also wants to take a direct hair sample. That's more complex. He'll have to go to the grand jury for a subpoena."

"Translate."

"The information on which the subpoena is based has to be such that would lead a reasonable person to determine that things that could lead to an indictment are probably to be found in the place designated to be searched. In this case, your head."

"And other sundry parts," I add ruefully. "Can he find a 'reasonable person'? I can't."

"They're around."

"Right. Anything else? Anything on Ballister?"

"His name hasn't been brought into the case, not that my source knows of. He's also a good personal friend of Chief Baddely's so we're going to need more than your suspicions in order to get someone in the department to go out on a limb. The way things are now, it would look like a desperate attempt on our part to deflect the investigation. Sorry, Albie."

"So what do we do?"

"Nothing, till we hear from Danno. Just keep calling in."

"Do you mind if I call collect?"

"Don't worry. We'll put it all on the bill."

Big spender. Why is it the biggest penny-pinchers of all are the ones who have more than they'll ever need? Billionaires who leave 5 percent tips. Moguls who stiff parking attendants. Wealthy comedians who take money for telethons. Beautiful people doing beautiful things.

The street map we get from Budget shows that St. John's address falls into an area of North Philadelphia called Germantown. Apparently, this is the earliest residential section of the city, settled by the Germans a hundred years before the Revolution.

It's been several decades since I've been in a snowstorm, much less driven a car in one. Navigating the barren, snow-covered parkway into Philly, its lane dividers and boundaries obliterated by the driving snow, I feel like I'm doing the Nome-to-Anchorage Dogsled Run, except the dogs know where they're going. I can't see a damn thing, so I white-knuckle the wheel, lean my face to the windshield and baby the gas pedal.

Mariah, in a misguided attempt to keep us alert, tunes the radio to a rap music station which sets my teeth on edge. How can she listen to that? I mean, I can appreciate the raw expressiveness of the form, but the music is like a vise on my head. I wouldn't ask her to turn it off though, because I remember the way my parents tried to stop me from listening to rock and roll and I would endure anything, even a rap migraine, rather than be like my parents.

We cross over the gray Schuylkill River, which looks like it could ice over any moment, and head into downtown Philly, where steam pours out of manholes and predawn snow-clearing crews struggle doggedly against the mounting drifts.

How do people live like this? I can put down Los Angeles as long as you can listen, but if this is the alternative—give me the mindless California smog-shine anytime. When the Apocalypse hits I'd much rather watch it from Zuma Beach. Or maybe Point Dume. For a wordsmith, that might be more appropriate.

Mariah suggests we look for a place to stop and get some rest. It's way too early to barge in on St. John and we're both getting ragged and bleary.

I find a Holiday Inn just outside of the town center and we clump into the lobby with our snow gear and overnight bags. Finances dictate that we take one room but I gallantly give Mariah the option of having a room of her own. To my surprise and well-concealed excitement, she declines.

The view from our room of the old city, America's first capital, cradle of the Revolution, birthplace of the Declaration of Independence and the Constitution of the United States, is awe inspiring.

Maybe because the snow has painted everything white and new, the way it looked almost three hundred years ago, maybe because I'm so tired and my feelings so raw, the magnificence of man, his hopes, aspirations and determination, comes upon me in such an overwhelming rush, that I feel a profound sense of dignity to be descended from the men and women whose

God-inspired vision created an Ideal that, butchered as it has been by the Gremlins of Greed and Apostates of Power, still stands, in its purest state, as civilized man's highest philosophical achievement.

Mariah is standing by my side at the window.

"Beautiful, isn't it?" she says quietly, her deep brown eyes letting go their hard edge of defiance.

"Beautiful," I agree, feeling the warm electricity of her closeness.

This must be the spot where I take her in my arms and kiss her. Every nerve in my body tells me so. But how do I do it? Will she stand for such impudence? I've never been this unsure of myself with a woman. Is it because she's the daughter of someone with whom I had a deep and intimate relationship? Is there something perverse in loving the mother *and* the daughter? No, I don't think so. I'd be nuts about Mariah no matter who her mother happened to be.

Is it because she's so young and confident? Is my age making me self-conscious? Will she push me away and make me feel humiliated? You'd think at my age, with all the dues I've paid, I wouldn't feel like a goddamn teenager anymore. Although, there is a kind of perverse pleasure in it. The realization that innocence is never completely lost.

"Albie . . . ?"

"What?"

"Why are you looking at me like that?"

What is she, the Virgin Queen? Doesn't she know what's going on here? "Like what, Mariah?"

"Like you can't decide whether to shit or get off the pot."

"That's charming, Mariah. You really have a romantic touch."

"You think so?" she says, and before I know it she's up against me and her arms are around me and her lips are moving toward me and I'm seeing it all in slow motion, the way you see someone get shot in the movies sometimes, only this is no killing and our lips are pressing together, our tongues searching each other out and I'm feeling like we've lifted off the floor and are circling around the room, our bodies and lips and spirits entwined. God, You sadistic joker, don't You dare put a stop to this or You and I are gonna really have it out, once and for all.

But God always has the last laugh. He doesn't stop the kissing, which goes on for a while, along with sighing and moaning and expressions of every possible feeling short of actual love for each other. But He does decree, through the mouth of this full-blossomed creation of His, that we retire to separate beds so we don't fall into the trap of "moving things along too fast."

I can remember when "moving things along too fast" meant screwing some girl in the men's room whom you met fifteen minutes ago at the bar. I used to think of those as the "good old days" but I'm not so sure about that now. If they really were so good, why did they bring me to heroin and the brink of death? If screwing every woman I met and taking every chemical I could find was such a treat, how come I'm not still at it? Because my body can't take it anymore? Because my soul's had its fill? Or is it both?

We wake around eleven, get some coffee and eggs in the Breakfast Shoppe, as they call it, and have the bellman call for our car.

It's stopped snowing and the clouds have fled, giving us an icy, crystal clear day to work with. The parking attendant gives us directions to Germantown Avenue, his vaporized breath flying off into the unseen world of molecules and atoms.

Some cities really have it together. The streets, which were buried under snow just six hours ago, have been plowed and salted and made passable once more. I guess after battling the elements year in and year out for three hundred years, these people have finally gotten it down to a science.

We find Maple Street off Germantown Avenue, two blocks away from the house where George Washington spent summers during his presidency. I wonder if George Washington ever felt compelled to declare, "I am not a crook!"

Felix's house is an old one, large, well maintained, in the Federalist style, with picket fence and a neat garden, now obscured by the snow. Some energetic person has already shoveled a path from the front door to the sidewalk. I park down the block and across the street from the house.

"Looks like Felix is mainline Philadelphia," Mariah remarks.

"What I'd like to know," I muse, "is who's the Fräulein with the thick knockwurst accent? She wasn't very congenial on the phone yesterday. When I told her I was a reporter."

"Probably his wife," she answers. "Who else would exercise that much control over who someone speaks to?"

"Then we need a plan to get by her. Maybe we should say we're from the National Security Board."

"You think someone would believe *I'm* from the National Security Board?" she asks incredulously.

She's right, as usual. She looks like a rock and roll singer or a high-class hooker or a Gianni Versace model. She does not look like a government agent. Although I wonder if her Uncle Newt is trying to make her into one. What a waste of a fine piece of ass. Stop it, Albie.

She says, "I think you tell her you're with the *Los Angeles Times.* Saying you're from *Up Yours* magazine isn't going to soften someone like that up."

"You're right. Maybe I'll say I'm from *Der Spiegel.*"

"Do you speak German?"

"I can speak English with a German accent. I'm their American correspondent. *Ve haff come to talk mit Herr Felix, Fräulein.* How's that?"

She doesn't bother to grace my feeble humor with a reply. Instead, her eyes focus on Felix's house. "Look, Albie."

I turn to see the front door open and a large, thick woman of perhaps sixty, sixty-five appears, all bundled up for a walk in the cold. On leashes at her feet are two cowering dachshunds, flinching back against the freezing air, despite the brown woolen sweaters that cover their fat little bodies.

Coaxing and tugging on their leashes, she gets them out of the house, then closes and locks the door behind her. She takes a deep breath, turns up the collar of her gray military greatcoat and straightens her shoulders, as if preparing for a forced march. Pulling her reluctant troops behind her, she heads down the block with short, powerful steps. Trailing behind the three is their freezing breath and their prints in the snow. We wait for them to round the corner.

"Looks like our shot," I say, and force myself out of the warm, cozy car.

Mariah walks beside me as I approach the house. Clomping through the snow, we move around the sides and the back, peering in through the windows and curtains, trying to see anything that speaks of Felix. We don't have any luck but the lights on the second floor tell us that someone must be up there.

I take out the plastic skeleton card I got from Shrike and slide it between the back door lock and the doorjamb. Luckily, the Prussian didn't set the bolt and the door opens squeakily. In a flash we're inside, closing the door behind us.

There's a back stairway from the kitchen that goes up to the second floor. We quietly make our way up the stairs and emerge at the end of a corridor lined with a series of closed doors. Silently moving from one to the next, listening for movement inside and then moving on, we finally come to one that is open.

It appears to be a kid's bedroom, full of toys and games and all kinds of gadgets and knickknacks. It's a big room, and as we get a better look inside, we see, sitting on the floor, wearing a bathrobe and pajamas and smoking a cigar, an unshaven, rumple-haired man of some sixty years. Like a six-year-old child, he's engrossed in his play. And what he's playing with is a fantastic collection of toy Revolutionary armies, with Redcoats and Colonialists and cannons and horses and everything else that was part of that war, down to the walking wounded, little boy drummers and some mangy dogs.

He's apparently marshalling the rag-tag Americans, behind George Washington on a great white horse, for what looks like a four-pronged assault on a numerically superior British force. Sensing our presence he looks up, gives us the once-over, then, without a word, goes back to his war. Unless I've gone color blind, one of his eyes is blue and the other is green. I look at Mariah. She's as baffled as I am. I clear my throat. He looks up again. I was right—one blue, one green.

"Excuse me. Are you Felix St. John?"

"I'm not Hopalong Cassidy," he answers in a gravelly voice, blowing a cloud of cigar smoke our way. This is a man I could learn to love.

"My name is Albie Marx—"

"That is *your* problem, sir," he snaps. "Good-bye and have a nice day—or whatever the current homily is." And he's back to his toys.

"That's some set of soldiers," I declare lamely, attempting again to engage his attention.

"How the dickens did you get in here?" he barks irritably.

"The door was open. We knocked but nobody answered."

"Where's Irmgard? Where are the boys?"

"The boys?" I ask, glancing at Mariah, alert for security guards we may have missed.

"Herman and Heinrich. The shitters and barkers."

He must mean the dogs. Unless some of the government boys have been acting up. "If we could just have a few minutes of your time—"

"What are you selling?" he grumbles impatiently.

"What are you in the market for?" I reply, changing speeds in an effort to lure him into conversation.

"*Privacy,*" he growls. "The door's where you found it." Assuming the finality of his words will finally vanquish us, he returns his considerable attention to the retreating Redcoats.

"Mr. St. John," I persist, "we've come a long way and we need to talk to you." He looks up again, his brow knit in annoyance. "We're here about NICE."

His eyebrows raise involuntarily. We now have his attention. "Irmgard is the Minister of Information in this principality, sir. If that's what you seek, petition her."

"I write for a national magazine," I press. "We've come into possession of classified material concerning the National Security Board and the 'NICE Campaign'—we know that you have personal knowledge of these secret plans. If privacy is your concern, I promise not to use your name."

Reluctantly deigning to reason with me, he explains, "You've come to the wrong person, my boy. I'm merely an infinitesimal cog in the promethean wheel of bureaucracy. I can do *nothing.* If it's NICE you require, you'll simply have to wait till it's legal."

Aha! NICE *is* a drug! I was right! They're going to legalize it and give it to everyone! God knows what it does—probably turns you into a grinning clod. Actually, given my present state, a grinning clod would be an upgrade.

"Does the name Harry Ballister mean anything to you?" I ask, taking a wild shot.

"The name *J. Edgar Hoover* means nothing to me," he replies pugnaciously. "Don't judge by my frame of reference."

But I have to try again. If St. John can connect Harry to NICE and the NSB, it will be the missing link that provides me with indisputable motivation for Harry to get rid of Linda—a terrified conspirator resorting to murder in order to save himself and the President from public exposure.

"Please," I plead relentlessly. "Think for one moment. What do you know about Harry Ballister?"

Grabbing clumps of his hair tightly with both hands, he closes his eyes and intones, "I am merely an infinitesimal cog . . ."

". . . in the promethian wheel of bureaucracy—I know." I must press on. "Do you know the name Ahmet Ludi?"

His answer is apparently to decide that I do not exist. He turns his motley gaze on Mariah, who's been standing quietly apart from the proceeding. Thankfully, she appears to be just what the doctor ordered—for the first time his face softens. A tiny twinkle sneaks into his eye—the blue one.

"And what do *you* do?" he asks velvetly, smoothing back his disheveled hair.

"I'm a student," she replies, the soul of youthful insouciance.

"That's a coincidence," he purrs intimately. "So am I." And the way he ogles her makes it plain that he wouldn't mind studying *her* for a while.

"What's that game you're playing?" she asks, beckoning to the toy soldiers.

"This? A local battle. Took place right across the street from here, about two hundred twenty-five years ago."

Inspired now, he sets the stage for her and moves the soldiers as he explains. "Washington conceives a daring plan.

With Generals Stephen, Wayne and Sullivan, he'll converge by four roads on Germantown at dawn, drive the British army back on the Schuylkill River and force its surrender.

"The morning comes. It's cold. It's misty. It's foggy. Washington surprises the British. He has them on the run. Now the fog closes in. So thick you can barely see your nose.

"General Stephen's brigade, on the left wing here, comes up behind General Wayne's brigade. Can't see in the fog. Thinks they're the British and commences to fire. Wayne's men fall back against General Sullivan's brigade, coming up on the flank.

"Wayne's men think Sullivan's men are the British, and fire on them. Sullivan's men fire back on Wayne's men. The Americans are slaughtering each other while Howe's Redcoats sneak out of the trap. A deadly comedy of errors.

"Now Cornwallis, alerted by the sounds of the battle, brings in two British brigades to join Howe. The Americans, thinking they're surrounded, panic and flee, running over each other in the fog.

"The British kill and take prisoner any Colonialists who haven't been killed by their own men.

"If not for the fog and the panic of his men, Washington would have carried the day and the war could have ended right here in Germantown."

He picks up the little George Washington figure on his heroic white horse and looks at it dreamily. "It was a daring plan—but often the fate of a man who dares is decided by forces greater than those he reckoned with."

In a wondering voice, a voice filled with the potential for anything in this universe being possible, he muses to the toy replica of Washington, "If you had known how to disperse the fog that morning you'd have saved a thousand lives . . . if the war had ended right there, you'd have saved twenty thousand lives . . ." Then he turns his gaze inward and questions his own muse. ". . . If the molecules of hydrogen in fog could be split off from the oxygen by some chain reaction initiated by introducing one new atom into the compound . . ."

He seems to have gone off into another world. I nudge Mariah to bring him back.

"Is this part of your work?" she asks.

He looks up at her, jerked by the mindstraps from the world of conjuring. The two different eyes make him look like he's everywhere at once.

"Are these part of your work?" she repeats. "These soldiers."

"I don't work," he declares. "Never have. It's play I'm interested in."

"Can we play with some NICE then?" she asks sweetly. I half expect her to flutter her eyelids.

He tries to reassert a stern look, but her charm's hit him right in his Achilles' heel. "What would you like to play?" he murmurs, mischievously twirling his cigar with his fingers. I think she's getting his number, whatever number that is.

"My friend Albie here—"

"The man on a mission," he mumbles with a desultory glance in my direction.

"He'd really like to try some NICE. And see—you know—what it's like." She looks at him beseechingly, and actually does flap her eyelids.

I look at her like she's out of her head.

Felix, catching my expression of consternation, is perversely amused. He actually smiles at me—patronizingly. Somehow Mariah has brought out the imp in him, which apparently doesn't lie very deep beneath the surface.

No longer the infinitesimal cog, he bends his cigar-chewing face next to mine and asks harshly, "You want some NICE, Albie? What's the matter? Life got you down? The pace too fast? Pressure too much? Can't catch up with your bills? Can't hold on to your girlfriend? Want to stop everything and just feel good for a while? Want to feel good all the time? Want to have a really NICE day?"

I'm sure I've taken drugs that make NICE look like St. Joseph's aspirin—and I'm the last one to turn down a new high—I just resent being offered as a guinea pig without being consulted. But she does have the horny old goat where we want him, I'll say that for her. I guess it's now or never. Before Eva Braun gets back with the weenie twins.

"What is it like?" I ask. "Is it a hypnotic?"

Puffing away at the cigar, Felix brushes the ashes off his pajamas and reties his bathrobe. "Come down to the lab," he orders, and takes Mariah's hand. She throws me a look of triumph as he leads her off.

I follow them along the corridor, then down the stairs to the kitchen, through a door and down another stairway into the basement, which has been converted to a slick high-tech laboratory.

Just as I get to the bottom of the stairs, we hear a distant door close heavily and then eight little feet scamper and scurry across the length of the house.

"Irmgard and the boys," Felix warns, then adds naughtily, "She'd love this."

"Is Irmgard your wife?" Mariah asks.

Felix coughs and spits up some cigar bits. "My wife? No, Irmgard is my cousin from Germany. She takes care of my life and my business and the house . . . so I can have time for important things—like you."

Then, tightening his grip on her hand, he leads us to a counter that holds a white mini-refrigeration unit. Opening the door, he extracts a small vial.

"For this precious elixir we must thank the tropical plant, *Salvia divanorum*." He beams at the vial like a proud new father, his bushy gray eyebrows alighting joyfully over his sparkling blue/green eyes. For some reason I think of the oxymoronic term, benevolent dictator. What we have here is a benevolent mad scientist.

The vial contains a clear liquid sitting on top of a fine, thin, red sediment. He sets the vial into the grip of an appliance that, when he switches it on, shakes it with super-human force and speed. When he removes the vial, the red is gone and the liquid is still clear.

"That's NICE?" I ask dumbly.

"Still in the liquid stage," he says. "I could give you a pill but this is pure."

We can hear Irmgard overhead in the kitchen. She starts up the back stairway to the bedrooms. Felix is looking through some equipment on the counter and Mariah whispers to me, "Better take it before she breaks up the party."

He finds what he's looking for, a tiny glass device that captures liquid in the smallest measurable amounts.

"Let's see that tongue," he says to me.

I stick out my tongue and he touches it with the little glass rod. "That's it," he proclaims. "You've been NICEd."

"How long before I feel it?"

"In this form, a minute or two. In pill form, fifteen minutes."

I turn my attention inward, in order to make note of each physical change that takes place. I have no idea what to expect, but I soon find out that with NICE, unlike any other drug I've ever taken, it's what you *don't* feel that matters. It has absolutely no physical effect whatsoever.

"Feel anything yet?" Mariah asks expectantly.

"I don't feel a thing," I answer. "Not physically."

"In the size dose I prepare, it doesn't affect the body," Felix explains. "It works specifically on the neuro-transmitter receptor sites in the brain. It affects only your thoughts and emotions."

"How do you feel?" Mariah asks.

"Fine. Good. I feel good."

An intercom on Felix's counter buzzes. Felix switches the toggle and answers, "Good morning."

He is greeted with the hard Teutonic timbre of Irmgard's voice. "Felix. You are down there?"

"Just puttering."

"I have the morning newspaper. The island will fall soon. You are ready to go?"

"Aye, aye," he answers and flicks closed the talk toggle.

"Did you hear that, Albie?" Mariah asks, trying to mask her alarm.

"Yes," I answer. What is she alarmed about? Why would she get alarmed about *anything?* I'm not alarmed. Life is too short for alarm. Not that I've forgotten about Danno and Linda's murder—but why should I let it all get to me? Danno's a decent guy, he's just doing his job. And the murder? Well, that happens every day, it's a fact of life, like death. People get killed. Linda's number came up and she went bye-bye. Why make myself miserable over it?

And come to think of it, life is too short to be unhappy. When I think of all the hours I spent worrying about the rain forests. It's crazy. There's nothing I can do about the rain forests. Besides, why should anything be done? So they pull down the trees and they put up cattle ranches. Ranches are pretty and cows are nice. What's wrong with that? Without those ranches there'd be no McDonald's.

I know my problem. I'm in the wrong business. How can I be in the protest business and be happy? Protest is synonymous with discontent. Why be discontented? There's so much to be happy for. So we have pollution, deception, corruption, deforestation . . . why go on and on about it? We also have sex, beautiful cars, houses and apartments in giant complexes so we never have to be alone, magnificent shopping malls where we can buy anything from a brisket of beef to taps for our shoes, leaders who dedicate their lives to preserving our freedom and purchasing power, we have zoos and families and movies and ice cream . . . Why was I such a crab?

"Albie, did you hear what Felix just said?"

"No, I'm sorry. What did you say, Felix?"

"There's enough *Salvia divanorum* in one beautiful field to supply the world with NICE for the next thousand years. A single leaf yields nearly a million doses of the size I gave you."

"That's wonderful," I say.

"It must be incredibly addictive," she asserts.

"If you call happiness an addiction," he replies.

"Are you getting happy?" she says to me.

"Well, I'm not *ecstatic*. But I feel good. I feel like I'd like to feel like this a lot more often."

"Would it bother you if Danno showed up and took you away in handcuffs?"

"Would it *bother* me? If I *let* life bother me, it would bother me. But why let life bother me? It's better than death, isn't it?"

"Would death bother you?" Felix asks, grinning.

"It's part of life," I tell him.

"What about *my* death?" Mariah asks. She's putting something on the line here and I don't want to disappoint her. On the other hand, maybe she can learn something.

"If you died I would feel good because I would know you wouldn't want me to feel bad."

"What if I wanted you to feel bad?"

"If it would make you feel good for me to feel bad, it would make you feel better for me to feel good."

Mariah looks at Felix. He chomps down and puffs away proudly on what now is a stub of his original cigar. "How long will this last?" she asks. "This happiness jag."

"Oh, about three hours."

"Then?"

"He'll be his old miserable self again."

God, that's a horrific thought. I'll be miserable again? I'd better get some of this NICE to take with me.

Suddenly the door at the top of the stairs opens and Irmgard's lovely fat ankles appear on the landing. "Felix. Is time for your breakfast."

"Are you two hungry?" he asks Mariah and me.

"Who you are talking to?" Irmgard calls. She sounds kind of gruff. Probably still shaking off the cold.

"Some friends of mine. Come say hello."

Here she comes, clumping down the stairs in her cute black matron shoes. Seeing Mariah and me she stops and twists up her face. I guess she's wondering if she has enough food for the four of us.

"This is Mariah," Felix tells her, taking Mariah's hand. "And this is Albie. Albie's a magazine writer."

Irmgard looks very cross. I glance around the room to see what it is that's got her miffed.

"Felix, you have not told these people anything?" If I didn't know better I'd say she was furious.

"We're just playing with NICE," he tells her. "Look at Albie. Five minutes ago he was a tortured soul."

"I feel great now, though," I say. "It's nice to meet you, Irmgard." I'll bet she's a pretty decent person under all that bluster.

"I must make a call," she says, turning abruptly and heading up the stairs.

"We'd better get out of here, Albie," Mariah says.

"Don't leave," Felix grumbles. "I have other things we can play with." He grinds his cigar underfoot and puts his lips to her ear. "You have to try my electrical anesthetic dental chair."

"That sounds like fun," I enthuse.

"Not you," he says. "Mariah."

"I'd love to, Felix, I really would love to get into your chair, but," and she looks at her watch, "it's getting late and Albie and I have a very important meeting downtown. We can come back later on if you'd like."

She seems very anxious to leave. I don't remember us having an appointment. "Let's play with the chair for a while and then we can go," I offer.

"We have to leave now," she insists.

Felix looks crushed. Like a little boy. She touches his cheek. "I'll be back, Felix. I promise."

"Is it Irmgard?" he asks. "Did she frighten you?"

"I like Irmgard," I say, to Mariah's great consternation.

"And she likes you," Mariah says. "She likes you so much she's making a call. Can you guess who she's calling?"

Who could Irmgard be calling? The police? So what? We're not doing anything to hurt anybody. Felix likes us. The police will like us.

Mariah comes to me and takes my hand, squeezing it so hard it hurts.

"Albie, we'll come back and play with Felix later. We have to leave now."

"Okay," I answer. Why make a fuss? Anyway, I don't mind leaving. Maybe we can go to a mall and do some shopping. That would be fun.

She turns to Felix. "Can I trust you with a secret?"

"Yes."

"This is important. Are you sure I can trust you?"

"Of course," he crows. "I've been trusted by people I wouldn't even trust myself."

"If you tell anybody, I'll never speak to you again. I'm staying at the Holiday Inn on North Broad. Room seven-twenty-two. Call me at eight and we'll get together. Will you do that?"

"I promise."

"You won't tell Irmgard?"

"Nobody. I'll tell nobody. I'm merely a cog. I have no tongue."

"You're wonderful," she says, and graces him with a lingering kiss on his scruffy, unshaven cheek.

I shake hands with him. "Thanks for the NICE," I say. "Can we take some with us?"

"No, no, no. Irmgard would be furious. You come back, I'll give you more. And *we,*" he continues, looking into Mariah's eyes, "will try out the dental chair."

"I can hardly wait," she promises. "Let's go," she says to me, and heads for the stairway.

"I'll call you at eight," he says.

"Room seven-twenty-two. And tell *nobody.*"

"A cog," he promises.

She throws him a kiss and I follow her up the stairs. It's nice that Mariah and Felix have grown so fond of each other in such a short time. Through the kitchen we go, where the dachshunds are licking their balls in a frenzy and out the back door into the bright, freezing air.

"That was fun," I exclaim.

"This place will be swarming with NSB agents," she says, her eyes alert for the slightest sign of trouble. "Hurry up."

We get to the car. "I'll drive," she says.

"I can drive."

"Are you sure?"

"No problem."

"Okay, drive."

"Where to?"

"As far as we can get from here."

The NICE wore off around three o'clock, after Mariah had explored my thoughts and feelings on a wide range of subjects, any one of which would have made my blood boil before I took the drug. We even talked about the night I spotted Mariah in LeDome with Newt, and I told her how nice it was that she could feel free to have secrets from me.

We walked around in a big mall, where I really felt good about myself and my country. Everybody was nice, people smiled a lot, there were pretzel stands and sporting goods stores and JCPenney and K Mart, which I particularly liked because there were so many fun displays and reasonably priced brand names to choose from.

There was even an incident in front of a Wendy's, a little drama we all got to enjoy. Somehow a homeless man had managed to get into the mall. He seemed like a nice enough person but he was awfully dirty and smelled not so good. He had all his possessions in a little plastic basket, the type you get in supermarkets when you just need a few things. Anyway, he installed himself in front of Wendy's and asked everyone who went in or passed by for either a job or money. Most people ignored him but a few gave him a nickel or a dime or some pennies.

Some people decided not to go into the Wendy's because of the homeless man begging at the door. The manager was upset because the homeless man put a crimp in their business.

Maybe the manager should have given the homeless man a job but he was so dirty that the thought of him handling the burgers would probably turn people off. So the manager called the police.

The policeman told the homeless man he would have to leave the mall but the homeless man said he'd been kicked out of everywhere but the freezing cold gutter and wouldn't go back to that. The homeless man refused to move and the policeman was forced to club him bloody and drag him off in handcuffs.

A pretty big crowd had gathered to watch this, and most

of them had no opinion. They thought it was a shame that the man was homeless but he shouldn't be begging in a nice, clean mall where people took their kids, who had wonderful new haircuts piled high on their heads, like birthday cakes. They watched kind of blankly as the policeman shoved the homeless man off down the gallery walk, and they mumbled something about it being a shame and went back to their shopping.

I thought it was all sort of nice in a way. I mean, there's life and death and everything in between is just kind of a play for our enjoyment. If we took everything seriously we'd all be drug addicts or drunkards or serial killers. The flow of life goes on, whether we're happy, unhappy, miserable or depressed. So why be unhappy, miserable and depressed? Where will it get you?

When I told her this, Mariah looked like she was nauseous and said she couldn't wait for the NICE to wear off. It didn't make sense. Before, she was always complaining that I was uptight, insecure and paranoid. Then, when I started to feel good about myself and the world around me, she wished I'd go back to the old me. Her attitude didn't bother me—I thought it was nice that she cared enough to make an issue of it.

But *now* I'm really pissed off. She wants me depressed, she wants me manic. She wants me mad, she wants me happy. What is it with women? Nothing is ever good enough. If I was smart I'd get a lifetime supply of NICE and a girlfriend with same. I wouldn't save the world but I'd live the rest of my life in peace. Who ever appointed me to save the world, anyway?

It's six o'clock and we're sitting in the car across from our motel, keeping a watch for government goons who'll come looking for us if Felix didn't keep his promise of secrecy. Mariah says she can tell NSB people by sight. Why does she

have this compulsion to constantly impress me with a reposi-
tory of knowledge far exceeding that which someone her age
would possess?

No one suspicious appears, so we decide to leave the car
where it's parked and head back to our room. In the elevator
going up to our floor I wonder out loud, "What can the
National Security Board do to us if they find us? They're not
empowered to arrest us."

"They don't arrest. They sanction."

"They would actually try to kill us?"

"They don't try. They do."

"How do you know?"

"Uncle Newt told me."

So there it is. If they find us we're dead. The stakes in this
game have gone up. Now that the NICE is out of my system,
I realize that people who want to kill me are *not* nice. And the
people who want to addict me to NICE are the same not-nice
people who want to kill me. Nice guys don't kill people who
get in their way and nice guys don't sell NICE to nice people
who think NICE will be the answer to all of their problems.
Then again, nice guys don't come out on top either, do they?
Oh, God, does it have to be true that nice guys always finish
last? Or in my case, *dead?*

The most frightening thing about NICE is that, given the
opportunity to take it on a regular basis, even I, who have
deliberately built my life on a foundation of healthy cynicism,
might find it impossible to resist. Yes, life in the nineties,
witnessing the devastating revenge of Mother Nature and the
insidious homecoming of Big Brother, might just have the
potential to be so depressing that even our most passionate
fighters for freedom will choose peace of mind over anguish,
serenity over despair. And when that happens, watch out.
Hitler and Stalin were brutes, but the men who want to give

us NICE have learned from the mistakes of their predeces-
sors—you don't need to kill the body, just the mind.

Inside the room we throw our few things together and then
sit, facing each other glumly, waiting for word from Felix. We
both know that, without solving the puzzle of Felix, Ahmet
Ludi and Libertad, we're helplessly stranded in this nightmare
maze of mystery and murder. That without actually going to
the island and warning Ludi of the government's threat to his
life, without learning firsthand what plans the NSB has for
that poor little country, our chances of getting out of this
thing alive are hopeless and none.

"You really think he'll call?" I ask skeptically.

"He has to."

"Why would he get involved? The man who created
NICE."

"Because it's the right thing to do."

"The right thing to do? That hasn't counted since 1962."

"Spare me your famous cynicism."

"Face it, the outlook is not upbeat."

"He's *got* to come with us to Libertad. Without Felix and
Ahmet Ludi we're two lonely voices in the wilderness."

"Or two dead voices."

She gives me a shitty look and I curse myself for being a
drag. I'll bet she wishes I was back on NICE.

I resolve to be more optimistic. "Let's say Felix agrees to
switch sides. How the hell do we get to Libertad? We can't fly
in—the NSB will have people all over the airport. The only
way to get onto that island without being caught is by boat.
A fishing boat. Or a smuggler's boat. Yeah, a smuggler's boat.
Even then it would be risky if the Navy is surrounding the
island."

My form of optimism isn't the purest, but it gets her going
anyway. "We can catch a cruise ship out of Miami or Fort

Lauderdale," she schemes, "get off in Jamaica or Grand Cayman and hire a small boat from there."

"A cruise ship? Like the Love Boat?"

"They'll never look for us there, they don't search luxury liners. It's totally innocuous. What choice do we have? Fly? Row? Swim?"

"Me, you and Felix on a Caribbean cruise? Sounds like Aaron Spelling's version of a Fellini movie."

"Can you come up with something better? I still don't know how we'll get down to Florida. We can't go to the airport."

"We'll drive."

"You rented the car on your credit card. They'll run a make and put out an APB."

"I'll rent a different car."

"Everything's computerized. We'd be picked up in a minute." Why is she so good at this?

"What about Amtrak?"

"Not bad," she grants. "It's an idea."

"Gee, I had an idea." She looks at me warningly. I snap back to my constructive mode. "If we're going through with this I'd better get ahold of Shrike."

"Shrike? Can we trust him?"

"Without Shrike there's no story. And without a story I get the gas and everyone else gets NICE."

"We trust Shrike."

"Right. Good thing you're smarter than you look."

"Sexist pig."

"I'll have him book a cruise for the four of us and meet us on the ship."

I get Shrike on the phone and run it all down for him. He barks at the prospect of adventure. "What did I tell you, Marx? The story of the year!"

"Or we all disappear in a mysterious boating accident."

"Good old Albie, the nattering nabob of negativity. Hang on a minute." He puts me on hold while he checks with his travel agent, then comes back on the line. "There's a cruise ship out of Miami, the Jamaican Queen, she makes Jamaica in a day and a half. Jamaica's only two hundred fifty miles from Libertad."

"When does it leave Miami?"

"One P.M. Friday. That's about . . . thirty-six hours from now. I got us three cabins."

"Three?"

"One for St. John, one for you and Madonna, and one for me."

"You're coming too?"

"Hey," Shrike says, "it's a tropical paradise and I can write it off. You'll have plenty of time alone with your girlfriend."

"That has nothing to do with anything," I answer, indulging in a quick fleeting vision of me and Mariah, under gleaming white stars on the bow of the ship, engulfed in each other's arms as the great ocean liner cuts a deep, foamy swath through the black night sea.

That's all there is to it. We'll meet on board the Jamaican Queen. Now all we have to do is get Felix to desert Irmgard and join up with the good guys.

I check with Amtrak and find they have a train leaving the Philadelphia 30th Street Station at 10:18 A.M. tomorrow morning, arriving in Miami at 11:08 Friday morning. That will give us a couple of hours to get to the ship. I reserve a pair of adjoining sleepers.

Eight comes and goes and no call from the mad scientist. At eight-thirty, Mariah's anxiety has us both biting our nails. Should we stay in the room and wait? And if we do, are we sitting ducks for the Philistines?

At 8:45 Mariah says it's not worth the risk, we'd better evacuate and get to Felix some other way. I try not to feel discouraged, but it looks like our plan has gone all to hell. And my big story with it. God knows what's happening back in Los Angeles. Danno probably has a warrant to arrest me for murder by now. Hey, maybe that's the *good* news—I stand a better chance on death row than I do with the government NICE guys.

We grab our stuff, check to make sure we've left no trace, and head for the door. As I reach for the doorknob, someone knocks loudly from the other side. I jump back like a cat suddenly face-to-face with a pit bull.

The knocker knocks again. I look at Mariah. "Yes?" I call out.

"Room service," a voice answers. Sure. Room service.

Mariah takes a small, steel-blue pistol out of her handbag.

"What the fuck are you doing with that?" I whisper.

"Stay behind me," she answers tightly, and stealthily wraps her hand around the doorknob. I don't want any part of this, I didn't bargain for this, I want out of here. I think back to the Lazy Leek restaurant and how masterfully she laid out the musclebuilders. I guess she knows what she's doing.

With one fluid motion she whips open the door and shoves her gun in the face of the man standing there.

Felix.

He's wearing an ankle-length fur coat and a heavy fur hat and his nose is bright red from the cold. He chomps down on his cigar, looks from the muzzle of the gun into Mariah's eyes, smiles, and mutters in his gruff, gravelly voice, "Is that a gun in your hand or are you glad to see me?"

"Felix!" she exclaims, in a tide of relief. She grabs his hand, pulls him into the room and shuts the door.

He looks at me and says, "Would you mind leaving us alone?"

"We'll be alone soon, Felix," she assures him, "very soon."

I go to the window to see if he brought any company along. From this vantage point I can spot nothing suspicious.

"I would have called first," he says, removing his coat and hat, "but I couldn't get any privacy. Irmgard's 'friends' were all over the place."

"NSB people?" Mariah asks. He shrugs. "How did you get out?"

"Easy. Irmgard made a big pot of coffee and I added enough NICE to put everyone to sleep. There's nothing more refreshing than a NICE sleep. They'll wake up in eight hours, rested and ready to take on the world again."

"What if you gave them too much?" I ask. "What if they OD? That's murder."

"You can't OD on NICE," he informs me. "Even if you drank a gallon, you can only metabolize so much. It's safer than mother's milk and twice as satisfying."

"Do you take it?" I ask.

"Wouldn't touch the stuff."

"Why not?"

"Because I'm an addictive personality," he answers, twinkling his blue and green eyes at Mariah. "If I'm going to get hooked on something, it's got to look like her."

Believe it or not, I actually feel stirrings of jealousy. She'd never choose Felix over me but we just had our first kiss last night . . . That's all I'd need. She runs off with Felix. I stand trial for murder. I wind up in jail, squeezing my eyes shut while some three-hundred-pound serial killer whispers his sex fantasies in my ear—from behind. Then I get lucky and the government NICE guys poison my food. Whew—I didn't have these thoughts on NICE.

"How would you like to take a trip with us?" Mariah asks Felix.

"Depends on the accommodations," he answers.

"Don't worry about the accommodations," I say testily, "there's a lot more at stake than your comfort."

Mariah throws me a dirty look and says less contentiously, "Felix, do you know what the government is planning to do with NICE?"

"That's not my department," he replies. "I just make the stuff."

"That's what Krupp said about the tanks he turned out for Hitler," I remind him.

"NICE doesn't kill people," he retaliates. "Your comparison is out of order."

"It turns them into robots."

"It makes them happy."

"It makes them stupid."

"It has no effect on I.Q., in fact, with some individuals, it frees their intelligence from negative emotions which incapacitate the intellect."

"Frees their intelligence to do what? Analyze the plot of a TV commercial?"

"It enables people to accept unpleasantness without becoming malcontents. Like you."

"It enables them to accept any atrocity perpetrated by greedy power-mongers for their own purposes."

"It enables them to face a world in which that's already a fact of life."

And I thought *I* was cynical. "That's sheer defeatism."

"It's elevationism."

"It's mind control."

"On the contrary, it's mind decontrol."

"That's bullshit, Felix, and you know it. You're the Revolutionary War expert. Did you forget Thomas Jefferson? 'I have sworn upon the altar of God eternal hostility against *every* form of tyranny over the mind of man.' "

"He also said everyone was entitled to the 'pursuit of happiness.' "

"The '*pursuit* of happiness.' He didn't say man should be *handed* happiness. It's the *pursuit* that makes it worthwhile, the process by which someone rises above his current state to achieve something better. If there's nothing to achieve, no higher rung of evolution to aspire to, what good is happiness?"

"I think Albie's right," Mariah says quietly, "and *my* philosophy is that's it's *all* a waste of time. But just in case I'm wrong, and there's more to life than death and more to death than nothingness—well, NICE makes people happy but it robs their souls."

Felix looks from Mariah to me, a scowl of deep inner conflict invading his face. He stops puffing on his cigar and suddenly looks for all the world like a guilty child. The gruff exterior crumbles before our eyes and the challenging, mischievous set of his face dissolves into a sagging expression of defeat. He slumps down into a chair and stares at the wall.

"I was playing with salvia and accidently came up with NICE," he says softly.

"The tropical plant," Mariah recalls.

" 'The winds of Belief are blocked by the mountain. High in the Windshadow lives the Divine Salvia,' " Felix quotes from a source I don't recognize.

"Ahmet Ludi," Mariah says, remembering the lines from *A Heretic's Handbook.*

"Very good," Felix says. "*Salvia divanorum,* or the 'divine salvia' as the natives call it. It's a red, heart-shaped leaf that incredibly grows in only one place on this entire planet—the side of a mountain on the tiny Caribbean island of Libertad."

Libertad. It's all coming together. Now I understand the reason for the NSB's focus on Ahmet Ludi's island.

"What is this salvia," I ask, "some form of psychedelic?"

"Chemically, yes. It's a trimethoxyphenethylamine, very similar in structure to peyote. The Mexican Indians have been using peyote for three thousand years in relgous rites and healing ceremonies."

"I know, I took it before Castaneda came out," I brag.

"The amazing thing about salvia," he continues, "as opposed to peyote or any other hallucinogenic I've known or read about, is how a slight change in the position of the carbon atom of the benzene ring can make a dramatic change in the nature of the effect on the brain or the duration of the experience."

"What kind of change?" Mariah asks.

"It's all about chemistry. Brain chemistry determines how you feel. Simply put, the brain contains neuro-transmitters which regulate the levels of the neuro-chemicals that affect it. Neuro-chemicals are substances like epinephrine, norepinephrine, ACTH—cortisol, for instance, is a chemical manufactured in large amounts by A-type personalities.

"There is one group of neuro-chemicals, though, that always has a pleasant, soothing effect on the brain. They're called endorphins. Harmless, natural neuro-chemicals that always make you feel good."

"The same endorphins you manufacture by exercising, right?" I ask. "Running always puts me in a serene state of mind."

"Exercising is one way. The manufacture of endorphins is a Pavlovian response to many different types of gratifying behavior. For you it's exercise. For some people it's eating. For others, shopping. Or sex. The activity generates the endorphins.

"The incredible thing about NICE is, it does two things simultaneously. It creates natural endorphins and at the same time directly occupies the receptor sites of the neuro-transmitters, allowing no other chemical to affect the brain.

"There's never been a substance that accomplished this so naturally and efficiently, without affecting the physical senses, motor coordination or speech and intelligence. It makes NICE the perfect drug."

He says this last, not with the pride of discovery and achievement, but in a hollow, cynical voice. Then, in a sudden burst straight from the heart, he confesses, "What I invented is a tool for mind control greater than any before it. A drug that makes people so happy and carefree that anything they do or anything that's done to them is rationalized and assimilated as a pleasant experience. Happiness. For a price. A horrible price."

We sit there in silence a moment as Felix suffers his own brand of searing regret.

Finally, I ask, "How did the government get ahold of your baby, Felix?"

"Irmgard. Irmgard has high government connections. She took it to them. She browbeat me into agreeing that NICE would be beneficial for mankind. And, incidentally, worth a fortune to us. I was so proud of my creation, I allowed myself to believe her. Now I am ashamed. Hubris and science—a deadly duet."

He's right about that. Think of the atom bomb. Or the Nobel Prize—Nobel invented dynamite. But still, I feel for the old fucker. He let Irmgard hoodwink him and he's paying the price. I wonder what their relationship is. Probably something really sick.

"Felix," Mariah says, laying her hand on his arm, "it may not be too late to change the course of events. Do you know Ahmet Ludi?"

"Yes, I know him. I've spent many hours in his village." His face seems to light with the remembrance. "He's a wonderful man, a very spiritual man."

"Did you know that the people who employ you are planning to kill him?"

Felix looks down at his feet, then answers meekly, "I heard that . . ."

"Did you believe it?"

For a moment he says nothing, then whispers, "I do now."

"Would you like to stop them?" she asks. He nods sheepishly at the floor. "Well that's what Albie and I are here to do. But we can't do it without you. Will you come with us to Libertad and take us to Ahmet Ludi?"

"Yes," he answers.

They're cementing their bond with a deep soulful look and it's making me puke. "Let's get the fuck out of here," I pipe up, resenting my part as odd man out.

Felix puts on his coat and hat and we warily scan the hallway before leaving the room.

"Maybe we should take the stairs," I say, feeling uneasy.

"I think we're all right," Mariah replies. "Anybody follow you Felix?"

"I don't think so," he answers distractedly, immersed in her closeness.

This doesn't exactly put me at ease but we enter the elevator and head down. "What is our destination?" Felix asks when the elevator doors open onto the lobby.

As Mariah answers, "Libertad," I recognize the man standing at the front desk and looking directly at us. It's Tom Rush, the "salesman" who was on the plane from Los Angeles with us. I nudge Mariah and she sees him, too. All of a sudden, everyone is moving at once.

■

It's about nine in the morning and I'm in a stall in the 30th Street Station men's room. I've been here most of the night, dozing on and off, my heart in my throat each time the door opens and a new pair of feet step into the room.

Despite her education by Uncle Newt in the ways of the shadowy government, Mariah failed to see through "Tom Rush's" cover on the flight from L.A. But there wasn't a millisecond of doubt in either her mind or mine when the three of us locked eyes in the hotel lobby. The son-of-a-bitch had been on our tail from the moment we left L.A. And when we stepped out of the elevator with Felix in tow, "Rush" and his associates were waiting for us with open arms.

My first instinct was to jump back into the elevator but the doors had closed behind us. I can recall everything that followed in vivid slow motion, which I have been doing all night in fitful dreams and starts.

As "Rush" and two or three others took a step toward us, Mariah drew her pistol and said "Run!"

The government men, four that I was able to spot in that brief moment, reached for their firearms but as they were doing so, Felix, who was standing beside me, took something from his coat pocket and hurled it at their feet. It must have been some kind of supercharged smoke bomb because the instant it hit there was a muffled explosion and the entire room was filled with dense, choking billows of gray-black smoke. You couldn't see your nose in front of your face, probably the same feeling Washington's men had at the battle of Germantown.

Suddenly guns were going off and people were screaming and figures were scurrying blindly in the smoke—a fucking nightmare. I have no idea what happened to Felix or Mariah, if they were caught or shot or if they escaped into the cold, dark night. No idea. Felix's contraption was so potent that the thick smoke filled every square inch of space, expanding into the restaurants and lounges off the main lobby itself.

Eyes burning, I found myself in one of the restaurants, tripping over people and tables and trays. I've never seen such panic and confusion, and that includes the day the Chicago police charged into us at the Democratic Convention. Maybe because this was an enclosed space and the people were picturing themselves in the morning newspapers: HUNDREDS DIE— TRAPPED IN HOTEL FIRE.

I eventually found myself in the restaurant kitchen and even there the smoke had pervaded. Felix is no ordinary scientist and his bomb was no ordinary device. It was almost as if some nuclear chain reaction took place, the smoke multiplied and proliferated so quickly and pervasively.

Somehow I found a back exit and stumbled into a dark, freezing alley behind the hotel. Rubbing my hot, teary eyes, I surveyed the alley up and down, and took off in the direction of least light. I ran as fast as I could over the slippery, icy surface of the alley. A couple of times my feet went out from under me and I landed hard and heavy on the ice but I got right back up and kept running, staying away from well-lit and busy areas.

After covering a couple of miles of back alleys and side streets, I found a deserted building vestibule and collapsed into its shadows, my heart and temples pounding like never before, even on my most prodigious runs.

Only then did I allow myself to focus on the myriad possible scenarios, any one of which could have been my present reality. Had Mariah been killed in the blind exchange of shots which followed the explosion of Felix's bomb? Had Felix been taken? Or had they escaped, like me? Would Mariah be on the 10:18 train to Miami? I wanted to think she would. But I knew she wouldn't.

I couldn't even begin to imagine all this without Mariah.

Fuck, I couldn't imagine *me* without her. Sure, I'd still be Albie Marx, but an Albie Marx without hope, without faith, without love. That's like being nobody, nobody I want to live with.

Time to face facts, Albie. The chances that two of you got out of that motel alive are slim and none. They must have had the place completely surrounded. You lucked out by stumbling onto the alley. You got out for a reason, a reason bigger than you can conceive. *You have to go on*—I guess that's the message.

So here I sit, brokenhearted, hunched over in my stall, waiting for the train to board. I'll meet Shrike on the boat to Libertad and together we'll take on the government. Without Mariah and Felix. Talk about long shots. How did I ever get into this mess? Or, better question, *why?* Oh, I remember. To save my ass. To save my country. To save the world.

What a putz.

"Born under a bad sign, If I didn't have bad luck I wouldn't have no luck at all." That's me, all right, old Moon-in-Your-anus Marx. Talk about bad signs—bet the same astrologer who did my horoscope told the Big Bopper it was a good night for flying.

The worst thing about sleeping in a men's room stall isn't the physical discomfort, it's the bouquet. God knows what these guys are eating but I don't think there's been one vegetarian in here all night. I've spent most of the time with toilet paper wads stuffed up my nostrils. My nose doesn't want to know what my ears tell me is going on. What the hell, it's character building, right? But why am I the one who has to keep building character? I have enough fucking character for *two* middle-aged writers.

All right! Enough self-pity! It's time to suck it up and do the job. Whether I like it or not, I'm the one picked for the mission. I have to put my feelings on hold long enough to bust those bastards in Washington. Then I can worry about what's left of Albie Marx.

The guy in the next stall leaves a newspaper behind. I reach under the divider and pull it over to my side. The first thing I see on the front page is a photograph of an aircraft carrier with the headline: NAVY BRACES FOR SHOWDOWN. Showdown? Who are they kidding? That one carrier has more fire power than the entire country of Libertad.

The story says that the refusal by the government of Libertad to grant additional land for the new American naval base is a thinly disguised attempt by the controlling party—led by a coven of right-wing Japanese sympathizers—to turn the base over to what could become once again a hostile military power. Which means that, in the name of hemispheric security, our government thugs have manufactured a justifiable rationale for invading a neutral country. And Americans fall for this shit.

At least now I know what it's all about. John Thomas and his cronies want the salvia fields in Libertad so that Felix can make NICE for them. And they'll stop at nothing to get them. Clean and simple.

The story made no mention of Ahmet Ludi. I don't know how he fits in but they certainly don't plan on taking any chances with him. And what is his connection with Felix? I hope they don't off him before Shrike and I get there. Without Felix, Ludi is our only hope of believable corroboration.

Over the tinny men's room speaker comes the announcement that the 10:18 Superliner to Miami is now boarding. That means me. In my snow parka and boots, with no baggage, a few bucks and one over-the-limit credit card, I edge out of the men's room and, eyes down, cover the distance to the ticket window without being stopped. A few steps for man, a pathetic shuffle for mankind.

Let's hear it for Albie Marx.

CHAPTER 16

"A critical assignment and you blow it like a rank amateur! What were you thinking? Did you forget everything I ever taught you? How could you let a time bomb like Albie Marx out of your sight for a single second?

"I don't think you comprehend the magnitude of the stakes in this game, the incredible damage the tiniest speck of blow-back could wreak on each individual up and down the line, and I mean from the top of the top to the bottom of this basement.

"Your orders were to clamp onto Marx like a vise, keep his dick hard and his nose clean. I had hoped it wouldn't be necessary to toast him—I didn't want to stir up trouble in the media—but you were authorized—you were *required*, in fact—to do whatever was necessary to keep him from getting involved. And you failed. You got careless. You didn't cover your ass."

Mariah sat in the spare little office in the bowels of the White House facing the head of the National Security Board, her boss, Walter Bates, and suffered his imperious tirade in silence.

"You leave Los Angeles without making contact, without even a drop to your case officer. Then you show up with Marx—at Felix St. John's home! *Felix St. John,* for Christ's sake! Have you lost your mind? What happened to you? Did Marx slip you drugs?"

Weary and overwrought, his right eye suddenly began to jump around in its socket like a grasshopper in a jar. Walter placed three steely fingers over the eyelid and clamped down fiercely. This girl was a proven agent. In three years of service she'd come through every assignment with flying colors, actions that called for discipline, guile and titanium balls. She was trained to kill if she had to—but when she had to, she didn't. He was bitterly disappointed.

"How do you explain yourself?" he demanded. "How do you justify your failure to act?"

"Albie Marx is an ineffectual drunk," she said simply. "The only thing he's a threat to is himself."

"A careless and dangerous assessment! For a story of this magnitude a drunk pulls himself together! He cleans up his act! He's no fool—he found himself a ticket back to the big time and you punched it for him! You let him into the barn and gave him the matches! Now we have a five-alarm fire and I can't trust my fireman!"

"There is no fire. He has odd pieces of information and no idea how to put them together. He's as harmless as he was before, even *more* harmless—he's on the run from the law."

"I'll be the judge of who's harmless, not you! How the hell could you let it get this far?"

"I have it covered," she insisted.

"You have *shit* covered."

"He has no story. He knows nothing."

Unbelievably brazen. "What were you doing at Felix St. John's house? How did Marx know about St. John?" Flinching at the memory of yesterday's red alert phone call from

Irmgard Menglemann, Walter's wayward eye again commenced, against all the force of his will, to pop open and shut a dozen times in rapid succession.

Mariah watched in rapt fascination. A man locked in mortal combat with his own face. When the convulsions stopped, she answered his last question. "Newt slipped Marx a classified memo with St. John's name on it. A memo he smuggled out of *your* 'Eyes Only' file."

"A *memo*? What kind of idiot writes a memo using real names?"

"It was signed 'W.B.' "

W.B.? That could only be him. He cursed himself. Was he losing his grip?

"St. John doesn't know anything either," she went on soothingly. "All he cares about are his toys."

"I have a report you took NICE together."

"Not me. Felix gave Albie a dose to distract him. The horny old goat wanted me to himself."

"There are no excuses. Marx knew too much. The code called for termination."

"What would that have accomplished? It would still leave Newt out there. He's more of a loose cannon than Albie—he knows *everything.*"

"*Newt and Albie Marx have nothing to do with each other!*" he screamed.

"But they do!" she protested. "I didn't eliminate Albie because he was going to meet Newt. My plan was to take them both out at once."

Where did this bitch come off having a "plan"? You do what you're told, that's your plan. Bates looked at her hard through his steady eye. The other one was doing some weird Highland jig. He considered punching himself in the face to stop the thing once and for all.

"Is your eye all right?"

"Yes! *No!*" Control, Walter. Control. "Where is Marx meeting Newt?"

"Miami."

"Why Miami?"

"I don't know. It was Newt's call."

"And you didn't report it to me?"

"I didn't get the chance. The idiot tailing me screwed everything up. If you weren't so paranoid and you trusted my instincts I'd have Marx in my pocket and we'd be on our way to Newt."

"Where in Miami is Newt?"

"His only instruction to Albie was, 'Amtrak, Miami.' "

Bates knew she was telling at least partly the truth because his agents had found a Holiday Inn notepad in Marx's room, noting the telephone number for Amtrak and a Philadelphia-Miami time schedule, in Marx's handwriting.

"If Albie made the train I can catch up with him here in D.C.," she said anxiously.

Walter leaned back and forced himself to look calm. He glanced at the direct line on his desk to General Mark Marmon, commandant of the 82nd Airborne Division, who was awaiting the call to activate Operation Long Bomb and lead his troops into Libertad with orders to defeat and occupy, sustaining just enough American casualties to prove they encountered armed resistance.

Then he looked at the other line, the one from J.T.—when that flashed, it would be the call for Bates to send Marmon's war machine into irreversible action. An operation of such consequential proportions, such sweeping size and scope, being jeopardized by a midget, a girl and a drunk—unbelievable.

"Do you still believe in me?" she asked, unnerved by his silence.

"Don't ask ridiculous questions," he shot back heatedly. "If

I didn't believe in you, you'd be dead. I'm keeping you on this. Take me to Marx. Take me to Newt. That's what I want you to do. That's your assignment."

What he really thought was, why not let her go? He didn't know what her game was but he'd watch her more closely than a cat with a lizard. She'd lead him to Marx who would lead him to Newt. And when they *did* get together, he'd clean all three of their clocks at once.

CHAPTER 17

Lieutenant Joseph Danno walked out of City Attorney Ira Franklin's office, forcibly resisting the urge to tap dance. His face was a mask of calm but his blood was already racing to the thrill of the chase. An hour from now he'd be on a United Airlines flight to Miami Beach, Florida. And, he was sure, a rendezvous with Albie Marx.

The night before last, when his pal Ike, down at the lab, ran an off-the-record, unlogged test and came up with a positive match of the hairs found under Linda Selby's fingernails with the ones from Albie Marx's head (so generously provided by Sally Keester), Danno knew it was time to lasso the doggie and rope him in. First thing next morning, he pressed Franklin to get him a search warrant from the court and he went to Albie's bachelor pad in Los Feliz.

Albie wasn't home but Danno and his men gained entry and conducted a first-class Search and Seizure. They turned up no murder weapon, but they did collect enough *lawfully obtained* hairs from Albie's brushes and clothes to take to the lab for testing. Armed with the *official* lab report, matching

Albie's hairs to those found on the victim, Danno marched into City Attorney Ira Franklin's office.

He ran down the case for Franklin, step by step, line by line. It took him three hours but it couldn't have gone any better. For every question Franklin asked, Danno had the right answer and every answer pointed to Albie Marx. He could see the excitement building in Franklin's demeanor as the implications of the case became more and more clear to him.

Franklin was a conservative Republican planning to run for attorney general in the next election. Because of left-wing bigots like Albie Marx and the liberal/progressive press, the people of California were questioning the dedication of Republican candidates toward preserving and cleaning up the environment.

The case was tailor-made to Franklin's needs. An innocent young woman, with blue-chip credentials as a selflessly tireless worker for the environment, had been murdered. A famous leftwing blabbermouth with a record of civil disobedience and drug arrests was her accused killer. The sides would be galvanized. A cold-blooded murder had been committed and the sham and hypocrisy of the liberal leftist press would be exposed when the killer was proved to be one of their very leaders. The Albie Marx trial would be a center-stage pulpit from which Franklin could trumpet his philosophy of crime and punishment to the people of California. Overnight he would become the Man on the White Horse, leading the crusade for truth, justice and the American way.

Franklin thanked Danno for the excellent work he had done so far, warned him that any missteps from this point on could be costly, and pledged full backing and support. He then placed a call to Judge Lester Stockard and, just like that,

Danno was armed with a warrant for the arrest of Albie Marx. The charge—first degree murder.

That's when he discovered that Albie had skipped town. He was nowhere to be found and no one knew where he was—or admitted to it. Danno called Gruntman, read off the charge and told him to produce his client, pronto. Gruntman claimed he didn't know Albie's whereabouts but would look into it and get back to him. Sure, Danno thought. You'll get back to me when you need to cut a deal.

Danno's first move was to put Albie's house and business under surveillance and include a tail on Shrike, Marx's employer and probable confidant.

Just in time, too. This morning, just an hour and a half ago, the tail followed Shrike to the airport and discovered he was booked on a 2:05 flight to Miami. Danno knew in his bones Shrike was off to meet Albie Marx.

He instructed his man at the airport to have United delay departure of the flight under the pretext of minor mechanical problems. Then he rushed over to Franklin's office to obtain permission to follow Shrike to Miami. With the assistance of the Miami police, he would put Marx under arrest and, upon extradition, escort him back to Los Angeles.

Franklin bestowed his blessings and now Danno was flying down the steps of Municipal Hall to the waiting squad car. A quick stop at his office on the way to the airport yielded a wig of bushy brown hair and a moustache to match, a disguise which he kept in his desk for just such occasions. He was so excited he took the fake eyebrows as well. This was the moment of truth and, after twenty years of waiting, there was no way on earth he would blow it by not being prepared. After all, no effort could be too great when it came to this final round in the battle against Albie Marx.

CHAPTER 18

When Harry Ballister got the call from Chief of Police Herman Baddely he could hardly believe his ears. Albie Marx charged with the murder of Linda Selby. It was stunning news. But did it take the heat off Harry? Would a murder charge put a damper on Marx's passion to destroy him? Or would it more likely inspire Marx to go on the rampage with the Waste Disposal scandal and even, possibly, God forbid, try to take the heat off himself by implicating Harry in Linda's murder? Knowing Marx as he did, Harry couldn't see him sitting still for a murder rap without kicking up a gigantic cloud of misdirection and rhetoric.

Coaxing the details out of Baddely, Harry found out that a police lieutenant named Danno had just flown from Los Angeles to Miami Beach on the suspicion that Albie Marx was hiding out there.

God, Harry thought—if I can only get to Marx before Danno does. Once Albie's nailed, he'll sing his damn head off—and who knows what he'll say? What does he know that I don't know he knows? Can he prove I was in Linda's house at the time of the murder? Jesus, that would be disaster, that would be worse than the bribery rap. I have to get to him. This could be my last shot at that sleazebag—a long shot, but the *only* shot.

Baddely told Harry that Danno was tailing someone he believed would lead him to Marx, a man named Shrike. Harry's mind raced ahead—if I can get to Miami in time . . . if I can find Danno and follow him . . . if he'll lead me to Marx . . . if I can get to Albie before Danno slaps the cuffs on him . . . if I can shut him up once and for all . . .

Danno was scheduled to land about midnight in Miami and would stay in contact with the Department in L.A. Harry figured he could keep in touch with Baddely and track Danno down through the detective's progress reports. Then, *if* everything went his way, *if* Danno got bogged down in the usual bureaucratic bullshit, *if* Harry moved fast enough, *if* he was incredibly lucky—then he could get to Marx before Danno did.

It was a plan with a lot of *ifs,* so many *ifs* it made his head swim, but it was the only plan he had. Farfetched and risky, yes—but what other options were there? Could he let Danno bring Albie back and suffer in silence while Albie blabbed his brains out about Harry Ballister and Linda Selby and the toxic landfill and Waste Disposal? Just the thought of it could drive him to suicide.

The next flight to Miami was a red-eye that left L.A. at 10:45 P.M. and arrived at 6:30 the next morning. He could check in with Baddely upon arriving and hopefully catch up with Danno. And if Baddely became recalcitrant about providing information, Harry would gently remind him of that little laundering favor Harry did for him not too long ago.

He makes a reservation on the red-eye. He's got six hours between now and flight time. He looks at the picture of Lesley which he keeps meaning to remove from the credenza and thinks, if only she could be convinced it was Albie and not me who killed Linda, she'd come running back to me. On the vague chance he might find her in, he dials her number.

"Hello?" It's her!

"Lesley. You're there!"

"Harry, I have nothing to say to you—" That haughty, up-your-ass British inflection . . .

"Lesley, don't hang up! I have news! I know who killed Linda!"

A pause. "All right, Harry—who?"

"Albie Marx."

"Impossible."

"Why impossible? You believe that *I* would do something like that but not Albie Marx? A crazy, drunken fanatic? Come on, Lesley. I may have bent a few rules in my time but do you really think I'm capable of murder? Me?" He can hear her mind chewing on that.

"Albie Marx? Who told you that?"

"The chief of police, Herman Baddely, is that a good enough source? They issued a warrant for his arrest for first degree murder."

"My God." She's hooked.

"But you know what the worst of it is?"

"What?"

"Marx has a copy of my Waste Disposal file. The copy you took from my office and gave to Linda."

"She gave that to Albie Marx?" she asks, angered.

"He took it when he killed her." Another long silence.

"Harry, why are you doing this to me?"

"Why am *I* doing this to *you? You* accused *me* of being a murderer!"

"All right, I was wrong. You're not a murderer. But you fucked me over, Harry. What did you expect me to do? Put my tail between my legs and disappear like all the others?"

"I love you, Lesley."

"You made me furious!"

"I can't go on, I won't go on without you." God, please let that work. Please make her go for it.

"Dawn is so young and beautiful . . ."

"I never encouraged Dawn. She came on to me."

"I was blind with jealousy."

"I can understand being jealous but destroying my career and ruining my life—that's more like hate."

"Don't say that, Harry! I could never hate you. I didn't stop to think when I took that file, I was incensed . . ."

"Do you love me?"

"I don't want to hurt you . . ."

"Do you love me?"

"I never meant to destroy you . . ."

"Albie Marx is going to destroy me."

"You have to stop him!"

"There's only one way. He's hiding out in Miami, they sent some detective to find him. If I could find him first, I could . . . do something."

"Something? What?"

"I don't know."

"God, Harry, I feel so bloody guilty."

"Maybe you could help me."

"How? I'll do anything—I could talk to him, plead with him, woman to man . . . I can be very persuasive for a cause I believe in . . ."

"A cause named Harry?"

"Yes. I do believe in you, Harry. Sure, I wanted to get back at you, but I never imagined it would come to this. Jealousy made me do what I did. My sick, overpowering jealousy got you into this horrible fix. Oh, Harry . . ."

She breaks down. She sobs. She sputters. "I'm so terribly sorry . . ."

Here we go, he can feel it, the scales are tipping his way.

"This may sound completely untruthful but . . ." She sniffles. She coughs. She blows her nose. *"I still love you, Harry."*

That was all he needed to hear. She was his again. She was pleading with him to let her help him. Take her with him. Be her partner again. Maybe, she argues, she could divert the detective while Harry makes some kind of deal with Albie Marx.

Maybe, Harry thinks, she could divert the detective while Harry emptied a .38 into the drunken son-of-a-bitch.

He finally "relents" and agrees to take her back. She swears she'll do everything she can to make herself worthy of his forgiveness.

He arranges for another seat on the red-eye and heads over to her apartment. On the way there he can't decide if he should fuck her or strangle her. This whole thing is her fault. If it weren't for Lesley and her lunatic jealousy, he wouldn't be in the mess he's in.

On the other hand, Lesley gives the best head in the world, and that includes that $1,500 hooker at the Republican Convention last year. And Lesley never complained about the hard, gristly scar on the head of his penis the way some of the other girls did. All in all, a good enough reason for keeping her around—for the time being.

CHAPTER 19

There's a bank of pay phones on the train platform. Melding into the crowd, I slip into the most sequestered booth and dial Gruntman's home number. The big man comes on the line.

"Don't tell me where you are," he says, "it's better I don't know."

"Just tell me what fun I'm missing."

"Danno called—he's got a warrant."

"For what?"

"Murder in the first degree."

"Jesus."

"He swore he'd hunt you down like a dog."

"So this is what it comes to."

"I'm filing for Discovery. To see what they've got."

"What can I do?"

"Nothing. You might as well keep doing whatever you're doing out there."

"At four hundred an hour, that's your best counsel?"

"Four hundred's charity work. I'm doing it for The Cause."

"You're all fuckin' heart, Gruntman. I'll keep in touch."

I hang up the phone and check around for inquiring eyes.

Hunt me down like a dog. What is this hard-on Danno has for me? Some kind of vendetta from the Janis days? Maybe he's just one of those guys who hate me on sight. There have been those in my life. Nat Bostwick is one. Big-ego guys, threatened by the fact that no matter how high they've raised themselves from the collective muck, I still treat them as the cosmically irrelevant schmucks they always were. It infuriates them. Makes them want to punish me, teach me a lesson, rub my nose in their power. I can't disguise my disdain for people who think they're royalty, even though it's bought me a lifetime of trouble. I'm the Common Man, the man who leads protests, sit-ins, mutinies, revolutions against the Wealthy, the Arrogant and the Powerful, the man who puts it all on the line, the man who says Fuck You, Hot Shit. So *fuck* the big boys, *fuck* Danno, fuck him if he's out to get me. As Shrike put it, "They've always been out to get you, Marx. That's why your readers love you."

The Superliner is idling at the platform, massive and sleek and silver, with its high, dark windows and wide stripes of red, white and blue running the entire majestic length of the train. It's final call and people are scurrying to board, cologned businessmen in stylish overcoats and leather gloves, young people braced against the cold in jeans and down jackets, women in high heels and winter ensembles with fake gold accessories, an ethereal blonde with a lost look in her limpid blue eyes, a beautiful, sparkling black family headed for fun in the Florida sunshine, a frenetic lady with bright magenta hair dressed all in black . . . and a middle-aged hipster in rumpled jeans and a war surplus parka, furtively sweeping the platform with sleepless eyes in quest of the girl with the rainbow hair.

I find my cabin, a safe, cozy nook in the maelstrom of my life, a sleeper for two with a sink and commode cleverly set into the small, utilitarian space. I immediately check the adjoining sleeper, reserved when it was going to be Mariah, Felix and me, leading the crusade for truth, justice and the American Way. Now it's just me. Hell, it's always been just me— why do I keep at it? Does the world really need my help? Would freedom and liberty perish from the earth without the unrelenting vigilance of Albie Marx? With my royalties from *Roger* I could retire to some sleepy fishing village on the coast of Mexico and stay drunk and dreamy for the duration. Meditation, writing and magical sunsets. Toasting the days in Margaritaville. Life at the end of the rainbow.

Not so fast.

"We made a promise we swore we'd always remember, No retreat, baby, no surrender." That fucking Springsteen song again. *"Like soldiers in the winter night with a vow to defend, No retreat, baby, no surrender."* Sure, Bruce. And you just bought yourself a twenty-million-dollar mansion in Beverly Hills. "Born To Run" in La-La Land. I picture The Boss, jogging cheek-to-cheek with Zsa-Zsa, trashing the pigs and trading names of Rolls-Royce mechanics. Lord, where is Bob Dylan when we need him? We made him yesterday's news and now we have the Beverly Springsteens.

The Superliner pulls out of the 30th Street Station and I yank off my boots, wincing at the stark, cheesy aroma of my three-day-old socks. I stretch out in my bunk, with a long, grateful groan, my crumpled body trying to dispel the aches and pains of a long, rancid night crammed into a toilet stall. The splint on my two broken fingers has long since been history and they're now fused together with a Häagen–Dazs stick and two rubber bands.

The gentle, rolling motion of the train and the womblike enclosure of my sleeper finally have their way with me and the faraway, surflike sound of the wheels on the tracks is a welcome salve to my troubled mind. Calmly, lovingly, I tell myself to ease off, you're safe, relax, relax . . .

Albie . . . Albie . . . It's her voice. We're in a plane high above the desert, a small plane and we've got parachutes strapped to our backs. We're going to jump out and I don't really want to but how can I back out? We've agreed to make the jump together and I'm going through with it to show her I have the guts. That I'm up for anything. That the years haven't robbed me of my passion, my daring, my charisma. I need her to know that I still love the challenge, the rush, the danger. She needs to know I'm as wild as she is, tough as she is, smart as she is, hot as she is. She needs to know it, God, because if she doesn't, *nobody ever will.* The famous philosophical question: If a tree falls in the forest and no one hears it, does it make a sound? If I am the man I think I am and nobody knows it but me, am I really the man I think I am? Ah, but then there's Rinpoche's inevitable disclaimer—"You are not who you think you are."

Albie . . . Albie . . . I don't want to open my eyes. We're out of the plane, floating over the vastness, the emptiness, the truthfulness of the desert. Nothing but sky, earth and us. Holding hands, free-floating, in the palm of God, but He won't pull the cord, will He? No, I must pull my own cord, Mariah must pull hers, we are all free to survive or perish of our own a-cord. But what if I make it and she doesn't? Do I want to take the chance of surviving without her? Is survival the only end? If I preserve my life, have I fulfilled my appointed task? Or is it meaningless to survive alone? Do I truly *survive* without her? Or do I *merely* survive without her?

Albie, it's me . . . And now we're no longer floating, we're plummeting, racing to the ground, to the end, to death. But we're together. Death Together. I am not afraid. Yea, though I fall through the fantasy of the imminence of death, I will fear no rejection. For she is with me, her voice and her body they comfort me . . .

I bring my right hand up from the depths, with astounding power and speed, and take hold of the man leaning over me.

No more dream, no more illusion, I'm on top of the bastard and ready to kill. My eyes open wide and I find myself nose to nose and hand to throat with a profoundly astonished porter.

"What the hell are you doing, Mister?" he manages to burble, as my thumb and forefinger threaten to cut off his air supply. Regaining my senses, I relax my grip, but not enough to let go. "Get your hands offa me!" he gasps, tearing himself free.

What's happening to me? Attacking innocent people. Violence. Hostility. I'm totally stressed. "I'm sorry," I say softly, sitting on my bunk with an expression of shame. "I was having a dream when you woke me. An old dream from Nam."

He's concerned with the damage to his collar but the Nam reference distracts him. "What kind of dream?" he wants to know.

"Hell-fire. A fucking Bosch come to life." I don't think the Bosch connection registers. So much for Albie Marx, Common Man. "I'm sorry if I messed up your uniform, man."

"I did time, too. Wounded in Khe Sanh."

Shit, I don't want to trade stories with this guy. The closest I got to Vietnam was my Army physical where they classified me 4-F for being psychotic. Who wouldn't be psychotic after staying up on amphetamines and watching old war movies for ten days? I came in screaming "Kill!" and the Army shrinks judged me too dangerous for war. I was actually a rabid antiwar radical and knew I wouldn't be any help to The Cause locked up in jail for refusing to serve. My mother supported my action for other reasons—she thought it was good thinking not to risk getting my dick blown off. There are times when Mother really does know best.

"I tried to wake you by knocking but you were dead to the world," the porter is explaining. "I wouldn't have touched you but I gotta see your ticket."

I dig out the ticket from my parka and he checks it, punches it and hands it back. "Were you Army?"

"Special Forces. Suicide missions." Like the one I'm on now. At least now it's the right enemy.

"101st," he says, with a palpable undercurret of pride. "Got two toes blown off."

Nice going, you idiot. While I was getting laid every night. I'll never forget that famous draft resistance poster—three pretty girls on a couch: "GIRLS SAY YES—TO BOYS WHO SAY NO."

"What's the next stop?" I ask, hopefully turning the conversation to the present.

"Wilmington, Baltimore, New Carrollton, Alexandria, Washington, D.C.—there's a tour guide in that pouch there. If you need anything, push the service button. I won't wake you up again."

"And I won't attack you again."

"Fair deal," he says and limps out with a smile, softly closing the door behind him. Ah, the charm of Albie Marx, Common Man.

I turn to look out the window. The melancholy sound of the great train horn drifts by as we whisk along, and I think of Ayn Rand's *The Fountainhead* as I ponder the deserted, monolithic thirties municipal structures built high on the hilltops overlooking the mad, brown Delaware River, repositories of things only man can make and throw away.

Through blasted rock, stubborn mountainsides that yielded to the relentlessness of progress, past snow-draped steepled towns, icy marshes, wooded coasts, lonely buoys on choppy bays, abandoned freight cars, passenger cars, cabooses . . . abandoned, burnt out, rusted over, ancient, buried alive with disuse . . .

■

When next I open my bleary eyes my window is bursting with clear bright sunlight and, in the distance, the Washington Monument is penetrating the cold blue sky with five hundred feet of hard white marble.

We're slowing to a crawl as we approach Union Station in all its "Beaux Arts splendor, the country's most magnificent depot (so says the Amtrak guide), modeled after the Baths of Diocletian." I'm impressed. *My* experience with train stations is limited to the New York City subway, modeled after the Inferno of Dante.

Leaving the sunlight behind, we pull directly into the station and I'm tempted to close my eyes again and sleep all the way through to Miami. But I see something that brings me to life like the live end of a twenty-volt wire.

Her.

She's wearing her parka, her boots, everything the same. She's standing in the shadow of a column, overnight bag in hand, looking grungy and ragged, checking out the crowd with raw, burning eyes. A million questions spring to mind—how did she escape from the shoot-out in Philly, why is she here in *Washington* of all places, how did she get here, what lies will she tell, will we fuck in the sleeper—I'm so goddamn happy to see her.

When the train finally rocks to a stop, I watch as she calculates her chances of being unexpectedly overtaken, then moves quickly to a door three cars down and climbs aboard. In a heartbeat I'm out of the cabin and on my way to her. I pass through two sleepers and a snack bar and then, at the other end of a crowded club car—is it wishful thinking, or do I really sense her heart pounding like mine when our eyes meet? I'm no Danielle Steel, but I know a romantic crescendo when I'm in one. The music swells, along with other things, and the ecstatic lovers move toward each other with "Thank God" in their hearts and "My love" on their tongues.

Of course, the two lovers in *this* story can't afford to be demonstrative, so I put John Williams and the philharmonic on hold, give Mariah an imperceptible nod, and go back through the door I came in by. Mariah follows me to the cabin, comes in behind me and closes the door. I reach behind her and lock it. There we are in that little cubicle, face-to-face, breath to breath. All I want to do is hold her, kiss her, have her beautiful smooth body become naked next to mine. But I have to be cool. For survival's sake.

"Thank God you made it," she says.

"He works in mysterious ways."

"How did you get out of there?"

"Through the kitchen, to the back alley. I spent the night in a toilet stall at the train station. You can put down your bag."

She tosses her bag on one of the bunks and takes off her parka. *The vibes are heavy* as we used to say. The tiny cabin is exploding with repressed energy. Then, almost too matter-of-factly, she says, "I couldn't stand the thought of not seeing you again." I'm looking at her incredulously but she goes on, "I thought I could keep you locked up in a compartment somewhere. A place in my mind that would always be safe."

"Is safety the best policy?"

"It didn't matter anyway. You escaped."

"Call me Houdini," I say in my steeliest voice.

"If I tell you I love you, will you hate me less?"

Do I detect an honest emotion? Couldn't be. "Did I say I hate you?"

Her eyes are doing quick-changes—defiant, wounded, challenging . . . "Aren't you going to ask how I got here?"

"I figured you'd tell me."

"You make a terrible phony, Albie. Why don't you just say what you're thinking? What's your worst thought about me?"

Interesting question. Is it that she's a lying, scheming,

manipulative, possibly government-employed bitch? Or that she doesn't *really* love me like I want her to? "I think you are not what you pretend to be."

"What am I then?"

"Damned if I know. I know what you're not."

"What am I not?"

"You're not the long-lost devoted daughter, relentlessly on the trail of your mother's murderer."

"You don't think Linda was my mother?"

"There's a birth certificate in the Hall of Records for Mariah Selby, daughter of Linda Selby, that much I know. Shrike checked that out for me. The question is, are *you* Mariah Selby?"

"Who else would I be?"

"You got me."

"Who do you think I might be?"

"How about an employee of the National Security Board? I think they're called *agents.*"

"You think I'm a government agent?"

"You asked for my worst thought."

"What's your second worst?"

"That you won't make love to me right here and now."

We're a foot and a half from each other and my temples are pounding like jungle drums. Or is it someone knocking on the door?

"Porter," my old buddy from Vietnam announces.

I tear myself away from her eyes and crack open the door. "What's happening," I say.

"Life's a bitch and then you die." He peers in at Mariah. "Ticket, Miss?"

She hands him her ticket. He looks it over, tears it and gives it back, then throws me a broad look of appreciation for my excellent taste and limps off. I push the door closed and lock it.

"If I'm a government agent, why have I done everything I can to help you?" she demands.

"If you weren't a government agent, why would you meet Newt in secret and lie through your teeth about it?"

"All right, I met him. He called me at your place, asked me to meet him. Newt is a dead man. They've got a team after him. He wanted to see me. I'm his niece. I'm the only family he has left."

"Why didn't you tell me that at the time?"

"Because he asked me not to tell anyone, not even you, that I'd seen him. He wants to stay alive. He wants to help us. He saved your life, didn't he?"

"Did he give you that gun you carry?"

"As a matter of fact, he did."

"Did he get you out of the hotel?"

"No."

"Who did? 'Tom Rush'?"

"You won't believe anything I say."

"So lie to me."

"Felix gave me a mask and led me out. We got to the car but my eyes were still burning from the smoke, so Felix drove. He shouldn't be allowed near a car. He ran into things, went down one-way streets, drove up 'down ramps'—like some boy gone wild with a giant toy. He's dangerous, Felix. But we got out of there and ditched the car. Believe it or not we spent the night in an all-night porno theatre."

"You and Felix spent the night watching pornos?"

"He watched. I slept."

I can't help but laugh at the sheer nerve of her, laying this preposterous bullshit on me. It's so ludicrous it's funny.

"Laugh all you want, but I'm telling the truth."

"The *truth*," I repeat, catching my breath. "You shouldn't be allowed to use that word. That word should be ripped out of your vocabulary. Don't say it, don't write it, don't use it.

You haven't told the truth since I met you. You wouldn't know it if it flew up and crapped on your head. You could be telling me anything."

"That's right, I could be."

"How the hell am I supposed to know *what's* true with you? How did you wind up in Washington, of all places? Why didn't you come to the station in Philly?"

"Because I was too hot to be seen on the street. It was Felix's idea to meet the train in Washington. He hotwired a car for me."

Now she's gone over the top. "You *drove* here from Philadelphia?"

"It's only a hundred miles."

"In a car Felix hotwired?"

"He's a mechanical genius."

"Why didn't he come with you?"

"He had to cool Irmgard down. He said he'll catch up with us."

This girl has an answer for everything. "Why didn't you board at one of the smaller stations? Why the most dangerous place?"

"The train only makes a few stops. Anyway, I got into the driving. Felix stole me a Porsche."

That's it. I'm drowning in bullshit.

"What about *your* story?" she challenges. "Would you believe it if *I* told *you* I spent the night in a toilet stall? At least give me the benefit of the doubt till you see Felix—he'll tell you what happened."

"Right."

"Everything I've told you is true."

"You're using that word again. I'm actually supposed to believe you?"

"Does it really matter?" she says, and we both know she's cut to the bottom line.

Well, Albie? Does it? Does it matter that you can't believe a word she says? That she's leading you down some path from which you may never return? "No. Not now. There's only one thing that matters right now. Only one thing I beg you to be absolutely truthful about." She looks at me uncertainly. "When was your last blood test?"

"About six months ago . . ."

"Mine was four months. HIV negative."

"Thank God," she sighs. "Me too."

And the moment she utters those blessed words, the moment I admit to myself that nothing else matters, my straining libido bursts through the bonds of my rational instincts, exploding my synapses, invading my blood, heating it instantly up to the boiling point.

Never have I tasted anything like that kiss, pressing my mouth to hers, her head up against the wall of the cabin, pushing my tongue into her mouth, taking hers into mine, my hands like heat-seeking missles, on her thighs, under her skirt, under her panties, enfolding and pulling toward me her fabulous, full, firm behind, welding my pelvis to hers, my steel meeting her furnace with nothing but denim and cotton between them. We're up against the wall and we're tasting each other's honey and her hands are working at my belt and zipper as mine are sliding her underwear down so my fingers can find the hot, hidden places they must touch and enter.

No words, only sounds, no resistance, everything for the taking. My pants are open, her hand is holding me, measuring me, squeezing me, strong, urgent . . . my fingers have investigated her folds and softer-than-soft spots and plunge into her pulsing tight wetness and she makes a sound in her throat like the release of a thousand secrets.

I'm coming in her hand and it doesn't matter because I'm staying hard and I know I'll stay that way and come again and again as I go to my knees to slide her panties all the way off and her fingers are in my hair as I kiss her sweet labia with the same urgent passion as I kissed her mouth, moving my tongue inside her as deeply as it will extend as she lifts one leg over my shoulder and I pull her closer.

I can stay this way for eternity, she's the fountain of life but she wants me in her mouth and I lie back on the narrow floor between the bunks as she bends over me, our eyes soul-to-soul as she caresses my hardness with her lips and her tongue and she takes me deep into her mouth, filling it, my tip hard against the back of her palate, her hand holding my balls, just right, just tight enough, perfectly, as though she's known me forever.

I don't want to come in her mouth, I want to go deep into her sex and, as I move on top I take her now bare nipples and one by one explore each hardening millimeter of sweet brownish skin with my lips and my teeth and my tongue.

We're moving together now, like we've moved together for centuries, our rhythm is perfect, identical, and it builds the same way in each of us, moving faster, holding tighter and now our lips are together and the kiss is of Love and I'm moving in and out steadily, slowly, building, feeding the fire, a little faster and as she arches up to me, deeper, then faster then deeper and my finger slides into her smaller, tighter entry and she catches her breath and starts shaking and moving faster and faster and we're both in a place where nothing exists but bliss, but love, but primal satisfaction and then . . . my body is out of my control, carried away with the approaching climax, thrusting, thrusting faster, harder, like a fabulous, perfect machine and then . . . we reach the top together, as one, our bodies one, our voices one, our identities merged beyond redemption.

■

We passed out to the hypnotic sway of our Love Train, woke up and made love again while a sassy orange moon climbed into the indigo sky outside our cabin window. We tore through the night, leaving the freezing North in our wake, and everything we did to and for each other was right, nothing went unexplored, unentered, unfulfilled.

If Mariah is not the Love of My Life, then sex and love have nothing whatsoever to do with each other.

We use the sink and washcloths to clean ourselves and the tiny commode to pee—unembarrassed, in front of each other. We talk only of feelings and emotions unconnected with the reason we're on this train, racing to Miami to catch a boat or boats to take us to a tiny island in the Caribbean where, chances are, we'll be killed, even if we do happen to make it that far.

"Are you hungry?" she asks. It's about ten o'clock, we're somewhere in South Carolina, halfway to Miami and neither of us has eaten in more than a day.

"Only for you," and I'm ready to taste her sweet pussy again—although I would like something to go along with it, like maybe a plate of pasta with tomato and basil sauce and some great warm garlic bread and a wonderful bottle of deep red Chianti Classico. Followed by maybe some thick, rich zabaglione or how about a crisp, fat cannoli? A little pussy, a little pasta, a little pastry, a little vino—what could be better? Of course this is Amtrak, so we head for the dining car with the hope of maybe getting some meatloaf and mashed potatoes. But it doesn't matter—I'm with my girl.

The dining car is empty at this time of night but still open for service. We sit side by side at a table covered in a near-elegant green and white tablecloth upon which is set a single fresh white rose in a slim pewter holder.

As we roll along the fat orange moon sets the Carolina

marshes aglow, giving eerie night life to huge oaks draped in thick Spanish moss, a tableside view unmatched by any other restaurant.

The waiter hands us a menu and, holy of holies, a wine list. I'm rapidly revising my meager expectations of Amtrak. Mariah orders a Bloody Mary and attempts to demonstrate how well she anticipates my desires by ordering a Corona and Cuervo for me.

"That's okay," I demur, "I'll just check out the wine list." She looks at me in puzzlement. "I haven't had any booze in a couple of days," I inform her. "Since we got off the plane."

"You're on the wagon?"

"The *tequila* wagon. I'm trying to stay drunk less."

"What led you to this lofty decision?"

"You. I had kind of a revelation on the plane. About my self-destructive behavior. I was thinking, here I am with an incredible woman and the opportunity to fall deeply in love— and what am I doing? Getting blasted and propositioning a stewardess."

She laughs. "She told me you came on to her."

"She did?"

"She thought you were cute."

Cute? Me? A cute old man, slobbering over some patronizing stewardess? Another slimy feather in my scuzzy old cap.

She sees me chewing it over. "You're not going to brood over that, are you? Would you be happier if she took you seriously?"

"Brood?" I ask innocently. "At a time like this?" I put my arm around her and pull her close, the sweet, exciting smell of her filling me up as I whisper in her ear, "From here on in, the only brooding I do will be over you."

She touches my thigh and slides her hand onto my crotch. "I'll make sure of that," she whispers back, squeezing harder than she has to.

If she expects me to flinch, she's disappointed. I let her make her point, then I smile lovingly, lean in and kiss her. "How about some champagne? To celebrate today. And our future."

"Whatever there is of it," she adds, nearly precipitating the inevitable moment when reality sets in. But I'm not ready yet, I don't want to let go of the unfettered romantic moment I have by the tail right now. Fuck it. We're here now, not later, and that's what counts.

I order a bottle of their finest and notice a black man, mid to late thirties, tweedily dressed, professorial, in the doorway. He proceeds to a table at the opposite end of the car. Something about him is familiar. As the waiter goes over and hands him a menu I recognize his face. There goes my romantic moment.

"That guy," I whisper to Mariah, "was on the train platform with you in Washington."

She glances at him surreptitiously. "Are you sure? I don't remember him."

"He was reading a paper. I didn't see him board because I left the cabin to meet you."

"A lot of people got on at D.C.," she says. "So what?"

"He's sitting there watching us."

"He's not watching us, he's facing us."

"Well, I don't like the way he's facing us."

"You want to go ask him if he works for the National Security Board?"

"No. But I'm not leaving this car before he does."

"Are you going to obsess over everyone who looks at us?"

"Yes. Aren't you?"

"I don't have enough energy left. You wore me out."

"I did? No, I didn't."

"I'm a little sore down there."

"I'm sorry," I lie. Not that I want her to be sore, but given our ages, that's kind of a compliment.

"I'm not complaining, it's the good kind of sore," she assures me. "You didn't let me down."

"I'll never let you down. No matter who you turn out to be."

"*It takes a woman like you, to get through to the man in me,*" sang the poet Zimmerman.

She takes my hand in hers and moves closer. Why couldn't we be two normal people on a honeymoon? An insurance agent and his bride, escaping the cold and concrete of Philly, heading for the sun and exploring a new world of delights in the partner we've chosen for a life of family and middle-class bliss.

Was there ever a time when that kind of life could have been mine? Was there a turn I took, a choice I made, somewhere back when, that led me into the Forest of Angst, from which I never quite find my way out? But wait—is it possible, after all this searching, that I finally have found my guide? My Beatrice? My Muse? My Mariah.

I sing the lyrics softly in her ear. "*Storm clouds are raging all around my door, I think to myself I might not take it anymore / It takes a woman of your kind, to find the man in me.*"

She looks at me with eyes of creamy brown and I kiss her lightly on the neck. The champagne is fine, the dinner is fine, the world is fine. Except for the man at the other end of the car. Whoever he is, he'll never see my back.

In the cabin we cuddle and neck through Charleston and Savannah but as we cross into Florida, Mariah gets fidgety. I assume it's because we're nearing Miami and all that it bodes.

"I'm too nervous to sit," she says. "Maybe I'll take a walk. Can you live without me for a few minutes?"

"No."

She kisses me and says, "Try."

Does she think I'll let her go somewhere alone? "How many minutes?"

"As long as it takes." Why so testy?

"I'm glued to the spot. Don't go too far."

As soon as she's gone I'm on her tail. Who is she meeting? Up ahead she suddenly turns to see if I'm following and my ass is saved by a winding stairway that leads up to the Observation Dome. A large, red-faced man in bright polyesters is edging down the stairs, directly between me and her line of sight.

She goes to the bar car, and, as I peer through the glass at the opposite end, walks over to the one person sitting there—the black guy from dinner.

That bitch. I could fucking kill her. I hate that I told her I love her.

All of a sudden she turns in my direction. I'm caught. Our eyes meet. I can't move, I'm frozen. She turns back to him.

I step away from the door. My stomach is churning. Everything seems suddenly hopeless, like a dream where nothing goes right—your car won't start, you can't find your papers, the police are chasing you, your friends don't know you, your gun doesn't work—impotence, paranoia and doom. Is this the inevitable crash that occurs when you fly as high as Mariah and I just have?

Back in the cabin I'm pacing and working myself into a frenzy. How could I have been so stupid? To open myself up in a situation like this. I wanted to *feel.* How naive can I get? I've had too much therapy. What am I going to do? Well, one thing's for sure—when she gets back here, she's gonna fucking come clean or say good-bye, I don't care which, as long as it's one of them.

I don't have to wait long. When she comes back her armor is on. As I suspected, her defense is an offense. Hard as titanium. "I don't appreciate being spied on." Colossal chutzpah.

"What world are you living in?"

"I don't care what you saw. There's nothing I can tell you."

"Who *are* you? Do *you* know?"

Acting oblivious to my anger, she takes her gun from her purse and checks the clip. "We're getting off in ten minutes. Just do what I tell you and you won't get hurt."

"Fuck you."

"I'm trying to save your life!"

"I've got news for you, baby—I don't need you to save my life. I've lived twice as many years as you have without your help. If you don't fucking level with me one of us isn't walking off this train."

She reaches into her tote bag and pulls out what I recognize from the movies to be a silencer for a gun.

"Jesus! I've been fucking a goddamn hit man! Who are you, John Gotti's sister?"

Screwing the silencer onto the barrel with a practiced hand she says, "You're a fabulous lover, Albie. The best I ever had."

"Skip the massage baby, my ego's on the blink. Just give it to me straight—who are you working for?"

"I'll tell you everything once we get off the train. Can you wait ten more minutes?"

"No more waiting. It's now or never."

She gives me a kind of sorrowful look, then pushes the button for the porter and steps back against the wall beside the door, gun ready. And I'm standing there, like a putz.

Seconds lumber by like dinosaurs as we stare at each other.

Is there a move to make? Is it up to me? A couple of epochs go by and then there's a knock at the door. "Porter."

"Tell him to come in," she whispers.

"Tell him yourself," I shoot back and suddenly hear myself sounding like some whiny teenager. What's the matter with me? This isn't a kid's game, it's for all the chips. This far down the road I'd better stick with the horse I rode in on.

"Come in," I call out, my voice registering higher than I intended. The door swings open.

"Your call light is on, brother," he says. "You needed something?"

"Yeah, I—I . . . I can't get the window open. Can you give me a hand, man?" Pathetic, Albie. You're a pathetic liar.

He steps halfway inside, then suddenly spins on his "lame" foot and plants a powerful roundhouse kick right in Mariah's stomach. How he knew she was there, I have no idea. Maybe my eyes moved and gave her away. She crumples from the force of the blow and her gun goes off with a *pop* that sounds harmless, but the bullet whacks heavily into the pillow in the upper bunk, a foot away from my head.

He tries to finish her off with his boots but the quarters are tight and she's squirming around and he can't get an angle on her. I jump on him from behind and catch an elbow to the mouth that cuts my lip, rocks my teeth and brings out the stars. Giant dental bills flash before my eyes as I stumble backward against the cabin window.

I've seen Mariah take out two men with karate but this guy outweighs her by seventy-five pounds and he must have a blacker belt than hers because all she can do is defend herself against his onslaught. Her gun, which he knocked from her hand, is getting kicked around on the floor between them as they slam into the walls and the sink and the bunks.

I shake off the fuzziness in my head, think to myself that

since I've met this girl I've gashed my forehead, broken two fingers, split my lip, probably fractured a bicuspid, and still I dive back into the fray with a flying head-down charge into his kidneys. I throw my arms around him and drive him into the wall but he grabs my hand and I nearly pass out when he twists my mangled fingers. The second I let go he spins around and as I'm going down, knees me in the chest so hard I hear my lungs cry out.

Mariah makes a stab at the gun but he's back on her, kicks her in the ribs and she slams back helplessly against the door, a trickle of blood coming out of her mouth. He moves in to finish the job when I grab the gun. *Pop.* He stops moving. *Pop.* He turns around. *Pop.* He starts toward me as the blood bubbles out of him. *Pop.* He stops, looks at the holes in his body, looks at me with a befuddled expression and collapses like a marionette at my feet.

I killed him. I killed another human being. I'm a murderer. I'm no better than the rest of them.

The blood's streaming out of the holes in the body. *The body.* A minute ago he was moving, breathing, kicking, alive. Now he's the body. Years, decades, a lifetime of struggle, then four quick *pops* and it's over. "Life's a bitch and then you die." He said it himself this morning. Guess he was rehearsing for tonight.

"Thank you, Albie," she says softly, taking the gun from my hand. "I owe you."

"Who was he?"

Unmindful of the dark syrup still oozing out of him, she opens his coat and searches his pockets. She finds what she's looking for and hands it to me. It's a short, thick wire with a small metal tie on either end. It's a garotte.

"That had your name on it," she says.

I suddenly remember the moment I woke from my dream and found him leaning over me. Was he about to use that thing? On my neck? The thought makes me shudder. How close did I actually come to buying the farm? Is God on my side? You are, aren't You, You crafty bastard. You woke me up at precisely the right moment. What was it? The dream? Of course! The dream about Mariah and me, flying, jumping, falling . . . and then her voice . . . calling me, calling my name . . . and then I woke up and caught him standing over me. She came into my dream and saved my life.

"You don't owe me," I tell her, "we're even."

She stands and I take her in my arms. She flinches when I pull her tight against me and I know he's hurt her and I hate him for it and I'm glad I killed him. I'll kill anybody who lays a finger on her.

Minutes later we pull into Orlando and slip off the train. Down the line I spot Mariah's black friend stepping out of a forward car, briefcase in hand, and hurrying off down the platform toward the terminal.

"All right, who is he?" I ask as we follow in the same direction.

"Howard Wattlington," she answers, and leaves it at that.

"Howard Wattlington. Of course." Let her play her games. Whatever she wants to do is okay with me.

Clinging to the shadows we traverse the terminal and continue out the exit marked, *Taxis, Buses, Rental Cars.* A few edgy minutes go by and then the newly ubiquitous Howard Wattlington pulls up in a white Pontiac with a Hertz sticker on the bumper. We throw our bags in the trunk and climb in, Mariah in front and me in the back. Howard gives it the throttle and the Pontiac blasts off, hurtling out into traffic, the rental car from Hell.

"We've got three hours and forty-five minutes to get to Miami," he says, checking his watch and swerving around a slow moving truck. "Two hundred and thirty miles. Don't want you to miss your cruise."

"Thanks, Howard," I bark from the backseat, "Whoever the fuck you are."

Our eyes converge in the rearview mirror. "Nice meeting you, bro. I read your stuff all the time."

"Howard's a friend of Newt's," Mariah offers. "An old friend."

"Kappa Lambda Phi, Cornell '73. Like brothers," he affirms.

"You work for them too?" I ask. "Our Guardians of Freedom."

"No, no-no-no-no-no . . . Politics is Newt's jones, not mine. We graduated college and broke into the ad game together but I'm still pitching toothpaste and hemorrhoid cream. I don't feature ducking car bombs for a living. This is a one-time-only gig for me. Newt asked and I couldn't say no. Besides," he adds with an avuncular wink at Mariah, "I have to look out for this guileless young lady here."

"Howard fingered the porter," she informs me.

"Got it from Newt. Somehow they picked up your plan and put the man on the train in Philly."

"Good old omnipotent Newt," I reflect. "Where is he now, Howard? In that briefcase of yours?"

"Could be anywhere. Don't look and you'll see him, don't listen and you'll hear him." The Mighty Midget of Zen.

Howard follows the arrows leading onto the I-95 to Miami and gaining the highway, pushes the Pontiac up toward a hundred.

"Newt and I were hired out of college as apprentice copywriters by Doyle, Dane and Bernbach. Newt was such a natural that he made account exec while I was still in the jingle pool. He was a wizard at hooks and buzz lines. He came up with the 'Think Small' campaign for Volkswagen. Remember that ad during the gas crisis in the seventies, 'Tank heaven for little tanks'? That was Newt's. He really had it, man. God-given talent." He shakes his head at the thought of Newt wasting his brilliance in Washington.

"If he had such great talent, why did he give it up?" I ask. "Patriotism?"

"Newt loves his country," Mariah asserts.

"That and his *guru*," Howard sneers, "John Thomas. When J.T. decided to make Donald Cale president and took over the campaign, he brought Newt and the cream of the agency with him. When they won the White House, J.T. made Newt second in command at the National Security Board under Walter Bates. Now *there* is a shitheel of major proportions, Walter Bates."

"Is Newt really your uncle?" I ask Mariah.

"My mother's younger brother. By two years."

"Well," I say, glancing at my watch, "we have two and a half hours and no bullets to dodge. I think it's time you told me the whole story. The *true* one."

And, miraculously, she does. At least she swears it's the truth—the whole truth and nothing but the truth—or, Help me, God.

According to Mariah, Linda was seventeen and living on her own when she gave birth to her in a Los Angeles hospital. Nobody but Linda knew who the father was. Nobody knew if he even knew he was a father. It was Linda's decision, for reasons she didn't divulge, not to involve him.

Mariah reiterates the part of the story she told when we met, that a New York couple, Annie and Paul, unable to have children of their own, made arrangements to adopt her at birth, came to Los Angeles, then brought her back to Long Island, where they loved and raised her as their only child.

They never told her about Linda, they never let on that she was adopted. It was Linda, in fact, who eventually sought out Mariah.

Linda was heading toward forty, unmarried and, knowing she'd never have another child, became obsessed with her abandoned daughter. She asked Newt to use his sources to find her. But she instructed him not to reveal Linda's identity. She didn't want to drop a bomb on Mariah's life, she just wanted to know that her daughter was happy and healthy and, if she wasn't, to help her in any way she could.

The year before Newt came looking for her, Mariah had become bored with college, bored with her friends and bored with her prospects. She was majoring in psychology at Hofstra College but she didn't want to be a psychologist. She was dating lots of hip young guys but they were all immature. Something inside yearned for adventure, real adventure, even for danger. She quit school, bought a motorcycle and, on her own, rode south to the sun, down through Mexico and South America, all the way to Cape Horn and back, just for the thrill of it, just to test herself.

When Newt found her, she had just turned twenty and had recently arrived back in the States. She was working as a bartender in an East Village skinhead joint, already restless for a new adventure.

The timing was perfect. He approached her as a government agent, offering a career of excitement and action. He told her the agency wanted someone young and racy—courageous too—to penetrate the radical youth groups its people couldn't get into. He gave no hint of his true relationship to her, never brought into question her version of her own history. For him, bringing her into the NSB was a way to keep his eye on her—and to keep Linda tuned in as well.

Mariah was titillated by the picture he painted—spies, plots, danger, life on the edge. She'd never been political so politics played no part in her decision. Secret agent work sounded like the kind of thing that could make life exciting.

The catch was Walter Bates. Bates was skeptical about taking in someone so young and green. He did an exhaustive investigation into her life—her friends, her beliefs, her parents, her lineage—but all the investigators' research went through Newt first and by the time it reached Bates's desk, it contained no mention of a mother named Linda or an uncle named Newt. She came up Ivory Snow clean, 99 and 44/100 percent pure.

Bates put her through intensive training and soon realized he'd been delivered a gem. He began taking a personal interest in her development and carefully selected the assignments she was given in order to develop her talents properly. And that's how things were until Newt became disillusioned over J.T.'s fascination with NICE.

When NICE was brought to J.T. and secretly tested by the NSB, Newt recognized it for what it was, a masterful tool for mind control. Then, when he uncovered Bates and J.T.'s master plan—to take over Libertad and reap profits from the drug—he determined to do whatever it took to stop them.

But what could he do? He couldn't go to the mainstream media. They were all too cozy with J.T. They would either belittle his story or bury it in the back pages. The alternative press was his best shot—and who better to run with a preposterous tale of government conspiracy than me, Albie Marx, a man with a national name and the gonzo mentality to bellow away until he gets heard. Not to mention the fact that I was sleeping with his sister.

"Wait a minute," I interject, losing a primary thread of the story. "Back up a couple of steps. When did you find out Linda was your mother?"

"Just before Newt contacted you. He knew Bates was having him shadowed and he was worried. He wanted me to connect with Linda, just in case something happened to him. Linda agreed and Newt brought us together."

"That story you gave me about taking years to find her and the 'emotional bloodbath' when you met—that was made up?"

"We *were* emotionally overwhelmed by each other. She'd been twenty years in denial for abandoning me and I was in a rage about being abandoned *and* being deceived about it my whole life. But we were so thankful to see each other . . . to know each other . . . talk about our lives . . . share with each other . . ." Her voice catches in her throat. "I only knew her a week before she was killed."

"I'm sorry," I say quietly.

"That's the way it goes," she says, and I can feel her steeling herself. "Life isn't pretty."

"So Newt took you to Linda and then he was killed. But not killed."

"They were having breakfast together when some poor slob came along and tried to steal his car. *Boom.* Instant capital punishment. The body was burned beyond recognition."

"A stroke of luck for Newt. Let Bates think he was dead."

"Exactly. He told Linda to play her part and tell everyone, especially you, that her brother was snuffed by the car bomb. It almost worked."

"Except for?"

"Bates didn't buy it. He's a cynical, paranoid bastard and he never lets go of anything. He had my mother killed because he was afraid of how much Newt might have told her."

"*Bates* killed Linda?"

"That's what Newt says."

"He's absolutely positive?"

"He wasn't there. He didn't see it. But that's what he says."

"I would have bet it was Harry Ballister."

"What reason would Ballister have? He's not involved in the NICE operation."

"If he's not involved with NICE then why is he after the memo? Why was he trying to get into the post office box the morning after Linda was killed? Why did he ransack my house? If he isn't afraid of being exposed, why did he try to run me over?"

"You're sure it was Ballister in that car?"

"I found the masks in his office. I'm absolutely sure."

She shrugs. Neither of us has the answer. Maybe there is no answer. Maybe there's only questions. Like the one I have to ask her now.

"Are you still working for Bates, Mariah?"

She looks at me with a deep melancholy. "No, Albie. I'm running from Bates, just like you. Running for my life."

CHAPTER 20

The Jamaican Queen is a luxury cruise ship eight decks high and five hundred feet long. It has nine Rolls-Royce engines and cruises at sixteen knots. It carries one thousand people, one crew member for every two passengers. It's an ocean-going resort, a Las Vegas at sea, a Caribbean nomad which grants temporary worldly amnesia to those who can pay the fare. Pack up your troubles in your old kit bag and sail, sail, sail.

What can compare with the fresh, azure wind in your hair, the sparkling gold sunlight in your eyes, the magnificent isolation of unbroken horizons, as you lean on the railing of the uppermost deck of the great ocean liner and become cosmically at one with all you survey? At a moment like this, would terrestrial turmoil dare circle your head like the dread albatross? Would the hell of your landlubbing ways insinuate itself so ruthlessly behind your eyes, that all of God's beauty before them is filtered through the horror of what they've left behind? These and many other questions occur to the nautical philosopher as he ponders the serendipity of his life and wonders why it's all so fucked.

Howard Wattlington turned out to be Evel Knievel in a three-piece suit and we practically flew down I-95. Mariah told me that when Linda was killed, she maneuvered Bates into giving her the assignment of watching Albie Marx, by postulating that, number one, my weakness was women and number two, only someone as crazy as she would be trusted by someone as crazy as me.

Unaware of Mariah's connection to Newt and Linda, Bates agreed and from that moment on she's been working with Newt to lead me to uncover and expose J.T.'s Orwellian plan to legalize, distribute and make a fortune on the insidious drug dubbed NICE.

But saving the world from NICE is one thing and saving my ass from the gas chamber is another.

Let's say, for the sake of argument, that Newt's theory about the NSB car bomb geeks is correct—that they killed Linda because she knew too much. It makes as much sense as the Harry Ballister scenario. How could I ever make anyone believe, in the face of the case Danno must have against me, that I'm innocent, that it was two mysterious unnamed government agents who murdered Linda so cruelly? I'd get laughed out of court—with a verdict of Guilty. And I'm trying to save the world? I can't even save myself. Even if I could lay open the real story of the invasion of Libertad and the mass distribution of NICE, would anyone, much less Danno, care? Would anyone even say thank you?

Down below, Mariah and I baptize our narrow cabin with the holy water of love-sweat. We bend and twist from bunk to bunk, making the tiny space work for us, driving each other to geometrically higher levels of creativity, achieving links and connections I haven't made since the tantric excesses of my youth. When the fat lady sings we lie hoarse and spent, basted together in the luminous perspiration of union superbly fulfilled.

The phone rings. We exchange looks and I untangle my arm just enough to reach the receiver.

"Yes," I answer, brusque and efficient, sounding like anything but the man who just bellowed like a buffalo in orgasm.

"Marx?"

"Shrike," I announce for Mariah's benefit.

"You made it. I was starting to worry about you."

"Leave the worrying to me, Shrike." Nobody's better at it.

"How was the trip down from Philly?"

His question brings instantly to mind the thick, red syrup bubbling out of the holes in the porter. I force that aside and take a deep, intoxicating breath of Mariah.

"It had its moments," I answer.

"I'll bet it did." He can make anything sound dirty. "Meet me in the bar up in the casino—if you can still walk."

"Half an hour," I say and, as I hang up, Mariah's touch tells me we'll be late.

Up on the seventh deck, the one they call the Rainbow Deck, there's a full-scale gaming room, the Monte Carlo Casino, with craps, roulette, blackjack and slot machines. In the center of the casino is the Buccaneer Bar—their imagination in names sweeps you off your feet, doesn't it? Mariah, Shrike and I are sitting at a table in the darkest corner, reconnoitering and bringing each other up to speed on the situation as it now stands.

"The reason the ship isn't packed this time of year," Shrike is explaining, "is the Libertad crisis. People see aircraft carriers on TV and get spooked. They don't want to go on a cruise that passes less than a hundred miles from a war."

"Some war," Mariah mutters. "Libertad has the military muscle of a pygmy tribe."

"Then why are they standing so firm?" Shrike asks. "Why don't they just give up the land? They must know they're feeding our propaganda machine."

"Because they assume that we're coming in no matter what they do," Mariah explains. "I suppose they want the U.N. and the world to see that we're doing it against their will. For the record."

"As if that ever stopped us," I groan.

"You think the Libertad government knows about NICE?" Shrike asks.

"They must know about salvia," she guesses. "They've had it for thousands of years. I doubt if they know Felix's version of it—or the plans J.T. has for it."

"*Felix.* I hope to God he shows up," I pray.

"He promised he'd be there," she says with manufactured optimism. She doesn't look like she'd bet the farm on it. For encouragement I take her hand in mine and hold it tightly. She leans close and we kiss, while Shrike stares at us blankly.

"Where are we with the issue?" I ask on a more constructive note. "Is everyone on red alert?"

"Standing by to put out a Special Edition. We've got the complete story of the island—history, culture, economics, religion—I've got dynamite pieces on the secret history of American aggression in the region, including Grenada and Castro's Cuban revolution—which was armed and financed by the CIA, by the way—we have statements by the usual assortment of ex-covert and military types, Democrats fishing for progressive credentials, drug dealers no longer employed by the CIA—the cover is done, the issue is ready—all we need is the lead story. We need hard evidence, testimony to authenticate that memo to John Thomas—"

"Newt will be there when the time comes," Mariah assures him. "We can count on his full disclosure."

"After Newt, the most critical piece of the puzzle is St. John—if he cops to everything, we're Woodward and Bernstein. If he flakes out . . ."

"We're Kitty Kelly," I conclude.

"God only knows what Felix will do," Mariah says.

"You don't believe in God," Shrike taunts.

"The *missing* piece is Ahmet Ludi," I go on. "Why are they so intent on getting rid of him? What's his position in Libertad? What does he know?"

Yawning and stretching, Mariah says, "I'll leave you boys to figure that out. I'm out on my feet."

"You going back to the room?" I ask, wanting time alone with Shrike and at the same time picturing myself coming into the room while she's sleeping and waking her softly with my tongue in all the best places.

She nods, stands and stretches again. She's wearing a summery outfit we bought at one of the ship's stores this afternoon and she looks younger and tastier than ever. The flouncy skirt makes you want to look up underneath and gawk at her stuff. She comes around the back of my chair, leans over with her arms around me and presses her face against mine. "Wake me when you come in," she purrs in my ear and bites my earlobe for emphasis. Confined in my pants, my hardening dick is bent over double and screaming for relief.

"Act like you're asleep for the first half-hour or so after I start," I whisper back in her ear. "While I work up a good head of steam."

"What is this," Shrike intrudes testily, " 'What's My Fetish'?"

She straightens up, goes over and plants a kiss on top of his black-thatched head. "Don't keep him out too late. He needs all his strength." And she heads off through the club.

We're watching her go—that body, that ass, those legs— and, near the door as she goes out, my eye is caught by a guy working a slot machine. He's got lots of hair and big, bushy eyebrows and I can't say why, but something about him is strikingly familiar. I look harder but can't quite make him.

"So how are you and your daughter enjoying the cruise?"

"You have no idea what I've been through."

"No, but I'd like to," he says in his lewdest inflection.

"Shrike—less than twenty-four hours ago I killed a man."

"You told me."

"Do you know how that felt?"

"I imagine it felt pretty good."

I look at him like the pig he is. "It did."

"He was trying to kill your woman. Anyone would have done the same thing—and, whether they admit it or not, enjoyed it as much. This forced remorse is just you fighting your image of yourself. Albie Marx, peace and love, child of the sixties. Forget it, these are the nineties. Kill or be killed, fuck or be fucked, don't go outside without a helmet."

"Thank you, doctor."

"That'll be a hundred and fifty bucks."

"Bill my insurance."

"I know what's really bothering you. You're upset that people whose salaries you pay with your taxes are trying to kill you. Perfectly understandable. You're spending good money to do yourself in. Maybe if you stopped paying taxes they couldn't afford to keep chasing you."

"Maybe if I stopped paying taxes, Danno would be out of work and Harry Ballister would have to get an honest job. Jesus, I'm being squeezed at the city, state and federal levels. I'm H & R Block's worst nightmare. My life is a joke."

"That's an improvement over its usual state," he observes without sympathy. "Come on Albie, cut the shit. What's the real deal here? What's going on with this chick?"

"What do you mean?"

"You're following some teenybopper James Bond like a

dog in heat. For all you know she could be leading you straight to the pound. You've paid too many dues to get sucked in like this."

"I believe she's levelling with me."

"I believe your brain's in your dick. Nobody ever got that kind of pussy for free."

"If I believed that I'd have to slit my throat."

"If you don't somebody will do it for you."

Please tell me he's wrong, God. Don't let her be another one of Your little tortures.

"Take a look over there," he suddenly says, "coming through the door."

I turn to look. "The Japanese chick?" He nods. "What about her?"

"What do you think?"

"I don't know. She looks like Yoko Ono's younger, flashier sister. Why?"

"Think I can score with her?"

"She's not exactly your style," I answer, knowing his feelings about the Japanese. As I'm saying this, she's heading our way.

"I didn't think so either—at first," he says, pointing his most lizardly smile in her direction. "But since her father's worth a couple of billion, how could I not give her a whirl?"

"Her father?"

"The buyer I have for the magazine. He's the chairman of Nakubishi."

I look at him blankly.

"The biggest publisher in Japan."

"You're selling *Up Yours* to a Japanese publisher?"

"Didn't I tell you?"

He says it so offhandedly I have to stop and think. My answer comes up, "So that's what happened to the Japanese issue."

"What fun is racism?" he asks, just before she arrives at the table. "Oonie, this is my friend, Albie Marx."

I stand and take her hand. "Hi, Oonie. John's told me all about you."

"Really?"

"He's been going on for hours."

She smiles at him shyly and says, "What did you tell him, John?"

"Only that we're planning to get married on the romantic island of Libertad, darling," he answers and I think that his brain cells have finally given out.

"You're getting married in Libertad?" I repeat like a dope.

"They're closing the deal for *Up Yours* as we speak."

"That was supposed to be our secret," she chides.

"It's still a secret," he assures her. "Albie's memory deserted him years ago. I'm surprised he remembered to stand up."

"You can sit down now," she tells me, as she settles in next to him.

I sit obediently. "So . . . what's new at Nakubishi?" I ask, at a loss for words.

"*Up Yours, The Enquirer,* and *Scientology Today,*" she declares.

"Attractive company you're in," I remark sardonically to Shrike.

"Don't be snide, Marx. Remember, it's the nineties."

"What does this do to our Special Edition?" I demand.

"Doesn't affect it at all. We combine it with the wedding story and it becomes a collector's item."

The wedding story? I feel like throwing up.

"Feel like some fun?" he asks. "We're going to dance all night in the Crow's Nest Nightclub."

Crow's Nest—another original moniker—these boat people take their clichés seriously. "No, I think I'll turn in. My fiancée is waiting for me."

"You're engaged too?" Oonie asks. Why is she so surprised? Do I look like the type no one wants?

"Didn't John tell you? I'm getting married in Libertad too. We'll make it a double wedding."

"That will be fun, won't it John?" she says happily.

"We'll discuss it later," he barks, never one to share his thunder.

"Well, have fun kids," I say, rising. "This old man's going beddie-bye. See you anon."

I leave them in each other's care, wondering what God has in mind when He plays jokes like this. Selling the magazine to the Japanese? Marrying a Japanese princess? Does anything make sense anymore? "A collector's item," he called our Special Edition. My last hope turns out to be Shrike's wedding album.

After two days at sea we dock at Port-au-Prince in Haiti, another island America will someday invade for their own good. Mariah and I have spent lots of time in our cozy stateroom, drinking champagne, or taking strolls on the deck and having a drink with Shrike and his Oonie, whose undisguised appreciation for a good set of male buns is only surpassed by Shrike's mesmerization by anything with nipples. Mariah even bought him a little porcelain cow from the gift shop, hoping it will occupy him—like prayer beads.

I've spoken to Gruntman several times, all with frustrating nonresults. On one hand he advises me to come back and stand up to my accusers, that my flight from prosecution could prove disastrous to my case. At the same time he admits that anything I can do to help myself at this point is worth

doing. From a great criminal attorney, that's not too encour-
aging.

Mariah and I are out alone on the top deck, sipping champagne at the first stirring of dawn. The starry sky is barely
inflamed with a faint pulsating hint of light on its eastern
fringe. Mariah's reciting an excerpt from Ahmet Ludi's *A
Heretic's Handbook,* which she seems to have taken to in a
major way.

> I laugh every time that you tell me
> All the things that you want me to do
> Get my mind off the stars
> And buy a new car
> Become exactly like you
> I don't want to be "normal"
> I don't want to be "sane"
> If I give back the money
> Will you take back the chains?

"He was rich, wasn't he?" she asks.

"He made a fortune in the record business. Before he
dropped out and gave it all away."

"People don't do that anymore."

"We're in the emotional Ice Age. Nobody gives money
away unless they get a tax deduction. People use money to
hide behind."

"They didn't do that in the sixties?"

"In the sixties? There was a brief, shining moment when a
lot of people looked beyond money and into themselves—a
light shone on something they couldn't deny, a beacon of Love
that illuminated a Oneness, an interconnection between all
life. It sounds so corny when I hear myself say it, but goddamn

it, it was real. I know it. I felt it. In those days, God was Love. Now He's a CEO."

"You hung out with a rock and roll crowd back then," she says, and I remember her looking at that old snapshot of me and Janis. "Did you ever meet Ahmet Ludi?"

"Ahmet Ludi? As a matter of fact, I did," I answer, my mental picture of that night suddenly as vivid as the expanding powder blue edge of the cobalt sky above us.

"We were talking—about the space between us all, And the people—who hide themselves behind a wall of illusion . . ."

It was '67—the spring—I was doing a European promotional tour for the release of *Roger Wellington Rat,* which was already an American phenomenon.

I was in London and of course I hooked up with the local rock and drug crowd. A girl named Pam, she was seventeen, a beautiful groupie, had loved my book and somehow equated me with a rock star. She wrangled an introduction and kept me busy the whole time I was there. Where is Pam now, I wonder? A middle-class mother in Manchester? A bag lady at Claringdon Station?

Back then Pam knew the whole scene and took me to a mansion in the country one night—we were on mescaline I think—yes, mescaline, big caps of purple powder that lit up the Inner Path, if you cared to see it. There were about ten people at this house, everyone was laid back, but it was like being in the presence of royalty because two of the people were George Harrison and Ahmet Ludi.

Ahmet Ludi at age thirty-five was already a legend, and George Harrison—well, the Beatles were the biggest thing on earth, bigger, as John Lennon said, than Jesus Christ. Harrison had come back from India with Ludi, and the Beatles were in the process of recording *Sgt. Peppers Lonely Hearts Club Band.*

Harrison had a sitar and was quietly playing "Within You,

Without You," a song he had written that eventually opened side two of the album.

"*We were talking—about the love that's gone so cold and the people, Who gain the world and lose their soul—they don't know—they can't see—are you one of them?*"

Ahmet Ludi had deep green eyes and long, dark hair, braided in back. His face was beatific as he listened and resonated to Harrison's music.

I remember thinking that I was in the presence of Holiness. Years later, when creeping cynicism overtook me, I attributed that feeling to the mescaline. But I know it was more than just the drug—we were reaching for the heavens in those days, and Harrison put our thoughts and feelings to music.

"*When you've seen beyond yourself—then you may find, peace of mind, is waiting there—And the time will come when you see we're all one, and life flows on within you and without you.*"

It never happened, the time didn't come when everyone saw they're all One—but that's another story.

I was talking to Ludi about a philosophical difference I was having with a friend back home. My friend maintained that in order to raise your Spiritual Self from the miasma of your Worldly Self, it was necessary to go through some form of psychotherapy or self-psychoanalysis. He claimed that your programming could never be changed unless you went all the way back and disconnected it from infancy.

I held that when you clean up the present, you clean up everything, that it's a waste of valuable energy to go through all that trauma over and over again.

I asked Ludi what he thought and he said, simply, "You *steal* the energy from one to use for the other."

It suddenly became very clear to me. He had given me a modus operandi, which to some extent validated both views and provided the most efficient use of my energy. You *steal* the energy locked up in your past and apply it to the present.

That was my contact with Ahmet Ludi. Not exactly earth-shaking, but a tidbit of philosophy that I've never forgotten. A moment in time that's lasted a quarter century.

As the fading night sky sops up the new light of day like a see-through sponge, Mariah reflects on what I've told her.

"I wonder about my father a lot," she says quietly. "My real father. Do you think that's a waste of energy?"

"Not if you steal that energy—the energy of wondering—to see yourself as a complete human being, regardless of *whose* sperm contributed to putting a body on your soul."

"You think I can be complete if I don't know who I come from?"

"If a tree falls in the forest and nobody hears it, has it made a sound?"

She looks at me with an irritated smile. "If I ask a question and you ask a question, have you given me an answer?"

"If I give you an answer and you don't hear it, have you asked me a question?"

Brilliant, no? Marx as Socrates. Groucho does Plato.

This morning the boat docked in Ocho Rios, Jamaica. One more day to Grand Cayman Island, where we'll look for a way to cross the last hundred miles of ocean to Libertad. Mariah was right about the safety of a cruise ship—nobody's tried to kill us.

Day turns to night and the ship finally heads back to sea. Mariah seems sad, but when I ask her about it, she doesn't really say anything. Kids are moody, I think, and I call Shrike to see if he wants to have a drink in the Buccaneer Bar.

"You haven't been drinking your usual," he observes when I order a glass of white wine.

"I quit tequila. Too much like a drug."

"Was that your idea or hers?"

"Mine. What's with Oonie? She stayed in the cabin?"

"She's at the all-night beauty salon. I left a note for her."

"Perfect. John Shrike and his Japanese American Princess—Leon would love that." I have an image of Leon behind the bar as Shrike struts into The Rock with an overdone JAP on his arm.

"I don't live my life to please bartenders," he says pissily.

"Since when did you change your philosophy?" Before he comes back at me we hear . . . "Albie Marx? Fancy meeting you here."

Standing over me is that redhead, the English girlfriend of Linda's, what's her name . . . ?

"Lesley Wentworth," she says, answering my thought.

"Of course. Linda's friend." Where did I run into this woman recently?

"LeDome," she reminds me, scoping my puzzled expression.

"Yes, that's right." The night I saw Mariah with Newt. Or thought I did. Why do I keep meeting this Lesley in bars? Retrieving my manners, I say, "This is my associate, John Shrike."

Shrike looks at her like she's the type of buffet where you load up your plate so high it takes two people to carry it.

"Charmed, I'm sure." She obviously isn't.

"What brings you to this part of the ocean?" I ask. "Vacationing?" Probably man-hunting. Tired of Club Med.

"I suppose I just needed some breathing space," she answers weakly. "Life has been a bit bumpy lately . . ." She's trying to hold back some tears. I think she cried last time we met. This is some weepy woman.

"Can we buy you a drink?" I ask, trying to act like a caring human being.

"Thank you," she sighs, and sits herself down at the table.

"Are you here by yourself?" Shrike asks, with all the detachment of a man who would fuck a woodpile if he thought there was a snake in it. This from someone who's about to get married.

I buy her a drink and we sit around and chat about the people on the cruise and the vastness of the ocean and pretty soon it becomes apparent to both me and Shrike that she'd like to talk to me alone, about things she and I have in common, like our relationship with Linda, to be exact.

Shrike reluctantly takes his leave, but not before mentioning the number of his room in an attempt to find out the number of hers.

Lesley asks if I feel like going for a stroll on the upper deck. I sign for the tab and we head out of the lounge.

That guy with bushy hair and eyebrows, whom I saw a few days back, is playing the slots again, his face turned away from me. Why does he keep registering *familiar?* Relax, Albie. He's just your old friend, Paranoia.

Outside, the sky is a wagon wheel full of stars, enough stars to make me dizzy, shining and blinking and spinning around in my eyes. It's late enough at night and most people are so tired from their big day in Jamaica that the upper deck is eerily deserted. The big liner slips through the sea as if through a hole in time and space—nothing exists but Lesley and me, the foam in our wake and the reflection of the heavens on our faces.

In days gone by, I'd take her right here. I'd enter her from behind as we looked out from the railing, whisper in her ear cosmic truths about the infinite nature of our desires and fuck her as slowly and sensually as the moon moves across the sky.

As a man in love, I stifle my loins.

"I read something in the newspaper that truly disgusted me," are the first words out of her mouth, and her tone is anything but weepy.

"Welcome to the nineties," I say, echoing Shrike.

She reaches into the pocket of her light blue blazer and takes out a folded article from the front page of the *Los Angeles Times.* She hands it to me and I don't have to read it—Shrike showed it to me the first night.

ALBIE MARX, 60's RADICAL, NEW WAVE JOURNALIST,
CHARGED WITH MURDER

The photograph is an old one, taken at a '67 press conference, when certain passages in *Roger Wellington Rat* were supposed to have incited blacks to a wave of rioting and looting in ghettos across the country. I never meant it to happen but I was sure glad it did. The horrible oppression of the blacks can never get enough attention. The sad part is, it didn't do any good. Things have just gotten worse.

"Doesn't it make you nervous," I ask, "being out here alone with a murderer?"

"Linda loved you, Albie, I'm certain she did. Why did you do it?"

I stop walking and stick my face in hers, glaring down into her core. "Where the fuck do you get off coming on like this? You're butting your nose into business that can only hurt you. What's your stake? Are you an aspiring journalist? How did you find me? Who the fuck else knows I'm here?"

My answer comes hurtling at me from the shadows. A figure in a frenzy of motion, intent upon one thing only—to hurl me into the smothering arms of the black night sea.

He grabs a handful of my clothing and, with the element of surprise, lifts me over the railing and attempts to dump me into the brine. So frenzied is my attacker that he's making sounds in his throat like a dog, a rabid little terrier, which has made up its mind to have the bone in the St. Bernard's mouth or die trying. The force of his animal thoughts give him animal strength, he's crammed to the skin of his teeth with rage and pure, unadulterated, primal fear.

These images flash on my screen instantaneously and disappear even before I can raise my hands to defend myself. He's pushing me, his feet digging into the deck, the railing, the life preserver, anything to get the traction to give him the leverage to snuff out my life—in the prime of my manhood yet, I think, as I fantasize a world without me.

Who would care if I died? My parents in San Diego, I guess. My sister in New York. They'd care because it's what you do when a son or a brother dies, not because of who I am or what I've become. Would anybody who really knows me be affected by my death, for more than a passing day? Does it make any difference? Would anyone's life be *diminished* by the fact of my death? Mariah? My soul tells me no. Shrike? He'd turn it into a conversation piece at The Rock. My son? He'd turn down the film rights. Tank? Look at the way he betrayed me with Mariah.

So who does that leave? Danno? Of course. He's the only one who would be devastated by my drowning at sea—it would rob him of watching me turn purple in the gas chamber.

Meanwhile, I have to stop thinking because this maniac has just about got me over the side. I'm grabbing on to anything I can but the force of surprise is in his corner, has irreversibly tipped the scales from his opening rush.

He's kicking, punching, pushing, scrambling, grunting—I can even see him foaming at the mouth—and I'm literally hanging on for dear life, my feet flailing high over the yawning ocean—when God intervenes.

Praise the Lord. Praise You, Lord.

My attacker's hands are suddenly ripped from my face, my neck, my chest. Eyes glowing with rage, he's lifted by an unseen force off his feet, spun around and slammed into a wall.

Clinging to the railing and gasping for breath, I think I'm watching a scene from *The Exorcist,* when my eyes finally pierce the shadows and tell me it's a man, a large man with a huge head of taut pink skin, gleaming in the starlight like the twinkle in an angel's eye, who has, at the last possible second, plucked a fresh morsel, *me,* from the hungry jaws of the sea.

Thank You for the Bald Demon, God, thank You for Lieutenant Joseph Danno, with his fake bushy eyebrows all comically askew but still clinging to his forehead, and his fuzzy toupee flopping around like a wounded critter on the deck under his feet. No matter what he does from here on in, no matter the reason, he has saved my life. I will judge You no more—Father knows best.

Astonished by the sight of Harry Ballister and Lieutenant Joseph Danno brawling under the lifeboats—over yours truly—I can only wonder in awe at how we all wound up on this ship together.

"He tried to kill me!" Harry screams as Danno twists his arm behind his back. "He jumped me in the dark! Who the hell are you?"

Danno pulls him out of the shadows into the starlight as I get both feet planted firmly on deck.

"He tried to shove me overboard!" I shout, in the ludicrous hope Danno will believe me. "Lesley is my witness . . ." But as I peer into the shadows, expecting to find her cowering from the violence, I realize the bitch has vanished. She must have been in on this.

"You can let me go," Harry says, regaining his composure. Danno releases him and turns his attention to me.

"You're under arrest for the murder of Linda Selby," he

announces, the fake eyebrows bouncing up and down crookedly. "You have the right to consult an attorney—"

"Hold it, Jack. We're in international waters, you have no jurisdiction here." At least I learned that much from Gruntman.

"Don't bust my balls, Albie," he says, but I know that he knows I'm right—he can't do shit to me here.

"I don't know how you got here Lieutenant, but I'm glad you did. This is the man who murdered Linda Selby—for the same reason he tried to kill me just now—he's up to his ears in a government scandal—"

"He's out of his mind!" Harry wails. "I was standing alone at the rail and he jumped me! I was protecting myself!"

"Don't blow your cool, Harry," I warn. "I know all about NICE."

"About *what?*" he asks, playing dumb.

"John Thomas. Felix St. John. *NICE*, Harry. I know the whole story." This, I imagine, will put him away.

"He's crazy," he says to Danno.

Danno gives me a look that would wilt a cactus, then turns back to Harry. "Who are you?"

"Harry Ballister. City Councilman from Los Angeles, California. I'm going to file charges against this man for assault and attempted murder. Who are you?"

"The guy you call when you want to file charges. Lieutenant Danno, Los Angeles Police."

"What a coincidence," Harry says in his oiliest public voice. "Pleased to meet you, Lieutenant. Good thing you showed up when you did."

"Wherever *he* is, I'll show up," Danno says, nodding in my direction. "You say he jumped you?"

"For no reason at all."

I want to bust Harry in the face so bad, but I have to keep my head. "This guy is a political sleazebag, Lieutenant. He's involved in a drug deal that goes all the way up to the President of the United States."

Harry looks at me in utter stupefaction. "You really have lost it," he says.

"Let me tell you something, Albie," Danno barks, his forefinger jabbing at my face. "You're out of line. You've been out of line from the day you were born. I've put up with your stupid antics for twenty years.

"You're right, I can't book you here. Not yet, but I'm working on it. First degree murder, that's a big one. You think you're safe now? You don't think the D.A. is working on the company who runs this overblown sailboat? Your ass is grass, mister. You won't take a leak without seeing me. I'll be in your face every time you breathe. Enjoy the cruise, pal. It's the last freedom you'll ever get."

Then, back to Harry, "You can swear out a complaint to me, Councilman. Although I don't know what we can do to him after the gas chamber."

After the gas chamber. Sometimes I pray there's such a thing as good karma. When a nice guy finishes dead he'll have something to look forward to. He'll come back as a religious leader instead of a Nazi—well, maybe those are too close. How about a movie star instead of a warthog? At least there'd be *some* reward.

But karma's a game in a whole other sport, a sport everyone bets on but no one ever wins. I'd better concentrate on the game I know—and take it one play at a time.

When I get back to the cabin Mariah is still up. She can't sleep. Too many things on her mind. Too many fires to put out. I recount my ordeal on the deck.

"I have to give Harry credit," I admit. "He didn't blink when I brought up NICE. Fucking politicians are better actors than actors."

"Unless Newt's right and Harry really doesn't have anything to do with NICE."

"That's the question which has to be answered, once and for all." Brilliant deduction, Albie. "And I know who has the answer—Lesley. She set me up for Harry. She knows what's going down. Lesley owes me some fucking answers and I intend to collect."

Albie Marx, Enforcer.

The next morning I start prowling the ship in search of Lesley, from deck to deck, lounge to lounge, restaurant to restaurant—she can't stay in her room forever.

As I'm doing this, that maniac Danno is behind me, everywhere I go. Sneaking around corners, ducking behind potted plants, running up and down stairways to beat the elevators—I don't know why he bothers to keep up the act—he must know that I know that he's there. At least he doesn't slow me down.

Night falls and I finally strike pay dirt. I'm in the Topsiders Lounge, an upholstered, glass-domed piano bar overlooking the pool. Lesley and Harry are snuggled into a deep, private corner but I find an angle where I can watch them without being seen.

The piano man is a silver-haired WASP, playing "(I Can't Get No) Satisfaction," and crooning it like a Broadway show tune, jazzing it up with little ad-libs. These fuckers have no shame. Makes you wonder who's going to be singing rap songs thirty years from now—Tipper Gore and the Daughters of the American Revolution.

A woman in an evening gown with hair like Marge Simpson walks over and drops a bill in the piano man's tip glass. The son-of-a-bitch doesn't miss a beat, just keeps on croon-

ing—"*I just got some—thank you ma'am—satisfaction, yes I
did, I said, I just got some satisfaction . . .*"

I'd go over and throw up on his keys but my moment
suddenly arrives—Lesley gets up from the table and consults
a waiter, apparently asking directions to the ladies' room. As
he points it out to her, I'm on my way.

I reach the door just as she does and I pull her aside. "You
owe me an explanation."

"I don't talk to murderers," she spits, trying to yank her
arm away.

"Don't fuck with me. I didn't kill Linda."

"She was my best friend."

"You know damn well I didn't do it."

"How do I know?"

"Because your friend Harry killed her."

"Harry? Harry couldn't kill anything."

"He tried to kill me!"

"But he didn't, did he?"

"Because he's inept."

"You're desperate, that's why you're trying to blame
Harry."

I tighten my grip on her arm—Jesus this bitch is built.
"Tell me, goddamn it! Why did he try to kill me?"

Grimacing but defiant, she demands, "Why should I tell
you anything?"

"Because. I'm an innocent man being framed for a murder
I didn't commit. Is that a good enough reason? Tell me why
Harry's so bent on getting rid of me."

"You have no idea?"

"He's afraid I'll expose his involvement in the conspiracy,
right?" She looks away. So that's it. "Harry's heading for
Libertad and the salvia fields, isn't he? Just like the rest of us."

"Libertad? Salvia? What on earth are you talking about?" She flashes that phony bewildered expression.

"Come on, Lesley, give up the dumb redhead act."

"I beg your pardon, how dare you speak to me like that? Harry has every right to protect himself from people like you. Blackmailers. How would *you* feel if someone threatened to destroy *your* career?"

"Who fucking threatened him? Shit, he's just a tiny fish in a great big pond."

"People are sensitive about toxic waste."

"Toxic waste?"

"He knows what you're capable of doing with that file."

"What does toxic waste have to do with NICE?"

Losing her patience, she blurts out, "None of this would have happened if I hadn't given that bloody file to Linda!"

"What file?"

"You know perfectly well, damn it!"

Something is wrong. *Newt* gave Linda the file. There's a weird mixup here.

"Let me go!" she demands. "Poor Linda, what a horrible life . . . such terrible luck with lovers. You, Harry, that other jealous maniac . . . "

"Who?"

"It doesn't matter. Let me go."

"What jealous maniac? What lover? Who?"

"Let me go or I'll scream!"

I let go of her arm and she lunges into the ladies' room, all teary and weepy again. Shit. Who the fuck was she talking about? Nat Bostwick? Was Linda having an affair with Nat Bostwick?

I look around and, surprise of surprises, Danno's standing by the piano bar, tapping his fingers to the piano man crooning Led Zeppelin's "Stairway to Heaven" and watching the scene I just played out with Lesley. I feel like I'm caught in a whirlpool, being sucked down and down and down.

When I repeat Lesley's statement to Mariah, about the mysterious jealous lover Linda supposedly had, she doesn't look surprised enough.

"What do you know about it?" I ask. "Did she have another lover?"

Her silence is ear-splitting.

"Did you know she had another lover?" I demand.

"Does it make any difference now?"

"You're damn right it makes a difference now! I want you to tell me everything you fucking know and exactly when you fucking knew it!"

"I know there was someone."

"*Someone?* A jealous lover of a murdered woman is *someone* to you?"

"I don't buy the jealousy part," she answers. "Lesley made that up."

"Linda had another lover? It wasn't Harry Ballister."

"No, he was ages ago."

"This is mind boggling. How could you not have told me?"

"It happened before you two met. It was something she was deeply ashamed of."

"Ashamed? What was it, a German shepherd? If she was so fucking ashamed, why the hell did she tell you?"

"She didn't. The other person told me first. Then when I asked Linda about it she made me promise never to tell you."

"Even if it could save my life?" I ask in disbelief. "Since when are *your* promises sacred?"

"If I thought it had something to do with her murder, if I

thought it would get you off the hook, don't you think I'd have told you by now? Please. Give me some credit."

"I'll give you credit—for being a moron. A jealous lover running around loose and I'm searching the world for *motivation*. Who the hell was it?"

"Don't make me break my last promise to my mother."

"Was it Nat Bostwick? She told me she never slept with that fool." She doesn't respond. "If you weren't a karate bitch I'd beat it out of you. Who the hell was it?"

"You won't let it rest, will you?"

"Never! Not even after I'm dead! Now who was this fucking lover?" I demand, on the verge of violence.

"Sally Keester," she finally answers, quietly.

I'm stunned. "Don't bullshit me," I warn. But her answer has the ring of truth. And now I recall, when I dropped her at Linda's to get her things, that she and Sally were in there together while I was waiting in the car.

"It was something that happened. They were both lonely. They were friends. Neither ever had an affair with a woman before. They tried it. It was good for a while, then it stopped working. My mother met you and they agreed it was over."

"I can't picture it. I don't want to picture it. Linda and Sally . . . ?"

"Sally was more upset about breaking up than my mother was, it nearly drove her crazy. But she said she got over it. She loved my mother. She wanted her to be happy. She was devastated when my mother was murdered."

"Who was she jealous of? Me? If she was jealous of me, isn't it *possible* she killed Linda and did everything she could to make Danno think it was me?"

"Linda killed by a jealous dyke? Please, Albie, you can do better than that. It's much too convenient."

"She's big enough, she's strong enough—and she had the *motivation*."

"I don't buy it."

"You're saying it's impossible?"

"Nothing's impossible. But do you really want to go back now, under arrest, and try to prove something you can't prove? Or do you want to go forward and follow through with our plan, the only real plan we've got?"

Her question is rhetorical. I have no choice. Lesbian jealousy does not necessarily equal murder. *Lesbian.* Linda. God, what else is new? Any surprises left? Here I am, God. Keep 'em comin'.

Over the cabin speaker comes the announcement that we dock in Grand Cayman in an hour. How the hell are we going to lose Danno?

"Look at this," Mariah says, handing me a guidebook on Grand Cayman Island.

She points to a paragraph in the book and I rummage around for my drugstore-special reading glasses. I hate that I'm getting old, I hate that I can't read a book anymore.

Jamming the oversized, fake tortoiseshell glasses onto my face, I read, "Don't miss the 50 foot Atlantis Submarine, which goes down 130 feet for a close-up view of tropical fish, Cayman turtles, sponges, coral and undersea cliffs. The sub leaves from George Town Harbor."

The light bulb goes on in my head. "Our ticket to Libertad?"

"For the right price."

Who has enough money, I wonder, to charter a sub? Then I think of Oonie. Oooh, Oonie of the Japanese billions. Good old Shrike, he never lets me down.

"I'm going up to the health club," I tell her. "Get Shrike and Oonie and be ready to split when we dock."

I take a little rubber turtle that says "Greetings from the

Jamaican Queen" on its shell, a souvenir I bought in the cheapo gift shop this morning, and put it in my pocket. At the door I take Mariah in my arms and we kiss like it's the last time ever. I take the elevator up two floors to the Caribe Deck, which houses the Sunburst Dining Room and the pool and health spa. I don't see Danno but I know he's behind me.

In the health spa I strip down, take a towel and my rubber turtle and go into the steam room. I love steam rooms, they enfold and relax me while the heavy gray mist provides mystery and illusion. I like to think in steam rooms, think about stories I'm working on, work out the details as great drops of sweat roll off my body and splash on the tile. Go out, take an ice cold shower and then come back in. I can spend hours going in and out of steam rooms, the hotter the better.

I dial the steam up to its highest level and hope the bait works. Pretty soon the door opens and in swaggers Dick Tracy, his great bald dome gleaming in the steamy light. He peers into the mist and, seeing me, grunts satisfaction and sits at the opposite end of the tile bench. It's hotter than blazes but he acts like it doesn't mean shit to him. He unbuttons the top button of his shirt. He's not only determined to follow me to hell and back, he'll out-macho me all the way.

After a while I stand, leave the room and step under a cold shower. Danno comes out after me and watches. Soon as I'm cooled off, I head back into the steam, the old bald eagle predictably glued to my footsteps.

I get real hot this time, then get up and go out for another rush of ice water. Simple Simon does the same. He's got to be wondering how long I'll keep doing this.

He follows me back into the steam room and the moment he sits I stand again and walk out, quickly turning to wedge the rubber turtle under the door and testing to see that it can't be opened by any amount of pushing or pulling. Quickly I grab my clothes and, wrapped in my towel, run like hell out of there, tee-heeing all the way like some kid who just pulled the all-time classic joke on the school principal.

I suddenly feel a slight fear that he'll die in the steam room. That would be a mistake. Hell, he won't die. Most likely someone will hear him pounding on the door or he'll break the glass. By that time we'll be history. Gone. Vanished.

Libertad, mysterious jewel of the Caribbean, we rush to your shores with our dreams of freedom.

CHAPTER 21

Harry looked over at Lesley, napping fitfully in her bunk and his mind raced on. What was Marx raving about out there on the deck that night? Of exactly what was Harry being accused? Some nonsense about a drug deal and the President of the United States? Marx was a raving alcoholic, that was a well-known fact—but had he finally lost his mind?

Drug deal? Harry was confounded. What in the world made Marx think he was involved in a drug deal? He'd never sold drugs in his life. There's a place where a man draws the line.

But Marx was so sure of himself. He really thought he had something on Harry. And he never once mentioned Waste Disposal.

Harry's head went around so fast it literally made him dizzy. He held onto his bunk and concentrated his gaze on the top bolt in the porthole. Center. Focus. Reality.

"Nice," Marx had said. "I know about *nice.*" What was that supposed to mean? Nice. Marx wasn't calling him nice. Nice going? Harry couldn't figure it out.

Poor Lesley. What she put up with was astonishing. The

Brits. They lived through the Blitzkreig, they can live through anything. He liked Lesley. He liked her more than ever. She believed in him, even knowing his darker side.

Maybe he should marry her. Of course, he'd get her to sign a prenuptial agreement. Not only a financial agreement but one that stipulated she could never discuss his business with anyone. Could he hold her to that? Maybe.

Marrying Lesley wasn't a half-bad idea, even though she slept with her mouth open. He'd been thinking of running for mayor and he needed a woman at his side. Lesley had the sophistication for the job, she would impress potential contributors. And she looked good, that's always a plus—good-looking women attract money.

But marriage? Day in and day out with Lesley? He didn't know about that. She had moods and could be mercurial. She could be overbearing. She's the type who would try to take charge. What the hell, let her take charge every once in a while—let her organize a picnic to the Hollywood Bowl, that's something she can take charge of. Let her decorate the mayor's residence, she can take charge of that, too.

She'd have to cut back on her jealousy, though. He'd known guys whose wives were so bad they made them stop reading *Playboy*. He wouldn't put up with that. In his business, *charm* was the primary currency and he'd charm whoever he had to, man or woman, to get what he needed. He couldn't have Lesley throwing fits over his relationships with women. That's how he got into this fix in the first place.

Lesley's breathing got louder, like a dry gargle. Maybe she could get plastic surgery to free up her nose for breathing. And while she was in she could get an uplift on her tits and whatever else needed fixing. Luckily, with her obsessive working out at the gym, there wasn't that much work to do, the surgeon's bill wouldn't be astronomical.

He just had to settle this Albie Marx affair one way or the

other. That police lieutenant, the bald-headed clown, had jammed up his plans real good. No way he could knock Albie off now, he'd be booked in a minute. He had to go to Plan B, make some kind of deal with Marx, cop to *some* of the Waste Disposal sins, but turn it around so that other people looked guiltier than him, like his fellow council members who voted for the toxic landfill and championed Waste Disposal for the contract.

He didn't know which, if any, of them took money from Waste Disposal but if he could make Marx think they all did, he could minimize his own exposure. That way he'd just be one of a less than ethical group of city councilmen. Who'd care about that? Soft ethics never ruined anyone's career.

So that was it. Revolting as it was, he would have to bargain with Albie Marx.

Lieutenant Joseph Danno realized a second too late that he'd been suckered by an amateur.

Albie Marx had jammed the glass door shut so tight that, though Danno leaned and pushed on it with all his considerable muscle, he couldn't get it to budge. Cursing himself like a sailor, he pounded and rattled the door and shouted in his official police voice—but nobody came. The billowing steam was building fast. He stripped down to his underwear, shoes and socks, but it didn't help—movement was becoming burningly painful.

He wouldn't confess it to anyone but himself but maybe this obsession with Albie Marx had taken him one step too far. Until the moment on deck the other night, when he saved Marx's life for his own private satisfaction, he'd been 100 percent certain that Marx had killed Linda Selby, in much the same way that Danno believed he'd killed Janis Joplin, twenty years before.

But something, some worm of doubt, had wriggled into his brain when he witnessed with his own eyes Harry Ballister's unprovoked attempt to throw Marx overboard. Why did Ballister try to kill Marx? What did Albie Marx have on the councilman that drove him to attempted homocide? Some drug deal involving the President of the United States? Ridiculous. Typical Albie Marx left-wing conspiracy rhetoric. And Ballister was convincingly astonished at the ludicrous accusation.

He had to have some other reason for his attack on Marx. Whatever it was, Danno's long years of experience with homocides and the people surrounding them whispered that things were not as pat as he wished them to be. Something was rotten but he didn't yet know where the stink came from. One thing he did know—if he stayed close to Marx, the stinker would never be too far away.

But he had to get out of here before he passed out from the heat. There was nothing to do except shatter the glass. What could he use? There was no instrument in the bare tiled room, nothing sharp or heavy with which to do the job, nothing but his fist. If he put his fist through the door he would probably wind up taking stitches all the way up his arm. Not a pretty picture.

Then there was always his head. If he gave the heavy glass a sharp butt with his head, a blunt instrument which, over the course of his long career had been exposed to all manner of violence and fury and had withstood assaults of amazing ferocities, he might just cause the thick glass to crack. With some strategic pounding and punching he could finish the job. Then he would finish Marx.

Lining up an angle where the boniest ridge of his forehead would strike the glass full on, he took a deep breath, pulled all his forces into himself, then reared back and struck with a blow that would knock out a heavyweight fighter. The glass

cracked just as he hoped but it didn't do Danno any good. He
crumpled like a sack of potatoes onto the hot wet tile floor,
his consciousness playing a game of hide-and-seek with the
flickering light show of images projected by his unconscious
mind . . .

He saw Sonny and Bruno, his boys, waving from the distant hole of an endless tunnel . . . he felt their youth, their
vitality, their red-blooded American exuberance . . . he loved
them so much . . . he wanted to talk to them, be the father he'd
never been, tell them about good and evil, women and sex,
humanity and garbage . . .

Then the tunnel suddenly dissolved into the gaping blackness of Patsy's mouth, growing blacker and wider and big
enough to swallow the Chrysler Building and suddenly he was
being pulled in, like a fish in a school, being sucked turning
and tumbling into the great nagging mouth along with the
tables and chairs and appliances . . .

And in the blackness of that vast void he then saw himself in a great rolling mirror, with hair, real hair, thick, luxurious black hair, washing it, tousling it, pomading it . . .
and a suit, an Italian suit and a silk tie too, with loafers
with tassles, with money in his pockets and dark, handsome mystery in his eyes . . .

And the mirror with his reflection flew off into the void and
was gone.

Then—the horrific image of Albie Marx sprung up full
blown before him, towering over him, one thousand feet tall,
in skyscraper boots and great, billowing blue jeans . . . with a
beer bottle big as a man and a penis the size of a dirigible
. . . aiming a torrent of urine down onto his head and laughing
a hyena's mocking laugh as Danno gasps and sputters, drowning in the yellow deluge of Marx's scorn . . .

And then there's just blackness and the need to sleep
. . . and a faraway sound of breaking glass . . .

"Shit, Frank, some bald guy passed out on the floor in here! Give me a hand!"

Walter Bates put his ear to the door. He thought he heard someone try the knob and waited until he was sure they were gone. He listened at the door a moment longer, then went back to the sink and looked again in the mirror. "You are *mean*," he hissed at himself, "you are *hard*," and he tightened the grip of his thumb and fingertips on the stubby but steel-hard protuberance at the mouth of his open fly and began pumping again, slow and hard, leaning over the sink and looking himself in the eye and telling himself he was the toughest son-of-a-bitch on the White House staff.

A sharp knock on the door. "Mr. Bates, your private line is beeping."

He clenched his teeth to fight back the swelling tide of self-adulation and answered in a clipped, businesslike voice, "Be right there."

He looked back in the mirror. Should he go for it? Could he bring it off in a few quick seconds? He was intrigued by the challenge but things were coming down to the wire and he couldn't afford to miss this call. He stuffed himself back into his trousers, adjusted the new black patch over his squirming right eye and hurried to the phone. It was J.T.

"What took you so long?"

"I was at the shredder." The lie felt good, natural. J.T. would buy it.

"I'm having a problem escalating the rhetoric. The natives agreed to give up the land for the base."

"They *agreed*?"

"They panicked. Thought we were going to attack. Backed down, said, 'Fuck the Japs, you take the land.' "

"You can't let that happen, J.T. We'd have no reason to go

in, we'd be twisting in the wind, we'd be . . . there'd be nothing to fight about."

"I'm telling you, Walter, it's not easy to start a war."

"Let's just go in—a preemptive strike. The public likes preemptive strikes, there'd be minimum blowback . . ."

"That's a last resort. First we'll make new demands. Things they can't possibly give us—without risking outright revolt."

"Will it work?"

"You just sit tight and keep your finger on that button."

"I'm here, J.T. I'm a rock."

And that was that. Could it happen? Could the Libertad government bend over so far that Cale and J.T. would be unable to justify an invasion? And even if the Libertadians held firm, there was still the matter of Newt, Marx and the girl. Marx and the girl had escaped from the train and were probably trying to get to the island with Newt at this very moment. Walter had three teams after them but they were still on the loose. Could they kick up a storm in the media? Could they screw everything up? Could the whole operation go up in smoke?

Walter couldn't allow that to happen, he just couldn't. If he had to, he'd give the go-ahead without J.T.'s authorization. That would provide J.T. and the President the safeguard of plausible deniability in the face of the inevitable congressional wrath that would follow. Poindexter, North and Reagan got away with it, why couldn't Bates, J.T. and Cale? If Walter was man enough, the button was his to push.

As he headed back to the john, Walter had no doubts. He intended to be man enough.

CHAPTER 22

The Jamaica Queen docked in George Town and we barreled down the gangplank like thieves, Mariah, Shrike, Oonie and me, praying that Danno was still cleaning his pores in the steam room.

George Town, the capital of Grand Cayman, heavily geared to the tourist trade, was surprisingly quiet and it worked to our advantage. Because of the Libertad crisis, tourism had bottomed out and the captain of the Atlantis Submarine was willing to hear our proposal, which involved a check from Oonie in the amount of ten thousand dollars. As luck would have it, Grand Cayman, once headquarters for BCCI, is a money-laundering wonderland, with zero taxes. Posters pasted all over the tiny tropical island feature the president and his enticing pledge: READ MY PALM TREES—NO TAXES. With banks stacked on every block, the process of verifying foreign funds was not a problem—a few punches of the computer keys and we were in business.

Once the money officially changed hands, we were on call. The captain would make his normal dives for the tourists during the day and then refuel at night for the run to Libertad, a hundred miles to the southwest.

I called to report in to Gruntman.

"Locked in a steam room?" he winced, when I described my dance with Danno.

"He's a big guy, he can take it," I said, disguising my creeping remorse with a shit-can of bravado.

"What if he doesn't get out?" he asks, asking the unaskable.

"That's not my problem. What I need to know is, what if he *does?*"

"And he catches up to you in Grand Cayman or Libertad? Say good-bye to your freedom. We have extradition treaties with both of those islands."

So that was it—if Danno caught me, he could keep me. Gruntman would continue to work on ferreting out their case against me. I would continue to fatten the price on my head by remaining a fugitive from justice.

We laid low in the storage room behind the submarine captain's office until it was time to set sail—or, as they say in the submarine game, "shove under." The captain was aware that U.S. Navy ships were ensconced around the perimeter of Libertad, but was familiar enough with the shoreline and little-known trade inlets not to be intimidated—he knew exactly what route to take and where to let us off.

The submarine trip at night, 130 feet underwater, illuminated most of the way by the sub's floodlights, was truly spectacular. Grand Cayman Island is actually the top of a mountain submerged in the ocean. The deeper you dive, the more massive the undersea cliffs and formations of coral, the more you are awed by the fathomless depth of the ocean and overwhelmed by the fathomless depth of your own insignificance.

And then there was the undersea life of the night, every creature that could swim, squiggle, dart or glide, stepping out

NICE GUYS FINISH DEAD 295

in the spotlights in all their finery, a Walt Disney version of the Grand Opera Ball. Of course, thinking of Disney made me think of my son and wonder if I'd ever lay eyes on him again, assuming we were able to work out that lunch date.

At the end of the trip the captain provided us with a rubber lifeboat to paddle ashore in—for an additional $1,500. We complained, but what could we do? When we saw how far out he was dropping us, Oonie coughed up the extra dough. Is there nowhere you can go anymore where a rip-off is frowned upon?

In the silent moonlight, we paddled our rubber boat to shore, while the lights of a Navy battleship twinkled in the distance. Mariah had a map of the island and the captain had pointed out where we would come ashore. We wanted to get to the capital, San Nicolas. Felix had given Mariah the name of a place where we could make contact with someone who would take us to Ahmet Ludi.

Tiny Libertad has one main ring road that circles the perimeter of the island, upon which the two or three major population clusters are settled. According to our map, San Nicolas is about ten miles northeast.

"How do we get there?" Oonie asks.

"How do you think?" Shrike answers tightly. "Walk." He's been short tempered with her since we left the ship.

"I'm not walking ten miles," she says, as if that's all there is to it.

"Then get us a limo."

"I got us a submarine," she challenges.

"Albie got us a submarine. You signed a check."

"You really expect me to walk ten miles, John?"

"We'll walk. You call a limo."

"I would if I had my cellular phone," she pouts.

"Come on you guys," Mariah soothes. "It's a beautiful morning. We'll be there before you know it."

"You would have walked ten miles for that cabin steward," Shrike taunts.

"Oh, please."

"Your eyes were glued to his butt every time he came in."

"Can you believe this?" she asks Mariah and me.

"You ordered enough tea to float an elephant bladder."

"Listen to you. The Drooling Cowboy. I need a mop and a bucket when you get near a big pair of tits."

"Excuse me," I interrupt, before they get going full swing. "We're gonna start walking. We'll see you at the wedding." I take Mariah's hand and we start down the road to San Nicolas.

"Come on, John, be nice," I hear Oonie say softly to Shrike. I glance back as he reluctantly takes her hand and they follow along behind us.

The island doesn't look like a typical Caribbean paradise. In the full moonlight we can see that it isn't lush like Jamaica and doesn't have endless white beaches like Anguilla or great fields of sugarcane like Barbados. It was settled by fishermen and farmers and that's how it looks—planted fields terraced among rocky hillsides that tumble down to the shore where fishing boats dot the shoreline awaiting the families that have piloted them for generations.

We stop a few times to snack on the crackers and water we bought from the captain and comment on the simple beauty of the topography. One great mountain stands above everything, with a translucent white cloud hooked onto its peak like a halo. I'd bet anything that that's where we'll find Ahmet Ludi.

The sun is just rising when we get to San Nicolas, a small, provincial, seaside town that's a Jekyll and Hyde of antiquity and progress. Several huge steel and glass buildings stand self-consciously in the midst of centuries-old whitewashed adobe and stucco houses. A handsome wide palm-lined boulevard, all spanking new, which traverses the quarter-mile center of town, is really no more than a lonely axis for an intricate web of ancient cobblestone streets and alleys that strip away the illusions of modern prosperity and bespeak centuries of simple, unpretentious existence.

Even at this hour, because of the high political tension, armed soldiers and army vehicles patrol the streets. They're beautiful-looking people, brown skinned, light eyed and handsome but so intent on the threat to their island that this morning they give off nothing so much as tight-lipped anticipation, answering in short, clipped tones when I ask directions to the restaurant Felix told Mariah to seek out. They speak English, in a dialect that's an unlikely combination of prim British and Rastafarian, mixing tenses and injecting a lot of *hey* and *mon* for punctuation.

"You goin down to de end of de street here, mon, you takin a left turn and hey, goin down four more blocks where you seein a meat market. De restaurant is right dere, mon, right across from de market."

"Thanks."

"Dey don't open till lunch."

"That's okay, we'll just kind of take in the sights till then. It's okay if we walk around town, isn't it?"

"Be careful, mon. Anythin can be happenin."

"We will," I promise, and lead my group off.

"Looks like they expect an attack," Shrike says.

"Let's hope it never comes," Mariah responds, squeezing my hand tightly.

We walk the town from top to bottom and by the time we arrive at the restaurant we're ravenously hungry. Incongruously squatting in the shadow of one of the tall new buildings, the ancient little eatery seems frozen in time, a relic from another age. Out on the patio the tile is old enough to be excavated and sold to a museum, and the bougainvillea looks like it's been growing for thousands of years.

The menu is strange and eclectic and I opt for simplicity, ordering fried bananas and pepperpot soup. Mariah experiments with codfish fritters and conch ragout and Shrike and Oonie share orders of wild pig marinated in pimento, hot peppers annd scallions and grouper Creole. We all order *mauvy,* a sweet drink made from tree bark and have, in spite of the tensions around us, a pleasant lunch.

We're just finishing up when I make the mistake of telling the old woman who's been serving us that we're looking for Ahmet Ludi. Her eyes suddenly go wide and lose all rationality. She shrieks, a piercing wail from the dawn of grief and comes after me with a shish kebab skewer. The sharp stake pierces the tabletop an inch from my hand and sticks, quivering like an arrow shot, into the wood.

Just as she's about to strike with another skewer, a young brown-skinned man appears, tall, maybe six foot six, and broad shouldered, with piercing blue eyes and short, curly blond hair. He wraps her up in his arms, taking away the lethal instrument and chanting soothing things to her in some strange tongue. Eventually she quiets down and, with downcast eyes, shuffles off, whimpering sad plaintive sounds down deep in her throat.

"Hey, mon," he says, "I am very sorry. You see, mon, my poor mom goes loony when she's hearin dat name. Please accept my apologies, mon. Hey, my name is Vitalia."

"I'm Albie Marx. This is Mariah . . . John Shrike . . . Oonie . . . "

"Felix St. John told us to come here," Mariah informs him.

"Felix," Vitalia repeats, in a tone of deep knowing and respect.

"He said someone would take us to Ahmet Ludi."

The gentle giant glances around warily at the mention of Ludi's name, then explains, "My mom, mon, she lost a son to Samadhi, my brother, Endamo. She is grievin for ten years now, hey mon."

"Samadhi?" I ask.

"Ahmet Ludi's village, mon. Hey, once dey go up dere, dey never comin back."

"Do you know how to get there?" Mariah asks.

"Yes, mon. Hey, I have been dere."

"But *you* came back?" Shrike asks skeptically. He isn't buying this.

"Ahmet Ludi, mon, he's a very powerful teacher."

"What does he teach?" Shrike asks.

"He teach Nothin, mon. Dat is how I can come an go. In reality, I do neither. Hey."

Hey. A teacher of Nothin. The most difficult concept to teach, something that gurus and holy men spend lifetimes learning, something I desperately need in my own chaotic life—a huge, healthy dose of good old, sweet, elementary Nothin.

Vitalia says he will take us to Ludi.

Oonie asks, "Do we drive there?"

"Not in de mountains, mon. Dere are no roads dere."

"Then we ride horses?" she asks.

"Does one ride a horse to Mecca, mon?" he replies.

"I've never been to Mecca and I am not riding a camel." Good old Oonie. Sure knows how to put her foot down.

"De only way to Samadhi, mon, is under de power of your own Life Force."

That just sounds like more walking to Oonie and she isn't thrilled. As for me, I'll do whatever it takes to satisfy this burgeoning curiosity about Ahmet Ludi, inscrutable world-class dropout and founding father of rock and roll. In the blink of an eye our intrepid little party, including the brooding Oonie, is following hulking Vitalia out of the city and into the mysterious mountains of enigmatic Libertad.

These Libertad mountains are quite beautiful, with their jagged limestone formations rising in counterpoint to gracious, open fields of long grass and wildflowers and great stands of nutmeg trees in full bloom. Our little expedition, now in its sixth hour, has been hiking higher and higher and still the cloud-ringed peak seems light years away. We don't have to go to the top, Vitalia tells us, although I myself would love to. Because I'm a runner, the climb has been invigorating for me. Mariah is young and strong, she can leave us all in the dust. Shrike, on the other hand, is seriously wheezing and grunting at the sun. Hiking-wise, Oonie, before she came to Libertad, had never covered more ground on foot than a couple of laps on Rodeo Drive. And they're miffed at each other again, which doesn't make it any easier.

I haven't felt this good since NICE, but this is for real and that wasn't. Mariah and I are grooving along, no fights, no arguments, no undermining suspicions. The sky is a perfect powder blue with white cotton clouds and the sun is friendly and warm and not blazing hot.

Vitalia tells us we're on the windshadow side of the mountain, and Mariah quotes from Ahmet Ludi, "The winds of Belief are blocked by the mountain. High in the Windshadow lives the Divine Salvia." A feeling of high anticipation flows through us—we're getting close.

While we rest in the shade of a nutmeg tree, Vitalia goes on ahead, promising to return. "We're almost there," I guess, biting into a sweet blade of grass.

"How did I ever get into this?" Oonie pouts, leaning against the tree trunk and rubbing her feet.

"You met me," Shrike answers, lying on his back. "The man of your dreams."

"Hah," she responds.

"Well, it was real for me."

"Oh really, John? My father's money had nothing to do with it?"

"Absolutely not," he lies.

"Would you marry me if I had nothing?"

"Would you respect me if I did?" he shoots back. "Do you want a man who wants to be poor?"

"Does this mean the wedding is off?" I ask.

Oonie and Shrike glare at each other.

"Don't make any decisions until you meet Ahmet Ludi," Mariah advises.

"We'll see," Shrike declares. "We'll see why everyone from the President of the United States to a crazy old bag in Libertad wants to wring down the curtain on Mr. Rock and Roll."

"Because he intimidates them," Mariah responds. "Obviously." She sounds defensive.

"We'll see," he repeats. "We'll just wait and see."

Shrike's point is well taken and we fall quiet, some of us listening to the sweet laughing breeze in the high grass and others to the incessant babble of thoughts in our heads.

When Vitalia finally returns he's holding a bunch of delicate, red, heart-shaped leaves on graceful green stems. "In a very short while, mon, we will be walkin through great fields of dese beautiful flowers. Hey, it's absolutely essential you ain't puttin dem anywhere near your mouth."

"What do you think, we're gonna start eating leaves?" Shrike bleats sarcastically.

"Hey, if you are touchin de plants, mon, you must not be puttin your fingers to your mouth. Dis powder,"—he runs his

finger along one of the leaves, showing a very fine powdery
veneer—"will rub off on everythin, mon. Hey, be careful,
mon, it is potent in de extreme. You do not want to be meetin
Divine Salvia without de proper introduction."

When we come to the first of the salvia fields I am awe-
struck. Stretching for hundreds of yards before us, with the
crystal blue sky for a backdrop, are billions of little red hearts
on long green stems, swaying and dancing in the nimble
breeze—the ultimate Valentine's card. And the sweet perfume
that floods my senses—more perfect than jasmine, more sul-
try than gardenia, more poetic than magnolia. I take Mariah's
hand in mine, wishing we could lie down and sleep in each
other's arms, right here, for eternity, in the embrace of the
Divine Salvia.

Vitalia senses I'm being seduced. "Hey, Albie mon, you're
gettin sucked in."

"It's so beautiful," I say, on the brink of an LSD flashback.

"If you don't keep movin, mon, hey, you'll end up like
crazy Leopole."

"Who's that?" Mariah asks.

"Leopole, he's layin himself down in de salvia field an
wakin up thinkin he died an come back as de emp'ror."

"Ridiculous," says Oonie.

"Crazy ole Leopole, mon, all he do is give orders since den.
Ever'body just laugh at him."

"An emperor? Does it affect everyone the same way?" I ask.

"Dey don't all become emp'rors, mon. One fellow become
a mouse. Just runnin aroun and squeakin all day. Without de
proper introduction, hey, salvia take you to very strange
places."

"And you never come back, right?" Shrike smirks.

"Mostly never, mon, mostly never. Much too dangerous to
be stoppin here, mon, we got to keep goin."

Suddenly, as if to underscore the point, we're reminded of

the urgency of our mission by the scream of a U.S. Navy jet, flying a low-level reconnaissance run right over our heads. Indeed, we have no time to lose.

The little village of Samadhi consists of a number of Tibetan yurts scattered around a centralized square. Yurts are round huts, made of tightly stretched skins overlaid on a framework of wooden struts. The windows and doors are flaps that can be rolled up or down and many of the yurts in Samadhi have wooden floors. Somewhere between an igloo and a thatched hut in shape, a yurt is larger, sometimes up to thirty feet in diameter.

On one side of this village square stands a most unlikely structure, a large, white, two-story plantation house, with handsome, high columns, sweeping gables, and a graceful veranda. How or why this house came to be built in this place must be quite a story.

But even more mystifying is the sight of a white-haired old gent sitting calmly on the porch, reading to a young, brown-skinned boy from a well-worn cloth volume of *A Heretic's Handbook* and puffing away on a short, fat cigar. My heart takes a giant leap forward when I realize it's Felix St. John.

The little boy's eyes are alive with interest as Felix reads:

Hey, Mon,
Who are you?
You think you know but I have news for you
Hey, my friend,
The dolphins sigh
They know you better than you or I
There's an eagle on high and he's got a better look
At the boy who's standing beside that bubbling brook
Hey, Mon,

You're in the flow
If you just listen to the water then you will know
That we're all living on a ball in the great big sky
We all need one another and you don't have to ask why
Hey, Mon,
It's time to start
To listen to the bubbles and listen to your heart
It's never too late to learn who you really are,
Can you see your face in that distant shining star?
Hey, Mon,
We're here for you
We do our daily work but we have time for you,
Listen to your heart and tell me what you hear
Is it love, is it gladness or is it fear?
Hey, Mon,
Don't be afraid
To stop and listen and do absolutely Nothing today.
Hey, Mon,
The time will come
When you'll see with your own eyes
Where we all come from—

   Felix senses our presence and looks up. He looks wonderful, with his striking green and blue eyes, smiling at us through the gentle cloud of cigar smoke.
   "Felix!" Mariah shouts, and runs up the stairs, throwing her arms around him as he gets to his feet.
   Shrike looks at me. "St. John?"
   I nod. Felix and Mariah are hugging so blissfully that all we can do is stand back and watch. When the clinch finally breaks, I greet Felix and introduce Shrike and Oonie. He gives Oonie the old up and down and decides she isn't his type. Felix promises the little boy, Juliano, that he'll finish the story later and the kid runs off.

"Where's Irmgard?" I ask, hoping for an answer that puts her continents away.

"Down in San Nicolas, at the hotel, waiting for the Big Sweep. I told her I was going out for cigars."

"When was that?" asks Mariah.

"A couple of days ago."

"Christ!" I yelp. "She'll have the whole goddamn NSB after you!"

"No, she won't," he smiles. "I left a note—if she says a word about me being gone, I'll tell the world about her father, the whole thing. Irmgard wouldn't like that, no sir, and neither would the White House. No, she'll just sit there and stew, waiting to hear from me."

"Who was her father?" Shrike inquires. "What could someone possibly be ashamed of in this day and age?"

"I didn't say she was ashamed." Felix smiles that devilish smile again, then directs our attention to the opulent white house, so incongruous in its setting.

"Irmgard's father built this beauty," he explains. "His name was Albert Menglemann."

"Albert Menglemann?" Shrike muses out loud. "The famous Nazi? The Butcher of Wiesbaden?"

"My uncle twice removed. He escaped here with two of his officers in forty-five, when Berlin fell. Two years before that, when he saw the handwriting on the wall, he sent Irmgard to live with my family in Philadelphia."

His uncle twice removed was a Nazi? What does that make Felix? A Nazi twice removed?

"He was a horrible man," Felix continues sadly. "He and his henchmen came to this place, a peaceful village where people had practiced their old-time religion for hundreds of years. He killed the priest and the leaders and pressed the people into service to build this house. After that, they became

serfs, harvesting the nutmeg and mace, which Uncle Albert
sent down to the market in San Nicolas."

"Until the Israelis caught up with him," Shrike interjects.
The magazine did a big story on that, back in the late sixties."

"That is correct. Ahmet Ludi came here after Uncle Albert
was captured."

He calls a Nazi war criminal "Uncle Albert?" I guess every
Nazi is somebody's uncle.

"Irmgard always wanted to live in this house. She'd heard
about it for years and two years ago she brought me here to
see it—but she realized it was hopeless as long as Ahmet Ludi
controlled the mountain.

"While she was snooping around the village, I found the
salvia fields. I smuggled some flowers home with us, played
with them in my lab and *voila!*—NICE. But I should never
have told Irmgard about it. She contacted certain elements—
some high-placed neo-Nazi sympathizers in the federal government—and they made a deal. She gets her house and the
mountain back—and they get the NICE."

"And Ahmet Ludi?" Mariah asks.

"They led Irmgard to believe—falsely, in my opinion—
that it was Ludi who fingered her father for the Israelis."

"I see." That answers a lot of questions. I wouldn't be
surprised if Irmgard made it a deal-point with J.T. and Bates
to eliminate Ludi, to get him off the mountain and avenge her
father. But Ludi doesn't strike me as the type who would
engage in political intrigue. Teachers of Nothin don't go
around turning in Nazis.

"Does Ahmet Ludi live here now?" Mariah asks, peering
into one of the large bay windows.

"Oh, no," Felix laughs, as if the question were absurd.
"This is for visitors, village gatherings, communal medita-
tions—Ludi lives out at the lake."

"Does he know his life is in danger?" she asks. "Does he know he's a primary target of the invasion?"

"Those things don't concern him," Felix answers.

"I will take you to him, mon," says Vitalia, "and you can tell him yourself. But, hey, I would be very surprise if he ain't knowin it already."

Shrike and Mariah and I are excited to finally meet Ahmet Ludi but Oonie is cranky and tired. She wants to take a bath and relax, and she wants Shrike to stay with her.

"Are you kidding?" he bitches. "I came all this way to meet this guy."

"You're going to go off and leave your fiancée alone?" she wails.

"But it's Ahmet Ludi—"

"It's not like you won't see him later, John. I'm sure he'll still be here when we're clean and rested."

"Who knows if he'll be here? Anything's possible in this *meshuggeneh* place." Shrike must be really weary, he's resorting to Yiddishisms.

"Maybe it's better if Mariah and I go alone," I offer. "Maybe he'll be less on his guard."

"Albie is right," asserts Felix. "You'll get to meet him at the float tonight anyway."

"*Float?* What's a *float?*" Oonie moans.

"Patience my dear, patience," Felix answers. To Mariah and me he says, "I'll see you two later," and, picking up his book, wanders off in search of young Juliano.

"Well, John," Oonie demands, "are you staying or leaving me all by myself?"

Shrike's defeated expression needs no words. I don't think he's cut out for marriage, he's not too good at this kind of give and take. Maybe it'll help him grow.

As we walk off with Vitalia we hear Shrike complaining

about the cabin steward again. I guess he doesn't want to grow. Why should he? He got this far, didn't he?

As we follow Vitalia's broad back along a narrow but well-worn path through a dense growth of tropical ferns and trees, some of them so large and vibrant in color that I feel like we're moving through a Rousseau painting, I ask, "What makes you think Ludi knows the Americans are planning to kill him?"

"Hey, mon, Ahmet Ludi he's nobody's fool. When he first come to Libertad, mon, the 'Mericans are buildin their big buildins and dere fancy boulevard, mon. People in Libertad, oh, dey are bein so excited, mon. We are goin to be just like de 'Mericans, rich an comft'ble, with a strong econ'my dat grow an grow an grow, hey, an never stop growin.

"My mother, mon, she see a future for my brother an my sister an me, a life of prosper'ty, hey, of makin lots of money, of never knowin de hardship she an my father have all dere lives.

"Hey, Libertad is goin to be somethin im*por*tant, mon, like de other islands, we will have tourists an savins and loans, an our own Gross National Produc, mon. Andrew Sinood, our new president, is bringin de 'Mericans here. De GNP is his anthem—*growth,* mon, it's all about growth. De people dey love him, he is de father of de new prosper'ty. Hey, mon, people have right to dream, right?

"But someone get hold of a book, mon, a secret book dat has no author. It talk about de heart, an de spirit, an how money an possessions an greediness, mon, dey loot de soul. Hey, dis book is suppress, it is ban, mon, but de young people, de young men an women who are suppose to lead de island into de new 'Merican age of prosper'ty, dey get hold of dis book an dey keep it alive an dey keep it circulatin.

"What you think happen, mon? Dey discover de book is wrote by a man who live on de mountain, a man who want nothin from nobody, just for de world to be livin in harmony, mon.

"So dey start comin here, mon. De best and de brightest of Libertad, dey come to see de man who write such inspirin words, who touch de chord of truth in dem, mon.

"An dey never leave. Dey stay, dey have children, dey keep passin de torch. Maybe, mon, like me, dere bodies go down below every once in a while, but dere hearts are here, mon, here on de mountain with Ahmet Ludi an Divine Salvia.

"But hey, people down dere, dey don't forgive, mon. Libertadians, dere good people, not mean, not violent. Dey don't think, if I don't like somebody I kill dem, mon. But many hope for de day Ahmet Ludi die, mon, I tell you dat straight.

"He never ask nobody to come to Samadhi, he never ask dem to stay. He live, he speak, he float. Many people want him dead, mon, he know dat. But, hey, Ahmet Ludi say, 'Here today, no such thing as tomorrow.' "

"What do you mean, he *floats?*" I ask.

"You will see, mon. Hey, you will see soon enough."

Ahmet Ludi's yurt is pitched on the shore of a small lake, nearly hidden by the dense growth around it. Vitalia tells us that this lake is the only one of its kind because it's a salt lake, fed from mineral springs below, mineral salt springs with a clean, fresh smell, no sulphur, with a temperature of exactly 93 degrees Fahrenheit.

"A salt lake," I muse. "That means you can float on it."

"And ninety-three is de skin temp'rature of de body, mon, so dere is no sensation of hot or cold."

"An outdoor sensory deprivation tank," I figure out. "Like the flotation tank in *Altered States.*"

"You got it, mon, a nat'ral flotation tank, big enough for a whole village!" He laughs for the very first time, a hearty rumble from deep in his stomach.

We wait outside the yurt while Vitalia goes in to announce

us. Standing in front of this primitive hovel in the jungle I tell
Mariah, "The man in this yurt had the world by the balls.
Millions of bucks, limos, houses, groupies—the American
Dream."

Vitalia comes back outside and motions us to go in.

"Well, here we go," she says, instinctively fluffing her short
rainbow hair.

He's sitting on the brown earthen floor wearing a ragged
old pair of pants and an even older T-shirt from a Jefferson
Airplane rock concert. He's got a small, blue earring in his left
ear and his long, gray hair flows into a braid that descends
halfway down his back. On his right forearm is an old tattoo
of a pair of dice pierced by a thunderbolt. He's about sixty
now but, except for the gray hair, looks no older than me. His
body is trim and his skin is youthful.

But the main attraction is his eyes, green as the deepest
ocean, a deep, dark green, so dark that even his pupils seem
green. I flash back on those eyes and the impression they made
when we met in the country outside of London, the feeling I
had that I could submerge myself in their fathomless depths
and come out renewed and inspired.

He smiles a greeting. "Welcome to Paradise, Albie."

Amazing. He remembers me. "It took us a while to get
here," I say. "We took a few wrong turns."

"How could they be 'wrong' if you got here?"

"I guess they weren't," I answer, seeing his point.

"I'm Mariah," she says, unsure of whether or not to extend
her hand.

He looks at her and his eyes go even greener. "Make
yourselves comfortable," he says, indicating the dirt floor.

We sit opposite him and, for no reason at all, nobody says
anything. This goes on for what seems like hours, but it's also
possible that it's only seconds. We're looking at him and he's
looking at us. No one is moving. The longer the silence and

stillness goes on, the more it seems like a massive energy is building inside this small space.

This energy, or whatever it is, is getting so intense and making me so high that my heart starts pumping a rhythm like an African drum and I feel like I'm literally about to levitate off the floor. I glance at Mariah and she's actually vibrating. Or is it my imagination? Or is this whole thing my imagination?

The energy expands and expands until it's almost unbearable and then . . . *BOOOOM!*

An ear-shattering explosion rocks the yurt to its foundation.

Mariah and I nearly jump out of our skins but Ludi doesn't blink. "Sonic boom," he says simply. "Navy jets doing low-level flyby's at supersonic speed. Puts fear into the populace."

"It sure is an icebreaker," I say.

"You can't stay here," Mariah begins. "There's a government contract on you. They'll come to Samadhi and kill you . . . " She leaves the sentence dangling because he hasn't stopped smiling. Either he doesn't believe her or he doesn't care.

"Is that why you came?" he asks.

She opens her mouth to answer but doesn't. Then she says, "Partly," like she expects him to know the other part.

"Why are you here, Albie?"

"Partly to warn you. Partly to stop certain people in the government from taking this island and using the salvia to make a drug called NICE. And partly to expose the killers of a beautiful person I loved very much—Mariah's mother."

"Linda Selby," Mariah enunciates clearly.

He absorbs this information with a gentle ripple of sadness in the vast ocean of his eyes, then asks, "Who else came with you?"

"My publisher and his fiancée."

"What do they want?"

"To do an exposé on the government's plan to invade Libertad and take control of the salvia fields—to get the story of NICE to the public before the invasion."

"I know about NICE," he says lightly. "Felix told me about it. I find it fascinating."

He plucks a red, heart-shaped leaf from a small earthen vase. "Felix takes the Divine Salvia, this holy plant that has the properties to open your heart to the reality of your true Self—and he chemically treats it to produce NICE, a potion that hides your true Self behind simple-minded euphoria.

"Two sides of the same leaf producing totally opposite effects—a perfect example of yin and yang. One is natural, one is altered by science. And the world equates science with progress. And progress with happiness.

"As if the only goal is to be happy. As if the worst fate that could befall mankind would be, as Huxley said, 'to lose faith in happiness as the Sovereign Good and take the belief that the purpose of life is somewhere beyond, some intensification and redefining of consciousness.'

"I'm all for happiness and I'm certainly into Bliss. But nothing which separates me from my own true Heart can bring me that to which I aspire."

"But how can I be *sure* I'm hearing my own true heart?" Mariah asks.

He brings the heart-shaped leaf to his nose, inhales its aroma deeply and says, "We float tonight. All riddles will be answered, all questions resolved."

Lieutenant Joseph Danno watched Harry Ballister thrash around on the ground making little short clucking sounds, like a chicken having a bad dream. This stuff *is* powerful, he thought, taking meticulous care not to brush against any of the millions of red, heart-shaped flowers that covered the hillside where Ballister had fallen.

The councilman had been having a private little spat with his girlfriend. Danno, bringing up the rear of the hiking party, happened to hear Ballister, up ahead on the steep pathway, complaining to the redhead, Lesley, " . . . and your goddamn jealousy! What did you *think* Linda would do with that kind of information?"

"I didn't think," the redhead had answered meekly. "I was incensed."

"Because I fucked my secretary? That was cause to annihilate me?"

"I didn't think she would give it to Albie Marx. She was my friend. I thought she would give it back."

"Hah!" Ballister barked sardonically, as Danno came upon them unexpectedly.

"Look, you two," he grumbled, his patience at its end. "I'm going to tell you something right here and now. I don't know what happened between you and Marx but I saw you try to kill the bastard back there on the boat."

"That's a lie—" Harry began, startled by Danno's intrusion.

Danno cut him off. "Don't give me no more shit, Ballister. I *saw* you. And you, sister, you're going to have to explain your part in this too."

"You leave her out of this—" Ballister had begun, but in the heat of his rising hostility, the councilman suddenly lost his footing, tripped over an exposed root on the path and tumbled down into this field full of what their guide, Josef, called Divine Salvia. As Lesley and Josef tried vainly to restore the stricken Ballister to his senses, Danno reflected upon how they all happened to get here.

After he was pulled from the steam room and recovered consciousness, he raced into George Town in Grand Cayman, determined to pick up the scent of Albie Marx. He was sure Marx had left the ship, or else he would never have pulled that stunt, and was frantically trying to track him down when he ran into Ballister and the redhead at the Atlantis submarine tour. The captain confirmed to Danno that he had indeed taken a party of four, including a nervous individual of Marx's description, to Libertad the previous night.

At that point Danno went straight to the Grand Caymanese authorities and invoked the *doctrine of fresh pursuit* to convince them to provide a boat to take him to Libertad. Eager to help, they checked out his credentials and supplied the boat.

At first he refused when Ballister insisted that, as an elected official of the City of Los Angeles, he be allowed to accompany Danno in pursuit of the criminal. Danno had saved Marx from Ballister once and didn't want to have to do it again.

But Ballister persisted, making the argument that Marx had attempted to murder him and he couldn't stand by and watch him escape.

Danno didn't mention at that point that he had, in fact, seen Ballister initiate the attack against Marx. But he decided it wasn't a bad idea to have all parties present when he arrested Albie. He didn't know what the beef was between them but it would all come out when they came together.

In Libertad, the political crisis was worsening and the island was bracing for an American attack. Lesley informed Danno that Marx told her he was headed for somewhere called the "salvia fields" on Libertad. Danno learned from a farmer where the salvia fields were to be found and he went to the Libertadian authorities to provide a guide for him and his party. Unlike the Caymanese who *weren't* embroiled in a hardball struggle with the U.S., the Libertadians gave him a cold reception and turned him away empty-handed.

That was when Josef came after them. Josef was a clerk in

the office they'd just left but he was also a secret devotee of one Ahmet Ludi, an American expatriate whose village of Samadhi was located in the mountains where the salvia grew. It seems that Josef, like all Ludi's disciples, had standing instructions that if someone came looking for salvia they were to be guided to Samadhi so that they could go down into the fields and fulfill their quest. Josef explained in his queer Libertadian dialect that he didn't know exactly why, but it *felt* right to take Harry, Danno and Lesley to Samadhi and he proceeded to lead them off into the mountains.

Now they had come all this way without incident only to have Ballister trip and roll into the salvia, getting it all over himself and ingesting the powerful powder in the process.

Mariah and I are walking with Vitalia back to the plantation house. Nobody has spoken and nobody needs to. I'm still feeling the buzz from the energy force I experienced in Ludi's yurt, a natural high of major proportions.

I remember Joseph Campbell saying in a lecture, "Follow your bliss," and how those words thrilled me when I heard them, even though it was later said that Campbell was an anti-Semite, a fraud and, at best, an opportunist. But the words still made sense. Follow your bliss, follow your heart. Joseph Campbell, Ahmet Ludi—people whose words inspire us to reach beyond.

I think about the mindset that exists in the world today, in America. About the fearful arrogance and small mindedness of the Supreme Court to declare the use of peyote illegal, with no exceptions, so that American Indians who have used the plant in religious ceremonies for three thousand years would be breaking our law—as if we haven't already taken enough away from them.

And the corresponding hypocrisy of the United States

Congress, declaring certain "approved" drugs to be legal, preparing the way for NICE.

And Rinpoche, saying to me, "You don't know who you are." And George Harrison singing, "Life flows on within you and without you." And Ahmet Ludi saying, "All riddles will be answered, all questions resolved."

We arrive back at the plantation house to find a bizarre situation in full bloom. Harry Ballister, of all people, is lying on a bed, eyes rolled back in his head, making little short clucking sounds like a chicken. People are clustered around the bed, staring down at poor Harry in various states of fascination—among them are Lesley, Shrike, Oonie and, the one person I hoped never to see here, Lieutenant Joseph Danno. The minute Mariah and I walk through the door he looks up and greets me with, "You're under arrest, Marx."

I realize it's useless to run. "Jesus, what happened to Harry?" I say, deflecting his charge.

"He rolled around in the salvia field," Shrike explains. "He thinks he's a chicken."

"Be quiet, damn you!" Lesley shouts wildly.

"You know about drugs, you son-of-a-bitch," Danno spits at me. "Do something for the poor bastard."

"Maybe it will wear off," I say.

"Oh, no, mon," Josef says. "If de salvia is not bein prepare exactly to formula, hey, he could be in dis state forever."

"Like a chicken the rest of his life?" Lesley explodes, on the brink of hysteria. "I refuse to accept that!"

"If it weren't for you taking illegal flight, we wouldn't be here, Marx," Danno declares. "I'm holding you responsible for Ballister's condition."

For some reason Danno looks smaller to me. Maybe he was trapped in the steam room too long and shrunk. No, he couldn't have shrunk.

"Where's Felix?" Mariah asks. "He should have an antidote."

"He's down in the basement," Shrike tells us. "Has himself a laboratory down there. He's working on some pretty far-out stuff."

"Well, bring him up here, whoever he is, and get this man some relief," Danno orders.

"There is no relief, sir," Felix announces, appearing in the doorway. "There is no antidote for pure unprepared salvia. It burns out the neuro-receptors which any antidote would have to occupy."

"Are you saying he'll stay like this forever?" Lesley shrieks. "What will become of him?"

"He could get a job in the circus," Shrike says carelessly.

"You shut up, wise guy," Danno snaps.

"We should get Ahmet Ludi," Mariah says.

"Hey, I'll go mon," Josef volunteers. He takes a last look at the victim, shakes his head sadly, then starts back to the lake.

Now Harry begins clucking more fiercely, as if the nightmare is getting worse. Lesley, out of her mind with panic, falls to her knees and takes his head in her arms, pleading poignantly, "Please, Harry! Please! It's me! It's Lesley! Can you hear me, Harry? Are you in there?"

Taking a menacing step in my direction, Danno produces a pair of handcuffs and pronounces, "You're under arrest, Marx. You have the right to remain silent—"

"Look, Lieutenant, I know you have something against me—"

"—you have the right to consult an attorney—"

"I don't know what it is and I don't care—but you have to give me some time—"

"I have to give you diddly-squat."

"You were following me on the Jamaica Queen. You saw Harry jump me, you had to."

He looks at me distastefully. "What if I did?"

"He did it because he's afraid of me. He's afraid of what I know."

"Yeah? Maybe he did it because you were beating his time with the redhead. I saw you and her in the bar together before you went out on deck. And in the piano lounge."

"There's nothing between me and Lesley. But I know who killed Linda," I bluff. "And Harry knows I know."

"I know who killed her too, pal. Hands behind your back."

"Just give me tonight," I plead. *All riddles will be answered, all questions resolved.*

"Your time's up," he says, moving closer with the cuffs.

Suddenly, like the sound of mercy on God's lips, a mountain materializes between me and this relentless arm of the law—a mountain named Vitalia.

"Hey, mon, I'm bein sorry bout dis, but we don't have none of your laws here," he states flatly, staring down at the sweat-beaded billiard ball Danno's brain lives in.

In case Danno has any doubts about Vitalia, two more jumbo Libertadians step into the room for emphasis. Danno quickly computes the odds and his conclusion appears on his face.

"What's gonna happen tonight?" he demands. "What's gonna happen to change the facts?"

"I'm going to name the murderer and you're going to know I'm telling the truth," I tell him, putting all my faith into Ahmet Ludi's promise.

"This place could explode any minute," he objects. "There's Army and Navy and Air Force all around this island. We could all get blown away."

"Harry's in no condition to leave."

"We'll lug him down like we lugged him up."

"Just tonight, Lieutenant."

"You *will* pay for this, Marx," he snarls, throwing Vitalia and his friends his ultimate look of contempt.

Will I pay? Have I not paid enough? What will this night bring for each of us?

All riddles will be answered, all questions resolved.

The call to float is sounded in the jungle, across the lake, through the fields, into the village . . . the deep, pounding drums, the big, brass horns, the throbbing bass with the delayed backbeat that makes you want to move . . . It's Wilson Pickett! Singing, shouting, pouring out that old-time rock and soul, bringing the night to its feet from giant speakers in the trees . . .

"I'm gonna wait till the midnight hour, That's when my love comes tumblin' down . . . "

The sun is gone, the earth is cool, God smears the sky with a blaze of galaxies and Ludi plays Wilson Pickett . . .

"I'm gonna wait till the stars come out, And see that twinkle in your eye . . . "

People are moving toward the lake, young people, old people, brown people, white people, fathers, mothers, children, lovers, monks . . . like moths to a flame, the crippled to Lourdes, actors to Hollyood . . . they come to the lake, walking lightly, joyfully, their hearts all aglow . . .

"I'm gonna wait till the midnight hour, That's when my love begins to shine . . . "

The record is scratchy but the music is forever . . .

"All right, play it for me one time now . . . "

And the trumpet and sax converge into the everlasting voice of soul as we reach the lake and see Ahmet Ludi standing where the water meets the shore, greeting each new arrival, shaking each new hand, smiling, laughing, letting his love flow . . .

"I'm gonna wait till the midnight hour, That's when my love begins to shine, Just you and I, Just you and I, Just you and I . . ."

Mariah and I move with the crowd toward the spot where Ahmet Ludi is seeing each floater off on their journey. Shrike and Oonie, Felix, Lesley, Danno—escorted by Josef and Vitalia—and Harry, borne on a litter, all proceed ahead of us in varying states of anticipation.

We have all been given small hollowed-out shells of nutmeg tree bark, which hang from our necks on braided salvia stems. Set into the shells are little bee's wax candles which will be lit as each floater pushes off onto the lake, the heavy salt solution of the water providing an effortless float.

The music ends and all that is left are the sounds of the night and the image of scores of people, each lit by candlelight, already afloat on the motionless surface, looking up at a cobalt canopy of space, planets and stars.

When we reach Ahmet Ludi and the jumping off point, I see that he has put out, with great love and attention to detail, a buffet of specially prepared salvia leaves, twinkling like tasty hors d'oeuvres in the heavenly light.

He asks nobody to take them. Some people do and some people don't. His affection and love for each person are always the same, whether they float with the salvia or float without it.

Shrike and Oonie are the first to reach Ludi and they elect not to take the salvia. They enter the water, Ludi lights their candles and then pushes them off toward the rest of the floaters.

Felix gives Ludi a big hug, then takes the salvia and pushes off.

Vitalia and Josef lift Harry from the litter onto the water. Ludi lights Harry's candle, places an extra-special preparation of salvia under his tongue, and pushes him off.

Lesley floats without the salvia.

Danno, refusing to lower himself to the level of this silly charade, breaks line and moves off to the side, alone, isolated, a stranger in paradise.

Mariah kisses me on the cheek, says, "I love you," then hugs Ludi, takes the salvia and floats on out.

I come face-to-face with Ludi. "All riddles will be answered, all questions resolved," he says. I connect with his eyes, take two servings of salvia, get into the water and, after Ludi lights my candle, push off on my float.

The feeling of floating is like lying on a velvet cloud. The water is neither warm nor cold, but exactly skin temperature. My head lies back, as on a pillow, and the water fills my ears so that the only sounds I hear are my thoughts and the distant beating of my heart which soon fades away into total silence.

I close my eyes and say hello to the Divine Salvia as it sweeps into my consciousness with a blinding shower of color and light.

CHAPTER 23

Lately I find myself thinking back to those days with disturbing regularity. It seems so long ago now, another lifetime. Linda's murder and Danno the cop . . . that strange island with Ahmet Ludi and Felix St. John . . .

Life has an inexplicable way of leading you around by the nose, throwing lessons in your path and daring you to learn them. How did we ever come out of that alive? It was a miracle, a fucking miracle.

God, it's three o'clock already. Mariah's picking Sean up from Toddler's Time preschool. Sean, our beautiful four-year-old boy. When I think about them, Sean and Mariah, I'm overwhelmed with gratitude for the luck I've had, the way my life has turned out, and I sit here by the pool, sipping diet Pepsi in the sun and thanking the Lord for His bountiful blessings.

When was it, five years ago already, back there in Libertad, when I thought I'd used up every drop of good fortune destiny had allotted me. But there's always hope, I found out, as long as we're willing to let go of childish fantasies and get on with the business of growing up. And if I ever have any doubts about that, I just have to look around me to put them to rest.

We bought this house the year after we got back from Libertad, the year I sold my first screenplay to Disney. The house wasn't much when we bought it, but it had good potential and it was in Benedict Canyon with a Beverly Hills address.

My son Jonathan got me a deal to write that high-concept dra-medy they needed for Goldie Hawn, and I turned out a romantic caper with more botched bank holdups, multiple car crashes and wacky helicopter chases than they'd ever before seen. They loved it. Goldie loved it. They spent 30 million bucks on the movie and it grossed 200 million. My reputation was made.

Since then it's been one script after another—a picture for Tom Cruise about the world's champion ice fisherman, a warm-hearted comedy about three five-year-olds who adopt Tom Selleck, a high-tech adaptation of *Roger Wellington Rat* for Arnold Schwarzenegger, a TV sitcom about a loveable racist and his kookie family—and a new wing on the house, a pool and cabana, a Mercedes station wagon . . . Mariah gave up government work, grew her hair long and opened a little leather store on Rodeo Drive . . . Life has been incredibly kind to us, Mariah and Sean and me.

But I can't stop from thinking, how did we get here? We were all floating on that stupid lake in Samadhi when the Marines attacked, with their tear gas, assault rifles and fire bombs. Overcome by the salvia, I literally thought I had entered Hell. There was screaming and crying all around me as bullets whizzed by, cutting angrily into the water and, in some cases, into people who didn't or couldn't duck under in time.

I quickly found Mariah and led her underwater to shore, where the Marines had surrounded the lake and were firing away indiscriminately. Fortunately, someone gave the order to cease fire and, as everyone was being hustled out of the water with their hands over their heads, we saw some Marines leading Ahmet Ludi, who looked neither frightened nor angry, off into the jungle.

Then they marched us all, Shrike and Oonie, Felix, Lesley, Danno and Harry—who had miraculously recovered from his clucking catatonia—back to the plantation house where they interrogated each one of us before letting us go.

I was released in the custody of Danno and that would have been the end of the story—except for the extraordinary effect that the salvia had on Harry Ballister. It worked on him like a truth serum, and he suddenly launched into an explicit confession, describing not only his part in the toxic landfill episode, but his gruesome step by step murder of Linda Selby.

He had gone to her house to demand she return the incriminating Waste Disposal file. She refused and asked him to leave. He began to rummage through her papers. She stopped him. He pretended to give in, then took from his attaché case the paraphernalia he'd brought along for just such an impasse. She struggled briefly but the chloroform overcame her. Knowing she would ruin him if she revived, he gave her the fatal injection of heroin. To make it all the more confusing, he hung her from the living room cross beam with her pink bathrobe belt.

Danno was skeptical. He asked a dozen questions pertaining to the details of the murder, but Harry answered every one of them to Danno's reluctant satisfaction. At last the truth had come out.

A tide of relief swept over me as Mariah and I fell into each other's arms. My life was my own again. It was time to go home.

Eventually, Shrike married Oonie, sold the magazine to Nakubishi and gave half the money to the Japanese Justice

Fund, the coordinating organization for World War II inter-
nees. Harry was convicted and sentenced to the gas chamber.
Lesley moved back to England. Danno got a lot of publicity
and bragged about how he solved the murder.

Felix went to work for Chemtech, the company owned by
J.T. and Walter Bates, and the FDA approved NICE for
public consumption. It's all over the place now, you don't
even need a prescription to get it. I don't use it myself but I
have to say, that with all my fears of mind control and Big
Brotherism, it's not such a bad thing, people being happy all
the time. After all, they buy Mariah's overpriced outfits and
pay ten dollars a pop to see my movies.

All in all, I guess my cynical, distrustful way of looking at
the world was wrong. Childlike fantasies of Oneness and
Higher Consciousness were okay for youth and the sixties,
but when it's time to grow up and live with reality, you either
shit or get off the pot.

What the hell, I think, pulling over the rubber raft and
getting onto it without tipping over, all that was a million
years ago. Pushing out into the clear blue water, I tell myself
to stop thinking about things that are past and enjoy the
present with my beautiful family, my beautiful house, my
beautiful pool . . .

There's one thing, though, that's still niggling at the back
of my mind, and I wish I could finally let it go, something
about Harry's confession and the way it didn't coincide with
what I remember about Linda and the day of her death.

I remember, the day before she died, Linda and I had that
fight over why I didn't go with her to the animal rights
demonstration, why I talked about commitment but never did
anything about it. She was upset because I never once said "I
love you," and when I tried to take her in my arms she asked
me to leave, claiming she wanted to be by herself. I remember

being stung by her rejection and saying, "Great solution. Be alone with the person who makes you most miserable," as I left through the back door.

Suddenly, now, floating on my raft in the pool, my fingers and toes trailing along in the water, I get a crystal-clear vision of that moment, a vision so clear, it's like I'm right there again.

I'm standing in the back doorway, watching Linda with her hands on the edge of the sink, looking down at the drain as if everything she ever cared about had just been washed down it.

I feel like a heel, I feel like a shit, I feel like a man in a plastic bubble. Inside I'm screaming, "I love you, I love you, I love you, you poor mixed-up beautiful woman." Outside I'm a fortress, unmoved.

Enraged at myself, I slam the door closed and stalk off down the driveway, deliberately stepping on every crack in the concrete, hoping that bad luck will find me and punish me for hurting this person who just wanted love.

As I reach my car I see a flick of the curtain in Sally Keester's window and curse her for being a big nosy bitch who should mind her own business.

The scene changes. It's the next day, exactly two o'clock—I know because I glance at my watch and it's as huge as Big Ben and I see every wrinkle and hair follicle on my wrist like I'm looking through a microscope.

I knock on Linda's front door and wait but she doesn't come. I know she's home because her car is parked in the driveway and I'm so aware of every vibration in the air, I can virtually feel the heat from the tires as they cool off from having been driven.

My senses are *animal sharp* as I open the door and call Linda's name. She doesn't answer but this time I'm aware of a jumble of angry half-whispers coming from the kitchen, both of them female . . .

She comes into the living room, flushed, pushing her hair back off her face. "Albie . . . What do you want from me?" "I'm sorry for yesterday," I answer. "I need you." "God, Albie, why are you doing this to me?" "I love you, Linda. Please forgive me." "Oh, God," she says as she comes to my waiting arms.

We make love for hours and, here on my raft I can taste, feel and relive every move, every sound, every touch as if I were living it for the very first time. The heat, the ecstacy, my hardness deep inside her, *her fingers tearing through my hair* in a blaze of passion—in this extraordinary state of perception I remember exactly, no longer blocking out, every "I love you" I murmur, every tear of happiness I shed.

Four hours later I leave. When I get home there is a message on my machine—from Linda. "Please come back, I have something very important to give you." I take a quick shower. I feed Tank. I gobble down a cheese sandwich I make with my last two slices of bread.

I get back to her place and walk in the front door. There she is, suspended by that pink terry cloth noose, looking down on me with horrified dead eyes. I choke. I reel. My cheese sandwich rushes up to my throat.

I hear the back door click shut. *So quietly it never registers in my brain.* Until now.

I smell the perfume. *So subtle that the shock of Linda's dead body blocks it out.* Until now.

Until now. Until this moment. On this raft. In the water. Floating. Floating. With the sun in my eyes. The *sun?* No, the stars. The *stars?* Where am I? In a pool in Beverly Hills? No. Wait . . . it's coming into focus . . . where I am, what I'm doing, why I hallucinated a life I could never live . . .

Suddenly a wild, indomitable joy overtakes me—I didn't retreat, I didn't surrender! I'm still floating on the lake! In Samadhi! On the lake in Samadhi with the Divine Salvia as my guide! It was all a dream—*The Last Temptation of Marx.* Temptation appeared in the guise of the salvia and took me on a trip to a life of material comfort and abandoned ideals, a *NICE,* painless life.

But the salvia tempted me for a reason, to show me what *could have been.* Then, with love and with mercy, it led me from there to those final, trauma-blocked hours and minutes with Linda, to show me what actually *was*—in glorious, exquisite, psychotropic detail.

All riddles will be answered, all questions resolved.

Now I have smelled the familiar perfume, seen the flash of red hair that flicked by Linda's window—but never registered in my consciousness because I was so deeply embedded in my own pain.

Lesley.

Now I have heard with sparkling clarity the angry whispered words that came from the kitchen—and recognized the voice that spit them out.

Lesley.

The salvia took me back, into my subconscious memory, and there I experienced everything. Now I know the identity of the killer—Lesley, the rejected lover, the vengeful paramour—Lesley, who murdered Linda because she was threatening to expose and destroy the man Lesley still loved.

LESLEY.

Mission accomplished. My eyes are open now, the salvia is taking its leave—but wait, there's more, there's still one more great healing gift—yes, it's a spectacular finale, it's the Vision I've waited for all of my life—the glorious, transcendent vision of God Himself, descending from Heaven in a great diaphanous white shroud, coming toward me in a cyclone of energy, moving and swirling and . . . crashing into the water in a flurry of cursing and thrashing?

With short, stubby limbs and a tiny torso?

Tearing at the harness of the billowing parachute which brought him kicking and flailing to earth?

This is God?

No, this is Newt, dropped by some daredevil pilot, guided by a thousand points of light from the floating candles, smack-dab into the middle of Samadhi Lake. A fitting grand entrance for this most indispensable soldier in the battle against J.T. and the forces of NICE.

Walter Bates set the phone down and tried to collect his thoughts. His right eye was leaping from its socket trampoline-style. It felt as if any moment it would pop through the patch and jounce around his face, like a novelty-store eye on a long bouncy spring.

"Sit tight," J.T. had said. *Sit tight.* The time had passed for sitting tight. It was time to act. Time to charge. Charge or retreat. And Walter Bates would never retreat. Operation NICE would go forward. He wanted it. J.T. wanted it. The President wanted it. The world *needed* it.

But someone had to step forward, someone had to lead the charge—and Walter understood that J.T. was saying, without saying it, that the hero had to be Walter Bates. That, because of the maddening acquiescence of Libertad to each successive demand by the United States, President Cale was simply not in a position to justify the invasion. And there was no guarantee that he ever would be.

So it came down to Walter Bates, the last brave soldier, to rise up and ignite the torch of Happiness, to insure that the world would receive science's greatest blessing, the ultimate salvation—NICE.

Walter sucked in his gut, adjusted his crotch and reached for the phone, the direct line to General Mark Marmon.

Within twenty-four hours, Libertad would fall.

■

For Felix, the great fog is an astonishing breakthrough in molecular research, an achievement so rarified that it is to his smoke bomb as nuclear fission is to the caveman's fire.

The way he later explained it, by isolating a small number of *condensation nuclei* and releasing them from the top of the mountain, he created a *conspiracy of atoms* to attract every free-floating molecule of H_2O in the atmosphere, thereby creating a colossal chain reaction and forming a giant, colloidal mass of condensation droplets—a mass that surrounded the island with a fog so solid that barely anything could be seen through it, a fog so dense that it made the Battle of Germantown look like a crystal-clear summer's day—in short, the thickest, densest, stolidest fog in the history of fogginess.

And he did it just in time. General Marmon's forces, the 82nd Airborne Division backed up by the Navy fleet, had been given the order to proceed with Operation Long Bomb. The island was to be taken immediately, at any cost. But thanks to Felix's great misty monster, the invading forces were stalled in their tracks.

Felix himself doesn't know how long the fog will last, but for now the Americans can't get started. Their boats can't navigate. Their helicopters and planes can't fly. They can't attack. They can't get through.

In the midst of this impenetrable shroud, a human chain consisting of Mariah and me, Shrike and Oonie and Newt and Felix, brilliantly led by Vitalia and Josef, snakes its way down the mountain and reaches San Nicolas in phenomenal time.

Shrike jumps into the first phone booth we spot through

the gelatinous mist and puts in a call to *Up Yours* in Los Angeles. Miraculously, the call goes through and he relays the story, as we've put it together with Newt, Felix and Mariah, to the eagerly waiting staff. They will rush to press with this *Up Yours* Special Edition, papering America with blaring CONSPIRACY headlines in less than twelve hours.

But the clincher is Oonie's father's satellite hookup. While Shrike's working the phone line to Los Angeles, the rest of us run the twelve blocks, nearly blind in the fog, to Libertad's one and only broadcasting station, a spare little facility squatting beside one of the shiny, new buildings at the capital's center.

Barging into the station we find the Libertadians preempting their regular programming with news coverage of the stalled American invasion and the fantastic, God-sent fog.

At the sight of our motley crew—middle-aged hippie, rainbow-haired rocker, wheezing old scientist, steely-eyed midget and Japanese princess—the station manager grabs a twelve gauge riot gun and bars our way.

But Josef and Vitalia explain to their wary countryman, who eventually confesses to being an Ahmet Ludi devotee, that our diverse but well-focused group is here to defuse the crisis and pave the way for the withdrawal of the invading forces.

Convinced we're legitimate, he grants Oonie's request to phone her father, chairman of the board of Nakubishi and owner of the Nakubishi Satellite, in order to get the necessary clearances to connect us up with the satellite so that we can broadcast live to America over the giant Cable News System, which turns out to be yet another astonishing prize in Shrike's future dowry.

Mr. Nakubishi faxes the official clearance and we scramble onto the set, arranging the seating so that I'm opposite a panel of Felix, Newt and Mariah. Eyes glued to the monitor, we watch as the CNS anchorman breaks into a program about preteen sex with the announcement:

"This is Ted Worley at CNS headquarters in New York with a special news bulletin. Early this morning, American forces in the Caribbean, commanded by General Mark Marmon, moved to take and occupy the island of Libertad in response to the ongoing crisis there. Nobody at the White House, the State Department or the Pentagon will confirm that the orders to attack were issued but we have an exlusive report, live from Libertad, from special CNS correspondent Albie Marx."

The stage manager points to me. I look into the camera.

"This is Albie Marx, on the island of Libertad, where this morning an independent nation's freedom and sovereignty hangs in the balance—the result of an evil network of deception and lies—conceived and propagated by President Cale's chief advisor John Thomas and his staff at the National Security Board. Here in Libertad there is grave and impending danger—carrying with it dire and lasting consequences reaching far beyond this tiny island and into the heart of America itself.

"With me in the studio in San Nicolas, capitol of Libertad, are Newton Selby, former second-ranking official of the National Security Board; Mariah Selby, undercover agent for the NSB; and Felix St. John, inventor and scientist, recently employed by the NSB . . ."

And that's how it began. I questioned the panel of Felix, Newt and Mariah to reveal and expose the entire story of NICE—from its invention and impending legalization all the way through to the trumped-up war to control the salvia fields—unmasking the secret, self-serving bureaucracy of John Thomas and the extraordinary lengths to which he has gone to control, distribute and profit from the insidious mind-control drug.

I induced Felix, the repentant creator of NICE, to testify as to its subtle and perfidious properties and the ease with which John Thomas and his stooges would be able to create a nationwide drug habit.

Mariah told of undercover murderers, empowered and directed by the National Security Board, and their ruthless attempts to kill anyone obstructing the campaign to establish NICE.

Newt filled in the details. He had salvaged enough paperwork from the NSB shredders to document every charge he made, from J.T.'s cynical misuse of power in order to perpetrate the invasion of an innocent country, to his formation of Chemtech to reap the profits of NICE for himself and the government insiders who hid behind the corrupt administration of Donald Cale.

When it was all over and I turned the airwaves back to CNS in New York, I was pumped to the max. On center stage, I had put the pieces together and drawn out a story of monumental proportions in a fashion that everyone could believe. Like Mike Wallace or Edward R. Murrow in their prime, I drove the machine of Truth with a steady and unrelenting hand. It was my finest hour. Finally, a victory for the good guys. Finally, nice guys finish first.

Mariah and I walk out behind the broadcasting studio into the curtain of fog that keeps defiant Libertad safe from the overblown might of the frustrated American forces.

"I guess it's time to go home kid," I say, putting my arm around her and feeling somehow like Bogey.

"Albie . . . you weren't the only one who saw Truth on the float last night."

"I'm sure I wasn't," I respond, wondering what she has in store for me now.

"My mother went to the Nirvana Festival in '68, didn't she?" she asks cryptically.

"She told me she did. That's where she got the poster in her bathroom," I answer, recalling Linda's colorful description of the famous rock concert in Big Sur.

"She was there all three days. Do you remember who promoted the festival?"

"Of course. Ahmet Ludi."

"She was seventeen then, wasn't she?"

"I guess so. Around that old. What is this leading up to?"

"You don't see?"

"See what? Linda at the Nirvana Festival in 1968—" Suddenly I know. As clearly as I knew Lesley Wentworth murdered Linda. It all becomes perfectly, synchronistically, symmetrically clear. "When did you realize . . . ?" I ask, feeling like a dolt for being so blind.

"Newt told me that night in LeDome."

"And you never said anything to me? Why?"

"Because I didn't really believe it—until we got to Samadhi and I looked into his eyes. Then I knew."

"Do you ever run out of secrets?"

"I hope not."

"You know," I say, moving closer to see her through the mist, "there is a resemblance. You have Linda's brown eyes but the coloring . . . the shape of your face . . . your mouth . . . Ahmet Ludi."

"He's my father, Albie. Ahmet Ludi is my real father."

Her eyes are brimming with joy. I've never seen her this radiant. A sickening bolt of fear pierces my heart. Can it be? Have I lost her?

"I love you, Albie, I truly do." She takes my face in her hands. "You're a beautiful man, a man for all seasons."

"But not for you?" I ask, desperately trying to hold back a tidal wave of desolation.

"Albie . . . could you be happy living in Samadhi?" It's clear that she's made up her mind to stay.

The words, *I could be happy with you anywhere,* would come spilling out of my mouth if I let them. But I don't. I take the moment instead to follow the gospel according to Ludi, to listen to my heart. And what does my heart say to me?

My heart asks, If you stayed here on this island, would you be doing it to please yourself? Or to please Mariah? Are you willing to give up your life as you know it—with its ups and downs, pains and pleasures, the constant, exhilarating battle against the Forces of Evil, within and without—and settle down to the quiet, meditative life of a transcendental nutmeg farmer? How strong is your love? You would think it outweighs everything. But does it?

"I'm going to stay here, Albie," she says. "At least for a while. I feel my power here."

"What about our love?" I ask, in a voice on the brink.

"Our love should be strong enough to withstand going our separate ways."

"That's something your father would say."

"He did. He said it to my mother, twenty-three years ago. I saw them together on my float, Albie. I was there when they met and I was there when they said good-bye. I know that they loved each other."

There it is, the Divine Salvia again. Maybe the truth should be banned sometimes. "It wasn't a very happy life for your mother."

"Would it have been any different if they tried staying together?"

I think of my ex-wife, Freedom's mother, of our brief tryst

in the park in Chicago and the miserable way it all ended.
"Probably not," I answer.

"My place is here, with him. That's what my heart tells
me." She leans her head on my shoulder. Sadness pervades me.

"What about vacations?" I whine. "Can I come for vacations?"

She laughs. "You see? You'll be fine. Your sense of humor
always pulls you through."

"Yeah. Right." But I'm grateful for the fog, still so thick
that she can't see the tears inching their way down my cheeks.

The American invasion of Libertad was aborted. Charges,
indictments and smears flew from every corner. Every pious
Senator and Congressman, down to the last staunch conservative, denied the wounded President and his bleeding administration. J.T. tried to circle the wagons but it was too late, the
massacre had begun.

The newspapers and news programs went to work with a
vengeance, leaving no scalp unlifted. The media insiders who
took J.T.'s "push money," sounded not a peep in his defense.
When it was over, there was nothing but utter disgrace. Richard Nixon and his men had a walk in the park compared to
the gauntlet of fiery wrath which immolated J.T. and the Cale
administration. As ye sow, so shall ye reap. Amen.

*"I'm gonna take you and hold you, And do all the things I told
you, In the midnight hour . . ."*

"All riddles will be answered, all questions resolved."

We all came or were drawn to Ahmet Ludi and salvia just
like Dorothy and her friends to the Wizard of Oz. We came
for the answers that would fill in the holes in each of our lives.

For Felix, it was a release from the tyranny of Irmgard and

a rousing conclusion to his lifelong deliberation on the Battle of Germantown.

Newt became a hero and was awarded the job that he coveted, running the NSB for the new administration.

Harry recovered from his catatonia and launched into a tearful, heart-wrenching exorcism of the person he could no longer bear to be—the lying, cheating, self-centered politician who would say or do anything to get elected or take any money that couldn't be traced and the fearful, scared little man, unsure of his masculinity, who compensated for his insecurity with women by using and throwing them away.

Oonie received the invaluable gift of self-esteem, by virtue of being regarded by everyone as a stand-up sister on her own, irrespective of her father's billions.

Shrike, who confessed to courting Oonie because of her money, was granted the dignity due him for his honesty and the realization that though it was fun to *think* about selling the magazine and settling into a life of luxury, it was *essential* to remain the hard-living, hard-driving, Harley-riding crusader for freedom and compassion in a world gone mad with coldness and materialism.

Danno didn't get what he wanted, which was me. Under questioning in L.A., Sally Keester admitted to seeing Lesley at Linda's house the night of the murder. Danno's exhausting interrogation finally forced Lesley to break and confess, so he did get a murderer. But, knowing Danno, he'll always be on the lookout for an opportunity to save the world from Albie Marx.

And Mariah. Who wanted to know where she came from, who longed for a history to call her own. I can't honestly say I was shocked when she told me her father was Ahmet Ludi.

I knew Linda was a rock 'n' roller way back then, a groupie with soul—that's one of the reasons we were so right for each other. She never told Ludi about Mariah, even if she had been able to find him. In fact, she never named Mariah's father to anyone—until she told Newt, twenty years later—and then swore him to secrecy. But when her life was taken, Newt took it upon himself to reveal to Mariah the identity of her real father.

It came as no surprise to Ludi but, then again, nothing did. He knew who she was the moment she entered his yurt. He knew because he had perfected the practice of listening to his heart. And his heart always told him the truth.

Mariah did love me. It wasn't a deception or convenience. When all the fireworks and acting were over, there remained a bond between us that will last as long as we both shall live.

But she had to stay with her father. It was he, not I, who was the object of her quest. And how could I blame her? Who wouldn't want to hang out in Oz when your dad is the Wizard?

As for me, what did I come out with besides my free ass? The simple realization that for all my pretensions to cynical indifference and hard-bitten stoicism, I am willing and able to engage in the exchange of unbounded, free-flowing, unconditional love. Not a bad reward for a few weeks' work.

CHAPTER 24

First thing I do when I get back to L.A. is grab a cab and head straight for the Jaguar body shop. The smog is so thick and acidic that I have to tie a handkerchief over my nose and mouth on the way.

Ralph Pierson, the head body man, brings the car out for me. My baby never looked better. She's a beautiful, deep British racing green, almost a forest green but half a shade lighter. "I put an extra two coats of glaze on her, Mr. Marx, no charge."

"Thanks, Ralph."

"We saw you on TV the other night. Takes guts to stand up to the establishment like that."

"You do what you have to do."

"Well, you're aces in my book, that's all I have to say."

Aces in Ralph Pierson's book. I still have to write him a check for three grand but I get two extra coats of glaze. A hero's reward.

Pulling into my driveway I hear the phone ringing in the house. In my dash to get to it, I nearly break my neck tripping over Tank's homecoming gift on the front step, a pile of dead rats with their heads chewed off.

Grabbing the phone, I notice with dread the digital readout on the answering machine—forty-three messages.

"Mr. Marx?"

"Yes."

"Thank goodness, you're finally there. This is Marcy Kennerly. Can you hold for Jonathan Grant?"

"Who?"

"Your son."

"Oh. Right."

He's on in an instant. "Dad! You were dynamite! The whole thing was incredible!"

"Thanks—"

"Don't talk to anyone about the film rights—we want it. As a matter of fact, I'm sitting here right now with Michael and he says you can name your price. Naturally, we'll negotiate, but you can *start* by naming your price."

"I don't know, I really haven't thought about it . . ."

"This is a perfect Goldie vehicle: deep and meaningful. All we do is change the part to a woman and it's a monster. We're talking Oscar."

"You mean, Goldie plays me?"

"Don't answer now, just think about it. Tomorrow we'll have lunch with Jeff and he'll tell you exactly what to write. This is big money, Dad. This is Disney."

I promise to meet him for lunch tomorrow at the Disney commissary on Dopey Drive. So that's all it takes to have lunch with my kid. Become a national hero. Why did I wait so long?

I suddenly feel exhausted, drained, as though I haven't slept in years. Who needs this life, with the smog and the rats and Goldie and forty-three phone messages? I should have stayed in Libertad. Fuck it, fuck the phone, fuck the messages.

I hit the erase button on the answering machine and deliver the forty-three messages to oblivion. Then I turn all the phones to mute. Let people call from now till tomorrow, I won't hear a thing. I'm going to sleep for sixteen hours. All I need is a shot of tequila to relax and I'm over and out.

I jump in the shower, scrub myself till my arms get tired, then rummage around in an ancient suitcase for something I can't remember the last time I wore—a pair of pajamas.

Comfy, cozy and clean, I crawl into bed and swallow one carefully poured shot of Cuervo. The last fading image in my mind as I sink into deep, blessed sleep is my beautiful Mariah, waving good-bye at the airport, the warm breeze ruffling her rainbow hair, her delicious, olive-skinned legs planted confidently on the soil she couldn't leave.

Next thing I know it's eleven A.M. What a beautiful night. No nightmares, no dreams, no tossing and turning. I put up some coffee, sort through my mail and get dressed for my lunch date with my son, the executive.

On the way out I notice the answering machine blinking, indicating one message. Must have come in while I was sleeping. What the hell, it's only one, I might as well play it.

"Mr. Marx, this is Ralph Pierson, down at the body shop. Just wanted to remind you to cover the Jag, they're spraying your area with malathion tonight. Thank you."

Jesus Christ, where are we living—Hell? I walk out the front door and there's the Jag, my $3,000 British racing green paint job peeling off in great frilly curlicues, like big bright green ribbons in a little girl's hair. And they swear that it doesn't affect humans.

"Get your motor runnin', Head out on the highway, Lookin' for adventure, In whatever comes our way . . ."

Well, what the fuck, it's life in the nineties. I get behind the wheel and start down the hill. The peeling paint is flying into my windshield as I point the Jag in the direction of Hollyweird, so I switch on the wipers and pump up the volume on the cassette deck.

"Yeah, darlin' gonna make it happen, Take the world in a love embrace, Fire all your guns at once, And explode into space . . ."

Thank God for the music. Thank God for Steppenwolf. Thank God for rock and roll.

"Like a true nature child, We were born, born to be wild, Gonna climb so high, Never want to die . . ."

ABOUT THE AUTHOR

DAVID DEBIN, a screenwriter, has escaped to Saugerties, New York. This is his first novel.